CRADLE
OF
MARS

CL FORS

Cradle of Mars

CL Fors

Epitome Press Publishing, Lancaster, CA

An Epitome Press Book

Cover Image and Design by CL Fors

ISBN-13: 978-1-943212-24-8

Printed in the United States of America

DEDICATION

Dedicated to my daughter Lilith, my three sons,
Ishmael, Beowulf, and Odysseus,
and the children of their generation and generations to come.
May their basic human rights and autonomy be preserved
and may the legacy we leave them be less bleak
than the one pictured herein.

ACKNOWLEDGMENTS

My father praised and encouraged.
My mother critiqued.
My husband and siblings supported and shared the journey
My peers read and reread.
Thank you, John Frederick Fors, Jason P Crawford,
Angelique Gunnels, KC Hobgood,
Aaron Fors, Alexis Fors, AnnElena Fors,
and so many more friends and family who helped, supported,
and encouraged me
to write and finally publish my first novel.
Special thanks to my Superstars family for helping me with
rebranding.

TIMELINE

2050: Terraforming of Mars begins.

2050-2064: Coastal cities are evacuated and new settlements are built further inland to avoid rising seawaters and mega-hurricanes.

2069: Mass beachings of marine mammals, increasing pollution levels, melting ice-caps, and overfishing wipe out most sea life.

2067- ~2074: The largest scale algal bloom in recorded history is caused by mass agricultural runoff and warming sea temperatures. Along with the decaying bodies of large sea-mammals and fishes, the red oceans are dubbed the "Blood Tide."

2080: The United States government suffers economic collapse when China redeems its foreign securities to fund relocation and relief programs for its citizens. The European Union follows the U.S. into default shortly thereafter.

2062-2099: Despite rapid reproduction and over-population, the human race suffers from declining health, lowered life expectancy, and poor quality of life. An epidemic of genetic and lifestyle-induced diseases and disabilities, including asthma, autoimmune diseases, severe allergies, obesity, gastrointestinal diseases, and autism spectrum disorders, prompts the "Blue Panic."

2099: The United Nations, partnered with the World Health Organization, release a call to action and form The WCRI-Worldwide Crisis Response Initiative-from prominent scientific minds, headed by Alexander Grimaldi and Lawrence Aarons. The WCRI is given broad enforcement authority for its mandates.

2099: The WCRI appoints a Reproductive Council to reverse overpopulation and resolve the health issues that are plaguing humanity.

2100: Contraceptive implants receive overwhelming support by the world population as a first step in reversing overpopulation and improving the human gene pool.

2104: China, India, Indonesia, Brazil, Nigeria, Pakistan, Bangladesh, Russia, and the Muslim Empire suffer economic collapse due to trade embargos placed by the WCRI for non-compliance.

2105: The WCRI assumes full responsibility for world government and becomes the World Governing Council, displacing all member nations.

2107-2111: Pneumonic plague sweeps the embargoed nations, dropping the world population by 35%

2110: 99.8% contraceptive implant compliance is reached and a ten year hold on reproduction is put into place.

2113-2129: Worldwide natural disasters, epidemics, food shortages, and mass poisonings result in widespread casualties in less technologically-advanced areas of the world. The World Governing Council organizes rescue and relief efforts.

2116-2120: Worldwide mass transit rails to accommodate electromagnetic transport cars are installed and all individual transport vehicles are reclaimed.

2120: The world population reaches 3.4 billion and the Reproductive Council lifts the hold on reproduction.

2122: The Reproductive Council institutes the genetic coding system in place of ID numbers.

2124: Selection of candidates for breeding is accomplished through genetic testing; progeny with clean genetics are lab-created and implanted via IVF.

2160: Droid Demolitions and Wilderness Cleanup Program is instated worldwide to tear down ghost-towns and clear landfills and other debris for recycling and clean-waste energy processing.

2184: The Reproductive Council achieves clean genetics in 95.65% of the world population and 100% of the breeding population.

2200: World population reaches 1.26 billion.

2205: The WGC relocates inhabitants of rural areas and largely uninhabitable areas to self-sustaining cities.

2215: Secondary education is abandoned for an early apprenticeship model.

2221: AI is installed into all buildings along with automated cooking, cleaning, temperature control, and 3-D printing systems.

2232: World population reaches 856.2 million.

2233: The Reproductive Council institutes the License to Procreate Program, allowing couples to receive authorization for home-breeding of progeny upon approval.

2259: Longevity treatments become available, extending maximum human lifespan to approximately two hundred years.
2276: The License to Procreate Program is supplemented by the Surrogate Program, allowing for the creation and placement of progeny in approved homes without compromising the health, wellbeing, or work assignments of the foster parents.
2315: The world population reaches the WGC's target of 500 million through carefully controlled breeding practices, leading to negative population growth as well as climate and natural disaster related deaths, age-related casualties, and DNR policies for the old and unwell.

PHASE FOUR

Lines of data filled the luminous red screen. *AUC1: Temperature 37.1, oxygen saturation 1.7, testosterone .9 nmol/L, estrogen .1nmol/L, weight .5 kg, FHR 156 BPM.*

Theresa scanned the large, rectangular screen above the northern section of AUCs, double rows of large capsules, each framed by four transparent arms and tubing where blood and milky yellow fluids swished and flowed. Inside, blood-engorged tissues and filmy membranes swayed in a filtration current.

She compared the data on the screen to what was inside each capsule, alert for any abnormalities that she might need to correct. Electronic monitoring ensured that any variation from standard values would set off an alarm, but still Theresa double and triple checked. *AUC2: Temperature 37.2, oxygen saturation 1.69, testosterone .3nmol/L, estrogen .9 nmol/L, weight .35 kg, FHR 160 BPM. AUC3...AUC4...*

The red glow from the monitors and the faint pink light emanating from each AUC provided the only illumination in the lab, leaving corners and side corridors in near darkness, their mysteries left hidden and unexplored. There were research stations once filled with mentor and apprentice in the early development stages of ectogenesis—the creation of life outside the womb, and storage rooms of older technology, equipment that was no longer needed but was kept as teaching tools and relics of the AUC program's long history. All that had been whittled down as the project advanced and gained focus and purpose. Now the heart of the lab was here in these capsules.

Reaching out one pale, manicured hand, she caressed the pliable surface of AUC2's chamber and leaned closer to gaze inside. Cradled by layers of endometrial tissue and shrouded by membranes, a small form curled within. Though faint, a glow emanated from the base of the Artificial Uterine Chamber revealing the network of newly formed arteries beneath AUC2's thin skin.

She was bigger today. Theresa blinked and shifted her shoulders. "Well, that's irrational, Theresa. Really? You think you can see a day's growth?" She mumbled to herself, a habit born of hours in her own company, then she pushed back her chagrin and spoke into her personal hand-held device.

"Overall profusion in AUC2's tissues has improved compared to last visual inspection, and..." A small foot struck against the side of the AUC unit and slid down the side, toes slipping against the membranes and spreading like that of a frog in a specimen jar. Theresa startled at the sudden movement so close to where she peered in, and then a smile replaced her clinical gaze. With one finger she traced the path of the splay-toed foot, the delicate nails just visible on the end of each toe.

"And stronger too. You'll catch up with the others yet, little Abby."

Theresa remembered herself and glanced up at the minute, silver security camera, glowing red motion sensor blinking, as its head swiveled like a watchful owl perched on the ceiling. She had spoken aloud. *Shit.* If they knew that she'd named one of the progeny, she'd be given a psych eval and a quick reassignment. They were careful like that, professionalism, no undue attachment…How else could she cull the weaker of the batch or make other hard choices? Theresa deflected the question in her mind. She'd never had trouble with the more unsavory parts of her assignment, but Abby was—well she was catching up. It was within her place to decide when to provide supplemental efforts and when to cull the weak. Or so she told herself. Abby was well below standards, new growth or not and now she'd named her.

The scientist exhaled and mumbled under her breath to the lab, empty save for one hundred growing progeny just developed enough to hear her voice through the capsules. "No more of that."

She took a step back from AUC2's chamber and pulled down on the pockets of her lab coat, straightening it and smoothing down what was already wrinkle free and well-ironed.

She took in the row of AUC's awaiting her visual inspection. Less than half done and there were no interns to lessen the burden. Theresa pictured interns busily attending to the chambers, following her instructions, asking questions and herself following after and double checking anything they'd touched.

She'd had some just a week ago, all reassigned now to other departments. They'd been more burden than help and yet, their absence left behind a vacuum that was filling up with unanswered questions. This Phase was meant to be the culmination of the AUC project, the most advanced. Why strip it of resources before the end if it still had the support of the council? True, it would either be the last phase or the template for many more depending on its success. Once this batch of progeny was delivered and assigned guardians, she'd grow the next batch or be moved to another assignment. The lab *could* run without interns even then, but would it? Would the council send new ones to train after taking the others just as they'd become competent?

That line of thought was pointless, best dismissed. Theresa turned away from Abby's AUC to scan the scrolling data on the main screen. She willed herself to focus on the details of her task, instead of the hollow in her gut that spoke of Abby's tenuous position on the cull list and the mysterious reassignment of interns.

There was a whole row ahead and so, heels clicking on the metal tiles, she examined each AUC unit for wear, each fetus for signs of vigor.

Sliding her hand along the transparent pipes, she assessed the flow of fluid, alert for blockage or stricture. Her brown eyes narrowed as she inspected the progeny themselves, taking in details others would have missed: profusion of blood in surface tissues, reflexes, beat-to-beat heart rate variability. All of these details went into her records but other things that she couldn't quantify or explain, like the way they *felt* to her while she watched them—that she kept in her head. AUC26's frenetic movements, that seemed to her like the twitching distress of waking nightmares triggered no alerts, so she watched and tested and tucked away the worry. Or Abby—AUC2 and the subtle signs of frailty that Theresa could *feel* before her growth ever fell behind standards. They each had their own qualities that were beyond clinical definitions. It was imagination fueled by long hours in the lab of course. That was what she told herself, imagination fueled by watching their small bodies grow from clusters of cells, to embryos, to fetuses…

Reaching the last AUC unit, AUC100, she rubbed the cramp in her neck and leaned in to trace the details of the last progeny. She pressed her lips together, and, finding them dry, became aware for the first time in hours of the aching, parched sensation in her throat. It was easy to forget her bodily needs when tending to the needs of so many—food, sleep and water often fell by the wayside…*I need a drink.*

A smirk pulled at the corners of her lips as she walked to the central control station and ordered water from the nearby serving console. At least she didn't say that one out loud. She retrieved the glass and took a long gulp to quench her thirst with the ice-cold liquid. The last thing she needed was the department head on her ass for breach of contract…drinking in the lab. Theresa chuckled. She could already hear him stutter.

Taking another long gulp she punched in the codes on the control panel to begin the day's education protocols, beginning with a recording of sound patterns and progressing to conversations in several languages. Earplugs, she searched a lab pocket and retrieved earplugs—she just couldn't listen to that today—and returned to her workstation for a chance to check her messages. *Too bad I can't give Abby some earplugs.* She smiled. *She's probably sick of it too.*

Three hours later, between Spanish and Farsi, she pulled out her earplugs and set the alarm system and data transfer to sync up with her hand-held. She unclipped her tightly coiled braid and, massaging her scalp a moment, unwound and neatened her fine brown hair before re-braiding it, then took one last look into each AUC before leaving. It was a quicker look, just a precaution really, not a fixation or anxiety fueled tick. She wouldn't want to miss anything that could deteriorate in her absence. "Adios ninos…ninas."

She grabbed her satchel and left the north wing, her breath quickening along with her pace. She wouldn't be gone long. The board knew close monitoring was necessary. *They won't keep me long…* But they might explain the interns and that was worth a short absence.

The glass tunnel between the north and south wings revealed the latest storm brewing outside, muddy-brown and coal-fire black clouds were building over the towering skyscrapers and cell towers of the Inland New York Settlement that rose in an equally discolored sky. A hailstorm of plastic debris swirled around the tunnel, whipping against the glass, and sticking to the sides like aging wallpaper with the first heavy drops of rain.

Several flights of stairs later, Theresa arrived at the High Tower, that rose some eighty stories above the rest of the Reproductive Council's Headquarters, nestled in the sprawling jumble of low-lying storm clouds.

She brushed lint from her lab coat and, checking her reflection in the floor-length mirror adjacent to the metallic double doors, pulled down on the edges once again. Her brows dipped down as she inspected her appearance, twin sparrow wings with creases of judgement between them. She pressed her lips together, tried on a confident smile, and turned to face the retinal scan in front of the sealed entryway.

The octagonal room, packed full of faces Theresa knew on only a surface level, was silent save for one voice conducting the meeting. She took her seat and looked to the head of her department, where he stood at the front of the room. *Lord, I hope he keeps it*—But Theresa's thought was cut short when she looked at the data displayed on the screen.

Greg Matthews paced within the circle of scientists and functionaries of the Department of Procreation, presenting data on a screen that took up one of the octagonal room's walls.

"Brain scans from each phase of the AUC project progeny show an imbalance— an absence—of activity within the central portions of the brain." Greg rubbed his sculpted patrician nose with the edge of his lightweight wrist cast, more a frame than a cast with the number of open spaces. His wide brown eyes looked more skittish than normal, the hollows under his cheekbones more gaunt. "The first group shows the most marked differences when compared to a control subject. While there are still dark areas where a 'normal' brain shows activity in the second group..."

Round eyes narrowed, the CEO interrupted, gesticulating towards the screen. "What does that mean exactly for those of us who don't work in neuroscience, Greg?"

Greg nodded several times, scratching the itch under the edge of his polymer-mesh wrist cast as he searched for the right wording. "Well...the, um...the progeny show clear signs...well, the brain scans at least...indicate..."

An elderly woman rubbed her forehead and gestured towards the fumbling scientist before them. "Do we need a translator?"

The CEO shot her a look, then turned back to Greg with a nod. Greg cleared his throat and started again. "The brain scans are consistent with a diagnosis of sociopathy—an old term, not fully accurate but an indicator of abnormal development nonetheless—."

Theresa looked at the assembled faces in the room realizing for the second time in a matter of minutes that she had no friends or close associates among them. She stood up, hands balled into fists. "The first group was essentially a prototype. We've accounted for several possible causes of poor outcomes and implemented more stopgaps in each phase." Her voice cracked. "Isn't it possible that Phase Three is developing at a slower rate socially, but will reach normal levels under optimum conditions?"

All eyes turned from Theresa back to Greg. The scientist rubbed his hands through thinning hair, leaving red marks on his scalp. He scrunched his eyes and then blinked. A sign of stress in him that Theresa recognized immediately. "Based on comparative scans, Phase Three shows a slight…a very slight advantage, but is progressing at the same rate as Phase Two and Phase One otherwise."

"Then it's possible that Phase Four will fare even better when they come to term. The technology has advanced significantly since the earlier phases." Theresa began scrolling through the most recent notes in her hand-held and offered the device to Greg.

He did not meet Theresa's eyes at first, nor did he take the device. When he did meet her gaze, his eyes were wide. He shook his head, lips turned down at the edges.

The CEO cleared his throat. "In light of the report given by the AUC project lead, the program will be terminated and the progeny already brought to term will be sterilized and channeled into the workforce as per their individual strengths. Leadership positions with proper oversight, surgeons…there are assignments where their deficits will give an advantage." Laughter bubbled up from several places within the circle and the tension broke.

The CEO tightened his lips, lowering his brows in disapproval. "Please, the termination of a project and waste of valuable resources is nothing to laugh at. Maintain order until the meeting is adjourned, if you will."

Theresa looked around at the circle of individuals seated around her, her vision blurring. Nervous smiles prevailed and several present fidgeted. Others rose from their seats, milling to the back wall to retrieve coffee refills from the automated culinary bot before the CEO continued on to the next order of business.

Had they all forgotten about the 100 AUCs in the north wing? There was a tour three weeks ago and many had seen them. Some of them worked in the same building, for Christ-sakes. They couldn't just terminate the project so easily… Theresa closed her eyes and breathed in through her nose, willing away the dark spots that were peppering her vision. When she opened her eyes, Theresa found the CEO's gaze on her.

She'd forgotten to sit. In fact, she was the only one still standing.

She looked away and sat down in her chair, her face burning with embarrassment.

"Virginia, will you give us your assessment of the available alternatives to the AUC program?" The CEO turned his controlled expression from Theresa to a well-groomed woman with fine lines around her eyes and a poise that always made Theresa wonder if it was put on or just the way she moved through the world.

Virginia stood and glanced over at Theresa before beginning in a subtle New York dialect, drawing out her vowels. "We already have in place two other programs for sustaining population growth, while ensuring clean progeny; the Surrogacy and Placement Program and the currently discontinued Application to Propagate Program."

"Why don't you run us through the risk-benefit analysis of the two programs in comparison, Virginia dear." The CEO smiled at Virginia, bringing a blush to her narrow features. "But don't go too heavy into the numbers. Give us what's behind the data."

Virginia's nails clicked against the screen of her hand-held as she synced up and displayed the numbers for each program. "While the Application to Propagate program held widespread appeal for the masses, popular opinion is quickly falling in line to support the Surrogacy and Placement program. It irrefutably decreases the biological and temporal burden on those in crucial assignments while allowing a pseudo-family to exist."

One of the board members gave a signal from his hand-held.

Virginia folded her hands, turning her gaze to the gentleman. "You have something to add?"

He shifted in his seat. "How does all that affect the overall results, if we look at variables like apprenticeship compliance, and lifetime satisfaction ratings? The family is, after all, a primary source of satisfaction…"

Virginia pursed her lips and continued. "Well…A more loosely knit arrangement of this sort provides an enriching home environment for progeny without impeding early apprenticeship; the mean age for the Surrogate to Placement Program is 13, right on target with the WGC's guidelines, compared to a mean of 15.5 for the Application to Propagate

Program." She gave a pointed glance to the gentleman. "And as for your concerns…the Application to Propagate Program has been put on hold to gather data, and the preliminary results are promising. The submission of applications to procreate is tapering off and satisfaction ratings have only dropped .75 percent…well within acceptable limits that can be expected to normalize within the year."

Theresa watched the storm clouds rage, pouring out their disgust—*or was it hers*— through the thick, glass walls just past Virginia's head. She imagined the violent winds whipping the grating sound of the other woman's voice over the building tops and away from her ears.

There were no calls for Virginia's jargon heavy presentation to be translated as they'd done to Greg. This was language the protocol pushers understood, the translation of family dynamics and life satisfaction to numbers and spreadsheets. Most of them had been born under License to Propagate, their parents put in those applications and waited anxious weeks, months, years, for the approval of a single child. There were no representatives of applications denied in the room because they hadn't been born, and any in the boardroom that wanted their own children, a dwindling want—had the surrogacy program.

None of that came across with numbers and percentages. Virginia didn't dwell on percent increase of failed placement attempts—progeny sent back because the prospective parents had changed their minds or percent decrease of tearful goodbyes when it came time to send them off for apprenticeship. Theresa was surrogate progeny, a rare case approved by a friend of a friend in the WGC, her mother's egg, some genetic contribution from her father, some from elsewhere, a little like Phase Four in her lab, but not a true precursor to the AUC program. They were already testing early AUC's before she was born and she wasn't one of those.

She'd been placed, raised and then off to a precociously early apprenticeship. Twelve years was just long enough for her parents to feel a strong sense of accomplishment and guilty relief when she left them and to video-call her bimonthly if she didn't call first. The system did work. She'd spent a successful decade and a half working on the AUC program that they were so unceremoniously scrapping.

Theresa's head hurt, a tightness wrapping her skull and squeezing behind her eyes. The CEO was giving closing remarks, the usual projections for next quarter and praise for this quarter's accomplishments. He expressed his optimism and confidence in this new direction they were taking...

The meeting ended with appreciative laughter for the CEO's speech and firm handshakes and back-patting all around. They seemed quite pleased with themselves, as they took on the CEO's buoyant perspective.

Theresa watched them go and waited to the last, hanging back until the CEO was finished with pleasantries. If she could speak to him alone—Still she hesitated.

"What is it, Theresa?" He drained the dark liquid from his cup, with a sidelong glance in her direction.

She ran a hand across the seams of her lab-coat, smoothing and straightening, searching for comfort in the habitual motion before stepping closer.

"Morton...the termination. This project is years in the making...with such promise. Don't you think there are other, less drastic measures—I could..."

He shook his head, lowering the empty vessel to the table between them and traversing the distance. "Look, it's hard to step away from such a big time investment…you've been on this longer than most. I get it. I really do." He put an arm around her shoulders.

"Take some time to distance yourself from this. You have my permission."

"But I couldn't just…" The distress in her eyes was clear, and the CEO held up a hand to stop her train of thought.

"Theresa. I know your work. Clean, impartial, practical, and, quite frankly, inspired by genius. If you take a step back you'll find that you agree with my decision on this. It's time to cut our losses and find a new direction."

The scientist took a breath, exhaling slowly and nodding in agreement. "Okay…thanks, Morton. I'll put in a request for leave."

"Don't do that. Just take the time. I've got you covered." He smiled, patting her back and guiding her to the door.

Theresa offered him a shaky smile, smoothing over her expression and regaining full composure. "Okay."

The hall was empty, all board members having returned to their own offices and assignments. She headed towards the central building that would lead to the main exit, focusing on the click of her shoes on tile and the flickering reflection of her lab-coat in the reclaimed wood paneling, polished to a high gloss finish.

The sounds melded in her ears, combining with the rapid beat of her pulse. It would be cold outside, strong winds whipping ice against her cheeks as soon as she opened the doors. *They'll never feel it.* The thought came unbidden, splintering and filling her mind like the sound of shattering glass in an echo chamber. She pushed it aside. *They shouldn't…like he said, I need distance.* She sighed, as the main corridor came into view.

Regardless of their genetic make-up, the time invested in them...they're just progeny—and they're defective. Her chest constricted, throat closing as she struggled to normalize her breathing. *They don't fulfill the mission...* The extended version of the Reproductive Council's mission replayed in her memory. *To definitively halt overpopulation and the mechanisms that caused it, and to produce clean, genetically diverse, and specialized progeny in carefully controlled numbers. To maintain quality above all else—achieving resilience of form and function in the human race and maintaining sustainability of the production of progeny using models for cost-effectiveness.*

Normally the words and rhythms of the mission brought comfort, a feeling of control, peace. But not this time. Instead, it called up images of the glowing AUCs waiting for her return in the lab. And Abby, slated for culling thrice over and just making the minimums due to Theresa's extra efforts. It didn't take much...no real sacrifice of efficiency—it wouldn't take much to get them on track.

The thought took hold the moment it formed like vines in rich jungle soil, sending her heart racing ahead of her. She stopped, turning back in the direction she had come.

She scanned the people walking past the AUC Program's logistics office and secondary testing lab, and caught sight of the man she was waiting for. He walked with the awkward gait of a tall man who is uncomfortable with his height: head down, shoulders curled, and hands shoved deeply into his pockets.

"Greg."

The sound of his name stopped him short in his single-minded mission and his head snapped up, pale blue eyes startled. Theresa took hold of his arm and pulled him into the shadow of the overgrown money-tree that shaded the alcove alongside his office door. "Hey, I need to discuss the AUC program with you. I have some ideas for bringing it back in line with the mission so we can reevaluate termination."

Greg opened his mouth and then closed it, gaze flicking over at the office door as if for escape.

"The AUC program has been closed. Mr. Steiner already put in your orders to terminate."

She grimaced against the scowl that pulled at her features and struggled to maintain composure as the storm of conflicting emotion mounted inside. "I know that, but he authorized time off. I can use that to reassess…get some new data for him to consider…it's in the best interests of the council—"

He stared off, not meeting her gaze when he spoke. "We have to let it go, Theresa."

"Why?" She gazed up at him, eyes searching his before he flinched away again. "You have to talk to them. Let them know there are options to get it back on track…I—Greg." The walls of protocol and composure slid away. "They can't just cancel the project. I…I wish you had talked to me…before…They can't terminate the project."

"Theresa, it's not my jurisdiction anymore…The—they took it over my head." He stumbled over his words in his rush to explain.

Her eyes narrowed. "*Damn* your jurisdiction, Greg. There are one hundred progeny in the north wing! You can't just throw them away based on a few tests and theories! You know neuroscience is more complicated than a few brain scans and you let that whole room think a few scans can map a whole person. What about—"

"The data is accurate. All four phases are at risk for psychological disorders. You don't see that from the lab, Theresa. The earlier phases have been tested and retested specifically because of behaviors they exhibit—atrophied ventromedial prefrontal cortex…and other areas of the brain being forced to compensate. Your phase four can't exhibit the tendencies yet but the scans show they will." He looked away, face set.

"Why did this get to Steiner before me. You needed consult, you didn't warn me—"

"We were asked for the data. Tests ordered with instructions to report back."

"And you couldn't tell me it was happening?"

Greg looked away again. "I thought we'd get instructions to adjust course instead Steiner scheduled a meeting. I think he already knew what he was gonna do with those test results."

Theresa watched him look down, away, fidgeting with his cast, eyes anywhere other than her face. He'd known something was coming and he hadn't told her. Fine, she just needed him to help now.

"Greg, please, I just need three more months to take them to term. Please."

"It's not my decision. You know—"

Theresa went up on tip-toe to turn his face back so he would look at her. "Greg, I know I'm supposed to be impartial, uninvested, but they're my project…they're unfinished—babies." The old word felt strange said aloud. It was dated, obsolete and it wasn't used that way except in old literature.

She'd certainly never used it that way before—to describe the pink wriggling figures in her lab. Her lips quivered over the word. It felt too soft, too vulnerable, as if her AUC's had been cracked open in front of her and the hundred unfinished bodies spilled out on the floor. She saw Greg flinch and it made her want to say it again. "They're like—like *our* babies. *We* started this phase together—they're more of us than the traits packets. I just...I know why you transferred into data. I know it was me, I do, but...please, can you buy me some time."

Greg nodded several times in quick succession, unable to cope with the forced intimacy of their conversation any longer. "Make a report, find proof that Phase Four will be different. Make them essential." He sniffed his nose and went to rub his sparse hair, instead hitting the side of his forehead with his cast. He winced, rubbing the spot and leaving more of a mark with his fingers than the bump had. "The Ectogenesis program has a long history. They are *not* giving it up lightly. Someone wants it finished and now the data backs up termination. I—I w- will...I'll personally support your data—If I can. That's all I can do."

"So I need to make the data back up continuing the AUC project...or at least Phase Four." A deep breath. "I can do that. I think I can do that." Theresa brushed her cheeks and found them wet.

Greg turned and shoved his hands back into his trouser pockets, the cast catching the edge and making his movements jerky and awkward.

"Thank you, Greg."

He turned and opened the door to his office without reply, cursing under his breath.

Catching the nail of one thumb between her teeth, Theresa scowled before pulling her hand away and tucking it between her thighs. The words on the screen of her console blurred together and she squeezed her lids shut, counting as the damp protest of her over-used eyes leaked between them. *One-one-thousand...two-one-thousand...three-one-thousand...* The numbers merged and danced, twisting into incoherent images.

Yawning without holding back in the solitude of the empty lab, she glanced at the time-stamp on her hand-held and climbed onto the fold-out cot next to her desk. *Three AM. And nothing.* She sighed, the breath a gust of hot wind from a guttering fire. *This isn't going to work—the lack of sleep.* Her ideas were growing less coherent, less useful as the hours wore on. She'd have to tackle it again after sleep if she wanted a chance but she didn't want to close her eyes. Instead she stared at the rows of glowing capsules, lava lamps—warm fluid filled nightlights moving with gentle breath. Sleep took her, a leaden curtain dropping over her consciousness.

She opened her eyes to the same dim glow. Struggling to sit upright on the cot next to her workstation, she swung her legs over the edge and stared out in front of her, confusion and grogginess warring in her mind. She turned her attention to the workstation, tried to recall the thought that had woken her, the thought that had sent her pulse racing. *They're all gone. Rows of empty AUCs.* Grasping the edge of the cot, she squeezed her eyes shut, fighting the rising panic from the recurring thought.

Blinking away the dream that surfaced with such force, she stared through the hazy red glow of the AUC units.

I can't see them. Theresa struggled out of the covers draped across her knees, dragging her tangled sheets behind her and limping out of the strangle-hold they had on her calf. One thought pierced her mind.

Abby...

She pushed back the panic that sought to claim her. *Where is she?* Grasping the sides of Abby's unit, she leaned in and pressed her forehead to the hot surface, searching, eyes frantic.

A hand drifted into view, then a face, upturned nose, eyes sealed like that of a newborn kitten. Abby bumped against the side of the chamber. Again. The small mouth opened, revealing pink tongue and naked gums, then closed, swallowing like a fish. Thump. Another hiccup.

Tears of gratitude slid down Theresa's face, burning her cheeks. Her heart beat wildly, breath hitching as she lost control. *She's here. She's here and she has the hiccups!* Soft gasps of laughter escaped her lips, alternating with pained sobs.

She looked across the room, really seeing it for the first time since she awoke. Each unit held a small figure, partially concealed by membranes, the sides of the endometrial lining, and the placenta. The soft glow illuminated the blood flowing through arterial cord vessels. The large screen on the wall above the AUC units was active, scrolling through each inhabitant's vital statistics and the parameters being controlled.

Theresa stood, her hand still resting on the side of Abby's chamber as if it would disappear should she remove her full attention. How could she have believed they were gone? *All systems are functional. God, it must be the pressure. Just dreams...* She turned away from the AUC units and withdrew her hand, clenching it to fill the emptiness, then glanced over at Abby once more before returning to her cot.

Morning found Theresa red-eyed and disheveled before her computer, coffee in one hand, a stylus in the other, tapping as she dictated notes into her console. A soft chime sounded, and she turned to the control panel to begin the progeny's daily educational training. Her hand paused above the command switch and she pursed her lips, hesitating.

*Who gives a shit if they are predisposed to language if they don't even make it to...*She cut the thought short and returned to her computer without flicking the switch. Taking her hand-held out, she synced it with the lab's speakers.

"Computer, access music files from external device. Theresa's cell-phone, playlist, Oldies. Save as, Updated Educational Training File. Title...interactive auditory stimulus. Subheading, Empathy 101. Full volume."

A smooth, carefully inflected voice spoke from the terminal. "Command received. Processing."

A cello sounded forth, filling the room with the vibrations of its deep bass as voices joined in, creating a symphony of sound. She closed her eyes, savoring the melodic layering behind the cello.

The music shifted, the sound raw and jarring. Theresa grinned. Swaying and pantomiming instruments midair, she sang along, a beat behind the lyrics.

"Get your boards out, get your boards out. Blood tide's rollin' in. There's bodies in the surf, and smoke on the wind. Oo-Whoa-o-o— now!"

A smile spread across her face as she pulled out a keyboard to type her notes.

Then she looked up, startled, spinning in her chair to face the AUC units. Every single one was filled with movement and alarms went off one after another.

Over two-thirds of the progeny had elevated heart rates, just outside the carefully controlled acceptable range.

Theresa stared at the data, eyes widening as she switched the alarms off manually. She raised a hand as if to cover her mouth and let it drop down to her chest just above her own racing heart— a thought formed, thrumming at the rate of the beating organ under her hand. *It's the music...* Realization dawned, the implications of this flickering into view. Each parameter of the progeny's development and how it would be affected ran through her mind and formed a map there.

Her eyes were bright with excitement, hope. "That's right children. Soak it up." A smile grew on her lips. "We're going to shake things up around here. *Cali's under water, but we can still play, surfin' on the blood tide, pushin' bodies out the way! Whoa-oh-o-oh-o, oh-oh-o-oh-o.*"

She switched to manual entry, her fingers skittering across the keyboard. Opening a new file, she typed in the heading *Preventive Measures to Occlude Abnormalities and Deficits in Fetal Brain Development.*

She rubbed her forehead and looked at the screen. A tentative smile matched the gleam of hope in her eyes as she entered the data.

This is something. This is a start...

Every few moments she switched over to her messages. *Why am I checking again? To catch it just as it arrives?* The message alert would do just that when it arrived—alert her.

As expected, the in-box was still empty. She returned to the screen where her notes were stored. The half-empty document stared back.

God, this isn't enough... She was going to have to do more, to find as many measures she could control and study as she could. She'd have to bury the council in them. She stood, stretching her back and rolling her neck in a circle, a sharp intake of breath at the pain between her shoulders.

Then she paced down the aisles, peering into the AUC units, brows knit in concentration. *What is it your brothers and sisters are missing, huh? Is there something you need?* She stopped in front of Abby, watching the subtle twitches of seemingly random muscle contraction forming early expressions. She told herself she was assessing for growth, for any measurable effects of her knew protocols, but she was just staring, watching the small fists open and close, transfixed.

A soft chime sounded from Theresa's work station. Her eyes widened and her head jerked up. *There it is!* Speed-walking, she reached her desk and opened the message without sitting.

Subject: AUC Program termination time-table

Ms. Theresa Marin
In order to finalize the decision to terminate Phase Four of the AUC program, data from your department has been requested by the project head Greg Matthews. Please be prepared to make your presentation, complete with all accumulated data and recommendations for the future of the project, by Friday March 17th.

Thank you,
Secretary to -Morton Steiner, CEO
Gwen Hardy

Theresa flinched. *Nice subject heading.* She read the short message, beginning to end, three times, allowing every detail to sink in and refusing to allow her thoughts to wander.

It's all on you, Theresa. You and your sub-par presentation skills. She glanced back at the screen, noticing again how incomplete her work seemed: only a working hypothesis and minimal data collection.

They're only giving me a week.

Several articles competed for space on Theresa's computer screen, including the complete data summary from the past twenty-six weeks of Phase Four's gestation and the genetic profile of each progeny. She squeezed her eyes shut, then opened them, staring across the room for a few moments to give them a rest from the screen. *Twenty-eight, twenty-nine, thirty.* Her vision was blurring, eyes watering. Hours at the screen, little sleep. It was understandable, and yet this was not the time for weak eyes.

She looked back at the screen and closed out three of the articles that appeared to hold no useful information. The remaining three were from widely different fields that, as most fields do, intersected around the topic of neurological development, psychology, obstetrics, and embryology.

A sharp triple beep echoed across the lab. She finished the sentence, forcing herself to break away, then turned towards the sealed and locked doors on the other side of the room, one eyebrow cocked, corners of her lips down-turned. It could be

Greg with bad news, unlikely, or Steiner in a rage that she was working instead of on vacation, less likely, but still it spiked her heart-rate. *Who would be here?*

"Virginia Blaylock requests entry." The automated computer doors answered her question before she could state it aloud.

"Let her in."

She turned back to her screen and continued to read, inhaling deeply as she heard footsteps approach, click-clicking across the room and pausing just behind her. Placing a light welcoming smile upon her lips, Theresa turned to greet Virginia.

"My, my, you keep busy!" The other woman had a tight smile, a slight squint to her eyes.

Is that a touch of pity or just confusion? Thanks but no thanks, Virginia.

"I haven't seen you in the cafe for *days*. Aren't you eating?" Concern creased Virginia's brow and for a fleeting moment Theresa wondered if it was genuine.

"Just eating in. As you've so astutely noticed, I'm quite busy." Theresa nodded towards the AUC units, eyes wide with impatience.

Virginia glanced over at the units and back to Theresa, her hands flitting up to her throat. "Oh! Well, I just thought, with the project set to terminate, I would be seeing more of you."

Theresa held her smile in place, but was unable to avoid speaking through clenched teeth. "Actually, the project may be continued."

"Well, I hadn't heard that! I can't imagine why." The woman turned to stare at the pulsing AUCs, leaning in with her nose scrunched. "I mean, if they're defective, it would only make sense to…"

"Terminate a project that is the fruition of my whole apprenticeship and adult career?" Theresa took a step closer to Virginia, no trace of the smile she had cultivated moments before remaining.

Virginia continued to stare at the units, reaching out a finger as if to touch the side of the one closest. "Can you imagine being host to one of these?" She shuddered, lips twisting. "Thank the Reproductive Council for the surrogate program!"

Theresa grabbed Virginia's wrist before she could touch the AUC. "Did you come here for something in particular? Because I have work to do."

Virginia pulled her wrist from Theresa's firm grasp, cradling it with her other hand. "You know, I have tried to be a friend to you. You would think you would be grateful! I just can't seem to understand you." She paused to consider. "You know, no one blames you for the failure of the AUC project, if that's what you think. We all know how dedicated you are."

"Really?" Theresa raised an eyebrow. *Does she really think this is about my ego?*

"Of course! I saw your face at the meeting. The way you stood up for the AUC program. When they started phasing out the Application to Propagate program, I fought it tooth and nail. That was *my* project. I had invested in it. But I let it *go*. It just wasn't a good program really, too much risk. You have to let this go."

"Let it go." A thin smile found its way to Theresa's lips, her eyes iced over.

"Well—yes. There are so many better things to devote yourself to." Virginia gesticulated as she spoke, pacing around the AUC units and peering into them with a look of distaste. She reached out a finger once more.

"DON'T TOUCH THE AUC UNITS!" Theresa glared at the other woman. The small form in AUC6, startled at the sound of her voice, kicking against the sides of the unit nearest to where they were standing.

Virginia's eyes widened and she took a step back. "You know, Theresa, I came to offer you a position in my department. But now I think you'll have to find somewhere else to go when they terminate your project! We could use another good scientist, but you're just—unstable." Virginia shook her head, an abrupt sigh punctuating the end of her speech, and walked to the door. She looked back once more to give Theresa a piteous parting glance, but Theresa was no longer watching her. She was looking down into an AUC unit, her hand resting on the side.

"Shhhhh, shh, she's gone. It's alright." AUC6 calmed in response to Theresa's soft tones, the membranes surrounding him swaying like seaweed as he settled into light sleep, pinkish eyelids fluttering in dream. Theresa smiled and watched the FHR value drop as he settled. 172…156…"Your little heart was beating so fast!" She put her hand to her chest. "I think mine was beating faster, though—if you could feel it. Can you imagine that? I can…"

Her eyes widened and her hand flew to her chest. "*My* heart rate…" She was frozen, staring at AUC6, asleep and oblivious to how *her* heart was racing even faster now. Her workstation…she didn't walk, she ran to her workstation.

"If you could feel what I feel! What someone feels…Yes." She pulled up several more documents, reading furiously and taking notes. *It's all too controlled! No outbursts of anger, no* *surges of love, laughter, heartbreak...*Phase four had none of the exposure to human emotion that surrogate progeny get in the womb. *God, this could be it!* Theresa worked as if possessed, inputting new code into the system and speaking aloud to lab full of progeny. "Didn't I say we were going to shake things up?! That's right!"

The sun was shining on the transparent walls of the boardroom when the meeting began, dimming as the glass tinted in response to the harsh glare. Theresa stood at the front of the room, control wand in hand. The members of the council arrived one by one and took their seats. Greg was seated next to the CEO's empty chair. Theresa smiled and nodded at him. He returned the nod and shifted in his seat, finding something to study on his hand-held screen.

Theresa frowned at his lack of an encouraging smile. *Just nervous.* He was always nervous at meetings, always nervous. And he didn't know how good this is going to be. He had her paperwork that was only half of what she had planned.

The CEO entered the room with a tight smile on his lips, his eyes distant behind the transparent visor he wore. He took his seat and nodded at the person on the other end of the call. "Yes, of course. We're well within parameters." A subdued laugh escaped him in response to something only he could hear and Theresa shivered at the ice in his gaze as he looked through her. "Yeah, I'm in a meeting now so...Friday. That's right. See you then."

The CEO pointed at the man no one else could see and waved, giving a quick wink that was slight enough to pass for a tick. He tapped the side of his visor. Its soft glow extinguished as it folded up, leaving only a small device next to his ear. Looking around the room, the CEO swiveled his faux leather chair and looked at Theresa where she was waiting at the front of the room, hands crossed before her.

She nodded at the CEO, then clicked the wand once, turning her gaze to those assembled before her. The three glass panels behind her lit up with scrolling data, *AUC1, AUC2, AUC3*, as she began to speak. "This has been the protocol for the AUC program since its inception with only small variations. The most notable changes were implemented at the beginning of Phase Four, including the educational training protocols, and the background heartbeat playback."

With another click the sound of a human heart filled the room and was joined by a recorded voice speaking in English and then Spanish. The data scrolling across the screen shifted. "As you can see…the altered protocols permanently changed the baseline values for all of the pertinent variables for Phase Four as well as increasing variability."

Theresa could see several pairs of eyes glaze over as she spoke. She took a breath to fight back the answering panic. *They don't know what you're saying… What would Greg not do?* "What that means is the development of these progeny—Phase Four, is closer to that of progeny in the surrogate program." She made eye contact with each member of the board, seeking confirmation that they had understood…aside from the CEO who was looking down at the table silently, tapping his stylus on his hand. Theresa scowled. *Is he listening or waiting for me to finish?*

She turned back to the screen and slid her finger across the volume portion of the control just as the protocols changed. Loud music filled the room vibrating the glass, a melody at high volume. She dug in, glanced around the room and then in a soft speaking voice began.

"*Yeah-ah-ah—eeyeah-ah—yeah.   Yeah-ah-ah—eeyeah-ah—yeah.*"

A sweet voice, an echo from over 200 years past sang out and Theresa sang along, her voice untrained but melodic.

"*I'm slippin' through the cra-acks. Yeah. And now it's crumblin' fa-ast. Yeah. Still I think to when...All that I could feel was, how we fit toge-ether. Blurring all the lines. Some days I could not find, the seams that were between. Makin' us of you and me-e, yeah. Yeah-ah-ah-eeyeah—yeah.*" Tears ran down her cheeks as she sang, the image on the screen switching over to a live feed from the security cameras in her work space. AUC units glowed large as life on the window screens of the boardrooms. Small human figures, their limbs thin and disproportionate to their torsos, blood vessels showing through their thin, mottled, skin, slept within the cocoon shaped artificial wombs. Several board members gasped. These were restricted images. Things most people didn't have the stomach or the clearance to see—Theresa hoped for wonder but saw more disgust. As they stared, unable to look away, the music they were hearing along with Theresa's voice developed an echo as it was broadcast back into the AUC lab. The effects were instantaneous and obvious. The progeny within the AUC chambers awoke and started moving, translucent limbs kicked, turned flips and wriggled in their chambers. A smile joined the tears on Theresa's face as she took up the next verse.

The boardroom had broken into side discussions, chairs pushed back from the table.

She lowered the volume on the music and pointed to the side of the screen that contained the scrolling data for the AUC units. "The readings achieved here closely mirror the readings taken on surrogate infants while their mothers are enjoying themselves, singing, dancing, light exercise." The image on the screen transitioned to footage of two surrogate mothers sitting close together and laughing, holding their rounded bellies as tears escaped their eyes.

The AUC units filled the screens again and Theresa turned back to face her audience.

"The earlier phases of the AUC program have not experienced the formation of a loving bond during gestation and possibly not during early infancy. The inability to bond and feel empathy is the hallmark of sociopathy, psychopathy—very old terms once used to describe maladaptive behaviors—meaning people unfit and unsafe for society. Later research reveals those terms to be oversimplifications…Our research suggests that in the absence of a genetic cause, bonding and empathy may be coded into the human brain during gestation."

She gestured towards the AUC units, larger than life-size on the screen behind her. "These children have no mother." She used the old term for progeny. "Unless it's me." The tears flowed again, hot against her cheeks a clear betrayal of her inability to remain impartial, clinical, and she scrubbed at them. The final display of data filled half of the screen.

"A week ago I implemented the Emotional Priming and Education Program for Phase Four progeny. The results as you have seen are promising. Phase Four has approximately three calendar months remaining before they mature to term and are delivered. This is ample time for us to see the results of this new protocol." Theresa glanced over at Greg where he sat. "The Ectogenesis program has a long history. We should not give it up lightly. The data does not back up termination."

The CEO stood, a tight smile etched on his face. "Thank you for that...creative presentation, Theresa. You may take your seat at the table and we'll be sure to take your data into consideration in our final decision."

She hesitated a moment.

"Now. Please. We have other business to attend to." His eyes were cold and held a threat.

Theresa shivered but held firm. "I believe Greg was slotted to answer questions and discuss whether or not my findings could be backed by his department." She looked over to Greg, who winced and turned away.

The CEO stood and joined her at the front of the boardroom. He placed a hand on both of her shoulders and squeezed as if presenting a beloved daughter to the audience.

"Thank you again. I don't think we need Greg to back your singing ability. After all, you were classed as a scientist and not a performer." The CEO turned an ironic smile to those assembled, and gave Theresa a gentle push towards her seat.

She crossed the distance, cheeks hot with embarrassment. She stared at Greg biting nonexistent traces of nail from his fingers. *Why won't he look at me?! Did you weasel out, Greg? Huh?* She couldn't count on him even for this, when it mattered...She narrowed her eyes. *It mattered before too, dammit!* Still staring, Theresa's attention was drawn to the raw and reddened fingertips that found their way back to his mouth. *God, he's made himself bleed.*

The CEO pressed his hands together, holding them to his lips. "Keep your seat, Greg." The project lead had made no movement to get up. "I think I can cover the FAQs." He glanced around the room. He was not looking for confirmation. The board was silent and all side conversations had ceased during his and Theresa's interaction.

The CEO stood, blank faced, with an intensity in his eyes that Theresa had never seen. "First question. At what phase are new protocols usually made to make sure they pan out?"

Greg mumbled but did not look up. Theresa's eyes narrowed. *Something's off.* Greg hadn't bought her time—a second chance. He must have bargained for this meeting on his own head and pissed Steiner off in the process.

"There is never a certainty that a new protocol will result in..."

The CEO cut him off, his voice cool and controlled. "Please, cut the blah-blah-blah-pie; just answer the question."

Greg flinched.

"And so we can hear you."

Greg took a breath and spoke in an even tone. "At the beginning of a new Phase, Mr..."

The CEO's face took on a faint look of surprise. "Not in the middle? Say, the last third?" He glanced over at Theresa and then spread his hands toward Greg, eyes wide. "Why is that, Greg?

Greg's mouth worked a moment, opening and closing bass-like before his voice emerged. "To ensure that the...the new protocols have the greatest effect p-possible. To prevent wasting time and resources and possibly resulting in defective progeny."

The CEO shook his head, a frown turning down the corners of his lips. "Defective progeny. Now that would be a damn shame—" He looked directly at Theresa, catching and holding her gaze. "Diverting resources that would not be needed to achieve high quality product under other circumstances goes against our mission. So without intervention we'd have, what? Another…Hundred? Sociopathic progeny to knife us in the backs while we are sleeping? There's a chance of that, isn't there?"

Greg was motionless, allowing the silence to draw out within the boardroom. Theresa sat at the edge of her seat, hands gripping the table, knuckles white. Then Greg turned to face her, his eyes hollow. "Yes, there is a chance."

Theresa shot out of her seat, rage contorting her features, as her self-control pushed to it's limit over weeks of sleepless nights and sustained effort, finally snapped. "This is ridiculous! You saw them! You all saw how they reacted! You saw the data. Don't any of you have any questions?" She glared around the room. The board members were pale and silent, avoiding her eyes. "Don't any of you have any spines? This... this is a sideshow, not a board meeting!"

"Theresa, I'm going to have to ask you to get control of yourself." The CEO held his hands up, palms facing Theresa as if to ward off the verbal onslaught.

"Get a hold of myself? You've already decided to terminate! Why did you even ask me to present this data? Huh? To preserve your image? To humor Greg?" She advanced upon the CEO, who towered a full two feet and 100 pounds over her. He held his ground and, taking the control wand from his pocket, flicked the small switch on the bottom.

His voice softened as he looked down at the trembling scientist before him. "The bottom line is that these Progeny of yours fail to reach minimum thresholds for social effectiveness—So, Theresa, I am going to ask you again to calm down before your escorts arrive. This project is very important to you, I know. As I said before, we will take your data into consideration, but in the meantime it would be best for you to wait in your laboratory."

The CEO placed a hand on her shoulder, a spark of concern in his eyes, and she shook it off, glaring up at him. The door to the boardroom opened and the CEO smiled as two uniformed men entered the room and stood at the door awaiting orders. "Ah! Good. Jamison, Tucker? Can you see that she makes it back to her laboratory? She has been working too hard and is beside herself." He looked down at her, brows creased in genuine concern as he ducked down and whispered in her ear.. "You should have taken the time off, Theresa."

Her eyes flicked towards the uniformed men at the door and she nodded, turning and taking a step towards the exit. She stumbled, tripping over the leg of Greg's chair and Jamison caught her arm, preventing a fall and escorting her out into the hallway.

Greg rose as the door closed and stood a moment, staring around the room. "…the bathroom," he managed before rushing from his seat and out the door. He took long loping strides down the hall, and almost ran into Theresa.

"Theresa!" Greg called out, grabbing her shoulder from behind. She spun on him, her eyes swimming with tears, fury sharpening them and holding back the flow that threatened. "Theresa…I…it's going to be okay. I just…"

She shoved her hand out towards him, palm almost touching his face. "Do not! Try to comfort me! You promised me! Do not pretend to be emotionally available when we both know you're not!" Greg opened his mouth, but no words came. It was not the first, nor would it be the last time that words would escape him. Theresa turned and walked down the hall, followed by her escorts.

Theresa stared at the message in her inbox.

Subject: Reassignment

Dr. Theresa Marin
It has been determined that your expertise and temperament will be better suited to another project. The finalization of the AUC program will be completed by Dr. Brant. Please prepare your data and your workspace for the arrival of your replacement, so that he may take charge of Phase Four by 3:00 PM. You are expected to report to the Colonization project at the W.A.S.A. headquarters in New Columbia City in four weeks' time. Your contact for the assignment is Brogan Hollder.

Thank you,
Secretary to Morton Steiner, CEO
Gwen Hardy

Finalization? What did that even mean? It sounded like a euphemism for termination. She pulled out her hand-held, the blood drumming in her ears like a dirge. There was only one person she could call. Greg answered on the third ring.

"Hello?"

"They're transferring me." She looked across her lab at the glowing AUC units. They were so calm. She wanted to think they knew, that they could feel her pain, her numbness, the sick way her heart beat in slow, heavy succession, one beat after the next. Better that they didn't. *Could all of them be sleeping?*

"Yes." Greg's voice sounded small and distant. *He already knows.*

"Are they terminating?" Theresa stared off, waiting for the answer. She was slumped in her chair, listening to that cacophony of conflicting, half-formed thoughts in her head.

"Yes." His answer, when it came, could have been a recording of his previous yes.

"Couldn't we bring it to the World Governing Council, make an appeal of sorts?" Her words tumbled out without forethought. "If we could get them to take interest, and overrule them, then..."

His voice came across the line as a hiss. "Theresa! Stop! They won't do that. You *know* the WGC won't step on the Reproductive Council's jurisdiction. It hasn't happened. It...it won't happen. You-you should n-not be talking like this. And you'd be smart to delete your cameras—I will if you won't."

"Fine."

She hung up the call on her hand-held and stood, wiping the moisture from her lashes and trying to steady her breath. *We have three hours. It might be enough.* Grabbing her office bag, she walked to the back storage room and scanned the alphabetically labeled, organized shelves. Previous iterations of the AUC unit were here collecting dust. Extra tubing, gloves, and neonatal resuscitation devices of various models filled a small steel crate.

She found what she was looking for and threw several of the vacuum sealed packages into her bag, keeping one out. Her movements were picking up speed, urgency, as the unformed idea grew and came together, taking on a plausible shape. Pausing in her frenzy and glancing around the storage room, she grabbed several more items, tossing them into her bag. She could still hit a vein.

Theresa sat down next to her discarded lab coat and undressed down to her waist, the chill of the storage room stinging her bare skin. She flipped over the sealed package in her hand and read the instructions, mumbling under her breath. "God, it's mostly warnings and contraindications. *Remove Remedial Placental Unit from packaging. Insert the blue needle into axillary vein and the red into brachial artery.* Wow. Color-coded for my convenience. Ha! I hope I can hit *my own* veins. Oh, and an artery."

Three tries later she managed both tasks. It took several attempts as well, for her to fasten each button of her shirt with trembling fingers.

Taking a breath, she straightened her lab coat, pulled out her hand-held, and walked back towards her workstation, several shades paler than when she entered the storage room. She sat down across from her computer and pulled the remote AUC control panel up on the hand-held screen. *Commence room sterilization.* Still trembling, she typed in the command followed by an authorization code.

"Okay. Time to pack." Theresa dialed in a thirteen digit code and the lights dimmed, the doors sealed, and the blinking red lights on the security cameras stilled.

She stood from the casual position she sat in and ran to the control panel as a toneless computer voice echoed from the security cameras. "Security camera malfunction. Corrective protocols implemented. Expected return to service in fifteen minutes."

"Shit. Fifteen? I should have just broken the damn thing." She brought AUC2 up on the screen. "AUC control. Prepare AUC2 for delivery. Stage Three."

"AUC2 has completed twenty-seven weeks of gestation and has not reached term. Confirm your command to prepare AUC2 for delivery?" The automated control spoke with an almost feminine voice.

"Command for delivery confirmed. Prepare AUC2 for delivery." Theresa's voice shook when she gave the command.

"Preparing AUC2 for delivery. Stage One and Stage Two delivery preparation have not been implemented. Without Stages One and Two the progeny has little chance of survival. Confirm command to skip to Stage Three preparation?"

"Confirmed. Skip to Stage Three." Theresa could hear the impatience in her own voice. Her fifteen minutes was ticking away.

"Command confirmed for delivery. Beginning Stage Three preparation."

She hurried down the aisle lined on both sides with glowing AUCs and stopped in front of AUC2. Opening her shirt to the waist, she dropped her bag and rifled through it. "Damn it!" She tossed several packages out of the bag and dug deeper, pulling out a sealed kit made of aged and polished mushroom leather. Theresa broke the magnetic seal, removed what resembled a small scalpel, and switched it on. The blade glowed with a soft white light as it heated. Theresa leaned over the AUC unit in front of her and sunk the tip of the glowing blade into the rounded fundus at the top of the unit. A thin seal covered the emergency access panel of the unit and Theresa broke it with smooth, swift cuts, then she lifted the upper portion of the translucent silicone shell and set it aside. The membranes were revealed before her, thin and vulnerable, rippling with small movements from within.

Motions brisk and economical, she ripped open a sealed bag from the storage room containing a thin translucent polymer sheeting. She held it in her hands a moment, staring from the flat sheeting and back to the small opening in the top of the AUC unit. *How do I get her out with this and still in the fluid?* Her eyes were panicked as she stared down at the plastic sheeting as if the answer must be written upon it. *Oh, okay. Maybe... just...* Folding it to form a bag-like shape she tucked the sheeting under one arm and lowered the scalpel again. The membranes sizzled when the heated blade made contact, giving off a smell that she had become accustomed to, though not fond of. *Almost like a cross between burning hair and cooking meat.*

The membranes gave way, splashing her bare skin with warm amniotic fluid that cooled quickly and left goosebumps on her arms and chest. Theresa was too focused to react to the discomfort—instead, she cut away the top of the chorionic and amniotic membranes, making an opening as large as the one she'd made in the top of the AUC unit, then dropped the scalpel on the tray next to her with a sharp clatter. Taking the folded plastic sheeting into her hands, she plunged it into the fluid like a collapsed balloon, maneuvered the sheeting over Abby's submerged head, then pulled it open and slid it down around her feet. In one quick motion she clamped the bottom of the plastic shut around Abby's cord and lifted her with both hands out of the Artificial Uterine Chamber that had been her host for the past 6 months.

Abby struggled, kicking and squirming against her hands. She could slip away so easily, fall to the hard ground. Theresa pulled her close—she wouldn't drop her—and leaned over the AUC to avoid exposing the cord to the cold air. It had to be wrapped in a tube of flexible plastic, kept warm and wet or Abby's blood flow would be restricted.

"Okay, Abby, this is going to be tricky. Bear with me, honey." The term of endearment felt strange in her head but sounded good spoken aloud.

Angling the open end of the makeshift capsule that was clamped shut in her fist against her chest, she alternately stretched the plastic open and pulled it tight against her skin. The plastic made a loose seal, only losing a small amount of fluid as Theresa struggled to prevent the seal from breaking and keep hold of the wriggling form inside. The leaking fluid splashed her chest, dribbled into her underclothes and down her legs as if she'd wet herself. Once she managed to flatten the plastic against her skin it formed a cocoon just large enough to hold Abby against her in the space between her breasts.

Taking up the scalpel once again, she pressed the flat edge against the seal between skin and polymer. The heated metal hissed against the damp edges, melting the adhesive beneath and securing the capsule. The glue was hot against her skin, hotter when the edge of the scalpel brushed her skin. She let out the breath she'd been holding as if anything but absolute stillness would have broken her focus and spilled Abby out of the precarious little balloon. But the seal was made and Abby was safe inside. Her AUC unit stood gutted and almost empty—just one last step.

"Shunt placental circulation to progeny AUC2." Her voice wavered, full of restrained emotion. "Not done yet. This used to work for us…so here we go."

With scalpel still in hand, Theresa reached down into the AUC and cut through the placenta in a small circle around the cord's insertion site. Only small tendrils of blood escaped into the fluid from the cauterized sides of the tissue, tinging it faintly pink.

She lifted the wrapped cord and placental tissue out of the water and, reaching into her sleeve from the inside of her open shirt, pulled out the RPU that was tucked there. Ripping off the sterile seal, she pressed the small chunk of placenta into the gel filled interior of the device and closed it around the wrapped cord. After checking all of her seals again, Theresa glanced down at the time on her hand-held display. Nine minutes and forty seven seconds had elapsed.

The sealed door to the laboratory hissed open, revealing a tall middle-aged man in a white lab coat, a young man barely out of his teens, also in a lab coat, and a young woman who looked to be in her mid-twenties. Dr. Brant and his assistants crossed the laboratory, peeking now and then into the AUC units and watching the large screens with their streaming data. Their steps were quick and energetic, eliciting the disrespectful echo of tourists in a cathedral.

Theresa turned in her seat and stood behind the desk that, only a few hours before, had held her belongings. The emotional education playlist played a soft ballad in the background, and she hummed along as Dr. Brant approached, holding out his hand to shake.

"Are you Dr. Brant?" Theresa scowled at the man in front of her, she stared at the hand he presented. What business did he have expecting a warm greeting? He was standing in a tomb with a smile on his lips. She did not take his hand.

Waiting a moment longer before giving up on a cordial greeting, Dr. Brant lowered his hand, rubbing his palm against his lab coat. His smile didn't slip.

"I'm Richard. Richard Brant. Ready to go, I see?" He motioned towards her tightly wrapped jacket and neck scarf, and the suitcase next to her chair. "I hope you aren't in a hurry. Maybe you can show me the ropes?"

He seemed to be trying for charm, the warmth in his eyes, a glint of humor, that smile. *Really?* Did he think she didn't know what was happening? Or that she didn't care? Theresa stood before him, the generally well-veiled inner thoughts and emotions clear in her pink and swollen eyes. "Everything you need to know is included in my records and notes, Dr. Brant, so if you'll excuse me…"

I have got to get out of here before I punch him in his damn teeth.

"Oh, you'll have to forgive me! These are my assistants, Jeremy and Elise." Jeremy stood close to Dr. Brant's side, hands in lab coat pockets, eyes skittering here and there, anywhere but the awkward scene playing out before him. At the mention of his name, he looked over at Dr. Brant, then met Theresa's gaze and lifted his hand a fraction to offer a shake. He shrunk from her stare and, thinking better of it, lowered his hand. Elise was a few feet away, looking into the only empty AUC in the room. She turned at the sound of her name.

"Hey, what happened to this one?"

Theresa stared at Elise, feeling her pulse quicken as she glanced over at the empty AUC unit. Adrenaline clouded her thinking, urging her to abandon the interaction and flee. Abby moved, kicking against her ribs. *She feels it too.*

"There was a demise. Just this afternoon." She turned back to Dr. Brant. "The progeny is in cold-storage and has already been examined. I intend to deliver him to department six for processing on my way out."

"Oh, what happened? I've read about the excellent survival rates of the program."

"As I'm sure you realize, it is the Reproductive Council's policy that progeny that are not keeping up with base-line milestones for growth and development be culled." Saying it aloud, despite the many times she had followed the protocol, left a sick taste in her mouth, burning, sour like the aftertaste of vomit. It was Abby she was talking about...It could have been her. Soon it would be all of Phase Four. "Up to this point I allowed his development to continue while I tried various measures to improve his growth rate, but found this morning that he was declining." The words were hard to say. Lies didn't come easily and this one felt like a betrayal. What was wrong with her?

"According to the protocols, I removed support and delivered the progeny. Upon further evaluation the placenta was found to have implanted poorly and was delivering insufficient blood flow."

"Couldn't that have been detected and corrected if you...'

Theresa cut him off. "Really, Dr. Brant, this is all in my notes. I have a new assignment to prepare for. What does it matter to you anyway, when you are just here to terminate the project?" *Did I just say that? It might have been better to punch him. Yeah, maybe I just will...*

Dr. Brant winked at her and leaned in to speak sotto voce. "I'm going to see about extending this project as long as possible, Theresa...Theresa, right? I hope you don't mind if I call you Theresa. Just between you and me, I think the AUC project is—fascinating, and important. I think it's a good project." He laughed, his proximity, the intensity of that look when he spoke about the project, unnerving her. Her nerves were worn thinner than electrical wires chewed down by rodents. That's what it was that was unsettling her, sending her thoughts racing and her insides fluttering. This man couldn't stop the termination. He was still talking.

"...And without the unfortunate and frequent necessity to interact with the hosts of the progeny like the surrogate program." Dr. Brant crinkled his nose.

Get it together and get the hell out, Theresa! She pulled in a slow deep breath. "It really was nice to meet you, Dr. Brant. I hope you can extend the project." She looked over at the AUC units and the progeny they held. Phase Four minus one. She wanted to cut each of them out of their capsules and strap them to her chest, take them with her. "There is a lot more riding on its continuation than your personal fascination. Good luck."

Lifting her bag in one hand, she turned and walked across the lab. She stopped at the cold storage to retrieve the cadaver progeny and left.

Department Six was a quick stop, three digital forms to be signed for transfer of custody, remittance of the deceased progeny for dissection or disposal. Each time she signed her name the script became more illegible, a spidery scrawl with dips and points in its legs that would have given her away to a handwriting analyst. She almost laughed at the thought of someone analyzing her name and declaring that Theresa Marin, declassed head researcher of the AUC program was smuggling live progeny under her jacket.

Was she delirious? It wasn't that funny. None of this was funny but she had to fight back laughter as she scribbled out the last signature, smiled at the secretary and placed the cold storage package on the counter. It held a long dead specimen from a previous Phase, not even Phase Four…not Abby.

Her steps echoed within the long tiled hallway. Each one brought her closer to the exit, closer to escape. Panic welled up in her belly when the door was in reach, the fear pushing her steps faster. She had to fight herself not to draw attention, not bolt for the door. *They know. How could they not? They're going to stop us here. Rip open my jacket. And take her. God, we've gotta get out.*

Cameras winked from the corners and above the door, the retinal scan that would authorize her exit another barrier. If someone knew and sent down an order to stop her, the door wouldn't open. But the scanner turned blue when she leaned in and gave a beep that meant she could go, no questions.

The AI voice spoke in cheerful tones as she came forward. "Good evening Dr. Marin, enjoy your new assignment."

The doors slid open, and as they shut behind her, Theresa stepped out into the wind.

ACCEPTING APPLICATIONS

A light rain pattered overhead, the sound a muffled tapping chorus that competed with the metallic hum of minuscule wings. David squinted dark expressive eyes up at the tinted poly-glass ceiling, thankful for the pigment that protected him from eyestrain and headaches out in the sun. They were such a dark shade of brown that they almost appeared black, like coffee reheated so many times it had condensed into a thick bitter remnant in the bottom of the mug. At least, that was how Joanna was apt to describe them. David flinched at the sudden memory of her words. Sixty-five years on this Earth and thirty years since they'd been together and she was still popping up unbidden in the middle of everyday tasks and random trains of thought. *Some things are built to last, Jo.*

He pushed a hand through his hair for the third time in so many minutes. It fell in messy brown curls around his forehead, not quite touching his shoulders, instead framing the sharp contours of his jaw. It gave him the lean, rugged look of a coyote left out in the uninhabited zone for too long after the land had gone dry and the small creatures had already moved on, fleeing from the rising temperatures into the man-made oases.

The poly-glass overhead was several layers thick and pitted by the frequent rainfall and the low PH. David turned his gaze from the ceiling to a row of miniature lemon trees that were surrounded by a haze of shimmering nano-bees, hovering and flitting around the blossoms.

Crushing the yellow, sun-burnt leaf of one tree between his fingers, he scowled up at the sun and pulled out his hand-held. "Increase UVA and UVB barrier tinting fifteen percent and increase LED lighting to compensate." *Darken it much more and we may as well garden underground.*

"Command confirmed. It has been brought to my attention that the rainwater being collected is registering a pH of 3.4 and contains several radioactive isotopes. In light of this, filtering components will need to be replaced sooner than previously estimated."

"I'll take care of it." David sighed and shook his head, watching the surface of the domed transparent ceiling dim and the white of the LEDs brighten. *If not for the rain or the light. What the hell are we doing all the way up here anymore?* His eyes narrowed and a scowl reshaped his lips. *Waiting for the surface to bubble up with life again, now that we've stepped aside? Like a house on stilts waiting for a flood in the uninhabited zone.* He pictured a house on chicken legs, old stories…The laugh that followed held little humor, laced with bitterness instead.

He strode towards the transparent wall overlooking the city, eyes pinching at the corners in response to the view in front of him. To the west, skyscraper-sized apartment buildings scintillated in the harsh sunlight that cut through the clouds, towering in front of the distant Pacific coastline. In all other directions, the abandoned ruins of the once-teeming Inland Los Angeles mega-city sprawled across the landscape all the way to the horizon where the Uninhabited Zone started, marked by the wall of heat distortion visible from afar. Even from the top of the multi-storied greenhouse, David could track the movements of bulldozer drones, tearing down the abandoned city bit by bit, reclaiming what was built in haste and excess and was no longer needed by so few. *Not that anything will grow down there if they ever get the rubble cleared away.*

David blinked the grim scenery from his eyes, loosening the set of his tightened lips and jaw, as he spoke to his hand-held. "New messages."

"You have fifteen new messages."

"Reread the one about reassignment options." He pushed a hand through the unruly dark brown curls that fell into his eyes, tickling the tanned skin of his brow.

The messages flashed across the screen and then paused on the requested missive. "Message found." The voice was expressionless and retained the echo of a voice simulation.

He rolled his eyes. "Read it aloud."

"Reassignment: Field research position. Nicaragua. Team lead required…"

He gestured for the machine to hurry up with a flick of his hand. "Skip to the end, please."

"Horticultural expert required for colonization effort. Mars. Medical evaluation, current psychological examination, and fitness testing required."

Despite hearing the message for a second time, he inhaled sharply, dark eyes taking in the familiar surroundings of the greenhouse around him, countless rows of miniature trees, tended by his hand from seeding to fruiting. *Could I leave it all?*

He caressed the dimpled side of a lemon, still green on its branch. *Joanna would go.* The thought brought the ghost of a smile to his long, pointed lips. He let the lemon drop, trusting to the branch that held it, and paced down the row of trees, disturbing the minute bodies of metallic pollinators buzzing in between the plants.

"And who would tend to all of this?" His eyes hardened, resistance crystallizing the hope in their depths before it was well-formed.

Someone else, David. The thought was clear in his mind, but it wasn't his own. *Someone who isn't made for more.* David snorted at the absurdity of the sentiment. *Someone who isn't slowly dying in here as the years pass.*

"I'm not leaving."

What are you staying for?

He paused mid-stride, eyes narrowing as he turned his gaze inward. "I don't..." The mumble came out in a tumbling rush of vehemence. "There's nothing here to stay for except for you and the plants. Even less to leave for."

Except to let go...forget.

"Never."

Never forget or never let go? The voice as he heard it was light, with the playful smile that would have gone with it.

Forget, Joanna...I can let go anytime.

You sound like an addict.

David laughed aloud, the sound full of genuine good humor. Reaching the security door that would admit him to the lower levels of the greenhouse, David leaned in for a scan, blue and gold lights flashing across his face.

"So you think I should go, huh?"

Clearly you think I think you should go.

"Same difference, Dear-heart." An amused smile lingered on his lips as he climbed onto the escalator and rode down to the surface.

Emily sat down in the chair, mild trepidation raising her blood pressure.

"Good morning, Emily!" The chair sounded excited to see her in its mechanical fashion. "You've lost twenty pounds since our last check-up. Great job!"

She smiled, blushing at the compliment, almost forgetting that she was conversing with a machine. The reflective sides of the alcove where the chair was enclosed flashed her own wide smile back a her, coral-pink lips pulling back to reveal small white teeth between freckled cheeks. Tentative as the smile was it was radiant with self-accomplishment and long-held hope-the sort that grows in fits and starts, held deep inside, languishing during rough patches when bouts of self-doubt prevail and flourishing once again during times of regained confidence, never winking out entirely and finally growing large enough to hold onto in the face of undeniable proof of progress—in this case, muscled shoulders and calves stretching her wardrobe and firmer curves, a clearer complexion, a healthy blush, signs that she was strong enough to pass this time. It was the sort of hope cultivated by the volatile of nature—such as Emily was.

"Yes, I have. I've taken all of our check-ups very seriously. I wanted to reach my ideal weight before this last check-up in preparation for getting my license to procreate. I've also improved my diet and taken up jogging." She smiled, the corners of her lips trembling as she struggled to rein in her nervous tension. The same nervousness lit her blue eyes, a rare blue that had become uncommon, passed on to her from her grandmother, having skipped her mother, whose eyes were instead a murky green that held a perpetual resentment. *It wasn't really Gram's fault-she would have been there if she could have.*

The sounds of the machine called her back from reverie. A soft humming emitted from the upper portion of the chair that craned over her and a blue light traveled down from her head to her toes.

"Your BMI is a bit low, Emily. I recommend an increase in caloric intake to sustain your new activity levels."

The corners of her lips turned down a bit before she pulled them back upwards, making a smile, albeit a shaky one, by force of will. "Oh…um…okay. I was aiming at 20% as was recommended at the last check-up. I guess I overdid it a bit." She laughed, the sound stiff and high-pitched like the laughter of an over-tired child.

"Commencing blood hormone level analysis." A robotic arm emerged from the side of the chair, its end effector a cylinder about the diameter of a pencil eraser. The cylinder pressed against Emily's skin, blanching the area white with pressure, and an even smaller cylinder within exerted strong suction to extract the least amount of blood necessary for analysis. She winced a bit and resisted the urge to pull back her arm. *At least it's not needles. I hate the idea of needles.*

Emily listened to the silence, as if by paying close attention she could hear the results sooner. A stinging pinch developed between her spine and both scapulas.

Blinking several times, she took a deeper breath. She could feel a build-up of mental tension as the seconds passed, like a brick wall being erected in her forehead, blocking her from any thoughts beyond it.

The computerized voice broke the silence and Emily caught the breath she was about to release, refusing to let anything interfere with her concentration. "Analysis complete. Hormonal conditions are not ideal for conception. Emily Brooks is otherwise in good health. Recommendations are as follows: continue exercise routine with an increase in caloric intake of three hundred calories. My records indicate you will reach your fortieth year before you are eligible for another fertility evaluation. Your request for a license to procreate is therefore denied, and we will schedule you for permanent sterilization due to advanced age at your next appointment. Would you like to remain on the foster list to await child placement at soonest eligibility?"

She couldn't breathe. The brick wall in her mind had melted down into something molten and had filled not only her head but her heart and lungs. Her vision swam, exploding into gray specks that expanded before her eyes and a sharp ringing cacophony filled her ears.

The friendly display on the preventive care and evaluation machine grayed out. Emily fainted.

Jon folded the page in half, then in half again two more times, closing his fist around the resulting small square of paper. He pushed a free hand through thin hair the color of a field mouse's and then paused to scratch the irritated scalp—it was a nervous habit carried over from his youth that not only left his scalp feeling angry and assaulted but thinned the fine hair that grew atop it—*leave that be, Jonny, it'll bleed soon!* It was a voice long dead—his mother's, the one who'd brought on his bout of nerves more often then not with her, *Jonny did you remembers* and *Jonny you just shouldn't haves*—in an incessant stream of verbal reproach fraught with her own worries. He'd soak up the strain and tension in the room, the reeking fear in her voice, and he'd start scratching.

The lights were out in the kitchen where he sat, decorative yellow flowered curtains—Emily insisted on such things—drawn over the automatically tinting windows. The sound from the other room was soft, unending, and damn hard to listen to. Jon glanced at the door to their bedroom, the door he was sitting across from, the door from which emerged a dirge-like moaning. The moaning ceased or differed only in short breaks, leaving instead of silence choking gasps and incoherent whimpers. *She's been in there all day. How long can she keep that up?*

Opening his hand, he unfolded the paper and smoothed it out on the glass table before him, pushing at the wrinkles and creases as if he could make it presentable again. He chanced another glance at the door, then down at the paper, pressed his lips together, and stood. Grasping it in one hand, he turned and took a step towards the bedroom.

The moaning coming from within transitioned to a higher-pitched keening and then tapered off, leaving behind sharp intakes of breath. Jon opened the door. The lights were out in here as well, but the curtains, drawn by a shaky hand, let in enough light for him to discern the crumpled form of his wife in the middle of their bed. He walked over, taking his steps with care.

Like a bull in a china shop, she would say. Now's not the time. Jon placed one long-fingered hand on his wife's shoulder.

"Please, Jon. Don't look at me. Not like this!" Her face was swollen and red when she glanced up at him, her eyes puffed, angry wounds rimmed in sodden lashes. The sharp blue of her eyes struck him as it always did when she was crying, and twenty years, for better or worse, could bring a lot of tears. Of course there was laughter, plenty of it, but when the tears flowed this heavy, as they had the last five years or so, the laughter got a bit damp.

"Em, I've seen you like this plenty." She shuddered and the tears flowed again, her face contorting in grief.

"Yeah. I guess so!" The last word trailed off into a sob.

"That's not what I mean, Em. Not at all. All this is…I mean, I know it hurts. You can cry as much as you need to. I just…Don't I do okay? You don't have to shut me out. This is both of us, right?" He kneeled down at the side of the bed and stroked Emily's soft, coppery hair.

She moved closer to him, resting her forehead against his. "It's not that, Jonathan. It's just me. It's always me. You got approved the first year we started this, and with me it's just one thing after another: my hormones, my stress, my weight! You could have a family by now if not for me." Emily tried to smile at her husband but the corners of her mouth turned down at the bitterness of the words she had spoken, the arsenic taste of apple seeds bitten by accident.

"Shhhh…Don't say that, Em! Don't ever say that." He locked eyes with his wife and nodded to punctuate his words. "Look, Emily. I have something for this."

He pulled the document from his pocket and started to unfold it onto the surface of the quilt. Emily looked over at what he was doing, wiping her eyes and sniffing her nose, now congested and swollen. She watched as he opened the paper and stared at the image, now worn by repeated folding and unfolding. A family stood together, a man holding the hand of a small boy, his arm around his wife with an infant in hers. Their faces held smiles of contentment as they looked out over a rugged landscape with sparse vegetation.

A caption explained in large bold writing: *Accepting applications for colonists! Apply now and claim your future! All accepted will be granted reproductive freedom as an integral part of colony life.*

She recoiled, pulling back her hand and curling in on herself. Her voice was small and muffled, holding back another wave of tears. "Jon, I can't."

"Can't what, Emily?" His face was still as he waited.

The tears came. "I can't apply anymore! I can't get shut down anymore! Five years of NO NO NO! I'm just done. I'm done."

He stood up and paced the room, restless hands finding his scalp and being none too gentle. "Emily, this is different! If we just... try. This last thing…We could just…" He paused in his pacing and stared over at his wife, curled up in a fetal position. She gave no answer, and, in fact, could have been asleep but for the ragged, hitching breaths that gave her away.

He waited a moment more, his frustration building. Emily's refusal to answer stretched into a chasm between them. Shoving his hands deep into his pockets, he walked out of the room, and shut the door behind him.

A smiling face was illuminated in the glaring light, and then fell into soft shadow, the subtle nuances made visible; then was lost to the sharp sunlight again. Leaning over the edge of her bed, Emily stretched her fingers out to their greatest length, overextending her reach and grasped the rumpled and discarded page in her outstretched hand. With prize obtained, she reached behind herself and grabbed hold of the coverlet, hauling her body back towards the upper surface of her bed. *What was I...* she lost her grip and slid to the floor with a loud thud and a sudden exhalation of breath.

Lying flat on her stomach against the bedroom carpet, fistful of coverlet in one hand and crumpled paper in the other, she couldn't hold back the smile that threatened.

Once the smile found purchase on her face and within her heart the laughter broke free as well, filling the room. She drew her knees up as she sat; still laughing, she wiped the moisture from the corners of her eyes and turned her gaze to what she held in her hands.

A husband, a wife, children. The light let in through the fluttering drapes illuminated the image and played across the words written below it. Emily stood, brows furrowed, lips a thin slash across her flushed cheeks as she walked over to the work desk where her hand-held waited.

THE GARDENER

The door sealed shut behind her last patient for the day, leaving Carla alone to contemplate the wet tear-stained patches on both shoulders of her shirt. *Seems to sink into my skin, as well as my clothes.* She massaged both temples, letting out a shaky breath and closing her weary eyes against the barren sight of her office. The only thing the room held that was personal to her was she herself despite the many years spent between these walls, slabs of recycled paneling with swirls of what they had once been, left behind as a constant reminder. The ghosts of soda bottles, milk cartons, and discarded plastic toys screamed at her from within the surface. The tinted poly-glass windows on the far wall curbed the harsh glare of sun that she would have welcomed, leaving the temperature controlled room dim and comfortable, much to her chagrin. Each time she'd thought to liven it up and bring in plants or some other such bit of home, she stopped herself. *I don't live here, I just work.*

She smoothed the damp fabric almost reverently with hands lined with experience instead of age. It was as if she was rubbing the dampness in instead of brushing it off. *Better I carry some of it for them, lest they drown in it...almost did myself once.* Even the silver rope of a braid that hung down to the mid-point of her back, the only badge of honor granted to her despite the treatments, was damp from tears.

She sighed. Not the usual uncomplicated exhale, but instead a long, heaving breath, releasing the barest amount of the tension she held from borrowed troubles. *You'd think with how much time and money is taken up on therapy to keep these women stable that the Council would find an alternative to the Surrogate Program. Maybe remove some of those damn implants and let the people take care of it. With the population so low it would take more than a little old fashioned random breeding to screw things up again.*

Carla unfolded her legs and stood, stretching the kinks out of her muscles, tired now from lack of movement and the drain of taking in the pain of others. At least she wasn't falling apart, as she likely would have been without outside help. The only difference she had noticed since she started closing in on a century was that her muscles and joints were less forgiving of misuse. Lack of use really. All day indoors, sitting too long, standing too long, virtually no walking, and her muscles would protest, pinching, aching. *No scrolling sidewalks for me on the way home, if I want to work out these kinks. Can't keep my old gears oiled up if I just stand around and let the sidewalks carry me.*

"I need my garden time today, sure enough." *Soak up the smell of tomatoes and slough off the stress.* Pulling out a small stack of papers, Carla tucked them into her satchel, making a space with her hand first and adding cushioning on either side. *Gotta get these out faster before the application period ends. Be a shame to let them waste even if they were just going to be reprocessed, but it can't be just anyone. That'd be like tossing seeds onto stone. None would take root and the effort would be wasted. Not to mention I'd be an utter fail-trout as a gardener. Now wouldn't I?*

The daily broadcast lit up the back wall of her office, startling her from her thoughts. She flinched at the cheerful melody that preceded the programming; it was loud in the small room and syrupy, the cloying taste of overripe fruit. A steady stream of dynamic images and footage lit the screen and reflected across Carla's face as she turned to watch.

A small group of young apprentices climbed into a transport drone, laughing as they conversed soundlessly. The voiceover started in—a warm female tone, narrating as the group of youths gave way to older versions of themselves, gathering in a home for drinks in the evening, the night lit up by paper lanterns, soft focus images of the natural world dancing across their filmy surfaces. *"Successful and fulfilled by your assignment and the comforts and security of modern life. Most of us have more than enough to make us happy..."*

Carla fought the soothing effect of the scenes, struggled against the contentment that descended in response to the familiar advertisement. *Happy or complacent?* Her lips twitched up in a bitter smile.

The next scene filled her veins with ice, like a sudden jump into freezing waters. Carla's jaw tightened, a grimace replacing the bitter smile with which she greeted the other images.

The narrator spoke again as the next scene faded in. *"But for those few, who want something more… a family without the inevitable sacrifice of health, safety, and career…"*

A banner stretched across the same comfortable home, *"It's a boy!"* printed in stylized blue letters. *"Welcome home, Eric!"*

The door opened and the couple stepped out, nervous smiles on their faces, eyes sparkling with wonder as a boy of seven or eight came up the walk, slowly at first, and then broke into a run, diving into their arms. Tears and hugs were shared, laughter and silent introductions as the scene faded out and was replaced by flowing script on the screen and the narrator's soft voice.

"There comes a time when the intensity of apprenticeship and budding relationships have given way to the routine and security of coupled life…for a select few selfless individuals, the next step is family.

Apply for Progeny placement today and meet the family that is waiting for you!

Carla turned away from the screen, the sinking of her stomach more of a nauseating lurch, dropping down past where her feet touched the cold tiles. Reaching for her satchel and hanging it on her shoulder, she turned to the door.

"Kendra Soulie would like to see you. Should I let her in?" The simulated voice of her office security door startled her.

"Sure you should. Of course, that isn't the same as saying I authorize it." Carla smirked at herself.

"Would you like to grant her entry?"

"Well I would, but…Oh, hell. Let her in. I guess I don't have to leave just yet."

The door hissed open, catching the woman waiting on the other side by surprise. Kendra's arms were crossed over her chest, hands squeezing her biceps hard enough to blanch her tawny skin a pale beige, and her face was tense, threaded through with suffering. The wide nostrils of her softly-rounded nose flared with each in-breath and her full bottom lip had a slight tremble when she loosened her jaw.

The anchorman on the news broadcast spoke as the musical interlude ended. "Top of our agenda tonight is the surface reclaiming progress report. The long-awaited data is in from two-thirds of the drones, and we have preliminary numbers for you this evening, so you'll want to stay tuned for details to the end of the broadcast. To give a little hint— camp-outs and trail-hiking may not be as far off as previous estimates indicated—"

A dark-haired co-anchor interrupted, her voice light with the tone of playful banter. "When you say sooner than projected...Are we talking sooner by a couple years or within our lifetime sooner?"

The smiling anchorman chuckled. "Within our lifetime sooner, Bridget, but don't make me give it away before—"

Kendra glanced at the broadcast, eyes sharp with irritation, and Carla scowled along with her. "Mute the damn broadcast, will you?

"Of course. Would you like to stay tuned to the end to hear about the..." The computerized voice dripped with pleasant undertones.

"No, I wouldn't. Mute it now and I'll practice my lip reading." She turned her attention back to her guest as silence descended. Kendra's breathing was controlled, too controlled, with patches of unevenness that reminded Carla of the residual hitching after a storm of tears.

Shouldn't've made her wait. Carla walked over to Kendra, arms extended for an embrace, offering up her already damp shoulders. Kendra pressed her lips into a thin slash and shook her head, pushing past and pacing the room instead.

"I should have known they'd take them *all* out on the same day. Of course Alissa and Nicole already came by."

Carla nodded. With only a few scattered confidences shared during the longer counseling sessions between them Carla knew Kendra's people. They were the sort that skirted modern custom and council regulations, breeding and raising their own as long as it was legal and keeping them from apprenticeship placement well past the upper limit of acceptability. You could hear it in Kendra's voice, the soft lilt that was hard to mask, and if she trusted you, word substitutions and added endings from an old-fashioned dialect that had mostly been bred and trained out of the population. There were many such dialects gone or still dying out, in Kendra's case a mix of Haitian Creole and AAVE from the west coast of North America. She'd only slipped once with that word after the first of her progeny had been taken out and Carla was called to calm her, *tiprogé-bébé*. There weren't many people left like Kendra. And yet here she was, from a line of individuals who still knew the meaning of family, the value of individuality.

The determined and clever young woman she'd come to know these past three years looked worn around the edges. A babe of twenty-eight years and the surrogacy had worn away all the care-free confidence she had exuded when she started and replaced it with bitterness and resignation. *Perhaps there's still some of the strength left though, buried underneath. That could be enough.*

Carla flicked her eyes down to the sheaf of leaflets in her bag.

"This was my last time. Third times a charm, right?" Kendra's laugh was tight, her eyes, a warm dappled brown like fresh ground nutmeg looked momentarily frantic. "But they're talking about extending me if I want. If I want?! There are some that love it, feel the gift of it without the pain. She fetched a deep sigh. "It's not for me anymore."

Carla looked away, the bitter frown on her lips turned towards the window instead of her patient. *Third times a charm when keeping them through ten to twelve birthings as they used to left too many angry, broken surrogates for me to piece them back together as useful, productive members of society.*

Kendra paced in front of her, stealing glances at the counselor's face. "I'm worried about Lissa and Coli, they've two more times and they're breaking like water on rocks." She shook her head and sat down in Carla's chair, rocking herself. "I don't think they'll put a request for reassignment in by themselves and I don't know where to point them. I have time to decide where to go next, I want to try some things before deciding, you know? Find what feels right."

Another nod. "Do you want to talk about what happened today?"

Kendra flinched, and then trying to smile managed a grimace. "No. I don't. I talked about the first one, and I talked about the second one and talking didn't take it back." The fire went out of her sharp eyes and her voice lost its vehemence. "I accepted the assignment, thought I was suited for it with what I'd learned from granmé and manma—Now I think I was impatient to experience it." She shook her head, closing off the memories attached to those names as if behind heavy oak doors. "I just need to... figure out where I'm going now."

Carla slipped one hand into her bag and pulled out the pamphlets. She rubbed her lips together, hesitating, and then placed the sheaf of thin paper into the other woman's hand.

"Now…you could take a look at this. You have a legacy behind you that most don't have. Maybe take it where it'll find fertile soil. Nurture it, pass it down."

Kendra's lips parted as she stared at the top pamphlet mouthing the words under her breath and then staring up at the older woman.

Carla spoke again before she could. "It's an option. You'd have choices. And if you drag the other surrogates along, you'll have family." Carla slid her arms into her jacket sleeves, pulling her silver-white braid out of the back.

Kendra stood and followed her through the door, holding up the pamphlets with a sidelong glance.

"I'm gonna take these, okay? See how it feels after a think about it more. I'll pass them on if it's not for me if—well, that's why you gave me all these, isn't it?"

"Yes." A smile pulled at the corners of Carla's lips and she nodded. "Alright then, so long as you make the application deadline."

"What about you? Will you be there?"

Carla nodded as she buttoned up her coat against the wind. "Count on it."

"Shit!" Long, narrow fingers grasped and clawed for the ochre-colored ceramic pot as it slid over the balcony's edge, scraping the side and then shattering on its way down. "It has a long way to go if it's going to hit bottom." Carla glared over the edge at her lost seedling. She turned to face her audience, several racks and carts shoved full of leafy twining vegetable plants, as well as hanging pots of flowers and repurposed tires holding struggling fruit trees. "And trust me…you won't want to go following that one. The dirt's all covered up down there and the bit that oozes through is sour!" The old woman cackled at herself. "Not the paradise you're picturing! Don't you give me that look!" She cocked an eyebrow at the tomatoes that were giving her sass. "We're all growing in captivity now, not just you. Just ask the bees. Some of them's been sneaking off at night to look for greener pastures. Ha!" She tipped her head and nodded towards a wooden box tucked into a corner behind an orange tree and an over-grown aloe plant from which a steady buzzing emanated. Minute furry bodies dressed in yellow-gold and black crawled along the edges of the box, some coming and others going, flying over to the nearest orange blossoms or the heavy red and pink blooms dangling from a pot above them that resembled bleeding hearts.

Carla brushed the potting soil, accumulated from her evening's efforts in her garden, off onto her jeans. She turned back to the balcony railing to shake her head at the loss once more, and then zipped the plastic sheeting through which the pot had escaped and headed inside with the basket of vegetables she had gathered.

Emptying most of the basket into her food storage and processing unit, she slipped a small portion of vegetables out of the basket and into a tall glass pitcher on the counter with a computerized base.

An old-fashioned blender.

Popping on a worn plastic lid, she placed her finger on the start button and looked over at her only companion, a small cinder gray cat who was currently napping on a bookshelf next to the only window. "Come on, Sisyphus! I don't have all night. I need to pack."

The muscular dark-gray animal sat up and, glancing in her direction, began washing his paw with a delicate pink candy tongue, eyes squinted to reveal just a sliver of yellow-green.

"Not interested this morning? Huh. Well, I'll just go ahead and push this then, I guess." Carla opened her eyes wider to punctuate her statement and tapped the button once, and then again to stop the roar of the blender. Sisyphus startled and darted from his spot before meandering in her direction, paws crossing as he made his way to his customary spot a foot from the blender. She chuckled and reached out to stroke Sisyphus' soft fur. Her hand was met halfway by the cat as he pushed his head into her palm and purred, rivaling the volume of the blender. "That's right, Sisyphus. I'm not old fashioned. The blender's for you. Can't watch it swirl if we use the FSP, now can we?"

The blender roared to life with another push of the button. Leaving it to swirl away, she moved into a crouch on the kitchen floor, and then lowered herself into a prone position. Arms bent and toes to the floor, she straightened and then bent her elbows, alternately, bringing the side of her cheek down to brush the floor, her back and knees straight as the floor she pushed up from. "One…two…three…Not bad, eh, Sisyphus?" Carla forced her breath out between pushes, managing to speak above the roaring of the blender so the cat would hear her. *Not bad at all for an old woman! Gotta stay tough. My time's coming. Bout damn time too. I've spent long enough nursing sick minds. Time to serve my purpose.*

"Forty-seven…forty-eight." The sinews of her muscles stood out like bunches of ropes and trembled slightly with the effort. Her skin held some wrinkles, like that of a woman in her late forties, but her muscles were strong and firm. "Forty-nine…fifty."

Carla bent one knee and slid it towards her waist to take the weight off of her arms, then sat back into a low squat, stretching her legs and standing tall before sliding back down into a deep squat one hundred times more before stopping. Her breath came fast and ragged by the time she was done.

She was flushed, glistening with sweat from the exertion and several strands of twisting silvery hair had escaped her braid. She pulled in a deep breath and allowed a smile to spread across her cheeks. There was a sparkle in her blue eyes as she savored the rush of sexy-warm feel-good endorphins that spread through her body like gentle waves in a hot spring.

Jabbing the blender with one finger, Carla stopped its cacophonous screaming and, along with it, the swirling of the now homogenous beet red mixture. Sisyphus pawed the side of the blender, and then trotted over to his dinner dish as Carla lifted it off of its base. She poured its contents into a tall crystal glass and took a gulp before pouring some into the cat's dish, along with a small jar of farm-raised sardines that she produced from a drawer full of the same. "One jar for you and one for me. Gotta make em last, with how tight the rations on these are."

Carla's hand-held let out a soft chime followed by a light simulated female voice. "Your grand-daughter is on the line. Would you like to speak with her or wait for her to leave a message?"

"Do I ever send my granddaughter to voicemail?" She set down the empty glass and wiped her fingers on a dishtowel before moving to pick up her hand-held.

"No. But there is a first for everything. Switching to speaker." The voice spoke with almost a sing-song inflection that mimicked human speech, but held little emotion.

"That's right. Thank you!" Carla picked up her device in one hand and with the other put her dishes away for sterilization.

"Thank you for what, Gran?" Emily's voice came through the speaker.

"Oh…um…nothing. I was just thanking my smart-ass hand-held again!" Carla laughed at herself. "Well, what's your news, miss? It sounds big."

She bustled around her kitchen, looking in drawers and cabinets and pulling things out to spread across the counters.

"You always do that, Gran! How do you know before I say it?" Emily's voice was more tremulous than usual. *Was that fear or excitement?*

"We're going to have children, Gran, as many as we want! If we can, I mean. If I can. I'm getting older and…This is just crazy but we're going to do it! We got accepted into the first colony! I haven't even told him yet. I wanted to but I just couldn't. He thinks it will work if we just try... I don't know, Gran. I think it's too late." Emily's voice had transitioned from excitement to despair over the course of her speech. Her erratic breathing could be heard through the line.

"Woah, Woah! Slow down there, Emily! Hold up. Breathe child, br-eeeathe." She took several slow, deep breaths herself to demonstrate. "I caught the gist of that, so you're doing fine. Just don't hyperventilate before you can get yourself packed up to go."

Carla smoothed the folded edges of a purple garment, tucked it into the small satchel that she had taken out and placed on the now cluttered counter-top. "Jonathan asked me to go with him, to try, but I just couldn't. Now I just have to. I think I'll just smother if we stay here!"

Carla nodded several times, a smile playing at the corners of her lips. "So Jon wants to go, does he?" *I'll bet he does after I tucked that flyer into his pocket. And bludgeoned him with the facts for a few hours. It's a damn good thing he trusts me or he'd have had me burnt at the stake.* She covered her mouth to stop the laugh that her absurdity brought forth. *I wonder if they'd make an exception to the rehabilitation codes so they could burn me.*

"Yes, I don't know where he got it, but he gave me a flyer when I…well, after my check-up." Emily's voice filled with excitement again, the tremble transitioning from one of fear to one full of wonder.

"Are you sure you want to leave everything behind? It's going to be rough and very different, you realize. I know you like your comfort, your routine. And it won't be easy having babies in a place like that." The old woman's eyes sparkled in anticipation of her granddaughter's response, bringing out the bright blue that she had passed on to the other woman, a blue that hadn't faded one bit in the past century.

"I know it will be difficult. I know…but can it really be worse than…Oh! Gran! You have to come with me! How else will I make it through pregnancy…and the delivery! I shouldn't even try by modern standards …I should just…but maybe if you came too…I'm sure there'll be physicians there, but I'd rather have you to deliver."

"Birth, Em. It's a baby you're talking about, not a package, but I'll come with you. I'll even catch if you want." Carla pulled a wooden box, mahogany red with a brass latch and covered in dust, out of the compartment over her bed. Running a hand around the edges and smoothing away the dust, a light smile played on her lips. She opened the box with just a slight shake to her fingers-*when did I last open it?*-and pulled out the small items on the top: an antique stethoscope, the flexible tubing cracking with age; a small device shaped like a pinard horn, flaring on one end and thinner on the other with a blank, lifeless screen on the thinner end; an old-fashioned storage device shaped like a small stick of gum; and a necklace, the silver charm depicting a humanoid curled around itself and half formed. Carla stared at the charm in her palm, conflicted.

"You really will?" Her granddaughter's voice broke through the reverie, breathy and animated with excitement.

"If they'll have me. They'll have physicians though. Don't expect them to take well to the idea of an old woman catching your baby."

Reaching in with both hands she pulled a relic, from days long past, out of the box and set it on the bed. The thick tome was bound in worn leather the same color as the box, the title gold embossed.

Women's Legacy

Her smile returned, creeping in from the middle and spreading all the way to the corners as she stared down at her great-grandmother's book.

"Well, that is what you did, isn't it, Gran? We could try, couldn't we?" Uncertainty shook her voice.

Carla tucked her relics back into the mahogany box and closed the lid, easing it into the rectangular luggage bag on her bed. "Sure we can, Em. I only have one grand-daughter, and for an old woman who loves babies that's just a travesty. I wouldn't miss watching her become a mother, not even for this world." She smiled when she spoke, but her eyes were sharp, her jaw set.

She opened her hand and held the charm up to the light, dangling it from its chain. Her brows smoothed out and she nodded. Opening the chain, Carla clasped it around her neck, before closing her fist over the cold silver charm once more. *If you only knew, Em. If you only knew.*

REASSIGNED

Genesis slipped the glasses over her eyes for the third time to see the message recorded within, a smile tugging at her lips. "Replay."

Virginia Blaylock materialized inside the lenses, red hair pulled back into a tight French twist, sallow skin, and voice nasal. "Genesis, you are being removed from the Progenesis Breeding and Repopulation Program and re-assigned. Report to my office in one hour to receive your new assignment and relocation."

"It's about damn time." Genesis stood from the side of the bed where she was perched, her movements echoing those of the long extinct panther as she crossed to the wall opposite. Her hair, the same color as the large jungle cat, hung in a sleek waterfall down her back over skin just dark enough to protect from the brutal rays of the sun but diluted enough to prevent an over-developed sense of individuality or clannishness, a safe golden-brown that was common in the nearly homogenized population. Her eyes were several shades lighter and much less common, a luminous yellow-gold with flecks of burnt-umber around the pupil.

She placed one hand against a small glass panel, awaiting the subsequent scan, and with the other reached into the compartment. She removed a set of folded men's clothing, turning to face her bed and its occupant.

Two steps forward, a flick of the wrist. She tossed the clothes onto the sleeping form in her bed, her movements swift and economical.

"Uhhh…" The man moaned and rolled over to face her. He flexed his pecs and shoulders, stretching well-muscled arms far above his head as a large grin replaced the grogginess. "Good-morning, Geny." Caspian sat up just enough to remind Genesis that he was dressed only in her slippery red sheets.

"Get up, Caspian. I don't have time for this." She stood with her hands folded behind her head, features and voice even, tone commanding. "Do not call me Geny."

"Hey, I called you Geny last night and you liked it! What the hell's this?" He sat up, swinging his legs over the edge and resting his hands on his thighs. The red sheets slipped to the floor with the soft hissing sound of silken fabric, leaving nothing of Caspian's nakedness for her photographic memory to fill in. "Last night we were getting somewhere, and now you've gone all robo-bitch on me again this morning!"

"Where exactly did you think we were getting to, Caspian?" She raised one black eyebrow and smirked. "The arrangement is over and, therefore, so are we. Now get dressed and get out."

"What? That doesn't make any sense. I would have been notified if I was assigned to someone else!"

Genesis walked over to Caspian, muscular legs turning just so to exaggerate the sway of her hips. She stopped next to him, and leaned against his bare chest. Nuzzling into his down-turned face to find his lips, she parted her own, allowing him to breathe her breath, warm and uniquely hers. Her tongue and teeth caressed his lower lip, full soft petals of her mouth brushing, teasing until he looked up into her golden eyes, his brown ones raw with restrained emotion.

"Get out of my room."

Caspian's brow furrowed, lips parting to reveal clenched teeth. He turned and reached down to retrieve his discarded shirt, jerking it over his head and forcing his arms through the fitted sleeves with barely-contained violence. He crossed the short distance to grab his pants.

"I don't know if you've been reassigned. I'm being transferred to something more fitting to my skills, and I don't have time for your delusions about our 'budding' relationship." Her voice rose in volume as she spoke, sharpening with each word, a blade in expert hands. She closed the gap between them again as Caspian pulled on his pants, struggling with one leg and almost falling over.

"Do you need help, Caspian?" Genesis stood with her hands locked behind her head where her cascade of thick black hair started on its way down to the middle of her bare back.

Caspian glanced up at the woman he had spent the last several nights with and shook his head, standing to his full height so that he was looking down at her. "No thanks, Geny."

He gave Genesis a tight smile and walked past her to the door, turning back in the doorway as it opened.

"You know, Geny." Caspian cocked his head and appraised her, his eyes lingering too long. "You might have some skills…but I've gotta say that you were the coldest fuck I've ever had." He turned and left, allowing the door to close and seal itself behind him.

"Access reassignment database." Genesis sat cross-legged on her chair in front of a large projected computer screen, dressed in a black tank top and yoga pants. Her hair, falling across dark, caramel-toned shoulders and down to her waist in a cascade of sleek tresses, opalesced like an oil-slick on the ocean surface under the soft blue glow of the computer screen.

"Access codes required." A small window coalesced on the screen in front of her, blinking in and out, and awaiting the entry of an access code.

Lips moving silently, she ran through the many possible combinations of numbers, letters, and characters that were pertinent to the creator of the access code. *Red-hair, forty-two, un-mated, swims, social security 593-17-5639...born 2282, May 19.* She typed in a combination of numbers and letters adding in an exclamation point for good measure and clicked 'submit.'

"Access denied. Perhaps you mistyped. Two attempts remaining."

Genesis licked her lips and turned her gaze downward in contemplation for a moment. She replaced two numbers and clicked submit for the second time.

"Access denied. Did you forget your Access Code, Ms. Blaylock?"

Pausing a moment to think, she ran the tips of her thumbs downwards across the smooth surfaces of her long pointed nails, reveling in their perfection.

A soft sound of delight escaped her lips, like that of a child discovering that water pours. Deleting the previous attempt, her fingers flew across the keys, barely pausing before tapping the enter key to submit.

"Access granted. Would you like to change your passcode to something more memorable?"

Genesis laughed aloud, a deep throaty sound that was full of satisfaction. She clicked enter again instead of switching to voice command. *Better not push it just now. We're not in the clear yet.* Reaching across the desk she retrieved her Virtual Com Glasses and flicked them open before sliding them onto her eyes. "Message recall. Virginia Blaylock. Image capture. Ocular imprints, code 376-21-7895-12. Lend me your eyes." A small grin played upon Genesis's lips and her eyes beneath the glasses were alight with the thrill of conquest.

"Commencing ocular scan." Lights glowed upon the screen and flashing numbers indicated the matching markers for comparison achieved.

"Identity confirmed. Welcome, Ms. Blaylock. How are you today?"

What appeared to be a large web-work of data opened up on the main screen. Upon closer examination, she could see that this was the master list of assignments within the Reproductive Council, mapped out according to their interconnections and the sectors that held jurisdiction over them. Genesis leaned in to the computer, her golden eyes scanning the options laid out before her.

Eyes swollen from crying, the young woman sat before Virginia's desk, hands folded in her lap and shoulders slumped. Virginia grasped her hand-held device with one hand and swiped a loose strand of red hair back into place with the other.

The bright pink color of discomfiture, as she was wont to call it, dominated her thin face and glowed through the concealer she used to hide her freckles.

An ever-present crease of concern that had taken up residence above her pointed eyebrows had deepened since Genesis came weeping in about a half-hour before. Now she scanned through the many pages of possible assignments, looking for something to suit the dejected young woman sitting before her. Her appointed procreation assignment had not taken the news of their reassignment well and must have taken it out on Genesis. The girl wouldn't say as much, but it was obvious, really. Virginia's insides fluttered and her cheeks burned with shame. It was an oversight, of course, but she should have personally informed Genesis's assignment of the situation instead of allowing the girl to handle it herself. *Still, clearly he's not professional, if he'd blame the girl for her reassignment.*

Virginia tapped one purple nail against the glass. *Let's see, but what to do with her, I can't send her into surrogacy.* Glancing up at Genesis, she found the girl had wrapped her arms around herself and was staring unblinking at the virtual fish tank display on the wall, eyes red-rimmed, lips trembling. Virginia's lips tightened into a thinner line and she shook her head. *Just not right.*

"Let's look at your previous assignments, shall we? Social Anthropology Research and Consultation, Software Development, Political Systems Analyst, Human Resources Specialist." Virginia blinked and arched a brow at Genesis. "My, aren't we eclectic?"

Genesis shrugged. "I enjoy a new challenge."

"Where do you *want* to be assigned? I'm sure I can find a way to ensure you get where you can feel challenged and avoid further...agitation."

Genesis's eyes widened, and she took a quick breath, shaking her head in indecision as her words escaped in a rush. "Really? I...well...I didn't think I could say...I've thought about it, of course, but...well, maybe somewhere I could start over? Somewhere outside of the reproductive programs. Maybe there's something else I could help with, something related but distant?

Virginia squinted her eyes and pursed her lips. "Actually. I think there is something. Let me see. For what I have in mind you'll actually have two assignments." She locked eyes with Genesis. "I don't think you'll be bored. It will require us to up your security clearance, though."

Turning to her main computer screen on the wall, Virginia entered the proper code to pull up a new assignment for Genesis.

PARTNERSHIP

Reaching across the chasm between the daybed and the end-table, Theresa's hand swiped at the expected location of her hand-held. Instead of the device, her fingers jammed against the edge of the table. Two nails, which had begun to grow back since the nerve-driven biting a week before, broke below the quick.

"Owww!" Theresa sat up, despite her grogginess, and placed her wounded fingers between her lips to soothe the stinging. Her eyes tried to open, but found the effort required too much in the face of the crusts of dried sleep-tears that held the edges of her lashes hostage. Peering instead with eyes half-open, she looked over to the table, fingers still between her lips, only to find that her hand-held was no longer where she remembered leaving it the night before. In its stead she found dishes still laden with left-over pizza turning crusty and flavorless, as well as half-full water glasses that had formed bubbles overnight.

Like fish-farts gathering in an aquarium... She smiled at her cheap sense of humor.

The soft chime that had awoken her repeated itself from somewhere beneath the cushion she was sitting on.

Theresa stood with the intention to turn and reach under the cushions, but instead slid down to her knees, resting her flushed cheek on the cushions to wait out the vertigo that washed over her. The spinning sensation receded, in part due to her stillness and her slow, deep breaths, but was replaced by a squirming, urgent feeling of nausea that kept her from standing again. She instead reached one hand beneath the cushions, careful not to move too quickly, and groped around for her objective.

Theresa's hand bumped against something solid. "Target acquired." She frowned. Her voice sounded dry and weak to her ears. Rising with more care this time, she climbed back onto the day-bed, her movements cautious, and rolled onto her back. Her call log had stored several messages while she slept, and she scrolled through them. The first two were follow-up details about her upcoming assignment, and the last three were from Dr. Richard Brant.

She hesitated a moment before opening them. A wave of excitement punctuated by the sharp thrill of fear rolled through her. A roller-coaster in the dark, hurtling around turns without warning or safety net seemed an apt comparison. *Better that I let him stay in contact than think I have reasons not to.* She lifted one pale, trembling hand to the hollow between her breasts, where Abby's cocoon was sealed to her skin, hidden beneath the robe she wore, and selected the message with the other.

"God. What is *with* this guy, Abby?" Theresa stared up at the first message on the screen.

<*Good morning, Theresa! Still enjoying your hiatus? I'll bet you're itching to get back into a lab. I'm sure I can get you a pass to come visit the kids. I could use your expertise. Let's compare notes over lunch.*>

She pushed the frazzled mess that her braid had become over the past few days out of her eyes and blinked at the message on the screen. "Seriously? Lunch? Yeah, because I really need a date with the callous prick who took over the assignment I've been on since I was like, eleven!" *Especially with an illegal growth nestled snuggly between my aching boobs.*

"Don't mind Abby! She was just a parting gift for my years of hard work. Oh yeah, they give underdeveloped progeny out to everyone they fire…"

The laughter broke free then, filling the empty room and leaving Theresa feeling like her grip on reality was slipping. Abby squirmed and kicked herself awake; aroused by Theresa's laughter, she struggled against the weight of the palm covering the whole of her back. Theresa pushed the robe aside and peered down at the impossible gift that grew and developed before her very eyes. It had been 3 weeks since their escape and Abby had changed visibly. Her skin was less translucent and her limbs longer.

"Hi, Abby." Theresa's voice took on a soft, lilting tone, crooning. "There you are! I see you, little love." Abby's small face turned up in the direction of her voice and her eyes opened, their color dark, indeterminate. Her small mouth was open as well, pink tongue practicing movements that would be needed once she was delivered. Theresa could not look away from those eyes as long as they were open and looking at her. She stroked

Abby's back through the translucent silicone capsule that sealed her against her chest and Abby wriggled around to place both feet against her palm and push back. Theresa grinned.

A chime pulled Theresa's attention back to her hand-held. Glancing at the screen she saw that it was another message from Richard Brant.

I haven't even read the second one yet. Slow down. She scrolled back to the second message and smiled. It was the current data for Phase Four, and it included the progress details for each of the AUC units. She scanned the data checking on each progeny's progress. The details from the previous update were already filed away in her mind for recall as she made comparisons and assessed each AUC unit. *There he is.* Theresa looked closely at AUC13's data. *Bram.* He was the only other progeny she had named. *If I could have taken two...*

The wetness of her eyes spilled over onto her cheeks. But he was doing well, excelling in all parameters measured as he had from the beginning. *Maybe Dr. Brant can succeed where I couldn't.* She looked closer at the numbers and glanced down at the now-sleeping child between her breasts. The leaden weight of worry that had grown over the past week resonated within. *She's not growing nearly enough.*

<So how about lunch?> The device called her attention to the last message received. She let out a forceful sigh, exhaling some of the tension she was holding and used the rest to type out a response.

<Sorry Richard. I'm not feeling well. I have parasites!> She deleted the last sentence before sending her message. *Probably better to avoid smart-ass remarks that sound like cheap excuses. We would like to keep getting updates, after all.* She smirked all the same, and glanced down at her little parasite.

The message chime sounded once again. *<Give me your address and I'll bring pie.>*

God, he is persistent. Theresa got up from the couch, pausing between movements to avoid another bout of vertigo, and walked to the kitchen leaving her hand-held behind.

"If I could hide you in the closet, Abby, I would invite him over. Just for the pie." The smell of congealing leftovers on the kitchen counter mingled with the imagined taste of strawberry rhubarb pie. The unexpected combination launched a joint assault on her senses. Though she struggled to vanquish a sudden bout of nausea, the stink of rich gravy from a half-eaten bowl of mashed potatoes sent her sprinting the last few steps to the kitchen sink.

The cold wind pushed back against Theresa as she walked, holding the front of her outer jacket closed around Abby as her breath condensed into small fog banks that the wind tossed behind her. She tried to keep up a quick pace as she crossed the last block to the small coffee shop. "Where's a scrolling sidewalk when you need one, huh, Abby? They need to extend construction to the outskirts of the city." She frowned at the familiar but dilapidated city block. It was a mishmash of new and old. Most buildings featured tinting windows to protect from the harsh sun, and even the small businesses were equipped with artificial intelligence-based security systems and solar-charged street lamps. The construction of this area of town was cluttered with businesses and residences, stacked and wedged in where they didn't fit. Instead of the convenience of scrolling sidewalks, pedestrians had a broken, pit-filled landscape to navigate that resembled many small fault lines.

The door to the coffee shop hissed open as she approached, welcoming her in with a blanket of warmth and the comforting aromas of hazelnut-infused coffee and buttery croissants. Taking a seat at the table nearest the door, she surveyed her surroundings. The shop was empty except for one gentleman in the corner in a worn brown trench coat. His skin fell in leathery folds around his features, swollen with age, and Theresa found herself wondering how old he must be to look like that. Or maybe he was one of the few who refused gene therapy in favor of the slow but inevitable descent into decrepitude that used to dominate that last thirty or forty years of life. *To each their own, I guess.*

The man's watery eyes glanced up at her, dark and shining with experience.

She bit her lip, flinching and looking away. *Yeah, staring at strangers is really going to keep you from being noticed. Right.*

"*May I get you something, or are you just here for the ambiance?*" Theresa was startled by the voice that emerged from the Coffee-bot built into the wall next to her table.

"Um…Hot chocolate? And a plain croissant…no, make that chocolate-filled." She smiled in anticipation of the decadent breakfast.

"*Coming right up! Would you like whipped cream on your hot chocolate? Or perhaps some fresh berries with your croissant?*" The programmed voice came very close to human inflection.

"Oooh…You do know how to please. Yes, and yes." She watched the chocolate percolate and the croissant dough rise through the glass front of the Coffee-bot, mesmerized by the spectacle. The food preparation system in her apartment didn't have a glass front for viewing. Too bad the novelty of food preparation wouldn't be enough to keep the coffee-shops open much longer. *Though it serves my purposes that no one comes here anymore, I guess.*

The whoosh of the coffee shop doors let in the smell of rain, and with it Dr. Richard Brant. Theresa turned in her seat at the sound, eyes wide like that of a cornered prey animal. A burst of panic traveled through her at nerve impulse speed, lighting up the fear centers of her brain. *Damn it! Theresa! How is relishing the ancient art of baking more important than Abby? You were supposed to be watching. God, this was a stupid idea.*

She turned away from the door and placed both hands over the front of her jacket, feeling for any gaps that might reveal her secret, only then checking visually. Satisfied that all was hidden, she stood and turned to greet Richard with a fresh smile pasted upon her lips.

Richard's face lit up and a grin, embellished with pure delight, laid hold of his strong features, youthening the mature face that was neither old nor young. His jaw and brow had the look of bones heavy and masculine from decades under the influence of testosterone, leaving nothing of the boy he had once been aside from an earnest smile, and even that had a maturity seldom found in youth. His hair was a dark auburn that looked almost black in the dim room and had fine streaks of silver emanating from his temples.

Just as he did the first time they met, he held out his hand.

Theresa bit back a rebuff. *He may be callous and forward, and may be trying to get a quick pre-flight lay, but he is keeping Phase Four going....and keeping me informed.* Instead of rejecting him, she raised her hand and placed it in his with a nod. *"Dr. Brant."*

He turned their hands palm up and placed his other hand over hers, turning the handshake into a full hand embrace. He looked into her eyes with a steady, warm gaze.

"Theresa. You can call me Richard, you know. If you can text it, you can say it." His gaze was unflinching and full of the same confidence that had seemed like callousness in the AUC laboratory, his eyes a luminous golden-brown in the center rimmed with murky green and flecked with a dark red-brown. She blinked and reclaimed her hand, sliding it out from the unwelcome embrace.

Taking a breath she turned back to the table and found something to notice.

"Oh, my hot chocolate! And croissants."

Richard slid into the space opposite Theresa and removed his damp jacket. "I thought you liked coffee?" He tilted his head and smiled, watching as she sipped the steaming liquid.

"Um…oh…I just...How would you know I like coffee, Richard?" She placed the emphasis on his name.

He smirked at her, forehead crinkling. "I'm sure you could guess, if you weren't so busy blaming me for your transfer. The settings on the bot in your lab. All coffee."

She narrowed her eyes and parted her lips to speak, but Richard spoke first.

"I'm sorry, that wasn't fair of me. I just feel like if you gave me a chance you'd realize we're on the same side. There's nothing to be wary of."

The ice that had grown in her eyes did not thaw. "Why exactly was it so urgent for you to meet with me before I leave for my new assignment, *Richard*? I have preparations to make."

"I guess I deserve that." He lowered his eyes and sighed, rubbing one hand across his face, pausing over his mouth. "It's Phase Four. The data indicates that your new protocols have definitively changed the course of the progeny's neurological development."

Theresa placed both hands on the table, sloshing hot chocolate onto the plate that held her croissant. Her heart was beating fast and her eyes could not conceal the emotions swimming there. "It's working? What did Greg say? You *told* him, right?" The words came out in a jumbled rush.

He held up his hands, a manual stop-sign. "Theresa, Theresa. Stop. They're still going to terminate. I've spoken to everyone in our department. I've done everything I can short of breaking the CEO's neck...and I'm not getting anywhere." His voice was low and deep with restrained anger.

Theresa shook her head, the movement extending out from her mental denial of what she was hearing, slow at first and then faster, harder, as if to shake loose the words that dug into her mind and crushed out the fleeting hope that had taken hold. Her face crumbled into a semblance of itself and the tears flowed, filling her voice with dips and cracks. "Why did you tell me? Why did you tell me it was working then? I'm leaving tomorrow!"

Richard reached across the table and placed his hands on her wet cheeks. He leaned in closer to speak where only she would hear.

"Because I'm going to save them. I'm going to do everything in my power to stop this. I'll go above their heads. I will take it to the people if I have to. Security clearance be damned."

Theresa's breath came in hitches and gasps but the tears started to abate. She stared into his eyes and could not look away. *He means it. I don't know why, but he does. Who gives a crap why?*

"If you want to stay I can get you reassigned nearby. We can work together on this."

Theresa blinked, startled by his sudden offer. "No." She shook her head. "I can't. I have to go. I would stay if I could."

He cocked his head and started to speak, a question in his eyes. "Why do you think…?"

"I can't, Richard. I just can't." She bit her lip. *God, I wish I could stay and help.*

He sighed and placed his hands together on the table. "Okay. If that's what you want. I need to be in contact with you then. You might have information or ideas that could be crucial. Phase Four was your project, after all."

"Of course! I'll give you my personal contact line that you'll be able to use once we've launched. Do you really think you can do this?"

He pressed his lips together and nodded. "Yes. It's not going to be easy and I'll lose my position for it, but yes. Yes, I do."

Abby wriggled beneath the many layers Theresa wore to conceal her and Theresa placed a hand at her throat to cover the movement. *I've risked us enough for today.* She stood then, wrapping up her croissant and tucking it into a pocket, and extended her hand for a parting shake. Richard stood and took her proffered hand. "Let me walk with you." It was more of a statement than a question.

Theresa nodded before she could think better of it and followed him out into the cold mist. *I should take my hand back before...* She stumbled over the first outcropping in the broken sidewalk and grabbed hold of Richard's arm as well. *Yeah, think I'll just keep that hand until I get back to the apartment.* The vertigo had returned and fainting in front of Richard was not an option.

His hand felt very warm over hers, in contrast to the icy air that whipped around them as they navigated the broken sidewalks, so much so that she considered taking her other one out of her heated pocket and handing it over to him as well. *And why not? Course I don't think we could walk like that.* Theresa smirked.

"What?" Richard was looking over at her, eyes quizzical and crinkling around the edges as if he sensed he was missing an inside joke.

She shook her head, reining in her humor. "Nothing. I was comparing the growth curve for the progeny that you sent."

"And that's funny?"

She gave him a wry smile. "No. But I was looking at AUC6 in particular and I noticed that even he has made improvement. It just floors me! He was at the top of the curve already, beyond perfect in all areas. Have you changed anything else? Is it just my new protocols?" She pulled him to a stop in front of her building, and turned to face him.

"It's your protocols. I mean, I've tweaked them, placing even more emphasis on the underlying principles that you built them on, as I'm sure you would have if you hadn't been…if you had the time. But the change lies in your protocols. Take Gavin for instance…"

"Gavin?"

Richard ducked his head, a crooked smile pulling up one corner of his mouth. "AUC6. I have to admit I've named him. I don't suppose you'll tell anyone?"

Oh my God. Theresa's heart raced and she felt a sudden heat spread through her like a solar flare melting the ice at the core of a dead planet. Her mouth hung open a moment, eyes swimming. She looked away, unable to speak.

"Well, I do spend an awful lot of time with them and it becomes tedious, I suppose, and awkward, calling them by numbers. For the records, I suppose it's best, but..." He released Theresa's hand and slid both of his into pockets, glancing away, self-conscious.

She turned back to him, looking askance. *Where did you come from?*

The motions were made before she could think better of them, leaning up, one hand pressed against his chest, lips still trembling, she kissed him. Cheeks and nose chilled in contrast to the warmth of her inner lips, her mouth questing, open, driven by an impulse she couldn't name. He returned the kiss, meeting her where she was, withholding nothing.

Theresa took a step back and pressed a hand to her lips, shock, worry, in her eyes. "I don't know what...I don't know why I did that."

Richard smiled. "I do. It was a kiss goodbye. And good luck."

"And for them." She sighed, relief spreading across her features.

He nodded. Taking a step forward, he gathered her into his arms. She stiffened, sliding both arms in front of Abby's cocoon before relaxing into his chest.

"Do what you need to do. I'll be here with them."

FAREWELLS

The sound of larks seeped into Emily's dream. She was sitting in the robotic physician's chair again.

"I don't think that's right. I don't. I feel differently than before. Maybe you can check my levels again before…" A syringe, oversized, and dripping a clear liquid from the end, had emerged from the side of the physician's chair.

She struggled to sit up, but found there were straps around her wrists, ankles, throat. "I really think that if you just check…"

The sound of birds singing, larks, grew louder, drowning out her words. Something was glowing. She looked up, distracted from the syringe. The sun had risen and a cool breeze, laden with dew, pressed against her face.

"Good morning Emily."

She opened her eyes, the pink-toned glow of her Virtual Rest Cycler receding as it registered that she was awake. Slipping the device from her face, Emily sat up in bed and looked out the window, licking her sleep-dry lips and taking a breath as she allowed her body to catch up with her mind. The sky was still dark, and would remain so by the looks of the thick blanket of clouds, a red glow just peeking through on the edge of the horizon. *It's today then!* Her insides fluttered like nano-pollinators in a lightning storm.

She looked over at Jonathan where he slept and pulled the covers, upset by her sudden movements, back over his shoulders. Her lips parted into a full smile and she slipped from the bed to cross the room, containing just enough of her excitement to take care that her steps would not wake him.

Clothes were set out atop the single suitcase, and all other arrangements had been made for them by the Colonization Bureau. Everything would be auctioned off and any mail would be forwarded to the Bureau, including unpaid debts. *At least everyone'll have a clean slate, no forgotten collectors or taxes. Except for mother. She has the number. I wish she were coming.*

"Nothing could budge me from my home! Not even you! I was here before I had you and I'll go on here after you're gone. Fool thing you're doing anyway; should have long given up on that." The voice of her mother exclaiming over a luncheon salad echoed in her head. While not unexpected, it hurt to hear it said aloud.

She's going to want to call, though. I know that as well as I know her. So the number is there right in her contacts whether she asked for it or not. Emily nodded to the empty room, her forehead bunched up in creases of worry that mirrored the knots in her stomach, but she was up and dressed and that was that.

The sound of water running carried from upstairs. *The shower. About time, Jonathan.* A smile played at the corners of her lips. *Well, I didn't say it. I only thought it this time.* She headed downstairs, the smile returning as she reached the threshold and was greeted by a soft tinny voice emanating from the vicinity of the front door.

"Your grandmother has arrived and is approaching the doorstep. Would you like to admit her into the apartment?"

"Oh! Um...no, I'll go out now." She set down her luggage and wrung her hands, the corners of her lips turning down. *Always surprising me, Gran.*

The door opened itself and Emily stepped out, almost colliding with Carla on the front step. She instead dropped her luggage and wrapped her arms around the old woman in a tight embrace.

Carla returned the gesture, holding her granddaughter longer than a customary hug would call for. Emily sighed. *Like I'm in her heart as well as her arms.*

After what seemed like several minutes, Carla pulled back to smile at Emily. She was a good five inches taller than Carla, making the older woman look up to meet Emily's eyes.

"You ready, Em?"

Emily's answering smile faltered and then recovered. "Gran, you've been crying!" *I thought that would just be me...well...are you sure about this? You could still stay, right?*

Carla shook her head, silver braid twitching behind her like a snake. "Oh, you couldn't keep me from going now. It's just the goodbyes."

"Mother?" Emily raised quizzical brows.

Carla snorted, wiping at the few errant tears that had escaped in response to her granddaughter's questioning. "Margery? She's wanted little to do with me since...well, for a very long time now. That's not about to change whichever planet I wait around on." Carla half-smiled at her, with the buried ache of an old wound shining in her eyes.

"No, it's Sisyphus. He's staying with your Great-Aunt Marianne." Hugging herself, Carla walked a few steps out across the gravel. "And the moon. She's been shining brightly like that all night. Showing off what we'll be missing, aren't you, lady moon?" Carla wiped her eyes again, shaking off the melancholy and turning back to Emily with a genuine smile. "Let's get Jonathan and head out. We don't want to miss our ride!"

Emily echoed Carla's smile. The excitement was infectious and it grew out from the two women until it was palpable. Emily's nerves and uncertainty gave way to the exhilarating thrill of anticipation. *We're really doing this.*

The hot winds whipping and howling around the magnetic commuter craft made a hollow moaning as the bullet shaped vehicle sped its passengers towards the W.A.S.A Headquarters. The craft hovered some thirty feet above the tracks, using them as a guide and failsafe should a system failure occur.

Inside, the passengers could feel the buffered tossing of the wind. None stirred or looked up from their hand-helds. Such was commuter craft travel.

Genesis looked down towards the ground from her window seat. Her vision blurred out with the view of the landscape that rushed by far below. Browns, the tans of tumbleweeds, reds and grays of rocks and broken up pavement, objects smeared and mixed together before her eyes. The scorched, barren desert below had been uninhabited for decades and, therefore, held nothing of interest for her.

Turning away from the window, she lifted her hand-held from the empty seat next to her. Three messages, fifteen document transfers. *Looks like Ms. Blaylock is on the ball.*

Genesis opened the first of the transfers, scanning the document. It was the list of recruited colonists, all one hundred of them. The next, some five hundred pages, a detailed history of each colonist, including all previous assignments, personal and professional relationships, personality traits, psychological evaluations, everything was there. *Perfect.*

She scanned over the message headings, *Welcome to the Colonization Effort!*, *Contract Details(signatures required)*, *Packing List and Regulations.* But not the one she was expecting.

Genesis turned back to the colonist biographies and tucked a stray hair behind her ear. The gleam in her eyes brightened as she digested the information before her and transferred it into a program of her own making.

Each colonist was represented by a 3D hologram of a person that, when accessed, dissolved into copious notes on the individual.

She pulled up one 3D file and it projected above her hand-held screen as a tiny glowing figure rotating there. She swiped the figure's head and a blank file opened. She labeled it. *Jacob Emory's Psychological profile.* She swiped its back. *History.* The chest. *Aspirations and core motivators.* The hand. *Possible uses.*

Genesis placed the virtual figure of Jacob Emory into a holographic box, hovering above the hand-held and moved onto the next. The further the commuter craft traveled, the more figures filled the box and the more her spirits rose. *So many possibilities.*

Her heart rate increased, the blood-pumping muscle positively dancing in her chest as she felt the pervasive thrill of the unknown, a new challenge, a new game. She could see the possibilities unfold in her mind, the images warm and clear, as tangible as if they were real.

Dozens of scenarios played out in her thoughts as she imagined the opportunities that would present themselves once she was safely ensconced within her new community.

A beep from the console beside the window drew her attention. Three digits with a degree symbol flashed on the screen and a light voice with predictable sing-song inflection broke the silence. "The temperature in the Death Valley Uninhabited Zone is 162 degrees Fahrenheit. Internal temperature has reached 94 degrees. Should an emergency landing become necessary, an endothermic WCC suit is stowed under the seat. In case of emergency, the first action that you must take is to remove all outer layers and clothe yourself in the WCC suit. If your neighbors need help with their suits, finish dressing yourself first and be sure to seal your suit before attempting to assist others."

Genesis waited a moment to be certain that the announcement had truly come to an end, the smirk that the recorded message had brought forth still lingering on her dusky lips. "Cool off."

"Is it too warm? I'm sorry, I'll turn on the air-conditioning and cool your seat for you!" The console lit up as the comfort programming complied with her request. She leaned back and savored the cool air pouring in from the vents and the iciness that seeped out from within her seat.

The endothermic suit was a more comprehensive version of what she wore now: clothes with a specialized core to pull heat away from the wearer and release it into the surrounding environment. Except the endothermic suit was a one piece garment that covered all parts of the body. 162 degrees Fahrenheit would make that necessary. *Good thing I'm getting off of this overheated rock.*

Her hand-held signaled the arrival of a new message.

"Hmmm. There it is, then." She spoke under her breath.

Primary Goals and Objectives (Time Sensitive)

Genesis smiled, tapping her lips. Time sensitive, so they weren't taking any chances with her assignment. Once she read it, all traces of the transmission would be erased, leaving only what she held in her memory.

Good thing that'll be all of it.

The W.A.S.A complex was much further from the coast than Theresa's previous assignment at the Center for Reproductive Management. The Headquarters was located inland and far south, just inside the area that used to be Columbia, South America, along the equator.

She stumbled on the last step as she deplaned, holding the guardrail several moments until her balance caught up with her and the nausea settled. *At least I'm the last one off.*

Scanning the horizon, Theresa caught herself staring. There were trees here-more than back home, at least. They looked to be struggling. What should have been deep green and glossy leaves were pock-marked and blighted with large dry patches and yellowing edges. *Why here? Maybe to avoid the hurricanes? But why not put the place in a populated area if it's for travel?*

As she surveyed the complex from a distance, it became clear why the near-constant coastal hurricanes had to be avoided by positioning the complex inland. She followed the shining structure that protruded from the top of the W.A.S.A complex with her eyes. Even tilting her head to look as far upward as she was able, she could not see the top. The silvery cylinder was the width of a small apartment and resembled an ancient French structure, long since demolished-the Eiffel tower-but without an upward taper and a solid core.

It continued up through the thick layer of cumulus clouds, and could be seen disappearing from sight in the open patch of sky higher above. It did not so much disappear as fade with the blurring of distance.

Theresa found herself unable to look away from the point where the shining structure blurred into the sky. She didn't notice the approach of her escort or the other colonists from behind.

"That's right. Go on and join her. I don't want you breakin' your necks trying to see it once we get to the building. No one stops staring till they're good and ready." The escort folded his arms and leaned back against the rail of the scrolling sidewalk that would take them into the building.

He was a large man, barrel chested and rough around the edges. He would have had a paunch as he neared his fifties if it hadn't been bred out of him. Sandy hair still covered his head in a thick but close-cropped cap, and his eyes were grey-green, sharp and cynical.

Theresa broke away from the object that held her attention to look at the man who would oversee the launch. "Is that how we'll be going then?" A skeptical frown touched her lips. "Does it have a name?"

"Well, that's the start of it. Armstrong's Ladder, Babble Express, Stairway-to-Heaven. We call it however the mood strikes around here, but they've got some acronym for it that no one remembers." He winked at Theresa, eyes glinting with good humor. "Unless the higher-ups are listening we don't even bother. GILE or something like that. But the Babble Express is only gonna take you out of the atmosphere to the geosynchronous station up there. That's where you'll hop on a ship and off you go!" He pantomimed a rocket launch with both hands. "I'm Brogan, by the way. Your liaison/escort."

The other colonists who arrived while she was staring at the space elevator had formed a small circle around her and the escort. "Does it really go all the way up into space?"

A young man barely into his twenties licked his lips and glanced back and forth between the space elevator and the escort. He pushed wavy, light-brown hair out of his eyes of the same color and gave Brogan a nervous smile. "How did they build the top?"

Brogan laughed and opened the side of the scrolling sidewalk. "Well, usually people don't get to the questions until they're done staring at it. Why don't we just go over the construction of the whole damn thing in detail! But on the way there, so we get you out on schedule and don't hold up the whole mission." Brogan winked at his charges. His words were harsh and straight-forward, but his eyes held just enough humor to soften them. He gestured each of them onto the sidewalk and then stepped onto it himself.

The curious young man was still asking questions when the scrolling sidewalk deposited them in the center of the main complex building. "So some of it was built on Earth and some of it was built in space, then?"

"Yep."

"But what about gravity? Shouldn't it just come crashing down?" The young man, Eli, pushed the unruly waves back again and scratched the side of his jaw still rounded by youth.

"The tower only goes 50 k up, and the cable running through the center of it is anchored to a meteor-turned-satellite. That's why we're at the equator here, to keep a geosynchronous orbit."

Their guide exaggerated catching his breath. "So if we're good for now, I'm gonna start briefing you all on the trip. The crew's already on board up at the station, so no need to worry about all that. The trip up will take you an hour. I'll be sending you in batches of ten to keep it simple. Ten batches of ten and you'll be the first up. You'll be strapped in. Some folks toss their cookies, vomit, gag, hurl, if you will. So your hands will be free and you'll have access to a suction mask to…well, toss out the cookies you toss. I just won't stand underneath the tower while you're going up, Eli." Brogan clapped Eli on the shoulder and gave him a wink.

Theresa lifted her hand to her throat and frowned, pulling her feathered eyebrows together and magnifying the fatigue and concern that she was attempting to bury in their depths. Even with the endothermic underclothes she wore, the outer jacket still left her feeling stifled and overheated. *Or maybe it's the thought of an hour long elevator trip up through the Earth's atmosphere while everyone, especially me, tosses their cookies into a vacuum.* She stifled a laugh. Brogan had gone on to more serious description of the expected course of events. *No need to stand out so early in the game.*

Theresa left her hand at her throat as she was wont to do of late. The position allowed her to rest her arm above Abby's back. It was comforting to have that extra contact, and the protective gesture made her feel more in control. *And at least it doesn't look like I'm feeling myself up like if I had my hand between my boobs.* She couldn't hold back the laugh that time.

Brogan raised his eyebrows. "You know, I just wouldn't have pegged that…I was expecting Eli to make the first crack about the Stairway to Heaven."

Theresa opened and closed her mouth like a trout and glanced over at Eli and the other colonists assembled in front of the dome shaped loading docks at the base of the elevator. Realizing the bent of the conversation and the assumptions that had been made about her laughter, there was only one thing she could do. She cocked an eyebrow and shrugged. "Well, it *is* pretty obvious. The designers had to have done it on purpose or it wouldn't be so obviously phallic." She shrugged, palms up, and put on a coy smile.

Brogan shook his head. "Nope, wouldn't a pegged it."

The other colonists laughed then, no longer holding back. It was funny, but there was a nervous edge to the laughter that made it echo a bit farther and go on a bit too long. This phallic structure that operated on principles that many of them only understood on a purely intellectual level was going to get them safely off-planet, or it wasn't.

The next two hours were taken up by emergency training, practice movement in simulated zero-G, and the issuance and fitting of space suits for wear, until they reached and boarded their ship, the Pinnacle. Theresa and the other nine colonists from her group boarded their shuttle at exactly noon.

Theresa leaned back in her seat and closed her eyes, allowing Brogan to check all of her straps and tighten them.

"You look pale, honey. It won't be as rough as you think."

She opened her eyes and inhaled with one long drawn out breath. He was looking down at her, concern evident in his expression.

She shook her head. "I'm fine. Just naturally pale, and hungry." *When did I eat last? Not since the bagels on the plane.* The thought of bagels made her stomach lurch in protest, an unappetizing mixture of hunger and nausea.

Brogan nodded and let go of some of his worry, replacing it with a half smile. "Ah! Well, the restrictions on eating will be lifted once you board the Pinnacle. Best to avoid a full stomach during launch."

She snorted. "I guess so." *Better to throw up nothing and then pass out from low blood sugar, I guess. But then, I'm the only one harboring a parasite.*

She rested her hand over the capsule, concealed underneath three layers including the space suit, and glanced around the interior of the small shuttle. It was just large enough to fit ten passengers in seats situated side by side in a semicircle. Eli was already strapped in and was speaking to Brogan as the escort adjusted the straps of the young woman in the next seat. The young man's hands waved about, gesticulating as he spoke and every movement betrayed his intense excitement. *He's likable at least, if a bit loquacious.*

Next to Eli was a woman of similar age; her arms and face still held that puppy softness that would give way to sharper angles and more predictably placed curves on hips and breasts in a year or two. Looking around the group, it seemed that even just among these ten they were split evenly by gender. Three pairs appeared to be couples no older than 40, and the rest were age matched.

Looks like the council is throwing them together in reality as well as for hypothetical reproductive pairing. Unease tickled the back of her mind. *Let's see... Eli and Bethany, Kendra and James, Nathaniel and Desiree, Lysander and Brianna. Looks like Donovan is mine.* She wrinkled her nose.

Donovan appeared to be in his mid-forties and had the classic appearance of an intellectual: slender build, clean shaven, with a narrow angular face and a long aquiline nose. *He does have nice eyes, but only if I discount Richard's, very dark, and his hands look strong.* She smiled as she closed her eyes to rest. *He could be my type if I was looking. Or I'm just that bored and delirious.*

She leaned back in her seat, running a hand across closed eyelids. *You may think that you can just pair people up, my dear colleagues, but it's more complicated than you think. You might be surprised.*

Theresa drifted in and out of sleep as the shuttle started to move. It gathered speed as it was pulled upward, hovering just above the tracks on the inner side of the space elevator, powered by electromagnetic propulsion.

"It's not just going to fall off, obviously," Eli's voice rose above the excited whispers and cheers of the other colonists as the shuttle reached full speed. "And the structure, of course, is made of the same thing quake-proof buildings are made from, that's what Brogan told me."

"Who are you trying to convince, Eli? Yourself or the rest of us?" Bethany's voice had a slight quaver. *Two parts fear, one part excitement.* Waves of sleep washed over Theresa, forming liquid layers that buried her deeper and deeper, distancing her from the voices of those around her.

The other colonists got up out of their seats and crowded around the transparent side of the ship, where they stared out at the sky's gradual transition as blue shifted to black. *Aren't they supposed to stay strapped in until we dock?* Theresa looked down at her straps and found that they had been unbuckled as well. *Well, I guess I can go see what they're all looking at then.*

She walked over to the group of colonists who all had their backs to her. They had been looking out of the window, but now seemed to be gathered shoulder to shoulder and they were staring down in front of them, whispering to one another.

She approached the cluster and looked for an opening to see what was so captivating.

"Well, it isn't really alive anymore, is it?" Eli was staring down at whatever held everyone else's attention with his brows furrowed and a quizzical smile upon his lips. He held something in his hands.

"It is alive, actually. But it clearly isn't human." Donovan reached out and took the object from Eli, tapping it against his cheek where Theresa could see it. It was a surgical tool, a laser scalpel like the ones she used back in the lab.

Theresa could feel alarms going off inside of her. The panic spread and intensified as she pushed her way into the inner circle.

"There are reasons that they told us not to bring pets with us."

She didn't recognize the voice that spoke, nor did she care who it was. The two who stood shoulder to shoulder in front of her stepped aside, leaving just enough space to wedge herself in. Lying on a table she saw herself, asleep and undressed. There was an open wound gaping between her breasts, revealing lungs and heart where her ribs had been cracked and pulled apart. Between her right and left lung a small wriggling form was implanted. Abby locked eyes with her and wrapped thin translucent arms around the glistening heart, tiny hands like claws, and squeezed.

"You have to get her out, Theresa!" It was the urgent, resonant voice of Dr. Richard Brant.

Theresa cried out and struggled, forcing herself to move, to climb up through the layers of sleep that had settled over her. *I'm not awake. Wake up! Wake up. Wake up!*

She opened her eyes, and could not stop her hands from feeling for Abby's capsule. Feeling the baby shaped lump between her breasts surrounded by a cocoon of liquid, she stopped short of ripping the many layers back to see Abby safe where she belonged. She did, however, prod at Abby's sleeping back until she could elicit a kick, to be certain she was alive. *Thank you, Abby. I hate not seeing you! How do surrogates survive damn near ten months of that shit?*

Theresa was startled by a hand on her shoulder. The hand's owner was looking over at Theresa, generous nutmeg-hued eyes full of concern. "Hey, hey. You're okay. That was definitely a nightmare you were having though. We're still flying, launching I guess, so everything's cool." Kendra gave a reassuring smile. Her features were soft and rounded, lips mauve tulips and skin the color of dark sage honey spread thin over almonds, a warm brown with sepia undertones that was uncommon. Beautiful, but what struck Theresa as she locked eyes with her, latching onto the other's face to banish the horror of her dream, was the warmth and maturity that softened her eyes and colored her smile.

Still in shock, Theresa stared, unabashed. *She must have stories to tell. But how old is she? My age…and home-raised by the accent, instead of council-born and placed.* She tried to rein in her breathing, still shaky from the adrenaline of the images that lingered even now that her eyes were open, and to focus instead on the curiosity that her seat-mate's subtle accent engendered; she was feeling light-headed, several long slow breaths in and out and her pulse started to return to normal. *No sense hyperventilating in here.*

"Oh…um, yes. A nightmare." She cringed at the remembrance that was more physical, more visceral than simple recollection. Casting a furtive glance from Kendra to the other colonists, most she found, seemed to be engaged in conversation or watching out the windows as the sky-scape went from deep indigo to inky black. Her brow was furrowed when she glanced back over to Kendra. Lifting her palm from her chest and clenching it, she lowered her hand to her side instead of placing it right back over Abby's nest as she would have preferred.

"Oh, them? No none of them noticed your conniption fit over here. They stopped paying attention right after wondering how you could sleep through the launch." Kendra gave her a crooked grin. "Anyway, I just figured you've some reason to be tired like that."

Theresa tried to keep her voice even. "Like what?"

"Oh, that's for you to know, I guess. We all have our reasons. Things to wake us up sweating and wide-eyed, looking for ghosts. Things we're leaving behind on Earth, maybe. Things we're looking for on Mars..."

Theresa relaxed. *She's just being friendly.* "Yeah, I guess. So, what about you. Are you leaving much behind?"

Kendra laughed and some of the humor drained out of her eyes. "Nothing that's mine." She shook her head and went silent.

Theresa winced and fumbled in her mind for something that would fill the silence. *I guess she does have stories.* "Sorry, I wasn't trying to..."

Kendra was looking away from Theresa, and her eyes had become wide pools, reflecting amazement along with a glowing blue light. A soft sigh escaped her lips. Following Kendra's gaze, she looked out of the large windows facing the sky, and found that it was gone.

The ship had gained just enough distance from the Earth's atmosphere to reveal the glowing blue curve of the planet, and the deep void of space beyond it. The colonists had fallen silent, and, though they were strapped into their seats, they could feel the sudden absence of gravity lifting them against their straps.

It was dark out when the final ship launched from the space elevator, shooting after its predecessors with the last ten colonists ensconced inside. Genesis had strapped into her seat by the wide-strapped five-point harness and engaged in conversation, face animated, velvet-smooth voice exuding subdued enthusiasm. Leaning in the small amount the seat straps allowed, she gave a playful wink to the young woman closest to her, eliciting peals of laughter.

Melissa covered her mouth and tried to rein in the mirth that had possessed her small frame, looking around the craft. No one seemed to mind. The other passengers smiled and conversed as well, pausing every so often to listen in to the conversation between Genesis and her seat-mates.

"It was really an honor, of course, to be chosen for the Progenesis Breeding Program. And I can't say it wouldn't have been exciting, but I prefer group interaction to one-on-one."

Melissa burst out laughing through her hand, wispy brown hair falling into her face.

Genesis crinkled her brow. She shook her head and blushed through her tanned skin. "I didn't mean…Well, I guess I did, but not *quite* like it sounded." She couldn't help but join in the laughter, which spread to the rest of the group.

Only David wasn't laughing, instead keeping to himself, scrolling through data on his hand-held and pausing to look out into the vast expanse of space that surrounded them. *He's going to take some work. What fun.* Genesis's eyes sparked with excitement. *And he came completely alone.*

"I have an idea: would everyone like to play a game?" She spread her hands and looked from one colonist to the next. "It's a guessing game. Each of us guesses what the others' assigned positions are within the group, while we give clues and hints. Everyone game?" Genesis smiled at her captive audience. "Let's see…David. Why don't you go first?"

David glanced up from his tablet at the sound of his name and brushed the curling front locks of his hair behind an ear.

Genesis stared, examining his every movement. *His eyes are almost black, they're so dark.* She widened her eyes and smiled at him, lowering her voice. "Don't you want to play with us, David?"

David remained silent a moment longer, caught in her gaze. "Sure. Um…okay, here's your clue." He tapped the screen of his hand-held and held it out in front of him as a 3D projection of a double helix materialized above it.

"So you work with DNA?" Melissa, who was still smiling, traced the double helix shape with her fingers.

"Genetic counseling?"

"Gene therapy? There's so many possibilities! How about another clue?" Ross shook his head.

David nodded, and spoke into his hand-held. "Display: mitosis."

"Well…That's not human DNA then." Genesis squinted at the glowing image that rotated before them and leaned in, examining it more closely. "That's plant DNA, isn't it, David? It's haploid, not diploid. So, maybe genetic engineering with plants?"

David's eyes lit up and he rested the device on his lap to clap for her. It levitated from where he placed it and he was forced to reach up and retrieve his hand-held before it got away from him. "I guess zero gravity will take some getting used to. But yes, that's essentially it. I'm responsible for engineering the plants that we'll cultivate for food, as well as introduction of these plants to the planet on a larger scale. I'm heading the department of horticulture. Plants from Earth won't thrive on Mars unless we tailor them to the environment. So that's me." David took a breath, but instead of continuing, fell silent as if he realized that he had been talking too much.

"That is so amazing, I would love to hear all about it. I think we'd all like to know what we'll be eating." Genesis laughed. "This is going to be a long trip without any gravity to hold us together and everything different than we are used to…but at least we'll be in good company." She glanced around the circle for confirmation and then back at David.

He nodded and pressed his lips together. The animation left his eyes and his smile was purely a physical arrangement of features.

Seeing his reluctance to be drawn further into the interaction Genesis moved on to the next member of the group. *Better not push him yet. There's something there getting in the way, I think.*

"So, what about you, Genesis? It's your turn now!" Melissa placed a hand on the padded shoulder of her suit.

Genesis covered her eyes and allowed a smile full of mischief to shape her sensuous lips.

"Aw, come on! You know we're curious!" A down-scaled Viking-framed woman with short black curls and olive skin flicked her wrist palm upwards as if to elicit an immediate response from her new comrade.

"Alright, Jessica! I'm already doing what I'm here for. Part of it, anyway. Any guesses?"

David looked up from his work and locked eyes with her. "Social manipulation?"

Genesis licked her lips and broke eye contact with him after great effort. Turning to the others, she offered up a smile. "Team-building and management of colony morale."

Melissa squinted at her and chewed at her bottom lip. "So…what does that mean you do, exactly? Cheer people up and assign teams?"

Genesis nodded. "Yes, Melissa, but more than that. A colony is a community, or at least it should be. We're going to be counting on one another exclusively when we get to Mars, and we can't afford to fall apart and die off or start fighting wars because of misunderstandings. It's my responsibility to make sure we build strong relationships, communicate, problem-solve, and work together. My other position is on the governing council, so that I can make sure social issues are taken into account." She made eye contact with each of the colonists as she spoke. Many of them were nodding, and those who weren't were hosts to enthusiastic smiles. Turning to David last, she confirmed her suspicion that he was paying attention again.

He stared at her as she spoke, his eyes narrowed, a look of concentration etched between his brows and the corners of his lips. He opened his mouth to speak when Genesis met his gaze, then turned his attention back to his tablet and his work.

Carla's ship reached the terminal end of the space elevator without event, aside from three instances of tossed cookies. The passengers with weaker stomachs found they couldn't hold back their heaving once Emily paved the way. They very nearly released the contents of their stomachs inside the craft, but instead managed to use the vacuum masks and jettison it out into space.

"Well, at least you're still smiling! The two that copied you don't look quite as chipper."

Emily ducked her head in chagrin and spoke in a whisper. "How could I not be, Gran? Smiling, I mean. We're about to dock with our ship, aren't we? I'm not really scared anymore. It was the weightlessness, I think, more than my nerves."

Carla gave Emily's hand a pat and raised her eyebrows. "A fresh start, right?"

There wasn't much more she could say. The excitement went beyond anything she had the words to describe. Instead, she squeezed her granddaughter's hand and smiled a smile that would have extended past the edges of her face if it could have. *She looks so hopeful- so fragile. We're gonna make this a fresh start whether that's what Earth has in mind or not. I just wish I could tell her everything.* She nodded at her granddaughter just as they came to a full stop.

The interior of the small craft went silent, the tension of the passengers palpable. Carla and Emily exchanged looks with the others in their group, each of them listening for some indication that they had docked. Smiles wavered, brows creased, as the seconds stretched into minutes. The corners of Emily's mouth trembled, clinging to a thin smile.

A deep thrumming hum became audible, growing into a vibration that resonated with the metal hull of the ship like a tuning fork. The tension broke as the colonists laughed, some clapping, others patting seatmates on their shoulders, teeth gleaming in their wide grins. Carla looked at Emily and smiled, brushing the wisps of hair back from her grand-daughter's wet cheeks. The cheer had reasserted itself upon Emily's face, but instead of the thin, trembling smile that had struggled to keep hold of her lips, this one beamed forth, full of relief and hope.

She's beautiful when she isn't scared shitless.

Carla looked past Emily's shoulder at her grandson-in-law, Jonathan. He was staring at his wife, eyes wet as well, but for another reason. He glanced up at Carla and mouthed two words before leaning over to kiss his wife.

"Thank you."

Carla nodded, and returned the silent message in Jonathan's eyes. *We did the right thing.*

The vibrating hum stopped as abruptly as it had begun, and was followed by the simulated voice of the transport craft.

"I am happy to report that docking with the Mars Colonization Transport ship, the Pinnacle, has been successfully accomplished. You may now retrieve your baggage from the storage compartments and proceed to the loading hatch."

Green lights lit up on the straps of all ten passengers, and with a sharp 'click' the magnetic locks released, leaving only the harnesses holding everyone in place. Carla pulled her straps aside and, grasping the rails next to her seat, allowed the lack of gravity to lift her before any of the others moved. Twisting one leg to the side from the hip and then the other while holding onto the safety rail with one hand, she stretched her cramped legs, spine crackling as she bent backwards and to the side, as cat-like as Sisyphus back on Earth.

"Come on now! You've even been authorized! We have a ship to board. Just make sure to hold on to something!" Carla snapped her fingers to illustrate the need for haste, smiling at her paralyzed companions.

Emily laughed and stood, holding the bars on either side of her seat with the gusto of a small child released for recess after long hours of study. The other passengers followed suit, one after the other.

Once released from the illusion of control, they talked amongst themselves, retrieving their luggage and stretching out the kinks in their limbs. Each movement had to be made with consideration for the lack of gravity and, despite the practice session they had done at the W.A.S.A station, the passengers were clumsy in their movements and giddy at the novelty of the experience.

"I see all luggage has been retrieved. If you will form a line in front of the loading hatch, one passenger will be admitted for boarding at a time. Thank you!" The Ship reasserted control of the passengers with its polite command voice.

Carla was the first in line, followed by Emily and Jonathan. While most of the passengers had reined in their enthusiasm and spoke in hushed tones, Carla danced at the head of the line, holding the rails on both sides. Pausing to think, she turned around and gestured Emily forward, pulling her to the front.

"You should go first. I'm gonna talk to our Computer science and tech specialist back here. Mario, right?" Carla waved at a tall swarthy gentleman in line just behind Jonathan.

Emily looked a bit disoriented. "Oh! Okay, Gran. I'll find our rooms on the ship."

Carla patted Jonathan on the shoulder as she passed him to move further back in the line.

"Will the first passenger to board step forward please?" Emily moved forward at the command of the electronic captain and grasped the parallel bars on either side of the hatch. With a hiss, the door opened. Emily glanced over her shoulder at Jonathan, brow furrowed.

"I'll be right behind, Em." Jonathan kept his voice low, holding back the trepidation lurking beneath the surface.

Emily pulled herself through the hatch and the door sealed behind her.

Carla leaned in closer to Mario. "I just wanted to see her boarding safe before I went up. She's my only grand-baby." She gave Mario a crooked grin and a wink.

He snorted a laugh and nodded. "Fair enough."

A video screen above the hatch allowed the other passengers to witness Emily's short climb upward to the second hatch that would admit her into the Pinnacle. As they looked on from below, a small green light and the hiss of the second hatch indicated that Emily had made it through and was safely aboard the Ship.

STOWAWAY

Theresa moved through the narrow halls of the Pinnacle, fighting the sensation that she was free-falling with almost every ounce of her mental focus. The last small portions were reserved for controlling the building waves of nausea and vertigo that threatened to send her spinning down the corridor, flailing and vomiting bile and water from her empty stomach.

Nice, Theresa. That is not a helpful mental image!

"The capsules you took before launch almost always prevent space sickness, but you look to be one of the exceptions." Captain Neil glanced back at Theresa with concern while still moving forward, his confidence apparent in his fluidity of motion. His lankiness would have left him thin if not for a wiry layer of muscle beneath his suit, apparent in the way he moved. His overall military appearance, with short-cropped brown hair and a clean-shaven face, inspired an odd feeling of confidence and trust. *Or maybe it's his crooked smile. Like a boy who cant possibly push a lie past you without giving it away with a grin.* Theresa paused to catch her breath, holding on with both hands.

I would be an exception if I had taken the damn thing. I'm not about to volunteer Abby for drug safety testing. Bringing her into zero-G is bad enough.

Kendra stopped behind her and put one hand on her shoulder, leaning in to whisper, "Are you gonna be okay? You look awful."

"I just need something to eat and I'll be fine." Theresa looked ahead to where the captain had paused to wait for her. "Do you have concentrated nutrient infusions available? In case I can't hold anything down?" Her skin and lips were pale and the cold sweat and shaking hands made it that much harder to grip the guide rails.

"I'm sure we do. That's the medic's domain. I'll give 'im a heads up." Captain Neil tapped the small earpiece he wore twice and waited until it emitted a faint green glow and beeped its readiness.

"Connect Desmond Fines."

"Connecting, Sir." There was a short pause and then another, much more human sounding, voice came from the Captain's earpiece.

"Captain?" Desmond's voice was full of excitement.

"Desmond, we have our first case of space-sickness in the batch that just arrived. She doesn't think she can keep anything down but needs to eat. Can you handle that?"

"Sure, sure…Did she take the PVD capsule before launch? Because usually that takes care of it. I could give her another dose along with a…"

Captain Neil spoke before Desmond could finish his thought. "She says she took it, so that's your call really. Just meet us in the cafeteria so we can get everyone else fed as well."

Theresa leaned in next to the Captain's earpiece. "With all due respect, I decline a second dose. I already have tremors and spotty vision, side effects of the PVD capsule. I just need to eat and wait it out. Space sickness passes, does it not?"

The Captain licked his lips and there was silence until the preventive medicine specialist's voice came through the earpiece once more. "Okay then…If you say you took it, I guess we'll just go with the nutrient solution."

The Captain tapped his earpiece once more and the glow receded. "What's your assignment for the colony, Theresa?"

Theresa let out her breath. "Reproductive technologies, Captain. I'll be making sure your future children survive to be born on Mars."

The look in the Captain's eyes took on a new respect for the pale trembling woman before him. "Oh, Theresa Marin then. I'm slow on names until we've met face-to-face." Reaching out a hand, he offered it to Theresa. "Let's get you something to eat, so you can do that." He looked past Theresa to the back of the line, where his second in command, a sharp-eyed woman with a bob of dirty-blond curls, was bringing up the rear. "Trina, can you see the rest to their rooms? Make sure no one floats away?"

Trina gave a lazy salute and answered his half-smile with one of her own. "Yes, sir. I'm on it, Captain."

"On Mars, on our new home world…" The captain paused to make eye-contact with his audience, a smile building as he continued. "It's dawn, daybreak, and when we arrive in two weeks time to see that dawn, we will be ready and as well adapted as possible to the differences between our old home and our new." He paused for emphasis and nodded.

"There are things we are leaving behind. Friends, family, the legacy of generations born and raised on the soil of Earth. The animals remaining on Earth and the plant life that is reestablishing itself more each year. But here we have a singular opportunity. We few will be the seeds of a new civilization, on a world reborn through centuries of hard work, dedication, and human ingenuity. What we build together will be the foundation of the future of humankind. Our children will be born on Mars and will know themselves only as Martians."

Kendra clicked her tongue, speaking just loud enough for Theresa to hear.

"*That* is a beautiful man! Looks like he's holding the ship up, and not the other way around."

Theresa put a hand over her mouth to stifle the laugh and glanced over at her.

Kendra fought her own threatened laughter with a warm blush reddening her cheeks. "I'm serious, though."

Captain Neil continued. "Together, we one hundred represent the best that humanity can be, each of us chosen for our unique skill sets, our strength of character, and our unshakable desire to be a part of this new world."

Genesis, two rows over, raised both arms and clapped above her head, eyes moist and a triumphant smile upon her lips, encouraging others to join in.

The small room filled up with applause, and several of the hundred assembled attempted to stand before realizing that they were strapped into their seats. Cheers broke out from all sides and, despite the captain's attempts to calm the colonists enough so that he could continue, the applause built to a crescendo before tapering off on its own.

"This *is* a big deal, isn't it? You know what? I'm gonna give you guys my applause now for having the guts to take this leap. I'll have to tuck my feet into the straps, though, because I'm not tied down like the rest of you."

Laughter filled the chamber along with the captain's applause. He grabbed hold of the handholds above him once more. "So, in the interest of switching ourselves over to a Mars schedule, all of the clocks are already synched up with Mars time and lighting on the ship will brighten and dim with the rising and setting of the Martian sun. While it's going to be a relief to get out of zero G at the end of this trip, the lower gravity on Mars requires that we wear the weighted clothing that we've been issued at least fifty percent of the time, to prevent losses in bone density and muscle mass. But really, it's just going to make it feel more like we are back on Earth."

Where she sat listening, Theresa raised a hand towards her breast to rest it above her secret. *God, I wish there was research on gestation in zero-G.* Before her hand reached Abby, she thought better of it, and grasped it with the other. *Yeah, because acting like I've got one crazy arm is better than casually resting my hand there.*

Theresa looked down to where her hands held each other hostage in her lap; they were still pale. She felt weak, but the nausea was starting to fade now that she had eaten and was sitting down. A soft chime sounded from within her pocket and she took out her hand-held, distracted from the introductions that had just started.

She stared down at the screen, where a message from Richard waited. An electric arrow of fear lanced through her as she read the words displayed there. It was one short sentence.

<Where is AUC2?>

Theresa's fingers flew over the keys. <What do you mean? You were there when I transferred the remains. AUC2 was terminated as per protocol with failure to thrive situations. It's all in the notes.> She pushed the hair back from her face, damp from the cold sweat on her brow.

The colonist next to her, a matured man with shoulder-length black hair, narrow jaw and prominent nose, stood up. He had the look of someone reluctantly friendly, with several layers of well-cultivated disapproval overlaying a kind heart, like loads of wet sand used to dampen a fire. "Hi. Um, well, I'm Donovan Sparrow. I'm heading up the Department of Planetology." He looked around the room, returning friendly smiles with a begrudging nod. "On Earth I was on the First Action Team to assess Earth's readiness for ecosystem repair— plant life, animal populations, pollutant levels, that sort of thing. So, on Mars, my job is two-fold." He paused, a bitter half-smile on his angular face. "Keep us from wrecking another planet, and monitor the development of ecosystems on Mars." There was scattered applause, along with looks of chagrin.

"Welcome, Donovan. Glad to have you aboard."

Theresa looked down at the small screen, hoping for a reply to her last message. *That delay is gonna kill me.*

She felt an elbow in her left side. Prodding. Kendra leaned over. "You're up."

"Oh." Theresa smoothed her forehead.

"My name is Theresa Marin, Reproductive Technologies."

Theresa heard a sharp intake of breath from her left and glanced over at Kendra. Her seatmate was staring at her, lips pressed together, eyes suddenly guarded. Theresa met her stare and mouthed a question. 'What?'

Kendra was silent along with the rest of the room. Theresa frowned and looked back down at her hand-held. *Nothing.*

"Okay. Thank you, Theresa. Maybe you could…give us a quick summary of, what that means?" The captain laughed.

She bit her lip and looked back up. "Sure. Yeah. Reproductive technologies mitigates the innate risk of childbearing through application of advancements in the field. I am responsible for developing and applying those technologies on Mars."

Captain Neil smirked. "Well, the way she explained it to me was…"

She glanced back down at her hand-held, the message there distracting her from the captain's words.

<Theresa. How are we supposed to work together if you keep secrets from me? What else do I have to do to gain your trust?>

She winced. *Trust him? What if knowing about Abby could save the others?* Her fingers hovered over the keys, brow creased, lips between her teeth. <It's in the records. She was terminated the day you took over Phase Four. There isn't any more to say.>

Another several minutes later, a one-word reply made it to her phone.

<She?>

David Raiklin, Head of the Department of Horticulture,

Jacob Emory, Head of the Department of Medicine,

Theresa Marin, Head of Reproductive Technology,

Emily Brooks, Head of 3D Engineering and Construction,

Donovan Sparrow, Head of the Department of Planetolog,y

Captain Neil Durran, Head of the Department of Colonization Infrastructure,

Genesis Shaw, Department of Social Science and Mediation,

Mario Palmares, Department of Nanotechnology,

Eli Straussen, Department of Bioengineering,

Melissa Espinosa, Department of Justice.

Theresa scanned the list of names and positions from the first council meeting once more before tucking it into a pocket of her suit.

"Coming?" Genesis stood in the doorway, her hands on the rails on either side of the door frame, the hall lights highlighting her hair with the simulated glow of a Martian evening. "I'd love to hear more about your previous assignment."

Theresa looked up, a bit startled to see that Genesis and two other council members were waiting on her. Digging deep, she found a smile and used the ship's rails to maneuver herself over to where they waited.

"What did you want to know?"

Genesis led the way down the hall, followed by Jacob and Theresa, with Donovan bringing up the rear. "Well, you worked in the Center for Reproductive Management, right?"

Theresa struggled to focus on the conversation without losing forward movement. *Some of them look awkward, but I'm the only one that can barely move with this damn zero-G.*

"Yes. I did."

"So did I, actually! I was chosen for the Progenesis Live-Breeding Program until they decided to scrap it altogether and focus on colonization. I'm surprised we never saw each other there, what with practically being colleagues." Genesis turned back to make eye contact with Theresa, moving down the hall backwards while conversing. She included the other two in the conversation, glancing their way and smiling.

Donovan nodded and brushed a bit of lint from his shoulder, letting it float away. "What sort of reproductive technologies were you working with—human? Animal?" He scratched the bridge of his nose.

Theresa looked back at the man who spoke from behind her, a slight scowl to his serious features. "My assignment was classified. Some of the technologies, as I'll apply them on Mars, won't be, though."

Jacob Emory, Head of the Department of Medicine, paused in front of her. He was thin and had the appearance of a man in his sixties, with small friendly eyes and a ready smile. A short-cropped neat beard grew close to his hollow cheekbones and he pulled at the hairs of it as he spoke.

"But what kind of technologies are we talking? Are we talking obstetrics or pediatrics or gynecology? How closely will we be working together? Because we can't have too many good obstetricians when the progeny start coming. And thank God our passengers still have their sterilization implants because I don't want to perform surgery in zero-G." Jacob widened his eyes for emphasis and gestured with one hand, miming spouting blood, and laughing at the absurdity of it.

Theresa frowned, wishing she could scratch the itch on her forehead without letting go, and instead blew the hair aside with a puff of air. "None of the above really, Jacob. I'm experienced with transitioning infants after delivery, but I have never worked with a living vessel. I primarily work with technologies that support or take the place of traditional methods of reproduction. The cauterizing scalpels you use in delivery...I designed those, as well as Caesarean Access Panels for repeat surrogates." She stopped to catch her breath. "I'm not an obstetrician. I'm making obstetrics obsolete."

Jacob blinked several times, a slow nervous smile spreading across his pointed lips. "I'm not sure what to say to that. But with a resume like that, I guess you might. I think we'll be working very closely, then."

Genesis applauded, her feet locked into the safety footholds on the floor. "That is precisely what we need to build a strong, harmonious colony. Why don't we all chat more over dinner?"

Jacob nodded at the suggestion, his gaze lingering over Theresa's face. Donovan shrugged in noncommittal fashion.

Noticing the silence, Theresa looked up to see that her companions were all expecting a response. "Oh. Another time for me. I'm just tired. Space sickness, Mars time...I guess I haven't caught up yet. Why don't you all go ahead? My room is just a few steps away."

The door opened with a hiss, and Theresa used the handholds to reach one of the six bunks in the room, wiggling into the sleeping sack attached to the bunk, grunting and huffing with effort now that she was alone. A sigh escaped from deep within her chest as she leaned her head back and let her muscles relax against the thin fabric. "Three days in. Eleven to go. Damn."

"Not taking the zero-G so well are you? It's tiring, I know." Kendra spoke from the top bunk on the other side of the small chamber where she was tucked into her sleeping sack.

Theresa's eyes flew open and her hands grasped the sides of the bed. "Kendra? I thought you were at dinner with everyone else!" She smoothed her brow. *She's going to think I'm crazy, or I just hate her*. Theresa pulled in a slow breath to calm her racing pulse. "You surprised me, that's all."

Abby squirmed in her cocoon, making the edges pull against the seal with Theresa's skin, and causing an itching burning sensation.

"I eat fast, I guess." Kendra laughed and then crinkled her small nose. "You know what, that's not even true a little bit. I was just waiting to pick your brain after the council meeting. That's the truth of it." Her eyes darted away, nervous, and she wet her lips.

Theresa stared up at Kendra from her bunk, brow furrowed. "Anything important from council meetings is noted to be shared with the whole colony..."

Kendra put a hand up, a pained look on her face. She fidgeted with a spiraled tendril from the soft golden-brown halo of hair she had tied back from her forehead. "That's not what

I'm looking for." Sliding her legs out from the sleeping sack and swinging herself down to the bottom row of bunks, she pushed off with just enough force and caught herself with Theresa's bunk frame.

"Wow. You make me look like a cripple, Kendra." She leaned up on one elbow.

"Well, you do move like a cripple in space. I guess you'll probably do better once we get to Mars." Kendra looked down at her lap, going silent, and then glanced back up at Theresa, brown eyes full of shadows.

Her words came out in a rush. "I need to know if we're getting what we bargained for. There's a council assigned and positions for all of us…is this going to be like Earth take two, 'here's your position, isn't it great? Don't worry if we break your heart for the good of man-kind three times!'" Kendra's voice had risen and become more impassioned as she spoke, her accent stronger.

"Hey, slow down. I don't know what you're talking about. Please."

"I need to know if it's going to be like they said, on Mars." Kendra looked down and went silent, breath heaving in and out of her chest.

"What happened to you on Earth?"

Kendra lifted one hand with the slow deliberate movements of one hypnotized, undoing the clasps on the front of her suit as well as the layers beneath that covered her abdomen. The skin was loose there, mapped with crisscrossing trails of silvery and pink scars. Across the bottom of her abdomen a half-inch thick, flesh toned, translucent seam, creating a long smile shape from one hip-bone to the other.

"I told them I wanted it taken out when they approved my request to be reassigned to the colony. Take the…I don't even know what it's called officially, out of me. They refused, of course. Said it was dangerous."

Theresa looked down, a slight grimace pulling at the corners of her mouth. "A Caesarean Access Panel."

Kendra pursed her lips as if Theresa's words had created an unpleasant taste in her mouth. "Access Panel? I guess you'd know, Miss Head of Reproductive Technology. They called it a C-panel. I call it invasive."

Kendra was silent a moment before finding the words to continue. "Three times I carried for them. And I felt the kicks and squirms inside, strong enough by the end to take my breath or wet myself." A ghost of a smile crossed her face. "But I didn't mind it. I laughed at their hiccups… Didn't feel tiny shaking my whole body, though." A slight shake of her head accompanied the soul-deep sigh that escaped her lips. "Three times they took them out." She made a horizontal cutting motion across the access panel with the edge of her hand. "They said the C-Panel…was the safest way. Maybe it was." A shrug. "All I know is they could take them out any time with that thing in me. Like I was just left hanging open all the time."

The tears ran hot from the corners of her eyes and she brushed them away before they could float off on their own. "I kept track of the days so I'd know how much longer I had, and I'll be damned if it wasn't always a different day for one reason or another. I didn't see them after that. Heard them, yes. I heard them wailing. But I never touched them."

Theresa struggled to prevent her blurring vision from progressing to the tears that threatened. "I'm sorry. I wasn't a part of the surrogate program. I didn't know it was like that…"

That's a lie, Theresa. You know surrogates don't raise progeny. They foster them out or raise them on site...but not with their surrogates or gene donors.

Kendra looked back up at Theresa, her red-rimmed eyes full of fire. "I need to know what we're in for here. Am I gonna have to fight you for what I was promised? I'm done giving up my progeny for the 'greater good' and getting sealed back up hollow like a gutted fish."

Theresa stared at her, mouth open, protests forming on her lips. "My assignment is to safeguard reproduction with technological advancements, not to take anyone's *children*. The Caesarian Access Panel is intended to make the surgery safer and prevent adhesions and ruptures. It's well designed and highly effective."

Kendra narrowed her eyes. "I don't know anything about that. I just know how it feels and how easy it makes it for someone to reach in and remove what's mine. And I want you to know I won't lay back for it on Mars. I want this thing out of me."

"Kendra, really. What exactly are you protesting? Why would we remove the access panel if you want to bear progeny, considering that without the panel your risks go up and we'll have to do the surgery the old way! And assuming you and the progeny survive...we don't have enough colonists to go taking it away from you!"

Theresa's heart was racing and her lips tasted of blood from their dry, cracked, surface.

Abby was kicking at her breast, sending pain shooting through the soft tissue. *God, how did this turn into an argument? It would be easier to tell her to stop being paranoid and crazy if I hadn't pissed her off.*

"I guess I'm not going to get a straight answer from you."

"*If you just...*"

Kendra moved from the edge of Theresa's bed without further discussion and pushed off, gliding towards the door and out into the hallway.

Theresa sighed and leaned back in her bed, massaging her temples. *Okay, we need to go get dinner before I get sick again.*

The cafeteria was full when Theresa arrived, despite the late hour, and the cacophony of voices competed for her attention like the buzzing of a thousand mosquitos around her head. She paused in the entryway, squeezing her eyes shut and breathing in through her nose to combat a wave of vertigo before making her way to the automated chef. *I don't even want anything!* Theresa scowled as nausea and waves of lightheadedness competed for her attention. *Ugh. Alright Abby, we're going to run tests as soon as we get back to the room.*

"High Protein, High calorie, smoothie, please." She leaned in closer to the console to be certain she would be heard without having to repeat herself.

"Certainly! Do you have a flavor preference?" The cheery robotic voice sounded loud to her. She glanced around to see if anyone else had been startled by the volume. *Nope! Just me and my frazzled nerves, I guess.*

"Something that won't make me vomit, okay?"

"I aim to please." The automated chef went silent as it processed her order and then produced a tall lidded container with a straw.

"Thank you." Theresa tried to smell the concoction through the straw but instead took a small sip of the thick reddish liquid. It had a light flavor reminiscent of strawberries with a hint of peppermint. She sighed as she took several large gulps through the straw. *Guess I was hungry.*

"Is the drink satisfactory? I would assume from your moans of pleasure that it is acceptable."

Theresa choked on the gulp she was in the process of swallowing. "Was I moaning? Never mind, don't answer that. Yes, it's just right."

She realized as she finished speaking that the cafeteria had gone silent. Turning to look around the room she found that all eyes were on the transparent viewing wall. She shivered, scenes from her dream on the elevator replaying in her mind's eye. After following their collective gaze Theresa found herself unable or unwilling to look away. The whole window was filled with the glowing, pockmarked surface of Earth's companion, the moon.

"Farewell, man in the moon. I don't suppose we'll meet again."

Reaching for the handhold next to the nearest seat, she aimed a foot into the foothold and pushed towards it without looking away from the mesmerizing view through the windows.

Without the guidance of her eyes Theresa's foot slid past its intended destination and collided with the seat. Her weak grip wrenched from the handhold and sent her into a free-spin towards the ceiling. Panic flooded her mind, muddling her ability to assess the situation and preventing her from maintaining equilibrium.

Oh, God, I'm falling! Which way am I falling? Her arms and legs flailed out in all directions like a startled infant as she struggled to combat her confused vestibular system through waves of panic.

"Help! HELP! Oh shit." Theresa's voice was sharp and hysterical. The moon-gazing colonists turned to look for the source of the cries and were paralyzed by the speed and unexpected nature of her plight.

Captain Neil unstrapped himself from his seat and pushed off with just enough force to send himself sailing towards Theresa's flailing form.

David looked up from his tablet and in a split second decision launched himself to intercept her from the opposite side. The Captain reached her first, grabbing hold of her left arm and shoulder and then reached out towards the nearest wall in preparation for impact. The change in trajectory caused by the Captain's impact with Theresa left David no choice but to grab hold of her leg, sending the three into a spin.

If I could just...I don't know where I am..stop the spinning...Damn it, what about Abby? Abby! In a moment of lucidity, Theresa marshaled all of her strength to curl up around Abby's cocoon. The action served its purpose in protecting Abby, but left the side of Theresa's head and right clavicle open for impact with the wall of the ship. A sickening thud echoed through the cafeteria as she hit the wall with the full force of three bodies.

"Crap!" Neil grabbed hold of the nearest handhold before the force of their impact could send them bouncing off in another direction. He clenched his teeth, muscles in his forearm bunching as he struggled to counteract the force that pulled them in the opposite direction. "Grab hold, David!"

David inhaled, nostrils flaring as he shook his head to regain mental focus. He scanned the wall for something to grab, and fumbled the first time before his hand managed a firm grip on the wall.

"Theresa? Theresa!" The captain placed a hand behind Theresa's head to tip her face where he could see it. She was limp, her skin blanched white. The Captain set his jaw, and pushed down to reach the floor faster, grabbing every fourth handhold and staining it red with her blood.

"Connect Desmond Fines. Status urgent." With one arm around Theresa the Captain pulled and pushed them down, coordinating his movements with David's.

"Desmond here." The medic's voice was thick, foggy with sleep.

"There's been an accident, a collision. She has a head wound. She's bleeding." The Captain's voice was steady despite the haste with which he spoke, the result of years of experience in command, and his movements were efficient as he strapped Theresa to a bench and started looking her over.

"Is she conscious?" Desmond's voice had taken on the uneven pattern of one in motion.

"No." Captain Neil pushed her hair aside to assess the head wound, and found it a clotted mass of deep crimson, already drying.

"Everyone stay back unless we request your assistance, please!" The full cafeteria seemed to have closed in around Theresa, Neil, and David, who was crouched at Theresa's side. "We don't want to have her waking up and getting claustrophobic, right?"

The assembled crowd edged back, eyes still glued to their captain and the unconscious council member.

Whispers ran wild among them as the crowd parted. Carla pushed her way through, exuding energy and purpose, her silver braid levitating over one shoulder as she approached. The Captain looked up from his examination of Theresa.

Carla didn't hesitate under his gaze and instead started double checking Theresa's torso. A faint stain of pink, and then red seeped through the fabric of her suit under the pressure of Carla's palm. "Oh! Well now, how far off is your medic?"

"He should be here any moment, And you ..?" Captain Neil cocked his head to the side, eyes narrowed. "Aren't you in mental health?"

"Among other things. The rest of the medical department is in a meeting, so here I am." Without looking up at the Captain, Carla unclasped the upper half of Theresa's suit revealing the pool of blood underneath. The Captain's eyes widened as he took in the extent of the bleeding that had been hidden from view. Theresa wore two layers of shirts underneath the suit and both were soaked through with blood.

Catching the Captain's look of dismay, Carla ripped the top button-up shirt and started unfastening the sturdier under layer, too thick to rip through and lined with a temperature-controlling core. "If this is all it is she has a chance. Not quite two cups I'd say, seeped around the edges of this one instead of through. Get ready to help me put the pressure on it when this one comes off in case the bleeding increases…"

Carla stared down at Theresa's bare chest and what the endothermic shirt revealed beneath. Hisses, gasps, groans of confusion, disgust, emanated from the crowd that had closed in once again. Carla blinked rapidly, dragonflies of alarm soaring across her already primed nerves. "Goddess help me! Guide my hands and heart."

She moved then, grasping Captain Neil's hand and placing it over the center of Theresa's right clavicle where the skin was broken by the sharp edge of bone that protruded from beneath.

Leaning in, Carla rested her ear over Abby's back through the thin silicone capsule, hidden between the unconscious woman's breasts just moments before and now revealed for the whole room to scrutinize.

" Three...four...five." Carla counted softly under her breath. *Never really leaves you does it?* "Bradycardia. Her heart rate's low and declining." She locked eyes with Captain Neil.

His expression was frozen, lips parted and eyes wide, as if he was about to speak and had lost the ability.

"She needs blood now if we're going to save them both. And I don't want to birth a premature baby on a space-ship."

The sea of bodies parted as Desmond arrived, laden with equipment and breathing heavy.

"I'll consider a transfusion after I assess her wounds..." The medic's voice seemed to lose momentum as he drew near enough to see Theresa and Abby.

"I already assessed it. She has a head wound, a broken clavicle with blood loss and a stow-away fetus draining the life out of her. High BP, low heart rate. I'm thinking she'll be pissed if you let the baby die while she's unconscious." Carla's jaw was set as she glared up at Desmond.

"Woah. Hold on there. Nobody is dying on this ship." Strapping himself to the adjacent seat, Desmond unloaded the transfusion equipment and started preparing it.

"So, you aren't a medic and you aren't one of our OB's. What is your assignment exactly?" His hands worked as he spoke, accessing Theresa's vein and attaching the pump designed for zero-gravity blood transfusion.

"My assignment or my calling? There is a difference."

Desmond raised an eyebrow at her statement. "Your assignment."

"My assignment is Mental Health Specialist. But that's not really...*pertinent,* right now."

"Oh? And what is?"

Carla looked up from where she sat with her hand on Theresa's pulse and waited until Desmond and Captain Neil met her gaze. A wry smile illuminated her face.

"I'm a midwife."

The blanket of dark grey fog thinned around the edges, a piercing, ringing sound heralding its retreat and bringing with it the muffled sounds of conversation. Theresa swam up through the dark layers of consciousness, hearing the room around her before she could see it or feel her body.

"I don't care if it's scarce! If you want them to survive the next thirteen days you're going to have to give her more, and maybe more tomorrow too!" The voice was strident, female.

"It's going to overload her! Not to mention that we need to have it available for other passengers!" This was a very nasal male voice.

A third voice joined the conversation with much more measured, even tones. "A non-pregnant woman can't handle that kind of blood-volume. And I must add that the theories you are operating on were never proven."

"Oh, for the love of the Goddess! She is pregnant for all intents and purposes, physically and hormonally. Her contracted blood volume is not going to sustain the baby much longer and she's likely to start having seizures. Have any of you even used an RPU to sustain a pregnancy after a premature birth?" Carla answered for them before they could open their mouths to speak. "You couldn't have because they were phased out entirely before either of you were born! I've overseen twenty birth to RPU transfers and brought all of them through to full term." She looked from one physician to the next, a challenge in her eyes. "That doesn't even take into account the two hundred plus women I served, before the Reproductive Council had cleaned up the genetic code and were still issuing licenses to procreate. So does anyone here actually need more proof of my qualifications or are we good?"

Theresa's vision reversed itself, fading in gradually. Her whole body tingled to life, one area regaining feeling at a time. She flexed one hand and then turned her head towards the vociferous voice that dominated her return to consciousness.

Carla stood in the company of Captain Neil, Desmond, and Jacob Emory, in Desmond's office, hands behind her hips, her stance strong and gaze steady. She raised an eyebrow and licked her lips, inviting a response from the group.

"Abby…Ow! " Theresa mustered the effort to raise a hand to her chest and felt the warm pliable surface of the RPU that held Abby entirely uncovered. She gasped, eyes widening and hands scrabbling to push herself upright. She was met by the resistance of the medical bed straps that kept her from free-floating while she was unconscious, and fought down the ensuing panic. *Enough of that for today.*

Carla turned from her one-sided conversation at the sound of Theresa's first movements. Her face softened as she placed a weathered hand on her arm. "Slow down there. She's safe. Don't start pulling at your straps, now. We don't want you floating off again."

Jacob moved closer and adjusted the remote blood pressure and heart rate monitor, noting their readings. "Your clavicle is setting, and we've immobilized it for now." His tone was casual.

Theresa turned to Captain Neil. "I want to sit up, and I want everyone out."

"She is not in any state to be giving orders!" Desmond's arms were crossed, a sneer on his lips.

Carla exchanged a glance with the captain. "She's the only one with her shirt off and injuries to recover from, so I'd say she is."

The Captain nodded in the direction of the door, making eye contact with each of the men in the room. He stopped in the entryway after the others had exited. "The monitoring system will notify us if she needs anything, and you have my direct line if *you* need anything, Carla." He tapped his earpiece and then turned to leave.

Theresa allowed Carla to assist her into a sitting position and then inclined her head to Captain Neil. "Thank you, Captain."

He turned back with a smile. "It's what I'm here for."

The door hissed shut behind him, leaving the two alone. Carla adjusted the lap straps so that Theresa could sit up or lie back without having to hold herself down.

"Well, that was fun to wake up to. It's like what I sound like in my head until I actually start talking, and I hear my voice shaking." Theresa spoke with her head back against the bed, eyes closed.

"A couple things about being as old as I am. You learn to bide your time, and you practice putting people in their place in your own thoughts so often you get real good at it." Carla sat down in a chair next to Theresa's bed, strapping herself down as well.

"Should have seen me in the boardroom going into hysterics in front of the entire Reproductive Council." She turned to face Carla, opening her eyes. "And there I go again. You don't even know what I'm talking about."

"I'm listening." Carla's eyes were still and fixed on her, posture relaxed.

Theresa shook her head, crinkling her brow. "This isn't something I can just talk about. It's not just mine. It's too much right now." Her lips were trembling and her breath came in quick inhales and sharp gusts. "And it's technically classified information." She almost laughed at herself.

Carla snorted. "Really? Because I'm betting your little stow-away is just as classified. No one uses RPU units anymore. They went out of style along with the idea of preserving the sanctity of life and the concept of motherhood." Carla narrowed her eyes and inclined her head towards Theresa. "You're not a surrogate. I know all of the surrogates in the Reproductive Council. I'm not surprised that the head of Reproductive Technologies has an RPU unit, but where did you get *her*?"

Theresa ran her one mobile hand through her hair and sat up farther. "You said you've brought twenty infants to term using RPU's. I know this technology, but I've never used it before now..." She grimaced at the blow to her pride. "Abby isn't growing well and I don't seem to be tolerating it. Can you do something?"

Carla allowed the change of subject and leaned in closer, raising both hands above Abby's cocoon. "May I?" Theresa nodded and Carla pressed her palms against the surface of the RPU, palpating the small body within. "My hands know better than my eyes. I've only seen twenty but I've felt hundreds." Theresa watched, eyes wide, as Carla felt Abby's size through the silicone capsule. Her touch was light and careful, and still the edges of the capsule pulled against Theresa's skin where they were adhered. Carla opened her eyes at Theresa's sharp intake of breath.

"Is it the seal?"

She turned her attention to where the edges of the capsule adhered to Theresa's chest. The skin around the seal was an angry red and looked swollen. "They don't usually get infected...but zero-G suppresses the immune system. We'll have to combat this aggressively."

She leaned back and looked at Theresa without speaking, her eyes narrowed as she nodded, taking measure of something in her mind.

"Well?"

"It's not going to be easy, Theresa...but you wouldn't have gotten into this if you weren't all in. So, here it is. You have the hormonal balance of a woman who's seven months pregnant thanks to the RPU, but you've got the workload too. Your blood volume is woefully contracted and your liver is showing strain. Abby seems to be struggling. She's on par with a six month fetus, a small one, and her survival chances are low right now, unless we work very hard at this. We need to shoot for keeping her in there for six to nine more weeks, ideally."

Theresa felt the built up stress and tension spill out from her eyes in liquid form. "She's been small from the beginning. I took measures to correct for her weakness and brought her this far. Whatever this takes, Carla. I'm in."

Carla raised her eyebrows. "How long have you been carrying her? It's never been done longer than three months, and certainly not for a whole pregnancy! I assumed she came from a surrogate and you salvaged her, and RPU's are made to be used on already pregnant bodies after a premie birth, not women who have never been pregnant."

"I've had her here for just over a month." Theresa leaned back against the bed once more and closed her eyes, ignoring the implied question once again. "What do we need to do?"

ACROSS THE VOID

Genesis stood in front of the door, allowing her features to be scanned instead of knocking. A moment later she heard the security system announce her presence and her identity before the door opened to admit her.

David was working, leaning over the front row of plants suspended in transparent tubing at waist level, and did not look up when she entered.

The soft white-blue light over the plants illuminated her skin and reflected off of the long black hair that trailed behind her as if underwater. She stopped just behind his right shoulder, close enough to whisper.

"That was quick thinking, in the cafeteria. The colony is lucky to have you."

David answered without looking up, leaning down closer to smell the water circulating through the long tunnellike tray. "Are you trying to flatter me or did you blink back there?"

Finishing the necessary adjustments to the water temperature and flow rates, he turned and found her face only a few inches from his. The incredulous scowl upon his lips and brows increased the severity of his expression. "I sent Theresa into a spin and knocked us into a wall. She has a concussion and a broken clavicle."

Genesis smiled and slid one hand onto David's shoulder with the air of a cat sliding against the nearest wall it passes. "The intent matters more than the outcome. If you and the captain hadn't decided to go after her at the same time, that wouldn't have happened. She's doing fine now, by the way."

He nodded, his eyes cold and unreadable. "What's your agenda, Genesis? I've spent too many years close to sincerity not to know a woman with an agenda when I see one."

She threw her head back and laughed with abandon, a laugh that would have seemed dramatic or contrived coming from anyone else. "Agenda? You make that word sound so dirty." She crinkled her nose and smiled up at David, who was nearly a foot taller than she. He couldn't help but smile a little, even as he fought to remain unaffected.

"I'm going to be honest with you, because I like you. Maybe you think 'You don't know me.'" Genesis put on a pout that was comical paired with her gruff imitation of his deep voice and surly tone.

"I'm quick to assess a person and either like them or hate them…and I'm never wrong. I do have an agenda. Several, actually; I'm a girl that thrives on agendas. My first agenda is this colony-to make it the most cohesive, successful colony one could ever imagine. My second agenda is you."

She leaned in closer, standing on tip-toes and sliding her hand from his shoulder to the back of his neck. "As I mentioned…I like you, and I like to have what I like." The last word she uttered against David's lips, allowing her mouth to brush against his just long enough to suggest a kiss would follow before she stepped back down from her tiptoes and walked away, pausing to turn back when she reached the door.

"So just think about whether an agenda is something to sneer at, David. And get back to me." Genesis walked through the door as it opened, allowing it to seal behind her. In a gravity environment she may have skipped, but instead pushed off from the sides of the hall with just enough force to glide.

"Did you see its eyes? The way it stared? It looked like a zombie."

"I didn't get a good look, too many people crowding in front of me." Melissa pursed her lips in disappointment.

Eli laughed. "Bet that happens a lot. You should carry a stool around with you."

Melissa glared.

"And the way it was attached, like it was growing out of her." Jessica wrinkled her nose. "Just. Eww."

"But was it even…I don't know, human? I mean, it didn't have any skin or anything."

"I don't know. I just think it's really fascinating. I'd like to pick her brain about it." Eli ruffled his own blond hair, excitement clear in his eyes.

"Go right ahead." Melissa's grin was full of disdain. "Maybe she'll have one of those things burrow into your chest.

I'm not getting first in line." She scrunched her face and shook her head.

David slammed his tray down and pushed himself over to the table next to him, eyes flashing. "Is this our shining new start as a colony? Gossip and mean-spirited judgments?"

Melissa gaped. "We didn't mean…"

Eli's face reddened and he looked away.

"Show some respect! The woman just lost over a pint of blood and had herself stripped down in front of the colony. We know nothing about her or her progeny." He shook his head in frustration.

"Well, we would if she'd tell us. Keeping secrets like that…what does she expect? I went to see her. Check on her and everything, and she wouldn't even let me see it." Eli stumbled over his words in a rush to defend himself.

"What do you expect of yourselves? Think on it." David turned then and pushed off towards the exit, taking care to avoid collisions.

Theresa smiled, pushing up to a sitting position in her bed. "Don't be ridiculous…David, right? It wasn't your fault. There's nothing to apologize for." Her uninjured hand pulled at the edges of her shirt. *The way they stared at her, as if she were a freak-show, other than human. Like my dream.* A scowl spread from her thoughts to her face.

"Still, I'm sorry it happened. Should have been more careful, judged the speed and distance faster, looked for others…"

She shook her head, the ghost of a smile retuning. *He isn't here to interrogate or judge us.* "What are you aiming to be, the Pinnacle's real-life action hero? Those are some pretty high standards you have there. If you usually live up to them, I'm impressed."

David laughed, dark eyes lighting for once as he rubbed the back of his neck with one hand. "Yeah, I guess so, huh? But you had a lot at stake. I regret that too. The trouble for you and…your progeny." He shook his head. "That just feels wrong. Is there a name I could use, maybe? If it's okay to ask that?" He put his hands up, palms out. "I have my own secrets. I don't need to be grabbing at yours, so…"

"No, no." She released her withheld breath. "It's okay. It's Abby. I call her Abby."

David's smile grew and his eyes softened. "Abby. A girl then?"

Theresa nodded, her smile echoing his.

"What did you make of that then, Em?"

Emily stared out into space, her stillness mirroring that of the stars beyond. "Make of what?"

"The accident, with the…what is she? Head of Reproduction? The…secret she was keeping." He shook his head. "Shook me up, I can say."

"I'm glad she's alright."

Jonathan moved closer to her, twin creases between his brows. "Has me wondering, though. How many secrets do we have among us onboard the Pinnacle? And what sort, if she could hide something like that right under our noses."

She shrugged. "I'm not really worried about it, I guess."

Jonathan aimed his full attention on his wife, placing a hand on her shoulder. "What's on your mind?"

"The trip. Where we're headed. Mars. It's going to change us, Jonathan." She stared out the window, her face pressed against the inner surface. A small green and black orb, with veins of orange, floated in the darkness. Her face was smooth of worry and her voice trancelike. "I can feel it already, just looking at her. It's like being called home to where we belong, to myself." A small tremor passed through her, leaving behind only the look of wonder and contentment that was there a moment before.

"Isn't that a bit premature, Em?" Jonathan looked at his wife and then back out at Mars, floating in open space. "It's going to be hard, adjusting to a new world. I wonder if I made the right decision, bringing us out here."

"If *we* made the right decision, Jon. It's not all on you." She shrugged without looking away from the vision before her. "It's just what I feel. The closer we get, the more I feel it."

Emily turned to look at her husband, a nervous smile crossing her lips as she came back to herself. "I'm excited. Gran is having another meeting this evening. She's asked all of the women to meet with her before we go to our appointments to have our implants removed, sort of a support meeting like she used to have years ago on Earth." Her hands were trembling just enough for Jon to notice and place his larger ones around them.

"What do you talk about in these meetings?" He smiled at his wife.

"Things…" Emily tried to look mysterious but fell short, laughing at herself instead. Letting go of her hands with one of his, he leaned in for a kiss, but instead tickled her ribs and under-arms, still managing to find the right spots even through her clothing.

She squealed. "Stop! Stop! You know I can't take that!"

Jonathan pulled Emily into an embrace, and then lifted his feet off the ground to hover next to the higher window in front of them. "Okay. Okay, but you're so fun when you're giggling and out of breath."

She blushed, more at her thoughts than any innuendo. As their breath calmed, the two looked out at the planet they were approaching and then back at each other with tentative smiles that were almost mirror images.

"You're right. We're going to be happy here, Em."

"Enlarge." Carla placed her hand-held down in the center of the circle.

The hologram tripled to life-size, rotating at her command; a simulated woman appeared, breathing and shifting her weight from one foot to the other, progeny wriggling in her semi-transparent womb.

"Alright. So if you watch her now, and this here is her pelvis…See the blood in her veins, the flow to her uterus. This is the placenta, the umbilical cord." She pointed at the bony structure under the skin, fading in and out, and then gestured to the veins and arteries flowing with minute blood cells like busy highways. "If you watch the baby…but watch her, too, now.

This is the mechanical process of birth. Labor is just starting. See there."

The holographic woman leaned forward, resting her hands on an invisible support and rocking her hips. Her uterus, visible through the skin, could be seen contracting, pulling the cervix open over the progeny's head and thickening at the top as it tipped forward ever so slightly. The progeny's feet pushed upward as it turned its head side to side, shifting it to find a better angle.

"You see, it's a dance, between mother and baby."

The circle of women leaned forward almost in unison, their faces glowing in the soft blue light of the hologram, eyes wide.

Kendra sat in the front, leaning in closest, and Nicole and Alissa were just to her left, Bethany to her right. Alissa rested her head on Nicole's shoulder and took her hand, her expression pained as she watched the simulated birth progress.

The cervix was open around the progeny's head, the woman panting, eyes shut as she knelt down onto all fours, waiting.

Tilting again and bunching up, her uterus heaved. The progeny rotated, finding the path of least resistance through the hologram mother's pelvis, feet kicking off again. Still, she waited.

"But she isn't doing anything." Bethany turned to Carla with a puzzled expression.

"Sure she is. She's doing everything. She's focusing on the task at hand. Relaxing her muscles, surrendering to the process, trusting her ability to birth. And maybe…no, *definitely* most important, she's waiting."

The hologram mother's mouth opened in a silent cry and she leaned up into a half squat, arching her back as the progeny spiraled out of her translucent birth canal and onto the ground in front of her, dissolving into pixels of light along with her.

"Can we see it again?" Bethany was smiling at the place where the hologram dissolved, awaiting an encore.

Carla laughed, eyes twinkling with pleasure. "You can see it as many times as you want to see it. And you can see about fifty variations of it if you're of a mind to."

"I don't want to watch that again! I just want to know…" Alissa dropped Nicole's hand and jumped up, pacing to the back of the circle and pressing one hand against her own shoulder.

"Know what?" Carla's answering voice was soft.

"Why, if it's this easy, does the council cut them out? Doesn't make any sense." Her eyes sparked, lips curling into a sneer.

"Well, because it's not easy. This is a simulation. Sped up and cleaned up. But a real labor takes hours to days and takes sweat, tears, blood, shit, and patience on the part of everyone there. That all went out of style a hundred years before the council took over the making and bringing of babies."

Kendra leaned back, looking from Alissa to Carla.

"Think about it, Lissa. What Carla showed us about birth hormones. If a surrogate's all revved up to be mother bear, how's it gonna be to take them out of us without us fighting them off or trying anyway, and who's going to sign up to do it more than once?"

Alissa stopped in her pacing and stared hard at Kendra. "It's difficult enough already. I said I changed my mind. Said I wanted her."

Kendra nodded, lips tightening. "But you didn't jump up and grab her, did you? Couldn't've, with your middle wide open and you strapped down." She shook her head. "Strap us down, pop us open, pull 'em out." Her voice was low and almost singsong.

Alissa's teeth shone through her grimace. She blinked several times and walked out of the circle, out of the room, through the automatic door. Nicole stared after her and then got to her feet, eyes full of apology as she glanced over at Carla, before following Alissa out.

The room was silent when she went…except for Kendra. She stared down at her empty hands, voice lower still.

"Strap us down, pop us open, pull 'em out, and off they go." She was silent for several moments before she looked up at Carla. "But we won't have any more of that."

"Thank you for coming, Carla and… and…I'm still working on my names…?"

"Kendra, Captain." The owner of the name reached out her hand for him to take, brown eyes meeting his with a warmth laced with wry humor.

The Captain took the small hand offered him and found the pressure of his hand matched by hers, the quality of the touch much more than casual greeting. Carla observed the exchange, brows raised. "Just following orders."

Captain Neil turned to Carla, forgetting to let go of Kendra's hand, his crooked smile in place. "Well, sure, but I don't like to frame it that way. I'm grateful to be your captain."

Carla returned the smile, nodding in agreement. "What can I do for you then?"

He glanced back to Kendra, releasing her hand, and taking a seat behind his desk. "Right. I just like to stay abreast of all goings on on my ship. You've been holding meetings, I hear?"

Carla nodded.

"Are those meetings within the bounds of your current assignment as mental health specialist or your...how did you put it... calling?"

A small smile touched Carla's lips and she spread her hands. "The meetings are entirely within my jurisdiction. I'm preparing the female colonists for the psychological aspects of reproduction and tending to any residual trauma that could negatively impact our success as a colony."

He blinked at the unexpected response. "Oh. Alright then. Just keep me informed of progress. And let me know if you have any intention to change your assignment so that I can clear it through the medical department."

Carla pressed her lips together. "Sure thing, Captain. Of course, midwifery isn't medical in nature."

He shrugged. "Let's debate that when and if you put in a formal request to pursue it."

Carla inclined her head, echoing the Captain's amiable nod.

He turned his gaze to Kendra then. "I imagine you just came along?"

Kendra smiled, not disputing the notion.

"I have a question for you though, Kendra. The surrogates, including yourself, were transferred to the colony without formal assignment. Have you thought about that? What you might like to do once we reach Mars?"

Kendra's focus shifted inward, uncertainty temporarily displacing the confidence that shone from her eyes just moments before.

Captain Neil opened his mouth to speak, concern wrinkling his brow. "You'll be approved for apprenticeship in any field that interests you. I can tell you that right now, having seen your aptitude tests."

"I'm still mulling it over, I guess. Shadowing Carla some... Did you have a suggestion for me, Captain?"

He smiled at the playful flirtation that had returned to her voice. "No. No, just shadow as many departments as you want. See what suits you and then let me know."

Jacob Emory squinted at the holographic representation before him, directing the nano-bot with precise swipes of his finger against the shimmering surface of the hologram. His concentration never faltered, though beads of sweat formed on his brow. This was the twenty-fifth nano-surgery of the day.

Kendra stared at the image of her right fallopian tube, the corners of her lips turned down in a frown.

"So what happens if you slip or something?" Her eyes narrowed as if she could guide the nano-bot by force of will.

"I don't slip." Jacob's words were spoken one at a time and with little inflection as he continued his task.

He sat back. Smoothing out his forehead and wiping the beads of sweat, he let out his breath with a heavy sigh. "Nano569, implant cleared. Relocate to left Fallopian tube." He turned to Kendra with a bright smile and a nod. "Halfway there."

Kendra broke her concentration as well, echoing his sigh. "So when it's finished…Everything will work as it should? Will there be scarring?"

He shook his head, pressing his lips together in a smile. "Full of questions, aren't we? No, the scarring will be very minimal, like a small scratch that will heal in a week or less."

"Well, since I'm here on the table and I've got you talking. I think it's fair to ask about what they did when I finished with the surrogate program. More implants so I couldn't conceive too soon they said, but I didn't question it." The bitterness of the memory seeped into Kendra's eyes like medicine, and, without any sweetness to help it go down, it welled up and twisted her lips into a grimace.

Jacob looked back at the computer screen, unable to hold her gaze. He flexed his fingers before turning back to the hologram that had shifted to show her left fallopian tube, glanced over at her, and then back at the hologram. "Nano569, activate. Begin clearing." He swiped at the edges of the second implant, directing the efforts of the nano-bot once again.

"That's like saying that I should know all of the details behind my psychologist's analysis of my mental health. It's not my assignment and I probably wouldn't understand two-thirds of it." Jacob paused a moment to point towards Kendra, widening his eyes to punctuate his statement, before turning back to the hologram. "Or maybe, more aptly, like saying that because you're a surrogate…"

She scowled, putting equal emphasis on each word she spoke. "*Was* a surrogate."

He blinked it away. "Okay, was. It's like saying, because you were a surrogate that you should have known all of the details of the delivery process that was used to extract the progeny. And I can tell you personally that the idea is absurd, considering the complexity of that process. It was my primary assignment on Earth. If you were suited to it you would have been assigned as an obstetrician instead of a surrogate."

Kendra grew silent, digesting Jacob's statement and its implications. When she finally spoke, her chin was lifted and she ran her tongue across her teeth making a soft click of punctuation. "Well, maybe that is what I'm saying. And maybe I'm not. I don't believe in too complicated, personally. When things are *too* complicated, usually it's because people want them that way."

Jacob stopped and really looked at her, his mouth open, brows encroaching on his eyes as he struggled to process her logic.

"That's why I signed on for the Mars project…to get back to simplicity and have myself in the driver's seat."

Jacob shook his head and blinked his eyes in one cohesive gesture of confusion, or perhaps disbelief. "Let me know how simple setting up a life on a new planet turns out for you."

Kendra pursed her lips and stared at the back of the physician's head.

"Captain Neil requests entry." The declaration from the security system startled her from her thoughts and she leaned up on one elbow, smoothing twists of hair back from her face with the other hand, unsure of what to do with the rush of nervous energy.

Jacob clenched his teeth. "Please, don't move Kendra. I have to reorient the entire system each time you move. Let him in please."

"Sorry." She held back a reflexive shrug and stopped moving, chagrin making her blush.

The automatic doors slid open, and the Captain stopped just inside the room, a smile pulling at the right side of his mouth. "Finished? Not quite? I'm just making my rounds... everything going well with the procedure?"

Kendra smiled at him, careful to keep her lower half entirely still, and nodded, giving an exaggerated salute. "Captain."

The tone of her voice, deep and melodic with sensual undertones, drew his full attention. "Ah... Kendra. Hello." He gave a half-smile, warmth creeping into his cheeks under her direct gaze.

He licked his lips, eyes lingering on her face. "Is she the last then, Jacob? Or are we behind schedule?"

Kendra returned the look, savoring the curve of his lips as he spoke.

"I'd like a full report once you're finished."

Jacob continued to direct the nanobot, his eyes unblinking, voice slow and measured. "She is the second to last. Feel free to stand by. About ten more minutes. And I need to discuss some proposals with you when you are finished, if you don't mind."

"Sure thing." Captain Neil nodded to the physicians back, his eyes flicking over to the woman on the table.

"I don't mind if you wait it out in here. I could use the company, you know. Better than entertaining myself." Her smile was not the look of a disgruntled patient and she was acutely aware of it as she forced down self-conscious laughter.

The Captain returned the smile, shaking his head as the words slipped out. "Why don't I just do that? I could use some good conversation." He did laugh, keeping his distance to avoid disrupting the procedure. "Didn't know surgery was so...lively?"

Jacob blinked but continued in his focused work missing the joke and it's intended recipient entirely. "Oh well…I'm good at what I do. Close to done now in fact."

Neil and Kendra exchanged a look and bit back further laughter.

Stretching his arms above his head, Jacob allowed himself to free-float in the empty room for a few moments before collecting his last patient. He found Theresa sleeping in the adjoining room, which held three rows of triple level operating tables, designed to accommodate ten patients within the minimal space.

The only bunks occupied were Theresa's and the one just above, where a medic had moved so that she could assist her until her injuries had healed.

"VSA system, rouse Patient 1A within five minutes." Jacob looked over at Theresa where she slept. Her color was better, if a bit blotchy from the effects of zero-G.

"Beginning arousal from stage four deep sleep."

Turning to face the large glowing screen, he accessed the most recent images of Theresa's healing clavicle.

"It's taking a long time to heal, isn't it? I'd like to have the use of my arms when it comes time to deliver." Theresa had removed the VSA headpiece and placed it in her lap, and was now looking up at the screen displaying the internal images of her injury. She brushed the stray hairs freed by sleep from her face, and used her one good arm to pull herself into a sitting position.

"Oh." Jacob turned from the screen to greet her. "You're up. How are you feeling?"

"Better, mostly. But this zero-G has me feeling so restless and ugh. I hate it. My energy is increasing since Carla started working on my diet with me. I'm not nauseous for the first time in, I don't know? Weeks, I guess."

Jacob pulled out a hypodermic pen and keyed in the correct information to activate the nano-bot held within. "Personally, I like zero-G. Didn't you ever have flying dreams?"

"Uh, yeah. The kind where I was being chased and I thought I could fly, but I could only hover. More like nightmares, really." She shrugged. "I like to have my feet under me. And there's no under in space ...is that for removing the implants?"

"Yes it is. And you're up." He walked over to Theresa's bed.

"Actually. Don't bother. It doesn't make sense to remove my implants. I've had them since I was twelve years old and I never even wanted a child until Abby. I don't need to get pregnant anytime in the foreseeable future."

Jacob massaged his temples with one hand, sitting down on the side of the bunk. "Okay. I see your reasoning. But we scheduled the reversals for today for a reason. We'll be arriving at our destination within a day's time and, if you imagine the unlikely scenario where we lose access to our technology, it will be too late to change your mind. In a colonization effort, it could someday fall to you to…"

She sat up straighter, her nose and brow crinkling in a scowl. "I'm not here to 'breed' for the colony! My assignment is to support the growth of the colony with reproductive technologies."

"Every colonist has two roles, or obligations, if you will. To perform their primary assignment and to produce the next generation of Martians."

Theresa shook her head, her lips pressed into an angry line between flushed cheeks. "Then I've already fulfilled that duty, haven't I?" Lifting her left hand, she placed it over the RPU that held Abby and looked Jacob in the eye.

After a moment, he looked away. "I suppose you have. I still recommend having the implants removed."

"Your recommendation has been noted. No, thank you."

Jacob rubbed his hands together and nodded, looking anywhere but at Theresa as he stood and tucked the vial from the hypodermic pen into his pocket.

Silence filled the room until the security door's tinny voice broke in. "Genesis requests entry to the inpatient room."

Genesis glided through the entryway and the door closed behind her. She was getting good at getting around quickly in zero-G, gliding from one point to the next and planning each point of contact several steps in advance instead of using the rails and foot-holds designed to allow for more cautious movement. A smile of greeting lit her face as she neared Jacob and Theresa.

"Hello, Jacob. The ladies can't stop talking about you today. Sounds like you're good at what you do." She gave him a teasing smile, eliciting a blush from the physician. "Am I interrupting?" Genesis glanced between the two, assessing the mood. *Definitely interrupting something. Good timing. She'll be grateful for the rescue.*

"Actually, we've finished our appointment. I was just leaving. I'll check on you again in the morning." He ran his fingers through his thin brown hair and waited for Genesis to reach them before pushing off towards the door. Theresa gave him a perfunctory nod and a wave. The door hissed open and then shut, leaving the two women alone in the inpatient room.

Genesis cocked an eyebrow. "That was heavy. Did he run out of his popular bedside manner I heard so much about?"

Theresa sighed, breathing out the tension that had built up during her confrontation with Jacob. "No. He was fine. It was me, I think. I'm not a very good patient. Most people don't argue with their doctors…or with the enforcement of policies. I seem to be making a habit of it lately." Theresa turned her face towards Genesis, giving a self-deprecating smile. "I often recommend against butting heads with authority. But I never seem to listen."

Genesis's smile turned into a laugh, entirely caught off guard by Theresa's candor and humor at her own expense. "How's that working out for you? I lean more towards leading authority to my way of thinking." Genesis gave a conspiratorial wink. *Confide just enough to inspire confidence. A bond.*

"Actually pretty badly, I think, but it sounds like your method takes more premeditation than I manage."

"Did *that* require premeditation or do you just manage smuggling progeny out of the Reproductive Council spontaneously?" She gestured to the bulging capsule that was just visible through the open front of Theresa's space suit.

Theresa's jaw dropped and her eyes took on a spark of alarm that Genesis recognized. *The cornered animal look.*

Genesis blinked, pulling up her eyebrows in remorse. "I'm sorry. That just sort of came out that way. I mean I lived there. I can't imagine anyone getting through their security."

Theresa narrowed her eyes. "You don't know where I got Abby. What makes you think…?"

"Theresa, really!? I think on my feet and I've never met anyone quicker. You're the colony's head of Reproductive Technologies and you worked in the Reproductive Council Headquarters. You're not part of the underground, breeding illegally, or you wouldn't be here."

Theresa didn't meet her gaze.

"The only thing I can't figure out is what program you took her from. I know everyone who works with the surrogate program, as well as everyone involved in the elite breeding program. Also, prematurity is a rarity and weak progeny are not kept." Genesis's voice had dipped lower and she placed a hand over Theresa's, hoping to regain eye-contact. "How did you get her out of a program that didn't even exist?"

Theresa looked up, red-brown eyes burning as she spoke each word with emphasis. "This is not your secret to claim, Genesis. And knowing will not benefit the colony in any way."

Genesis remained silent, unblinking, expressionless for several seconds. "I know there are other programs for reproduction that aren't in the records." The statement came out flat and without emotion. "I've searched the databases and I didn't come from any of the surrogate programs or selective breeding programs. My genetic code comes from five women and four men. I have no surrogate on record."

"Why are you telling me all of this?" The fire in Theresa's eyes was replaced by confusion and fear.

Genesis looked away to gather her thoughts. Her golden eyes widened into twin pools of anguish, deep and haunted. "When I was a child, I wondered about myself, and when I couldn't find the answers in my records I made up my own stories: my parents were killed in a tragic accident, I was acquisitioned by the council because of my abnormally high intelligence and potential." She shook her head, a soft half-formed laugh escaping her lips. "When I met you I was reminded of that, and seeing Abby revealed, a complete enigma with unknown origins..." She shrugged. "I guess I felt a connection."

"I'm sorry for freaking out. I need to keep Abby safe. I need to keep my secrets."

Genesis sighed, nodding and biting her bottom lip.

Theresa licked her lips. "I have connections in the Reproductive Council still. I may be able to find out what you want to know. If you want."

Genesis looked up at her, a small smile forming on her lips, bringing contrast to the forlorn darkness in her eyes as a small seed of hope took root. *She'll be an asset if aimed correctly.* "You'll do that?"

"Yes." Theresa inhaled before committing any further. "But only if you can promise me that anything we discover about you and anything you know about Abby remains between us."

Taking Theresa's hand, Genesis gave it a soft squeeze. "I swear, on my life. It stays between us."

Leaving Theresa to rest, Genesis made her way to the council room. *Soft like the rest of them. With some spine, true. But display some emotion and she gets all gooey and stops thinking clearly.*

Jacob looked down, nodding, one hand over his earpiece. It wasn't any different than it had been on Earth. *Did I expect a difference?* His conscience twinged, just a small nagging itch in the back of his mind, like the new exposed flesh under a burn sending out mixed messages that were best ignored. Scratch it. God don't touch it! Rip it off!

That small voice could be distracting, but only if he let it.

"Doesn't the request make some sense, though?" He pursed his lips and listened awhile to the response before cutting in.

"Okay. But couldn't it be brought before the council? We do have one separate from Earth, after all." *A collective of figureheads.* He sighed, the sound much louder than he expected, forcing his mind to run through practice exercises and drills while he waited for the reply.

"Fine. Yes. I need to know if there are going to be any exceptions, though. And what's the story going to be when the few who refuse later find themselves pregnant?" Saying it so plainly brought on another faint twinge of guilt. *Policies exist for a reason.* "I feel it would be most effective if we, if I, formed a Reproductive Council on Mars to handle these decisions and interface with Earth."

"Alright. Understood. I'll take care of it." Jacob ended the call and turned to the paneled wall in the small room that served as his office.

He typed his password into the panel above the secure medical supply storage.

8625970Asklepios

The soft yellow light on the bottom of the panel turned green, and the pressure lock disengaged with a soft hiss before the panel slid open. Reaching inside, he took out two small vials. The first labeled PDE4 Patient A1, the second Nano570. He placed both vials into his pocket and resealed the panel, leaving his conscience in the dark storage compartment, and returning to Theresa's room to administer her medication.

Carla made her way down the hall, alternating between the more cautious option of gripping the foot and hand-holds to pull herself along and the much quicker and exciting method of pushing off and free-falling in the chosen direction. *Ah, physics! Fun. Not awe-inspiring like biology, but fun. It's too late to still be up.*

Or up or down or sideways! Carla cackled at herself as she did a slow spin in the empty passage-way. *Let's see. A good number have got their eyes opened now, and we've only had three group meetings.*

She pushed off on one side, increasing in speed. *Not bad, for an old woman and almost fifty broken ones. They were holding onto more sense than I expected, what with the way the whole population rolled over during the crisis.*

Carla pursed her lips against the anger that thoughts of the World Governing Council elicited. *They had solved the crisis though, hadn't they? The human genome entirely clean, and health and long life a given. We're no longer tripping over each other. Hell, we could parcel out all the land on Earth and be unable to find our neighbors if it came to it.*

She narrowed her eyes, resisting the pull of years of propaganda echoing in her head.

But the stories she had heard in those first two meetings were the same as the ones she had been hearing from her patients the past fifty years, and yet, for some reason, these seemed to burrow deeper into her heart, claws out and clinging, digging in and burying themselves there. What was different?

You know what it is, Carla: these women have hope, they have a chance. Because you've decided to climb out of your cave and try again.

She put out both hands to stop her motion with the nearest hand-hold. *The others over the past fifty years blurred together, one faceless every-woman, a mishmash of grief that you couldn't vindicate. Validate, yes, but never vindicate. These ones are your last stand. Ha! Your only stand! They'll be the last ones you fail.*

She pushed herself off into another spin to contain the heavy sick feeling in her chest, spinning to condense it down and choke back the burning rage that emanated from its core, the anguish that bled through and seeped into her veins. *What have we done to our humanity? Is there a chance for us? Do we even deserve a second chance on Mars?*

The malaise growing within tried to settle over her, weighing down her thoughts and casting them in deep shadows. She swallowed.

This is what you stuck it out for. There's a chance. So take it. Carla sighed. *Need to pick up some stragglers, though, before we arrive tomorrow.*

Grabbing hold of the nearest handhold, she paused to regain equilibrium and take mental inventory. *Kendra's on board, along with all of the retired surrogates once Alissa comes around. That's thirteen. In fact, she might drag the others kicking and screaming if she has to. Brianna, Sarina, Bethany. Ariel is in limbo but leaning our way.*

Most of the stragglers just need more time and more information. Only ten are vocally against it and I'm seeing chinks in even their armor. Pushing off to change direction, she moved down the hallway towards the room she shared with Alissa and several others. *Or is that just the ship-sized holes in their indoctrinated logic? Now, now, Carla! Contempt won't win them over. Easy does it.*

Theresa made her second slow loop around the room, using her one good arm and the footholds along the path to move with caution, her headset on voice-activation mode. *I've had enough 'flying' for one space-flight—make that lifetime.* The walking would improve her circulation and was also good for helping her combat the boredom of waiting several minutes to hear back from Earth.

"Greg, I need you to check the records for all of the classified reproduction programs for an individual named Genesis Shaw. You can also check the numeric equivalent 7514519919."

Theresa paused at the sound of the security door chime and locked her feet into the footholds to free up her hands.

"Sorry, Abby." She stroked Abby's back through the silicone wall and then gently pulled the left side of her suit to cover her.

"Carla Schoen seeks entry. Would you like her admitted?"

"Yes. Let her in."

Carla glided through the door, silver-white braid trailing behind, and caught herself a few feet from Theresa with the side of the bed frame. "How are you and the little stow-away this evening?"

Theresa smiled at Carla's term of endearment for Abby.

"Isn't it a bit late to be checking in on us? And flaunting your zero-G skills. Seems everyone is floating around the ship now, instead of crawling like me." She glowered, exaggerating the true frustration at the core of her statement.

"Ahh, yes! That's what happens when you become a parent. Either you bust your bones protecting them or you are just generally handicapped by perpetually meeting their needs."

Carla chuckled. "And everyone on this ship is in for a shocking realization when they start popping out babies and learn that they don't come out like mini-adults. You do realize that everyone on this ship has had almost no exposure to babies and young children, don't you? Course, when you start out right the other pieces fall into place more easily, and having a childhood development specialist on board won't hurt."

Theresa opened her mouth to speak, but found she had not really decided what to say.

"That's part of why they stare at Abby, if they come near you before you think to cover her up. You don't have to do that around me, by the way." Carla placed a hand on her shoulder. "The other reason is we aren't really meant to see them unfinished as she is. Mind if I...?" Carla gestured towards the front of Theresa's suit and waited for her affirmation that a quick peek would be alright. Theresa nodded, pulling aside the flaps covering the RPU.

Carla smiled, a soft curl of her lips in reaction to the little rounded head and butt, noting the perceptible changes from the night before. Her cheeks were starting to fill in, rounding her small face and dimples marked her knees and elbows as well. "She's plumper, just a little. And she's getting hair."

Theresa stared down at Abby, tracing her contours with one finger. "She is bigger, isn't she? Her growth rate has improved drastically. The only changes I made are the dietary ones you suggested. And the nausea has subsided since I started eating more often."

"On the hour every hour? Something balanced, protein plus carb?"

Theresa nodded.

Abby kicked against Theresa's ribs, pushing hard as if she knew she was being talked about and stretched the back side of the RPU, distorting its shape. "Woah!" Theresa placed her hand against the small bulging back. "I keep worrying the seals will break."

"I've never had that happen, but if it did we'd have some time to get her stable."

Theresa shuddered at the thought of Abby naked to the world before she was ready to survive. "I've never delivered progeny that had not reached full term. There are reasons for the policy of allowing premature progeny to fade away...or for culling them."

Carla snorted. "Money and obsession with perfection."

Theresa's features twisted, her eyes clouding with contempt. "How can you say that? The policies that guide reproduction on Earth brought us back from the brink of extinction! Is that what you want for Mars, a repeat of Earth?"

"That is the last thing I want." Carla's eyes shone with a sharp light. "Not one of you knows how to be a woman-biologically-or a mother, for that matter. It is a fool's folly for us to remain dependent on technology that could be lost on Mars. Hell! How many natural disasters do you think it might take to knock out your ability to perform a 'safe' surgical birth? Or your ability to print the tools you need?"

Theresa's cheeks flushed pink, her eyes meeting the challenge issued by Carla's. "You are absolutely mad!"

"I am saying this to you because you are an intelligent woman and this is our only chance to take back what's ours. I know cognitive dissonance is a bitch, but it's time to wake UP!" Abby jumped at Carla's sharp tone. "Don't tell me that taking a sickly, premature infant to Mars with you was within the Reproductive Council's policies! Because I'm not buying it."

Theresa shook with repressed rage, her eyes sparking with the words barely withheld. "Because I respect you, I'm going to ask you to leave before I say something I might regret."

Carla held Theresa's gaze a moment, willing her to see the truth. She was met by the equivalent of a steel wall in Theresa's eyes.

Exhaling the breath she didn't realize she had been holding, Carla pushed herself towards the exit. Catching hold of the door frame, she turned back to Theresa and held up a hand. "I may have misstepped here, but consider this. Assume that Kendra's next child is premature. Shall I tell her it's best to let him die, or would you like to do the honors as the head of Reproductive Technologies? And are you going to tie her down when she refuses a surgical birth?" She shook her hand to stay Theresa's answer before it came. "You have the unique opportunity to use your technology to work *with* our women…instead of blindly enacting policies created for desperate times on a dying planet."

Theresa did not meet Carla's eyes, but instead stared across the room at the blackness of space showing through the window...and the fast-approaching mottled green and black planet.

"Our next Women's meeting is in four days, on Mars. I hope you'll be there." The door sealed shut behind Carla, leaving Theresa to her muddled thoughts.

The thoughts came one on top of another, interrupting each other with the force of transport craft collisions. Upon examination, Theresa found that each thought was so incomplete, and so closely followed by a conflicting thought, that she could grasp little but a strong sense of unease. Unease and the visceral sensation of being in the center of a war zone, bombarded by explosions from overhead, and the dying screams from thousands maimed on the field rushing in on her senses.

She forced her eyes shut, shaking her head and attempting to slow her breathing. Disjointed thoughts crowded in, mixed with mental images layered one on top of the other, lingering despite her attempts to make them dissipate. ~*She hopes I'll be at the meeting?* ~*2055:* Millions in filth splattered hospital beds, their discolored limbs hanging over the edges, with glowing ventilators strapped across their sallow, sweating faces, tubes draping by the tens from various parts of their bodies, arms, scalps, and buried between their thighs. ~*Why?* ~*Tie Kendra down!* ~2015: Wild-eyed, feet impacting with the stunned faces of the surgical team, nails drawing blood before the straps found their mark and restrained her, the mask descending to cover her screams, her pleas, the scalpel descending.~*The policy was to terminate the weak at the end of the first trimester.* ~*To listen to more of her madness?* ~*Surgical birth is necessary.* ~2062: Bloating corpses, skin once a shining silver, swelling, splitting and flaking in the sand, black, pink, white and tawny, sands as well as pebbles covered in the lifeless corpses disgorged by the seas, eyes clouding and fly dotted. The tide rushing in red.

Abby would be dead.

The final thought, which came louder than the others, was accompanied by the very real sensation burned into her memory five long weeks ago: Abby's wriggling body, slick and struggling as Theresa transferred her from the AUC unit to the cocoon she now inhabited, her warmth a sharp contrast to the feel of the cadaver fetus as she carried him to department six to cover her deception...and brought down a wall of silence, a reprieve from her inner turmoil.

A soft chime announced the arrival of a voice message, making her recoil from the earpiece she wore and bump her head against the bed-frame. "Ow." She could not afford to spare a hand to rub the throbbing.

Greg appeared in the VR com glasses as she came back to herself and slid them down over her eyes.

"Theresa, I'm glad you are well and approaching your destination, if my calculations are correct. I'm pleased to help you in any way I can. As for the records you requested...I found the person that you seek in the database, but unfortunately her records are above our clearance level. I'm sorry to disappoint. Just...Well, just ask if there's anything else. I'll do what I can."

"Damn." Theresa swore out loud. *He must have recorded a few times to avoid stutters until the end.*

She closed out the messages on her hand-held, ignoring the folder of unopened ones, all bearing Richard's name, that was almost full and pushed down the twinge of regret. *Maybe I should check them. We're supposed to be collaborating. They may have terminated by now. Damn your curiosity, Richard, your goddamn questions! Sorry, but I'm not ready to answer them.*

She bit her lip, struggling to regain focus on the task at hand. *I could ask Richard...if I was talking to him.*

She hovered a finger over the messages folder, bottom lip between her teeth. With a single swipe, she opened the folder and selected the first of the messages.

Richard appeared in her VR com glasses, lab coat open in front to reveal the tailored black and silver suit he was wearing beneath. He steepled his fingers on the desk, a humorless smile twisting his lips. "Theresa. I thought we had an accord. A shared purpose, if you will." His anger was clear, flashing in his dark eyes, as he stood to pace closer. "I respect your privacy." The look in his eyes softened a measure, but the frustration, laced with equal amount of confusion remained. "I really do. But we won't win this by going into hiding and cowering like prey animals." He spread his palms in appeal. "You have the advantage of distance. You can take that and leverage it if you are willing." He stared at her, willing her with his sharp gaze.

To what? What does he expect?

"In the meantime I am tending the children. Watching them grow for as long as I can keep this going." He gave a two finger salute in her direction. "Be well."

Theresa's heart pounded in her ears as she pulled the VR Com glasses from her face and tossed them aside, a laugh escaping when they continued to float in a slow spiraling motion across the room. *The advantage of distance? As if the council can't reach us on Mars! No, Richard.*

She pulled aside her scarf, using a shaking hand to gently scratch the reddened, irritated skin around the RPU capsule's seal on her chest. wincing at the raw burning, throbbing sensation the light touch elicited.

Forget about Earth, I guess. Let's be self-sufficient. Theresa pulled her hair back from her face as she strapped herself down in front of the computer console to think. *What can I do from here?* Squeezing her eyes shut and rubbing the lids, she struggled to banish Richard's face, and the challenge in his eyes, from her mind.

You're pushing her too hard. Gonna lose any chance you have if you don't back off a bit. Carla shook her head, letting out a sigh as she crossed the medic's adjoining room outside of the recovery ward.

"Everything alright?"

She startled from her musings, stopping and turning to the source of the voice.

"I heard raised voices. A bit late to be checking in on our patient, isn't it?" Jacob Emory swiveled his seat to face Carla from where he sat at his desk.

"Thought I was the only one up and working…but then, healers don't have off hours, do we?"

"You consider yourself a healer, then?" His tone was light with feigned interest.

She stared at him, the suspicion percolating in her eyes. "I do."

"Psychiatry is a healing of the mind, I suppose."

She turned to face the security scanner. "If you'll excuse me, I have…"

"You wouldn't be referring to the tradition of pseudoscience and perpetuation of ancient mythology that you mentioned to the captain, I imagine."

She straightened, moving out of range of the scanner.

A small smile played upon Jacob's lips. "Midwifery. Plucked from the days of appendectomies, circumcisions, and hysterectomies. I have trouble associating those times with…healing."

Carla's lips tightened and she swallowed, choking back the hot words that threatened to bubble forth. *Don't take the bait now. Just breathe.* "Barbaric times indeed. I wonder if our 'healing' will appear in the annals of history as barbaric or humane?"

Jacob nodded, the smile deepening as he looked up from his hand-held to stare at her back.

"No identity detected. Please lean forward into the scanner's range if you intend to exit." The security door's lights flashed from red to green and back to red, signaling a failed scan.

She wet her lips and leaned in for the scan. "Good night, Jacob."

Genesis looked up and smiled from the side of her bunk, where she sat sliding a translucent comb through the black waterfall that floated around her shoulders.

David narrowed his eyes, wariness tightening his features. "How did you know I was coming?"

Eyes a shade lighter than her tawny skin sparkled up at him as he glided closer, catching himself with the frame of the bunk opposite her.

Soft laughter escaped from her lips, leaving a smirk behind. "I didn't know you were coming tonight. I admit I wasn't sure when you would come."

"Not if?" He caught a floating lock of Genesis's hair, sliding it between his fingers, savoring the silken texture without looking away from her face.

She paused in her rhythmic brushing. "Are we playing games now, or are we putting our cards on the table?"

David's face smoothed out and he held her eyes. The look was not one of contrived contemplation but serious reflection, his voice low and smooth when he spoke. "I came here tonight to put my cards on the table. Since you keep pulling up a chair, I need you to know how I work."

Genesis closed the gap between them and knelt on the bunk a few feet away from him. "Alright." Her voice was resonant, replete with warm humor and patience. "I'm listening."

"I won't be your tool, Genesis. Games, manipulations, and hidden agendas…if that's what you have in mind, it's not going to fly with me." He paused to read her reaction.

Her eyes hooded and smile dimmed. "You think me insincere." It was a statement more than a question.

He wet his lips and shifted position. "I don't know if it's insincere, but I watch you interact with the others and they just lap up everything you say. You say all the right things, but the empathy in your voice doesn't touch your eyes."

"You confuse sincerity with sentimentality. I do not say things that I don't mean." Each word was underscored by the quiet intensity of her voice and the liquid fire in her eyes. It was a cold fire that simultaneously elicited a shudder and an electric thrill. "I've said nothing to you that I didn't mean, but if you'd like to see my cards…"

Her breath was hot and fragrant as she leaned in closer to David, speaking in conspiratorial fashion. She smiled and parted her lips as if about to continue. Letting go with first one hand and then the other she turned her palms facing out, wiggling her fingers to highlight their emptiness as she started to float away.

David reached out reflexively, pulling her back with both hands on her waist, his feet locked into the footholds on the edge of the bunk.

A grin spread across her face, a grin that lit her pale eyes sunset gold and filled them with triumph. "Still a bit jumpy, aren't we?"

He pulled her against him, sliding one hand up her back, tangling it in the hair at the nape of her slender neck. He hesitated, searching her face. Genesis returned his gaze, eyes luminous, fathomless, and grazed her lips with her teeth and tongue to wet them.

David drew a breath. He tightened his grip on the back of her neck and, without further hesitation, claimed her lips with his, allowing tongue and teeth to delve deeply into hers. Her lips parted slowly, providing resistance before allowing him entrance. Her tongue teased, a dance to his ardent questing, and then drew his deeper, refusing any retreat until she pulled away, covering his wet lips with one hand.

"What about my cards? Didn't you want to see them?" Her voice was low and breathy from the kiss, and her look belied her interest in further conversation. David shook his head.

"They're on the table, right?"

She nodded, eyes wide in mock innocence intended for their mutual entertainment as she slid one hand between the seams of his suit, releasing the seals to allow her access to the layer beneath.

"Then I'll see them later."

Reaching behind Genesis, David grasped the dangling straps attached to the bed frame and wrapped them tightly around her wrists, pinning one arm and then the other up and behind her head.

"Are we breaking the rules?" Genesis arched one delicately feathered black eyebrow and David paused. He opened his mouth as if to answer and instead gave her a crooked grin, full of mischief and shook his head before lowering his face to the front of her spacesuit. Unfastening the clasps with his teeth, he found only a light cotton shirt between his lips and her breasts... breasts which, without the pressure of the spacesuit and the force of gravity, stood out in front of her round and high, like full moons in the dimly-lit room. Lowering his face, he brushed his jaw along her flesh through the thin fabric and kissed their contours, avoiding the dark, pointed nipples that begged for his attention.

"Because as members of the council, it wouldn't look good to..." Her breath came in short gasps, interrupting every few words and causing her to trail off into a sigh as he nuzzled her. Sliding one hand up to her face and trailing a finger across her full lips, he slid the cotton aside and pulled one hard nipple and the surrounding soft curve of breast into his mouth, sucking hard. Genesis moaned and pressed into him. She bit down on the finger that probed her mouth and caressed it with her tongue.

Leaning back on his heels, David lifted his mouth from her breast, leaving one hand there in its place to stroke and tease. "To disobey the ban on sex the last night before we reach Mars?"

Genesis pulled against the straps and narrowed her eyes, lips parted and white teeth glinting in a predatory fashion. "Of course, as members of the council…we could decide to use our…authority…to overrule the ban." She arched her back, pressing herself against his hand.

Squeezing her breast, David traced Genesis's lips with his tongue, allowing her to taste his warm, salty breath.

"Or, we could obey my rule of no sex before we've played a few games of cards and all of the aces are accounted for."

She breathed in slowly, her jawline tight, eyes glinting with something he couldn't quite place before she regained control of her features.

"You aren't used to a man stopping, are you?"

"Untie me." Her voice was smooth and even again, with a slight chill.

He ran one finger down her forehead, nose, lips, and chin in a straight line before he unfastened the straps.

Genesis rubbed her wrists and then pushed off from the bunk, catching herself opposite a computer console on the wall. David leaned against the back of the bunk frame, watching her as she brought up the full list of colonists and their assignments.

"You're angry."

"No. I have work to do before we arrive at Mars orbit." Her full attention was now on the computer console as she made notes and rearranged the names on the list, like pieces on a chess board.

David stood, using the foot- and handholds, and headed for the door. "Goodnight. You know where to find me, I guess."

MARTIANS

The curve of the planet filled all viewing screens and windows. Earth's darker twin, floating just within their reach as the ship slowed to dock with the un-manned space station. Patches of black and rusty orange were interspersed with large expanses of green and swirls of white and gray.

"It's so dark…" The colonists stood gathered in small groups in the central room mesmerized by the sight of the planet growing before them.

"Where is the water? I guess those are clouds, but I don't see any oceans." Melissa pushed short wisps of brown hair behind her ears with both hands and leaned closer to the window crinkling her nose at the planet below.

Donovan placed a hand on her shoulder. "Maybe you should ask a planetologist." He looked away, a slight smile on his lips threatening to turn into laughter.

Melissa shook her head at Donovan, but with a patient smile. "Yeah? Too bad I don't know any worth their salt."

Kendra laughed at them both. "Okay, I'll bite. I actually *want* to know what we're looking at here."

Donovan gave Melissa a meaningful stare as if to rub in his small victory and moved closer to Kendra to point at the planet beyond the window.

"Alright. The Black and red portions are land. The black coloration comes from lichen." He paused and turned to Kendra with a quizzical look. "How much do you actually want to know? Detail, I mean."

She shrugged. "We're going to live there, it's all exciting. I mean, I spent the past twenty-something years learning about Earth; I may as well get a head start on Mars now."

Donovan's grin broke free then, and his whole body became animated, hands telling the story as his words poured forth. "The lichen covers most of the landmasses in a thin layer. It's a genetically modified version of an Earth species, *Lichina Pygmaea.* It's designed to be a fast-growing species, and it serves three purposes. One, it provides a dark blanket, if you will, to heat the planet; two, it breaks up the upper layers of the rocky terrain to build a topsoil; and three, it's edible!"

He paused again, checking to see if Kendra was still listening and, finding her full attention on him, carried on with renewed enthusiasm. "Now the oceans are very exciting! You see the green patches? Those are all bodies of water. Lakes, rivers, oceans, seas, all teaming with life. Well, algae anyway. And the beautiful part is that it's already differentiated into fifty plus species to fill each niche. The lichen too, of course. Our most recent data shows about thirty species of lichen spread out across the land masses."

"Is that going to pose a problem for the introduction of other plant species?"

Donovan looked behind him to find the source of the voice that had spoken and found his words delayed a few moments beyond his intention to speak. Theresa had approached the small group from behind, the front of her suit pulled closed with a scarf draped across the opening. "Oh, I'm sorry. I wasn't trying to interrupt." Theresa looked from one member of the group to the other, shifting her feet in the footholds, her cheeks coloring as the silence drew on.

"Ah, no. No, it's fine. We just haven't seen you out of the infirmary. Since the...ah...accident." Donovan stumbled over his words, drawing a hand through his long black hair and struggling to keep his wayward gaze from sliding down from Theresa's face to her chest area. "How is your, um..."

"Clavicle?" She offered, brows angled upwards with a slight lopsided smile. "It's healing slowly, and as you can see, still immobilized. The healing rate should improve now that we'll be getting out of this zero-G." She turned her gaze to Kendra and Melissa, catching Kendra's obvious stare and Melissa's nervous glances at the scarf covering Abby, and pretended not to notice. It was the same sort of looks that anyone outside of the AUC project gave when first allowed into the lab. *Is it because no one sees progeny up close any more, or because they look unfinished, like Carla said?*

"I didn't want to steal the spotlight, though. Go on, Donovan, please." She gestured towards the window that was now almost entirely filled with the surface of the dark, murky planet below them.

Turning back in the direction Theresa suggested, but at an angle as if he did not want to turn his back on her, Donovan continued his narrative with less gusto than before. "The breakdown of the rocky soil into topsoil is already underway, according to analysis…"

His words blurred together as Theresa stared ahead, lost in thought. *Wow, Theresa. You sure suck the life out of group gatherings. Guess that's why we like to lurk in shady, top secret laboratories.* A wry smile pulled at her lips. *Okay, that's just melodramatic.*

They were treating her differently now, though, since the incident. Was it Abby? Or was it her? A few had come to see her the day or two after the accident and, while she wasn't particularly warm or forthcoming when they asked questions about Abby, she wasn't unkind, and she hadn't told them to stay away.

"Theresa." The smile was evident in the voice before she turned. David propelled himself towards her using the hand rails, his gaze warm and friendly, filled with genuine pleasure. "It's good to see you up!" Leaning in to hug her, he thought better and instead took one of her hands in his and gave it a squeeze. "How are you and Abby?"

Theresa's brows tipped up and she could not help but emerge from her maudlin thoughts, a smile breaking through the ice and causing her lips to tremble with emotion. "I'm well enough. Better. And so is Abby. I still have my concerns, but she's growing again."

David's smile widened. "That's great. Is it a lot? They grow faster the last couple of months, don't they?"

She cocked an eyebrow. "Not a lot yet. She's likely to be small when I deliver her. But, yes, they do. Don't you work with plants, or did you have a previous assignment in obstetrics?"

David flinched and looked away before turning back to her, brows furrowed and eyes dark. When he spoke his voice was low and seemed to travel a long distance from where his thoughts were replaying, the words fighting to remain unsaid. "I was married once. We had an unexpected pregnancy." He looked ready to stop but then noticed her puzzled gaze. "She and the child are no longer with us." He rubbed his hand across his brow, fingers digging in as if to rub away the memories stored there. He turned and looked around the room as if to find some other focal point, something to distract.

No wonder he's interested in Abby.

"Docking with the Mars Space Station is now commencing. Prepare to board the elevator in ten minutes. Thank you." The smooth emotionless voice of the Pinnacle's autopilot was amplified to drown out the low din of the many excited conversations going on in the room. David seized upon the opportunity to avoid further discussion, at least on certain topics.

"Ah! I'm going to double check that the seedlings are all loaded properly and set to transport down." Before striding away, he placed a hand on her shoulder. Instead of explaining his reticence to speak on the matter, he smiled, his eyes speaking the apology he couldn't utter. "I'll see you on the surface."

Theresa nodded and watched him go, a sigh escaping her lips with the downward turn of her thoughts. He was, after all the only one who didn't seem afraid of her, and even talked about Abby as if he wasn't creeped out.

"Checking in with your little victim?" Genesis stood on the outskirts of the loading area where several other colonists were busy filling the large capsules with equipment that would be automatically loaded and transported down to the surface. Her voice was a low purr, eyes hooded, a soft smile on lips parted just so to reveal the pointed tips of teeth.

David stopped short, pushing in front of Genesis in the midst of his flight. Brows furrowed, he licked his lips and shook his head.

"Jealous much?"

"Not really. Unless you say there's cause to be. I enjoy a challenge." Genesis leaned in.

Brows that began the conversation furrowed, crowded together over David's eyes, and his lips pulled back into a grimace as he spoke.

"Now is not the time. I've told you I don't play games and this isn't chess." Turning to leave, he was caught by the small hand that shot out, nails scraping his bicep as Genesis gripped hard to hold him in place.

"I'm not blind. I saw the conversation turn. She upset you somehow and now you're taking it out on me." She shrugged. "Fine. But if you're going to go brood, the least you can do is tell me what it's about." Her eyes held his, unwavering, and while cold and hard in their gaze they lacked any sign of dissembling. She was being frank, and inviting him to do the same.

David's eyes lost their sharpness, but were still full of the shadows that darkened his expression. He allowed a faint sigh, but held back from any true release of tension.

"As I said, not now. It'll have to come later, sometime. But not now."

"Now is as good a time as any, David. While it's fresh. Doesn't it help to share these things?" She molded her features, aiming for compassion, concern.

She *was* concerned.

"No. It doesn't. It just gets worse. It's like ripping a fingernail off each day after it's started to re-anchor itself. So please, be patient. If you need to know that damn badly, I'm sure it's in your records." His smile was bitter, mocking. "What's a community relations manager without personal records?"

"Fine. I'm not asking for stats and third party recounting. I'm asking for what's in here." She released his arm and placed her hand on his chest. "For what's behind those brooding looks."

"To do what with? To file away for future use." His voice was low and resigned, the weariness that had crept in permeating not only his tone of voice, but the set of his jaw and the look in his eyes.

Genesis stared back a slight lift to her chin. "I don't know." She looked down for what seemed a long time and when she looked up her eyes held a darkness that seemed to come from her very core. The veil of many faces had slipped away, revealing something raw and unnamable. "But we won't know where this will lead, what it could be, unless we go all in. I don't know if I have that to offer, but I don't even know where to start if you don't."

David closed his eyes and inhaled slowly. Opening them, he pressed his lips to hers, their pressure light, not a tease or a promise but a peacemaking offer instead, meant to ameliorate for his inability to give more. "I'm going to check the seedlings and hydroponics." He left then, his movements brisk, and was aware of Genesis's hooded gaze tracking him as he headed towards the hydroponics crate.

Short moments after, his retreat was followed by the almost human intonation of the Pinnacle's AI. "Docking complete. Please, commence boarding the elevator to the surface, ten passengers at a time."

The weight of gravity descended onto the colonists' frames as they neared the surface. A sensation, not unlike the comforting press of warm hands massaging the life back into cold sleeping tissues and sluggish veins, progressed into the oppressive and fatiguing weight of sandbags laid over each surface of their bodies. With it came the buzzing, spinning, nausea-inducing sensation of equilibrium lost and regained in fits and starts. Carla laughed as she felt herself free-falling in her seat, and was compelled by instinct to reach out and grab the nearest landmark, which happened to be just to her left-Jon's face, in fact. Emily already had her arm twined around Jon's on his left side, and while her face was blanched of all color, her eyes were wild with excitement, giddy with the experience.

Jon placed a steadying hand on Carla's shoulder while she found a more suitable hand-hold, despite the unsteadiness that he was feeling, and smiled at his grandmother-in-law before turning to Emily, his look that of a child on a roller coaster that has turned out to be a bit more wild than expected.

"I'm starting to miss zero-G. How about you ladies?"

"I don't know about the ladies, but I'm thinking I can do without gravity if it comes with a raging headache and feeling like my guts are in my head and my head in my guts!" Eli groaned to accompany his description of the sensation of gravity descending on him.

Jon snorted. "Well, that's a colorful way to put it. Em?"

Emily took a breath and spoke with her eyes shut. "I just can't wait to feel the ground under my feet again. I can manage this if it gets us home." The silence wore on long enough to make her open her eyes. Ten pairs of eyes met her curious gaze, some moist with unshed tears, most glowing with a level of anticipation that was unmatched.

They *were* descending to their home.

But not Earth.

Emily put a hand out as if to reorient herself, eyes unfocusing for just a moment as her equilibrium was further compromised. Taking a breath, she closed her eyes again and leaned back against the seat.

"What is taking so long?" Kendra sat, arms folded, next to Captain Neil with her brow furrowed, lips alternating between a pout and a slight frown.

The captain raised an eyebrow and pulled one of her corkscrew twists between two fingers before answering. "Remember how long it took to ascend from Earth up to the space station? You wouldn't like to be dropped to the surface, would you?" His look was teasing but his tone serious.

Kendra cocked her head giving him a begrudging half smile. "Well, it *would* get me off of this ship faster!"

"I wouldn't be so anxious. It's going to make you feel dizzy, and heavy, and off-balance when you transition from zero-G to gravity, and that's if you're lucky. We've lost some muscle mass and bone density despite our zero-g diet and exercise regime, and our brains have acclimated to ignoring our vestibular systems. So, in other words, it's going to be hard to know which way is up once we hit gravity again."

Kendra's smile spread slowly as she watched him talk, half-listening to his words and half-admiring the curve of his lips around the words and the way his overly large hands punctuated his sentences. "I have two questions, then." She waited for the raised eyebrow that she had come to recognize meant he was listening. "Why do you continue to go on missions in space? And how much longer until the elevator makes it back up?"

Captain Neil laughed, resisting the urge to tweak her hair again despite the temptation the unruly mass of fine fluffy corkscrews provided. "Why do I go on space missions? I like zero-G. I like pushing boundaries." He gave her a crooked smile. "Mars. All of my missions have been leading up to this one."

She bit her lip. "So this is your last mission?"

"Mmm…last mission? I'm still on assignment with Earth. For now, my mission is to head the council on Mars and establish the colony government securely. After that, I don't know." He shrugged, turning one hand palm up in a gesture of uncertainty.

Her eyes flicked away from his, guarding the emotion beneath their surface. "How long till we get down from here?"

He nodded. "Well, seven have gone down, and it takes about forty-five minutes for each car to descend and unload and forty-five to come back up. So if you are still going to wait until the last car with me, then that's four and a half hours left.

Kendra puffed her breath out through pursed lips. "Well, I've had enough of space-food and exercise machines for a lifetime. How else can we kill time on this damn ship?"

The captain winced. "Now, don't curse the ship after she's gotten us this far. You'll make her angry." He placed a hand against the nearest wall of the ship and patted it, eyes warm with sentiment and humor.

She laughed and shook her head, unstrapping from her seat to stretch in mid-air. "Alright, alright. But I'm bored out of my mind. I'm itching to get to the surface. I don't know how you do it." She grinned. "Why don't you show me how *you* have fun in zero-G." Kendra's eyes sparkled with mischief.

Neil looked askance at her. "Well, I can think of a few ways to kill time in zero-G pleasurably, but most of them require practice, planning, and break at least two regulations for this flight."

Kendra blushed at the innuendo she had been fishing for but not expecting and allowed a full smile to round her cheeks and brighten her eyes. "You are too much, *Too much*!"

Genesis looked over her shoulder, irritation flickering in her eyes, independent of the smile she had placed on her lips for the occasion. She was last in line to board the elevator. But where was David?

Her eyes narrowed, spotting him gazing out of the transparent viewing wall, off into space. His arms were crossed, showcasing the well-developed muscles of his forearms through his suit. Genesis felt an electric thrill rush through her as she pictured those arms binding her wrists.

"David." He gave no indication that he heard her call. She opened her mouth to call out again, louder this time. *Oh, hell.*

Dropping her arms in frustration she strode across to the viewing window where he stood.

"Are you lost?" Her voice was a purr in his ear.

David flinched. "Yes."

"Well, that wasn't what I expected... we can talk on the way down if this means you've had a change of heart."

"No." David sighed, still staring out into the star-speckled darkness of space.

Genesis returned the sigh. "One word answers are hardly effective, you know...and if you think..."

The Pinnacle's voice cut her off. "Two more seats are available on the elevator craft heading down. Will two more passengers please board the craft? Descent will begin in five minutes."

David turned haunted eyes to face her, a failed attempt at a smile dropping from his lips. "Your ride is waiting."

Genesis glared at the infuriating man before her. "You're on the list for this trip down too! If you don't want to talk that's fine. But you're holding up the craft."

David looked askance at her. "Genesis, you're yelling. Not very diplomatic."

She took a breath, smoothing her features. "Will you please just get on the elevator, David?"

Taking her hand, the curtain in his eyes lifted just enough to allow concern to show through. "Hey, I'll see you on the surface. And we'll talk, okay? I just want to go down with the hydroponics equipment in the last batch. Take Brian down with you. He's anxious to get his feet on the surface."

Genesis stared at him, expressionless and unresponsive to the half-smile he offered with his words.

"Fine." Turning and walking toward the open door of the elevator craft, she leaned down to whisper in Brian's ear.

"Why don't you ride down with me?" The request was simple, but her tone held just enough innuendo to make the man blush and stumble over himself as he followed after her.

The horizon was red. Dust kicked up to the east, dispersed and hovering, painting the midday sky the color of bricks darkened by the elements.

Holding the support rails that surrounded the elevator complex, Carla pushed through the vertigo to make her way out into the Martian landscape. She dropped her bag outside of the complex, causing a small cloud of the same reddish dust coloring the horizon to blow into her face. The dust set off a fit of coughing, bouts of laughter coming in between each one, but she knelt down despite it, sifting the maroon colored soil between her fingers. "Look at this color... it's like blood. Isn't it?" Her voice was low, blue eyes wide, as she took in the alien surroundings. Donovan leaned down, toppling onto her bag and planting both hands to wait out the spinning of his senses as he laughed, a wild, almost hysterical sound filling the silent landscape around the group of colonists.

"It's the mixing of lichen and the iron rich sand. It used to be orange, you know." He paused to catch his breath again.

"Before we terraformed it. All the topsoil should be this color. Still needs work, though, to grow anything but lichen and aspens, first trees to grow after a volcano." He opened his mouth to speak and then paused, giving Carla an embarrassed smile. "Am I rambling too much? I'm rambling...yeah."

Carla laughed, her smile genuine. "If anyone knows how to go on and on it's me. You go right on ahead. You've got things to say. Say them."

Donovan smiled back, eyes gleaming in gratitude, as he stood and offered her a hand. Carla took the hand and surveyed the horizon.

Craggy black mountains soared to the south and the west, dark clouds rolling and tumbling over them, changing shape as they moved faster than any clouds on Earth, amorphous dragons and sky ships bearing rain. Tharsis Montes if she'd looked at the Pinnacle's maps right, but why keep the names that Earth had given them... Carla felt a pull towards those mountains, whatever the name, and stared with longing at the blankets of dark mist that meant rain in the distance.

The sound of retching pulled her back. The mountains would have to wait.

She turned, pausing several times to wait for her senses to catch up with her motions so the spinning in her head would cease. Emily had exited the elevator complex and was bent over the ground, emptying her stomach onto the red and black rocks. *An offering, Mother Mars.*

Carla smirked, making her way over to Emily and Jonathan, and placed a hand on both their shoulders where they crouched, shaking.

Jonathan's face was full of gratitude when he looked up at her.

"We don't seem to be taking to Mars just yet." His smile was weak in his pale face, beads of sweat gathering at his hairline as if it was taking great effort to hold down the contents of his stomach.

"Come on, then." Carla offered them both a hand. Emily stared up at her in alarm.

"I don't think I can."

"Of course you can. Gotta get you away from this little mess, or the smell will bring up another round. Come on."

She held her hand out until Emily took it, then pulled the younger woman upright. With Emily on one side and Jonathan on the other, Carla walked toward the southern horizon, where the small group of colonists gathered in a cluster, and stared at the dome shaped structures in the distance and, just beyond that, the algae green sea spread out before them.

The doors leading into the elevator car hissed open, revealing the cramped cylindrical interior. Through the windows that exposed the black nothingness of space, the view was punctuated by distant stars and broken by the curve of the planet below. The last ten colonists aboard the Pinnacle glided through the opening and climbed into seats lining the walls, strapping themselves down against the lack of gravity for the last time. Nothing was spoken, aside from a few soft murmurs and unintelligible grunts of effort. Their faces glowed with contained excitement. Their descent would herald in a new chapter for the group of one hundred colonists, and none were oblivious to the momentous nature of this final ride to the surface. The Pinnacle would remain docked here, unmanned, and yet, as soon as they touched Martian soil they would no longer be citizens of Earth, but instead, Martians.

A soft chime sounded as the doors sealed behind them.

"Final descent commencing. Have a pleasant ride!" The enthusiasm in the space-station's simulated voice was a bit off, as if the programmer from the time the station was crafted and imbued with AI hadn't quite understood the sentiment behind an exclamation point.

A few soft laughs and titters broke the silence, easing the built up tension of several hours. As the last down, they had waited the longest, and somehow collectively felt the importance of their safe arrival.

Breaking convention, Kendra leaned her head on the captain's shoulder as the sensation of gravity descended upon them with the movement of the craft downward. In the next seat over, David leaned back, eyes closed, preferring the weight of the planet on his limbs to the weight that had settled in his heart like a lead mantle. The descent was slow, gradual, and gave him the reprieve he needed. Wanting to descend in the same craft with the seedlings and hydroponics equipment was a good enough reason to be among the last ten to descend, as he had explained to Genesis, but it wasn't the only reason.

Letting his thoughts drift, he found himself unwilling to push aside the memories that flooded his consciousness, kept under tight lock and key to be taken out only when he was alone. Wispy auburn hair tickled his cheeks as the ghost of a memory—*or was it the memory of a ghost*— leaned in and kissed the tip of his nose, scrunching her own and then laughing, the sound like soft chimes, full of glee. In his mind's eye, David indulged.

What the hell. There will be nothing of her but what's in me once we reach the surface. He pulled the playful figment into his arms for an embrace, drawing on memories stored in his senses and replayed countless times over the past ten years until it was effortless to feel her there with him. The softness of her arms when wrapped around him. The moist imprint of her lips against his bare chest, unique like a fingerprint, and the way she would inhale through her upturned nose as she kissed his skin as if to breathe him in, tasting and smelling at the same time. His hands slid down to caress her slim waist, slim but with just enough softness, and found it instead grown round and full, like one large firm breast.

A wonder, moving of its own accord against his hand. Staring down at the albatross between them, David lifted her chin with the tips of his fingers to meet his gaze.

Couldn't we just skip this part, Joanna? Joanna's brows crowded together, pushing upward, and she shook her head, a frown on her lips.

"We were happy, though. Scared, but happy."

He sighed, bitterness evident in his eyes and the twist of his lips. "It wasn't supposed to happen. They said it wasn't possible. They thought we caused it." He laughed at the absurdity of that statement.

"Let's just be together, here. Until I reach the surface." His eyes pleaded with the figment in his arms.

She looked up at him, frowning. "You don't think I'll come with you there?" David thought a moment, not wanting to speak the answer that came to mind. He kissed her, slow, lingering and full of pent up longing. Longing for this to be real, to be a beginning instead of an ending.

"You know I want you to be happy, right? I didn't ask you to stay alone…" Her eyes were so intense, that deep blue suffused with such sincere…*God, what was it? It was as if she not only knew his internal landscape, and she had, as if she felt his feelings as deeply as if they were her own.*

"But she doesn't have anything to offer you." The sapphire eyes grew stormy, as she scowled. "You know that, right?"

He pressed his lips together and looked away, flinching at her choice of topic. "She doesn't have what you had to offer. No one does." He stared down at her, the tears coming then. "I can't replace what we were. I don't even want to." David brushed her face with his fingertips, stroking it as he had so many times in the past, lying there wrapped up together, feeling the soft downy curve of her cheek as he drifted into sleep each night.

"She needs someone she can't pull one over on. Being who I am and having been with you, I'm uniquely qualified." David sighed then, the breath releasing years of frustration. "And I need someone that I won't, no, *can't*, compare to you."

Halfway through the final trip down to the surface, the elevator car stopped. Imperceptible tremors grew into thrumming, jolting vibrations, and then fizzled into a sudden lack of downward motion. David opened his eyes, sitting up to survey the other passengers, and was struck by a sudden bout of vertigo as he caught sight of the curve of the planet, closer now but still far below.

A friendly voice from the craft speakers filled the silence. "Attention. Your descent has been halted due to technical difficulties and will resume once orders from the captain are received."

Captain Neal was already in motion before the announcement began, rising from his seat using the overhead handholds and standing to access the control console above his head. The sudden movement forced Kendra to sit up straight, and she instantly regretted it for the sharp pain it caused in her neck and the waves of nausea that came with the attempt to right herself.

All passengers were alert to the unexpected cessation of movement, their eyes darting to the captain as if trying to discern the severity of the situation by his expression.

"Alright. Now here's a trick for you when we get down to the surface…" The captain closed both eyes tightening his grip on the handholds above him, knuckles white with the effort it took to keep his feet despite the spinning in his head. *Easy now. Easy. Count down until the spinning stops. Ten, nine…and keep talking to them.* "When you feel off balance, just hold onto something and picture the horizon steady out in front of you." *Eight…seven…six. Hold it down.* "Once you start to regain equilibrium." *Breathe…five…four. Keep smiling.* "Open your eyes and hold your focus on the first steady object out in front of you. Just like that. And it will make the adjustment easier. Keep you from losing your feet and your lunch." He opened his eyes, facing the viewing screen before him. *Do I look confident or desperate? I'll assume confident.* He allowed himself to laugh at the inner monologue in hopes it would lend credence to his display of nonchalance, all the while scanning the data displayed on the screen. "Stay seated for now, though, and I'll get us down to the surface so you can try it." Digesting the information before him within moments and weighing the possibilities, he directed the AI system by touch response. He sent the pre-composed message for a scenario of this sort to the ninety colonists waiting below.

Genesis stood against the cold Martian wind, one hand on each rail, head bent down against the steady gusts left unchecked in the absence of trees. Lifting one hand, she removed her VR glasses and shut off the transmission as it replayed for a second time. Possible courses of action raced through her mind, scenarios with varying degrees of risk, some simple yet with far-reaching consequences, others more elaborate and with lower risk. *There isn't that kind of time. The captain has already made his decision. Damn fool!*

She kept her face impassive, features carefully arranged, as she stared across the rocky terrain toward the incongruous, frothing green sea. The vivid colors and sharp smells of the planet assaulted her senses, making it hard to concentrate.

One thought kept repeating. *David should have listened.* It was unacceptable that this would affect her personal interests. Especially when it wasn't guaranteed to achieve her other goals. *Of course, the captain is non-essential, but the hydroponics equipment...and David.* It would be unfortunate to lose what was developing so nicely there.

She straightened her shoulders, turning mind from doubts and futile attempts at guessing the outcome of her actions. *What's done is done.*

Turning to Theresa at her side, she slid the VR glasses onto the other woman's face, her movements abrupt, and replayed the message. An image of the captain appeared in the lenses before Theresa's eyes.

"A malfunction has occurred with the elevator. As the last car down, the necessary course of action involves some risk. Return to the space station to run repairs could result in permanent stranding of ourselves and crucial colony equipment, so I have chosen to continue our descent despite the risk of full-on failure. Should this occur, a quick descent and crash is likely and medical personnel are to be fully prepared at a safe distance from the crash site."

Theresa, who was kneeling instead of standing, blanched, her skin shifting from its already bloodless pallor to a drained and sickly gray. Placing a hand onto the dusty red brick of the rough path, she removed the VR display and handed it back to Genesis. "What do you and I need to do from here?"

Genesis's eyes narrowed, catlike, gold gleaming between hooded lids. Licking her lips she softened her expression and spoke in lowered gentle tones as if explaining the situation to a wayward child. "Theresa, I'm sure you couldn't forgive yourself if I delayed taking charge of the situation at hand to wait out your readjustment to gravity. Just wait here and I'll take care of it."

The irritating sensation of scattered focus, shattered pieces of her puzzle bouncing and colliding around her like broken marbles, subsided as she strode away from where the other woman knelt staring after her, closing the gap between herself and the group of council members that gathered around the second in command. *Nothing like imminent disaster to pull people together and lift me up.*

Genesis pulled the ecstatic smile from her lips and buried it beneath a look of controlled concern, sliding onto that a mask of calm determination. *So many layers. And best case scenario David will survive the crash. So no wasted effort there.*

Theresa stared after Genesis as she took up a light weaving jog to the large domed complex that housed the terminal end of the Space elevator. She couldn't remember the official name of the space elevator, and instead thought of it, with a level of humor that was boosted by the fear coiling in her gut, as the Stairway to Hell. *Well, it'd get you back to Earth and the council. And Morton Steiner, CEO of hell. And Richard.*

Thinking of her colleague while she sat frozen in the Martian dirt in the midst of a crisis made her cheeks burn with shame, and her heart race with an answering echo of anger. *I never claimed to be competent outside of a lab.*

A faint screeching sound broke through her thoughts, building from the high-pitched whine of a mosquito in her ear to the piercing shriek of a rocket, let loose in a small space. Her eyes widened, glinting ochre-red in the sunlight as she raised them to the sky.

A spray of white-hot sparks bloomed out from the metal frame of the Stairway to Heaven as the craft carrying the last ten Mars colonists hurtled towards the landing pad within the complex. Theresa retreated within herself, wrapping her arms around Abby, unable to look away as the craft fell.

A red balloon of fabric was expelled from the top of the craft, catching air. Theresa caught her breath. *Is it slowing? Will that do it?* She narrowed her eyes, watching for the change in speed. *It would be hard to see from here.* As the red fabric expanded the craft seemed to slow, at least to Theresa's eyes, but just as it reached full size, filling the interior width of the space elevator, the chute began to smoke.

She couldn't see the flames until they engulfed the right side of the parachute, from which point they raced around the thing, encouraged by the strong winds. Still the burning fabric held air and slowed the craft as she watched, mouth wide in horror, hands at her throat.

"Oh God." The winds carried away her mumbled words as she watched the burning chute and elevator car plummet and disappear through the top of the complex.

The dull thud that echoed from the complex was softer than she expected, not matching up with the reality that there were people inside of that craft. People she knew. Pulling herself upright with the bar nearest her, she stared towards the complex, eyes resolute and lips pressed into a line of determination.

The towering red rocks, purpling smoke, and cloud-filled sky spun around her as she stood, and she cried out. *Just like on the ship.* Terror shot through her and she flailed out, wrapping her arms around the rail as her legs crumpled beneath her. Arms weakened by weeks in space lost their grip and Theresa crumpled into a heap, cheek resting on the rough pumice ground cover. *It will stop spinning... it will...*

She drew in one breath after another, fighting the rising tide of nausea as her vestibular system struggled to determine which way was up and which was down. Several long minutes later, she opened her eyes and the landscape was still. She glanced over at the entrance to the scrolling sidewalk a few feet away.

"That's not far." Rising to her hands and knees, she moved across the crunching gravel, ignoring the rocks digging into her and the burning, stinging sensation of the RPU seal against her chest that had started as soon as she hit gravity. A faint wave of vertigo returned and she paused, closing her eyes. *Or I could just wait until someone comes to get me.*

She pushed forward, with eyes shut, feeling her way. *They might need me in there. For what I'm worth right now.* A smile at her own expense pulled at her lips and kept her moving towards the crash site.

The captain strapped himself into his seat and passed around his largest 'this is gonna be fun' grin. "There's been some asteroid damage to the elevator cables, so the ride down is going to be bumpy. If we crash-land, we only have a third Earth's gravity, so it'll be a much softer landing than on Earth." He held each pair of wide rabbit-near-the-stew-pot eyes long enough to watch the immediate panic settle down into low level anxiety in some, contained terror in others.

"David, I saw you eyeing your equipment. No need to cushion its landing with your body. The parachutes should slow us. It's safe enough in the side compartments."

"Alright. That's good." David's tone was even and respectful; the only sign that he was as frightened as the rest of the passengers was the hard set of his jaw and a slight pucker of his brows. The captain held his eyes a bit longer, dropping the edges of his calm in-command demeanor.

His silent message was clear. This was a serious situation, and if the cables snapped and they found themselves in a crash scenario, David's ability to step up in a crisis would be needed. David nodded understanding, and then smoothed his features out as best he could, grabbing hold of the handholds on either side of his seat.

"Alright. Let's finish this. Recommence final descent." Captain Neil gripped his handholds and nodded to the passengers to do the same.

With an abrupt jolt and a rumbling vibration the elevator car moved downward again, struggling towards the surface. Data streamed across the Captain's control screen, allowing him to track how close the cables were to breaking.

Kendra sat beside him, watching the images and the values on the screen flux and change. Her face was impassive, her demeanor calm, with just the hint of something else in her eyes.

Leaning closer to him, she spoke, taking pains to keep her comments between the two of them. "I'm not fool enough to think this is a walk in the park." She ran her teeth over her bottom lip, flicking her eyes across the other colonists. "Well done by the way…very smooth. But what are our chances of coming out of this?"

The Captain looked away from the data that held his attention to meet Kendra's gaze.

"That depends on when the second cable breaks. And how well the parachutes work, being small enough to fit in an elevator shaft." His look was serious, lacking the humor and bravado of a few moments before. "We are just over halfway down. We need to split the distance to the surface in half again to avoid a very hard landing with injuries likely."

She nodded, listening. "Anything I should do?"

"Help everyone stay calm and distracted. If you can. I know that's a tall order."

Kendra snorted. "If I can cheer up a room of surrogates after they've had their progeny passed off, I can distract a few colonists scared of falling."

Turning the slant of her body back towards the center of the craft, she surveyed the scene, waiting for the right moment to break the silence, and decided to make one instead.

Her voice rose slowly from a soft murmur to clear deep notes like her mother sang, pouring out slowly as smooth cane syrup on a cold day.

"I said baby hold the door, I'm comin' through. Baby hold that door if you know what's good for me…"

She paused just long enough to exaggerate a look of shock and a fumble for words. "I mean you. There's a whole lot of what you need headin' atcha. Don't lemme catcha' sneakin' anyone else through. " Kendra delivered each line with a twinkle in her eye, her voice deep and throaty. It was untrained but rich, like smoke from green wood tossed on a campfire.

'Baby climb on up, let's ride it like a pony. Baby climb on up, it's gonna be real good for me…I mean you."

The Captain stared at her, mouth agape, transfixed. It took several verses for him to step out of himself enough to notice that every single colonist was watching her performance with equal interest. Several more for him to turn his gaze from the mulberry lips shaping the words and back to the data on his control panel. During those stolen moments the second cable trembled its last and let go of itself, snapping in two.

The craft fell the remaining two miles to the surface of Mars, sending up curtains of white and yellow sparks each time it scraped the sides of the metal shaft, the screeching of metal-on-metal melding with the screams coming from within. Kendra sang louder, switching to an old hymn about a God she wasn't certain she believed in but wouldn't have minded some help from. A mile and a half above the surface, the small parachute deployed to slow the craft's descent from "free-fall into pile of smoking rubble" to "oh shit, we're going to crash."

Fire engulfed the top portion of the elevator craft as the burning parachute came down upon it, a blanket of flame.

The Pinnacle's second spoke into her handheld, struggling to rein in her frustration and keep her voice even. "Sync to Captain Neil, please."

"The Captain's hand-held is not responding. Would you like me to shut down, or do you have another command?"

"Shit. Come on, Neil." She stared at the handheld a moment, before trying something else. "Sync Martian Space Elevator Transport Controls with handheld number 321459."

Trina didn't wait for the inevitable reply but instead scanned the room for Mario and, catching sight of him, closed the gap between them as quickly as she could manage without causing her senses to spin.

"I need you at the manual controls ASAP to put out this fire. It's burning itself out but I'm not taking any chances, and the automated system isn't responding like it should. Are we clear?"

Mario nodded as she spoke, a knuckle to his lips. "Yes. Alright, I don't know how quick it will be though."

"Unable to sync with the MSETC system. Please check the status of MSETC before trying again." Trina's hand-held repeated the same message for the seventh time since they reached the surface, bringing a scowl of irritation to its owner's face.

"Son-of-a-bitch!" She shoved the offending device back into her pocket and turned her gaze back to Mario, her eyes sharp. "Our Captain and crew are in that oven and they may have injuries that need tended to."

He flinched at her tone and nodded again, this time with a determined glint in his eye, and hurried towards the control panel despite his inability to run or even walk a straight path.

Trina turned back to face the craft. Large puddles of melted parachute oozed down the sides of it, still ablaze, and formed puddles of fire on the landing pad. As she watched, a waterfall of white foam poured down over the craft, smothering the remaining flames, and was followed by a rush of water from the same source.

"About damn time." The words were mumbled under her breath as she turned to face the control panel, giving Mario a nod and a thumbs up.

Waiting not a moment longer, she trotted over to the impact site, catching herself the first two times she stumbled, but not the third. Her face and hands, which had just started to list forward like a top-heavy one year old taking her first running steps, caught the side of the fallen elevator car, still warm to the touch and slick with water.

"Goddamn it!" Her headset lit up and came to life, the voice of the captain filling her ears as she leaned against the door, waiting out the vertigo that pulled at her with the insistence of an undertow.

"We have four confirmed injuries in here and the door is stuck. I need a team at the side ladder to help everyone down. We're coming through the top."

Trina's sigh of relief was audible. "Will do. The fire's out, and the metal's cooling. I'll send Genesis's team over to collect the injured." She turned and gestured towards the first of four teams organized in stations in a semicircle around the platform. Genesis stood in the center of the semi-circle, addressing the teams with one eye on Trina to catch her cue. "Oh and Neil...How are you doing?"

"Same as ever. Sending the first two up."

"Well, me too, I guess. I tripped. Rookie move, right? You'd think this was my first time." Trina shook her head.

"Hits you hard, but at least *you* always get through it quick. Up and running marathons again six hours after landing, huh?" The captain laughed and Trina laughed with him, releasing the tension built up while she watched her captain free-fall in a flaming tin can and hit the landing platform at a rate that looked enough to shatter spines.

"Keep me posted on the status of our injured while I'm in here, alright?"

"Of course, Captain." The first officer rapped on the metal door in parting, then took up a jog toward the nearest impromptu medic's station.

The blood matting David's hair into dark, slick patches that shined crimson in the hazy sunlight was the first thing Genesis noticed. The disturbing way that his head tried to loll back before it was stabilized as he was lifted under his arms and lowered down was the third. The second was the sick feeling in her stomach that felt as if it had been filled in with the murky water of drowning along with her lungs. *Four injured and the first is him. That means he's the worst. How bad is it?* She tapped the shoulder of a team member.

"You're in command."

She escorted David and the two carrying him over to the first station. The sick feeling sloshed around within, splashing her internal landscape with the sludgy poison of a feeling she couldn't quite pinpoint.

You're supposed to be witnessing my leadership skills, not unconscious and bleeding out. She sat still, leaning in to watch as the doctor used first her hands and then a hand-held MRI scanner to assess David's head and neck.

"What are his injuries?" Her voice was sharper than usual, like falling ice.

The middle-aged woman glanced up from the scanner at Genesis to read what she could in her face.

Genesis stared back. "Well? How serious is it?"

The physician set her scanner aside. "He has a concussion, deep lacerations to his scalp, and several other cuts, scrapes, and bruises. I'll seal the cuts to stop the bleeding, and he'll likely wake halfway through and start moaning and grabbing my equipment."

The pestilent waters drained from Genesis's stomach and lungs as she breathed out, lancing the wound. *Who would want their newest interest taken off the shelf without being consulted, right? I don't like having my choices made for me, or being forced to start over.* She closed her eyes a long moment and then glanced over at David's unconscious form, thoughts wandering from the here and now as she waited.

Like when her first pairing with Jacobi had been ended prematurely and without her consent. Of course, that had made her angry, and determined. And they'd given him back after she had come up with a different scapegoat for her inability to conceive. Not the teas she was drinking, of course. That was between her and her provider.

David's eyes opened on the makeshift table, and he did groan, though instead of grabbing the physician's equipment he looked over at her without moving his head, and then back at Genesis.

"What happened?" Genesis smoothed her features, her voice impassive.

"Hmm? We crashed. Cables broke I think. Songbirds sang us down. The fall was fun, nerve-wracking, but something hit me. I think." Each sentence was punctuated by grimaces as the doctor worked to seal up the large gash in his scalp.

"Birds? There are none. Are you delirious?" Genesis's brows were furrowed and eyes narrowed as she tried to decipher what sounded like the speech of a drunkard.

"Mmm-hmm. Kendra sings. Like a bird. Not a lark, I guess, more like a raven or a dove. I think." He started to lift his head, but, feeling the press of the physician's hand, thought better of it and, wincing, dropped back to the table.

"Baby I'ma comin' through..." He mumbled the line several octaves lower than Kendra had.

"Why did it hit *you*?" Genesis shook her head at her own question and David chuckled.

"Careful. You're not making any sense, honey. Gonna get me thinking that you're emotionally compromised by worry over me. Thinkin' this isn't just a game of chess." He closed his eyes. Genesis stole a glance at the physician to see if she had been following their conversation and found the woman staring straight at her, eyes quizzical.

"Are you sure it's just a concussion? He isn't making much sense." Genesis gave a wry smile and arched a brow before turning to see how the rest of the teams were doing.

Scanning each station and making mental notes, she caught sight of Theresa at the first station, assisting Desmond with one of the wounded. *She must have crawled over from where I left her. Better smooth that over later. She's even upright, imagine that!*

At the platform, the third to last of the colonists, one of the surrogates, was being assisted from the craft, a bit banged up but otherwise sound and stumbling only as much as the rest of them were. There was a huddle next to the dented and charred craft as the team leaders converged, waiting for the final two to emerge from the top hatch. Disliking the length of the delay, Genesis stood without a backward glance, and, using the handrails for maximum effect, crossed the distance in several smooth strides.

"Trina. Is there a problem?"

The second-in-command pressed her lips together, withholding a laugh and shook her head.

"Naw. Captain's orders are for us to move ahead with getting everyone acclimated and settled, seeing as though the injuries appear to be pretty minor, and everyone is being tended to. He'll be along with Kendra when he's ready."

"There seems to be a joke I'm missing." Genesis raised an eyebrow at Trina's barely-contained humor.

Trina leaned in to whisper. "Captain doesn't acclimate well. Never has. Stumbles and vomits like a drunkard for hours. Best if he waits it out in there, and keeps his image of fearless leader untarnished."

Genesis frowned. "Oh. Well, it's physiological. There's no shame in that. I'll help you pick up the slack until he's well."

"Thanks for pitching in. An extra pair of hands is always welcome. At least until we get some medi-bots up and running." Dr. Alexander smiled, sliding his hands into the remote sanitizing unit one last time before returning it to his medical bag. "And you're getting a little cross-training experience as an added bonus." He gave Theresa a wink.

Theresa half-smiled. "So long as shaking hands are acceptable. I have those." She snorted at herself, the sound revealing the bitterness under her words.

"Tsk, tsk... your... condition... comes with limitations. Especially considering the uncommon nature of it."

The look she gave him was full of gratitude, and with a resigned smile, she slid down to rest on the rough-hewn brick floor. "At least we all made it down. I admit my heart was all the way up in my stomach watching them crash."

The doctor shook his head. "You and everyone else down here."

He lifted his bag to his shoulder, glancing up just as Donovan and Alissa approached the impromptu first-aid station, with Nicole propped between them. Alissa had worry etched into her brow as she struggled under the weight of her friend, and Donovan had the shell-shocked look on his face that many of the colonists hadn't yet recovered from, so soon after the crash.

"It's just cramping." Nicole's face was pale, and a light sweat had broken out on her skin. "Maybe I wasn't done healing yet, you know?"

Alissa dug up a faint smile, still not touching the worry lines that creased her face. "Sure, Coli. Makes sense. But we should just check, okay?" She rubbed her friend's cool, damp shoulder and caught Alexander's gaze.

The doctor dropped his bag and gestured to the bench in front of him. "Why don't you lie her down here. Did you trip over your feet? Most of us have been, you know, so no shame in that." He smiled at Nicole as she leaned back on the cold stone, shivering as she made contact.

Alexander narrowed his eyes, taking a closer look at the woman on his table. "Theresa, can you get a reading on her pulse and BP, please, while I examine her?"

Theresa edged closer to the bench without standing and dug into the physician's bag. "Mmm-hmm."

Nicole started to sit up and then, wincing, placed a hand over her midsection and thought better of it. "Really, it's not all that bad. Just these stomach cramps. And I'm lightheaded, you know?"

Alexander looked into her eyes, placing a device against her forehead at the same time that Theresa located the one she was seeking and pressed it against her carotid artery.

Alissa knelt down next to the bench, brushing the hair back from her friend's face. "She was fine right after the crash. Even climbed out herself, without a hand up. Maybe it's the gravity?" A nervous, hopeful smile formed on her lips as she watched Nicole close her eyes.

"She was in the crash?" Alexander's voice was quiet, each word spoken with care as he set his device aside and turned his gaze to Alissa.

"Yeah, we both were, but…"

Theresa's device let out a series of high-pitched beeps. "Alex…Her BP is really low."

"What's really low?"

"Eighty-five over forty." Theresa's eyes widened, a nagging suspicion taking hold. "You have stomach cramps?"

The woman on the bench shook her head. "Mm-mm, more like period cramps, lower…and pulling at me."

Theresa stared at Nicole as her insides turned to jagged ice, the growing alarm freezing her from the inside out. *They've been tested for trips and falls, for stairs, not crash-landings on another planet.*

"Alex, get her clothes off. These two are both surrogates."

Nicole reached a hand out and brushed Theresa's shoulder. She crinkled her nose, a sleepy smile on her candy-pink lips. "My blood pressure's always low, though. I get lightheaded every time I'm incubating progeny…Don't I, Lissa?" She turned her head to wink at her friend.

"Yeah…" Alissa laughed, the sound soft and laced with worry. "She does, I guess."

"We need to check your access panel, okay?"

Nicole shrugged, closing her eyes again. "This gravity is so *heavy*…making me sleepy."

The doctor hesitated, about to speak, but instead started removing Nicole's outer suit, his movements deft. "You're worried about her access panel?"

Theresa nodded and pulled the doctor's bag closer, digging through until she found what she was looking for, a transfusion device with the blood pre-prepped.

With the suit removed, they could see that Nicole's abdomen appeared normal. *Oh thank God.* Theresa sighed. "Okay…but we need to remove the rest so I can examine it. Alright, Nicole?"

The reply was faint. "Sure…" Shivers interrupted her speech. "I thought…I thought it would be tomorrow… though."

Alexander pulled her shirt up to her ribcage, revealing a thick wrapping of fabric encircling the woman's abdomen.

"Thought what would be tomorrow, baby?" Alissa kissed her forehead.

Nicole mumbled something, then opened her eyes. "That's not right. They already took him, didn't they?"

Alissa frowned and whispered to Nicole before answering Theresa's confused expression. "Were you falling asleep, Coli? That was two months ago now…She likes to wrap up for awhile after each pregnancy, makes everything heal in place." She gave a half smile and shrugged. "Says it's an ancient tradition, or something."

Alexander felt the tissues through the wrapping and Nicole pulled a breath in through her teeth, hissing; she jerked away from his touch.

The head of Reproductive Technologies and the physician exchanged a look.

"Start the transfusion and then get up here, I'm going to cut this off." Alexander's voice took on the clipped and direct tones he used in surgery as he turned on his heated scalpel and sliced through the layers of woven fabric. "Lissa, take the heated blanket from my bag and wrap her upper half...and keep her talking, plan for the move-in or something else cheerful."

He gestured in Donovan's direction without looking away from his task, lest he cut too far and wound the skin beneath. "You...contact the second-in-command; we need the rest of the medical department over here, now."

Theresa moved quicker than the spinning of her senses allowed, and started the transfusion despite shaking fingers. *Maybe it's something else...let it be something else.* The lead weight of dread said otherwise.

Reaching into the bag again, she pulled out the medications kit, full of vials, and dug around until she found the ones she needed: clotting factors, AntiShock A1, and anesthesia.

Alissa scrubbed at her cheeks, brushing away the tears that escaped, and pressed her cheek against Nicole's. Digging into her reserves of resilience, she found a smile and worked to keep her breathing even and her tone cheerful.

"We'll share a room, just you and me. And we'll go out and map the whole planet like you said...become wild women on Mars..." She laughed. "Open your eyes, Nicole..." Alissa caressed her cheek. "Hey...are you listening?"

Nicole turned to Alissa and opened her eyes, revealing the traces of fear that were taking hold, as a trembling smile touched her lips. "Mm-hm...I am...sounds perfect, Lissa."

The bandages fell away as Doctor Alexander cut the last few threads, both he and Theresa kneeling beside her, surgical tools at the ready.

There was no blood at first, not where they could see it, but the skin of her belly, mapped with long rippling, vertical, scars, had a purplish blue appearance, and released from the pressure of the wrappings was taut and distended around the Access

Panel's flesh toned seal. Placing the hand-held MRI scanner over Nicole's abdomen, Theresa gazed at the image. The outer seal was intact but the inner seal had broken away from the walls of her uterus and her peritoneal cavity was filling with blood.

Theresa gave the doctor a panicked look and mouthed her words. "*I don't have what I need to fix this.*"

He gave a quick nod, as he crouched next to her, speaking his reply for her ears only. "Then we do what we can. We'll take it out and seal her up."

The muscles in Captain Neil's shoulders bunched under his uniform as he leaned over the receptacle, hands trembling when he heaved for the third time, nothing left to vomit but bile and the sips of water he had taken short moments before.

"Uhhh...That's probably the last one." His voice was rough from the acidic burning in his throat. Managing a weak smile he lifted a canteen of electrolyte solution to his lips, swishing before spitting into the receptacle and sealing away the evidence of his weak stomach.

Kendra clicked her tongue, sympathy softening her brown eyes. "This happens *every* time you go on a mission?"

The Captain lowered himself into a crouch and looked up at her, a slight shrug accompanying his nonchalant expression. "Every time." He laughed, the sound strained and broken coming from his raw throat. "Guess I'm just lucky huh? Trina, my second in command, runs circles around me, literally, the day of." He took a small sip of the liquid in his canteen. "While I'm puking my guts out and holding the rails like a cripple, she starts up jogging again. Guess that's good, though, if I'm gonna be on my ass."

Kendra laughed, taking up a seat across from him on the floor, and laying a hand on his shoulder. "What makes you do it then? What do you get out of all this?"

Neil narrowed his eyes in thought, taking in a shaky breath before catching hold of an answer to her question. He lifted a hand and pulled it closed into a loose fist as if plucking the answer out of the air between them and holding it there in his palm. "There's adventure, sure. Doing something few have the opportunity to do. Being on the front lines of history." He paused, taking time to formulate thoughts that were proving elusive. "It's more, though. Each time I go up, I'm living out the potential of what I can do. Or really, what *we* can do. All of us. There were research missions first, and I didn't do the science but what I did do was make sure my passengers could do that and get home safely." He shrugged again. "And what are we doing here? Something... far beyond anything we have ever achieved."

Kendra's eyes shone, a smile of admiration spreading her full lips as she took the Captain's hands in hers. "You know, you *do* hold up a whole ship."

He looked startled by her statement, crooked smile returning. "What?"

She laughed, a throaty sound that was akin to her singing voice. "Just something I thought before... and I'm glad you're our captain. That's all"

The Captain's hand-held lit up and chirped its alert. "*Connecting Trina Markison. Status urgent.*"

"Put her through, then." Neil stood up, grabbing hold of the gripping bar above his head as the world spun around him.

He closed his eyes and pictured the interior of the craft still, beginning his count to ten. "What is it?"

Trina's voice, hesitant and stilted came through the hand-held, on speaker. "Captain, we've…had a casualty."

He opened his eyes and stared at the hand-held. "What… happened? You reported all four injured as stable just a half an hour ago."

"I know. It was one of the others from the crash. Apparently a delayed effect…a ruptured access panel."

Kendra stood up, and grabbed hold of the Captain's hand-held. "Who?"

"Oh, Kendra… forgot you were in there for a second. It was…it was Nicole." A pause. "I'm sorry. I know you two were friends."

Kendra sat down hard, massaging her temples with both hands. "Coli…"

The second's voice came through again. "Hey, Neil. I'm sorry, but Theresa and Dr. Alexander want to see Kendra right away to check her access panel and…"

Neil cut her off. "Of course. We're coming out." He shut off the call and put his hand on Kendra's shoulder. "Hey…"

She slid a hand down to hover over her belly where her own access panel was concealed beneath her suit. "Pretty sure I'm fine." She tried to hold a shaking smile, but it cracked and trembled on her face. "But Alissa's gonna need me out there… she and Coli were a thing. I convinced them both to apply for this, you know."

He extended a hand, brushing her cheek with his knuckles when she didn't take it. "Come on, Kendra, honey. We need to get you out of here… have you checked out."

CLEARING THE MARTIAN DUST

Theresa startled awake, struggling against the bowling ball of weight upon her chest, and making several attempts before finally achieving an upright position. Something in her dream had woken her. There were eyes, black, staring. So many of them, and tangled human shapes. Small, unfinished limbs kicking and writhing, suspended in a sea of green.

As her vision cleared, she struggled to recall more details, and the urgency of her dream faded. Fragments of other dreams came clear like ghost ships rising out of the water. There was blood, on her hands and arms, and the glow of her scalpel as she and Dr. Alexander worked to stop the flow. It seemed she wasn't so much sleeping or dreaming most of the night, but instead reliving.

Well, that's enough to wake most people, I guess. She stood, pushing down the rising tide of emotion, and turned to the window that overlooked the same green ocean-scape from her dream.

She lifted a hand, resting it on the surface of the capsule that held Abby, in what had become an unconscious gesture over the past month and a half. The skin around the RPU's seal was sore to the touch, aching as it had on the Pinnacle. *Maybe it's infected again.* Theresa frowned, wincing against the pain that came when she applied counter pressure to the heavy capsule that was no longer free-floating in zero-G. *I'll go see Carla when I'm done here.*

She stared across the jumbled landscape, populated by large red boulders spotted with snowflakes of black lichen and carpeted by a thicker version of the same, to the expanse of bright hopeful green extending to the horizon.

Waves rose and fell, frothing as they crashed and forming a barrier of viscous foam between land and sea. Theresa gazed at the algae-filled mystery, her chestnut eyes darkening with melancholy.

"What do you think, Abby? Should we go swimming once you're out?"

She tried to remember the last article she had read on Earth about ocean life, something about the balance of microorganisms needed to begin repopulating the oceans. *I wonder if there will be birds, eventually. And fish.*

But Earth's oceans were still a dingy gray-brown when viewed from space, or anywhere for that matter. *At least we're starting clean, on Mars.*

Theresa glanced down to where she was tracing circles in the thin layer of dark red dust that covered every surface. *How many years have these buildings been waiting for us?* She sighed, looking for somewhere to wipe the dust from her fingers, and, finding nothing devoid of Martian red, brushed it on her clothing.

"It's about time we clean up and move in. Get up close and personal with the Martian rust."

She turned to survey her three-room dwelling, a triple dome made from smooth red bricks, recessed into the soil several feet to take advantage of insulation offered by the ground itself. The floors looked like more of the same material, but, instead of bricks, was one seamless surface made by pounding the Martian clay until it was smooth and solid.

The far corner of the room that she had reserved for her bedroom held several metal crates containing everything she would need to continue her research, including computer equipment and a 3D-printing machine.

Searching out a washcloth and filling a sink full of warm water, Theresa fell to cleaning, enjoying the monotony of the work. She held one hand against Abby's capsule for support and scrubbed with the other, pushing through until she finished every wall and floor. Working quickly, despite the aching of the seal that progressed from a burning, stinging sensation to numbness interspersed with sudden shooting pains, Theresa pushed thoughts of the crash from her mind, aided by fatigue and pain.

The loud knock startled her from her task. She stood a moment, unable to place the meaning of the sound, her eyes distant as if staring into a set of binoculars, and then shook her head at the absurdity of her initial confusion.

Setting a small wooden box, now thoroughly dusted, on a shelf above her bed, she went to the door. *I need to install the security programming next, I guess.* Pulling her light robe closed over Abby, Theresa felt a flutter of apprehension; it was so much easier to avoid thinking about things she preferred to forget if she stayed in solitude. Irritation overtook the unease as she became aware of the clinging layer of red grime and sweat on her skin, and the halo of stray hair fuzzing out from her braid, left in from the night before.

She opened the door, struggling to push the stray hairs back from her face as she did so, and stepped aside. She ducked her head, trying to mask the chagrin with a smile, and gestured for Genesis to enter.

"I've been cleaning." Theresa shrugged, dismissing her disheveled appearance. "I'm glad you're here, though. I have something to discuss with you, actually."

Genesis ran a hand over one of the built-in stone benches. "You seem to have conquered the dust." She rubbed her fingers together, a frown on her lips. "It's on everything." Turning to face Theresa, Genesis reached out for one of her hands and leaned in, brows pulling up in chagrin.

"That's not why I came, though. I wanted to apologize for being abrupt and unhelpful at the crash site. You didn't deserve that, regardless of my hurry." Genesis looked away, then forced herself to meet Theresa's gaze a short sigh escaping her lips. "I was worried about David…and the others."

Theresa nodded and smiled at Genesis, who looked genuinely puzzled by the reaction. "I didn't brood over it more than a day. Don't like to feel like a burden, you know? I pull my own weight and then some under ordinary circumstances, so if someone calls me out when I *am* a burden and doesn't pull me along, I can cope."

"Well, I guess you proved that, didn't you? And what you had to deal with afterwards was just…That must have been horrible for you."

Theresa grit her teeth, swallowing down the bitterness of pent up emotion, buried deep and festering. "Do we need to talk about this?"

Genesis shook her head, eyes full of sympathy. "Of course not. Not if you aren't ready. Carla's room has been so full of mourning colonists that she hasn't even unpacked, but I'm sure she'll make room for you when you're ready."

Theresa pressed her lips together and gave a quick nod. "I'm sure."

Genesis looked Theresa up and down with an appraising eye. "You seem to have acclimatized well already."

"I can walk without stumbling or passing out, true, and my clavicle is almost healed, but I won't be running in the Martian sand or surfing the algae anytime soon." The color that rose to Theresa's cheeks and the sharp glint in her eyes when she laughed spoke more accurately of the extent of her recovery. "I'm still tired though, and being careful." She crossed both arms under her chest to support the RPU, hiding the pain the motion caused with tightened jaw.

"How much longer then? Until the...?" Genesis gestured towards the large bulge under her robe.

"Mmm...About seven weeks if we can make it that long. Assuming she keeps growing and her lungs are ready by then. I'll hold out as long as I can."

Genesis didn't respond. She was staring off towards the computer screen set into one of Theresa's walls. A thin smile grew upon her lips and spread across her cheeks.

"Genesis?"

She turned back to Theresa as if she had been waiting for just that, a call to return and explain the thoughts behind the smile. "I have a proposal for you."

Theresa raised her eyebrows at the sudden change in the flow of their conversation.

"Oh, well, okay; I do too, I guess, but you first."

"You are the head of Reproductive Technology, and you were the pioneer in your field on Earth. But there is a need here on Mars for technology that was obsolete back home."

Theresa arched a brow, intrigued. "Really? Alright. I'm listening."

"Birth control. The women of Mars need the ability to delay conception when they see fit. Carla has mentioned that pregnancies are healthier, safer, when they occur at the best time for a woman psychologically as well as physically. The Council on Earth directed that everyone's implants be removed on the ship, but many of the colonists aren't even acclimated, let alone settled in. We need to buy time, and, honestly, we just need to have full control of our reproduction."

Theresa frowned, twirling the long end of her braid in her hand. "Doesn't that sound like what the colonists were trying to get away from? Someone controlling when they can conceive? Having to get permission?"

"You are missing a key element of my proposal, Theresa. I…We need something in the woman's control. Something that will allow her to turn her fertility on and off as she sees fit."

Theresa's head was tilted, her brows pulled together as she paused in her hair-twirling to consider what Genesis was describing. *Is this for her? Why? She seems earnest, though.*

"I can think of several options, of course, but this sounds like something that could go against the Reproductive Council's directive for us. We may need to get permission from them."

Genesis shrugged. "That's something for you to consider. In the meantime, I know that one matter on the agenda for our council to discuss is our autonomy, which issues we will decide on our own and which we will defer to the Earth council. You'll want to think about that, I imagine."

Now it was Theresa's turn to retreat into the caverns of her mind, where designs for potential user-controlled birth control were already formulating themselves.

"What was it you had for me, by the way?"

She was startled when Genesis broke in. "Oh, um…Are you still interested in learning about your origins?"

Genesis's eyes clouded over, and her answer was slow in coming. "Yes. I still am."

Theresa clapped her hands together and walked over to the one piece of luggage lying open on her stone desk.

"Then I'll need your blood."

"Why would you wait on something like this?" Carla frowned at Theresa's bared chest, where the capsule had pulled away, taking several layers of her skin with it, and blood pooled around the upper edges of the RPU.

"I thought it was just irritated again…until it started bleeding." Theresa leaned back onto Carla's bed, her eyes watering from the raw, nagging, pain.

Carla sighed, taking out a vial of clear liquid and pouring it onto an applicator. "This isn't going to feel good." Sliding the applicator around the edge of the seal, she spread a thin layer of Rapid Heal into the raw wound that gaped where the top layers of Theresa's skin had pulled away.

"As if it felt good the past several hours while my skin was ripping off...Does this usually happen?"

"No. *Usually* an RPU is worn for a few weeks, not several. *Usually* it isn't used in zero-G and then tossed back into gravity weeks later, and *usually* a woman tells me if she's in pain and needs support straps." Carla's eyes held just enough humor to temper the censure.

"Okay. I get it." Theresa released her breath in a hiss, shaking in her effort not to move away from Carla's prodding. "I was just...I guess I was distracted."

"We've all been. And you have reason enough. Just...don't forget that your well-being is Abby's well-being, and well, Abby aside, your health and safety matters." Carla pressed the wound closed, maintaining the pressure despite Theresa's scowl, for the requisite ten minutes while the initial healing began.

Theresa looked away, rubbing the back of one hand across her eyes. "If I can't...if I'm not strong enough to handle this with her at this size...what about later? I mean, I thought I just needed to push through this." She sniffed, rubbing at her eyes again and leaving them reddened. "Nothing is comfortable right now, so how do I know what to come whine about?"

The midwife gave her shoulder a light squeeze, her eyes gentling. "You *are* pushing through. You're doing fine. Just let me help you before you end up bleeding all over yourself...or if you don't want to come to me, then take care of yourself, or see Dr. Alexander if he suits you." Carla continued to work as she spoke, wrapping several layers of gauze in a criss-cross pattern over the RPU capsule, and creating a makeshift harness. "Just keep this on until I can have Emily print us a permanent one with clasps, alright?"

Theresa nodded, watching as Abby squirmed against the elastic straps. "I will. Thank you, Carla."

"You were angry when I stopped." It was a statement, not a question. David rubbed the small scar on the side of his forehead, already smooth and pink just a few days after the crash, thanks to the inducement of rapid healing. *Thank God for modern medicine.*

Genesis laughed. "Sexual frustration and anger are not one and the same. It was a predictable move on your part, and thus could not make me angry."

"Predictable?" He scratched the back of his head, messing up the hair that grew there, curling in the high humidity. It was a hot day, and damp as close as they were to the seashore.

"Cards on the table, right?" Genesis looked at David as one would a small child incapable of consistent logic.

"That's right."

"You don't trust me, yet. I don't know if you will get there at all. Am I on track?"

He winced and spread his hands. "I'm not gonna lie to you. I'm not the type for that. No, I don't trust you…yet."

"It's alright, of course." The look in her eyes belied her words; a surface layer meant for his consumption, that was the epitome of patient understanding and nonchalance, hid a subterranean layer, much more raw, resembling the look of a cat struck twice and prepared to remedy the situation.

David filed the fleeting glimpse away and responded to her words instead.

"No, actually it's not. I want to trust you. I want this to be something solid if it's going to be anything at all." He held her eyes, not flinching from what he saw there. "But I think you had a point you were making."

Genesis blinked, looking around at the lichen covered red stones and benches made of the same that filled the garden in the center of the colony's dome complex. She searched for the point that had eluded her without and within, looking for just a moment lost, a small girl so used to having her way grasping for her upset equilibrium. She scowled. *I never lose my train of thought.*

"Oh." She shook out her sleek black tresses and with the same movement her fleeting uncertainty.

"You, are a simple man."

David laughed, head back, and hands clapping.

"What I mean is…" She could not help but smile back. "What I mean is that you see the world simply. Black and white. Right and wrong. You can conceive of one sort of relationship. Bonding, devotion, trust, commitment…"

"Don't forget sincerity." His eyes sparked with the light of playful thoughts.

"Yes. Sincerity." She raised her brows. "Then perhaps sex and another heavy dose of commitment."

David leaned in as if to whisper and instead tickled the back of her neck with his lips at the same time as the underside of her knee with his fingers. Genesis hissed, a sudden intake of breath as she recoiled from his playful touch and pushed against his chest to put further distance between them.

David allowed the distance between them to grow, holding his place on the bench they had occupied a moment before, hands up in a gesture of surrender. He watched, eyes wide in dismay as she rose to stand a few feet away, arms wrapped around her chest.

Several moments passed, the only sounds between them the low moan of Martian winds around the domes and the sharp exhales of her breath slowing as she regained composure.

"What did I do?" His eyes were cautious, his brow creased in worry, confusion.

"I don't like to be touched…like that." Her voice was softer than usual, muted by some unknowable emotion.

"Okay. Um…like what…like how, I mean?" His confusion deepened. "I can't not do it if I don't know what it is."

Silence. David waited a moment in hopes that she just needed time to formulate, but after many seconds had passed, decided an answer was not forthcoming.

"What happened? Seriously, Genesis. I've touched much more than that. Is something else going on here…is this about our disagreement on the ship, that I wouldn't ride down with you, maybe?"

She met his eyes. There was just one persona gazing at him from the yellow gold depths instead of the two or three usually there.

"No…It's not about that. Honestly, I don't know how to describe it. I don't like…touching without…clear intent."

"Clear intent? I don't know what that means." David shook his head, a frown on his lips.

"Sex is fine. Sex is more than fine." A suggestive smile replaced the vulnerability that had been there a moment before, and she took her place on their bench at the opposite end.

"Other touching, without some clear purpose, makes my skin crawl." she wrinkled her nose to punctuate her meaning.

David's frown smoothed out. "Now I get it." He shook his head eyes wide as understanding dawned. "You don't trust *me*."

She looked askance at him. "I don't trust *anyone*. Or maybe more accurately, I trust everyone…to play their parts, to fulfill my estimations of their characters. I'm never wrong."

He snorted. "So you've said. But I don't buy that."

Her eyes narrowed. "Do tell."

"You're offering me something simple. A contract. A partnership, if you will. All cards on the table. Not your usual, I imagine. I bet that idea was liberating once you got used to it. You could play it straight, speak your mind, and we could have a convenient relationship for mutual gain."

Genesis smiled at his astute estimation of her plans for them.

"So where does my lack of trust come in?"

He held out a hand. "I'm getting to that. But first we need to add an addendum to this contract."

It was her turn to laugh. *Not so predictable. Stimulating, in so many ways.*

"Let me have your hands. Holding, touching. I promise there will be underlying sexual intent if I touch anything else."

Genesis recrossed her arms, blinking several times. "Why? And where is the point about MY lack of trust that you claimed you would address?"

"First, I need my addendum." He shrugged off her impatience.

She opened her mouth to protest, but then stopped herself. Closing the gap between them, she placed one hand on David's knee, allowing it to slide upward towards his waist. "There are so many things more gratifying than casual handholding."

David caught her hand in his before it reached its final destination, and, turning her palm up, traced gentle circles against her skin with one finger.

"You're changing the subject, Genesis." She withdrew her hand, a shudder running up her arm and along her back to rest in the center of her belly.

He rubbed his empty hands together. "Consider it an experiment."

"Why would you ask me to do something that makes me feel sick? It makes me want to rip my skin off!" Her lips twisted, disgust clear in her eyes.

"I'm not asking for blanket permission. I'm asking you to try this. If it's too much you can pull away." He looked off at the jumbled mountain peaks across the garden. "You know what, maybe this is pointless. I'm just at a loss as to how to be involved with you if I can't touch you unless it's a precursor to sex!" He threw his hands up and stood, kicking the nearest red pebble towards the center of the rock garden.

"I don't even know what a relationship like that looks like." David sighed, his eyes burning with a mixture of hurt and frustration. He thought a moment. "Okay, you know what? I'm going to disengage here. You do what you want. You know where to find me." He turned to leave, heading for the garden gate that led into the complex.

"Do you want me to find you?" Her voice was flat, emotionless, taking on the character of the alien landscape as it traveled across the garden to reach him.

David stopped mid-stride and stood without turning back to face her. "Yes. Yes I do." He stepped forward, allowing the gate to swing shut between them.

A gust of wind found its way into the enclosure, whipping a storm of black hair into Genesis's face as she sat watching his retreat.

Carla stood in the shared dining room, tucking her hand-held into her pocket with abrupt movements, fingers trembling and catching on the fabric.

Emily stared up at her from where she sat on the nearest stone bench, a 3D printer and small tools to calibrate it in her lap, her blue eyes wide, concern casting shadows within them.

"Is everything alright? Am I in your way here?"

Carla shook her head, lips a thin slash against her face. "No, Em, I'm ruffled. I've been cooped up all day with grieving colonists. Going out for some air. It's damn stuffy in here!"

"Oh, should I open a window? Should I come along?"

Carla's lips loosened into a fond smile, lending a poignant sadness when it reached her eyes. "No, no. I need to collect myself, process. I'll let you in on my thoughts once they make sense." She ended with a nod and gave Emily's shoulder a gentle squeeze.

The corridor that led out to the garden was a wide curved tunnel lit by small skylights and arched windows at regular intervals. It was warm inside, still holding the heat that had seeped through the layers of clay and stone throughout the day. Carla approached the door to the garden with a sense of urgency, the suffocating feeling of being indoors growing more oppressive as she walked, then jogged, down the hall.

"Exit." Her tone was sharp. The door opened on her command, a whir as the motor came to life, followed by the soft hiss of suction breaking as the door opened. There was no sassy, clever, or friendly reply as she left. AI had not been installed in the security system yet. *Funny. I'm even missing my Earth robots. Batty old woman.*

The wind hit her first, along with the sudden temperature change. Early evening and it was already cold. Not icy, but chill. She stood still at the edge of the garden, breathing in the scents on the wind, eyes closed. Sharp bitterness of wet lichen; coppery, warm Martian clay; salty fishiness of ocean algae. *Rain's coming in off the water tonight.*

Eyes still closed tight, she pictured green, sharply pointed leaves swaying as the moist air caressed her skin. A buzzing sound came, not from without but from within the recesses of her mind, recorded there by her senses and replayed along with the vision of fat-bodied, winged miracles, life-giving wonders, so small as to be insignificant, yet so very essential.

Carla opened her eyes to the reality in front of her as the first fat drops of rain fell on her forehead, her bare sun-spotted shoulders. Rain rolled down her cheeks, saltier after having met her eyes and joined with her tears. Her exhalations trembled from her chest, protesting the contrast between her sense-memories and what surrounded her.

Turning to the west she allowed her gaze to trace the outline of the hulking mountain range whose roots wound all the way to the colony, its steep outcroppings hugging the western domes. Without pause or outward sign of the thoughts that motivated her, Carla slipped the sandals from her feet and broke into a run, leaving them abandoned on the red ground. She covered the distance to the garden wall in several bounds and pulled herself up and over, dropping into the dampened stalagmites of lichen below.

With barely a pause of motion Carla leapt over the sharp volcanic rocks sticking out from the ground, keeping to the balls of her feet as she scaled the uneven slope of the lowest point of the west mountains. She ran uphill where the slope was gradual, hands trailing to brush against the growths of wet lichen, and climbed with hands and bare feet as the incline grew steeper and the light rain made the rocks slick and treacherous.

Breathing in the Martian air, she sucked it in deeper with each breath, tasted the salty tang of it and welcomed in the many foreign scents on the wind as it whipped around her. *I'm here. Blow right through me. Brush away the last traces of Earth… fill in the empty spaces with Mars.*

Carla's arms shook, thin rivulets of rainwater running down her hands and forearms and dripping from her elbows as she pulled up and scrambled over the rocky edge. Leaning her back against the rock wall at the rear of the small ledge she found herself perched on, Carla smiled and brushed the accumulated rain and sweat from her face. The setting sun lit the eastern sky on fire and glinted off the ocean surface, painting the waves into a molten lava flow as she watched.

Looking down from the precipice, Carla traced the path she'd come down to the faint outline of the colony, symmetrical domes, archways and thin curving garden walls, her eyes sparkling with the light of the sunset that cast its orange-red glow on the domes. *Deceptively simple compared to what we left on Earth, but can we get the people back to the heart of things? Depends on if there's any heart left to them, I guess…or just microchips and circuit boards.*

Carla inhaled the cool wind once more before sliding to the edge and dropping down. Loose rocks skittered away from her feet, bouncing and clattering down in front of her as she loped down the way she'd come, back to the newly inhabited colony, and the walls that surrounded it.

Are you going to let us stay, Mother Mars, or shake us off like so many fleas off a dogs back?

The sky had darkened from a dark purple to indigo by the time she found herself back in the barren garden, transforming the rocks and lichen shrubs into hulking shapes a shade darker than the sky.

Sinking to her knees, Carla dug her hands into the Martian dirt, rainwater pooling in the small depression. She lifted a handful of the deep red soil to her face, inhaling its scent. Such an iron-heavy, salty smell, like the life blood it resembled. Splitting the dirt into her two hands she spread it across her cheeks, her forehead, her lips, and then down her legs to where her toes dug into the mud. *This is home now. This is my garden.* The mud was cold and soothing against her skin, a mixture of silky clay and grains of decaying lichen and sand. *I need to plant something. My seeds.* Carla stood, answering impulse, then stopped short. *Should I do it now?* The rain flowed in small streams through her silver hair, wiry with rain and damp.

"They'll probably shrivel up and die here." Turning away from the moonless night, Carla dropped the handfuls of soil and walked to the door that opened for her on command. *I'll just try a few seeds in the morning.*

Emily stood, the tools falling from her lap, and raised a hand to cover her mouth.

"Gran! Did you fall? Are you hurt?" She hurried over to the doorway where her grandmother had reappeared. Emily frowned, placing a hand on her shoulder, her face, patting to check for injuries.

Carla lifted her own hand to touch the remaining red on her cheek and held it up for inspection. A laugh broke free from her chest as she inspected the smear of blood red soil on her fingertips, and with the laugh her spirits lifted. Rubbing the soil between her fingertips, Carla touched it to her tongue to taste.

"Just communing with Mother Mars, dear heart."

"Oh." Emily's smile was tentative, her look sidelong.

"She says I can stay. You'd better ask her yourself, though. It's a bit wet out!" The old woman's eyes sparkled with humor as she brushed droplets from her arms and squeezed the rain from her braid.

"I'll see to that, Gran." Emily bit her lip. "Feeling better then?"

Carla tilted her head, searching her inner landscape before replying. "Yes. I am. A bit expatriated, but Mars and I are making friends. We've built the groundwork."

Emily smiled and shook her head. "What of the first meeting? Do you have concerns there? Because I was wondering…do you feel you're making progress with them?"

Carla pursed her lips, unprepared for the sudden change in topic.

"Time will tell. I'm just uprooting weeds and planting new seeds. Never know what'll take root and sprout unless you water and wait. The last meeting was all about weeding. I've been planting since we started, but no telling when the seeds'll come up. Suppose we'll water and fertilize at the next one."

"What about Theresa?" Emily was used to her grandmother's gardening metaphors and didn't miss a beat.

Carla's smile dimmed. "Mmmm?"

"I know you've invited her several times. But she hasn't come yet. Will she? Does it matter?"

Carla sat on the nearest stone seat a bit too hard. "Were cushions too much to ...ah hell!" She rubbed her throbbing backside. "Em, Theresa is from a whole different world. Not just the other side of the tracks but the other side of the planet. Hell, she practically *is* the Reproductive Council, or was, anyway." Carla's volume grew as she vented the concerns that Emily had unearthed, causing the younger woman to flinch.

Carla slowed her speech and lowered her voice. "She might show up. She just might. And whether she comes around depends heavily on how deeply rooted her beliefs are. A person can only take so much cognitive dissonance at once."

"And if she doesn't ...will you still bring your concerns to the Council meeting?"

"If she doesn't we hardly have a leg to stand on. We need Theresa or Genesis to stand with us."

"What about the Head of the Department of Medicine? Jacob Emory? Couldn't we speak to him?"

Carla shook her head and stepped over to the food preparation mechanism in the stone wall. "Coffee, please." *I hope David is working up an alternative for when our black gold runs out.*

The machine hummed, lighting up with a stream of blinking green and blue. "Acknowledged."

Carla winced, her lips and brows twisting. "Acknowledged? You need reprogrammed! Might as well not talk back at all. Stick to the blinky lights if you've got such a tinny voice and no personality."

The front panel of the machine slid open to reveal a steaming cup of hot black liquid.

"Affirmative."

Carla turned back to Emily, ignoring the reply. "Where was I, then?"

"Head of the Department of Medicine." Emily smiled.

"Jacob Emory. Right. No. No chinks in his armor. He won't come around unless Theresa leads him by the nose, and even then he strikes me as having his own agenda, so maybe not."

"Theresa has chinks?"

"Hell, chinks?! She has gaping *holes* in her armor. She doesn't see it yet, but she well might."

Turning on his heel, the Captain faced the tail end of the procession. The crimson and black pumice crunched underfoot, or else tumbled over the edge and disappeared into the mists below to be heard clattering and echoing to the bottom of the chasm. He wiped the beads of sweat from his forehead with the back of one hand and then cupped it to his mouth. "Bring up the rear now, and we'll rest at the top of this ridge!"

Trina trudged up to him, a large pack on her back, and stopped to survey the long line of colonists snaking up the mountain. There were large gaps in the line, and clusters where narrow passages between the jagged outcroppings and thick, mossy underbrush caused bottlenecks, impeding the hikers' progress. "You want me to go down and encourage the stragglers again?"

Neil pressed his lips together and shook his head. "Naw. Don't want to push them too hard, so soon." He smiled then, eyes lighting up with humor. "It's better than the first hike. Couldn't go ten feet without someone tripping or sitting down for a breather."

The Captain reached for Trina's pack. "Why don't you go on up ahead and find a good stopping point for lunch at the top of the ridge? I'll go down and make sure everyone makes it."

She raised one eyebrow and looked askance at him. "Is that because Kendra is down there?

He snorted. "If I suggest that Kendra needs looking after, she might help me off the mountain."

Trina shook her head, laughing as she turned and jogged towards the top of the ridge line.

The Captain took up a quick pace, taking care to watch his footing lest the gravel slip out from under him or a boulder trip him. "Looking good Eli, Melissa, Bethany. Keep it coming, okay? We're stopping at the top of that ridge." He gestured over his shoulder, with one hand, smiling when the two answered with out-of-breath nodding. Melissa's hair was slick with sweat but still whipping around her face in the brisk wind, and Bethany's skin was flushed scarlet from the exertion.

Eli called after the Captain as he passed. "Is that an actual stop, like for lunch maybe, or just one of those ten-minute pauses we've been calling 'breaks'?"

The Captain continued down the path and, passing closer to the line of hikers, he put up his right hand, giving out high fives and pats on the shoulder for encouragement. "You'll see when you get to the top of the ridge-if you make it, Eli!"

"Would you look at the diversity here?" Donovan leaned in gesturing to another colonist. "See this one? The planet was seeded with a *single* species of lichen and it's filled every niche! This on the rocks is flat and scaled, and here we have a variety that hangs down from the cliff edges." He crouched down to inspect a two-foot-tall, ragged, soot-colored shrub resembling an upright version of the hanging lichens. "Even these here come from the same source. Just, wow!"

Donovan turned to see that his one man audience had wandered off to another small cluster of colonists that were settling in to eat lunch. "Huh."

"You wanna talk evolutionary biology and plant species, you might need a new audience." David gave Donovan a half-smile from the top of a large boulder. "I'm game."

Donovan shook his head and sighed, climbing up to stand next to him and survey the land below. "Yeah, guess I was pretty much talking to myself anyway." Far below they could see the colony's complex of domes, just peeking out of the fog that rolled in from the sea, bright green on the horizon. "How are the aspen saplings coming along?"

"Beautifully. They looked a little battle-weary the first couple days after we landed, but they're leafing out now."

David watched as the next group of colonists came into view on the path. Genesis was among them, her golden eyes bright and flashing, cheeks flushed, with black hair coiled and twisted in a tight French braid. Several others were with her, many of them out of breath but cheerful, their looks full of gratitude for the pleasant distraction her conversation provided.

David slid down from the boulder and gave Donovan a smile of apology. "Be back in a minute."

Donovan laughed. "Sure you will."

David approached the group, listening through the wind to Genesis's voice.

"At least we'll notice the difference even more when we take our weighted layers off tonight." She winked at the man to her left, a blond-haired young colonist named Gideon.

David smiled at the mental image her comment elicited, raising his voice over the wind. "Good morning, Genesis."

She looked at her companions, a smile playing on her lips, revealing the points of white teeth. "If you'll excuse me. I'm going to see if Captain Neil needs help with the last group."

"Do you want me to…" David neared the group just as Genesis loped back down the hill without backward glance or response.

He clicked his teeth, and brushed the red dirt from his hands, as he watched her depart, braid swinging as she ran.

"Okay then." He turned to the group, most of them too tired to notice anything beyond their aching muscles. "There's some room to sit down in the shade over here, if you're ready to eat."

On Earth— Reproductive Council Headquarters

Greg's voice was broken with pauses and stutters. "Why don't you just...you could just...just, tell her! Maybe I should tell her...she'd stop expecting me to intervene."

The two men's hologram representations, identical to the men themselves aside from slight rippling distortions and shimmers around the points of movement, faced off.

"No." Richard shook his head, his tone conversational. "You won't do that. Because if you do you'll face the Council's penalties for falsifying research documentation. I know you don't want that any more than I do."

Greg threw up his hands, motions jerky and fumbling. "I don't... just don't want to be a part of this anymore!" His cheeks and forehead were flushed with agitation. "It's not my assignment, and I don't know why you're asking for me to get involved! I transferred out f- for a reason."

"You did it because of Theresa." It was a statement of fact.

"No... yes. We don't need to talk about it... about her."

Richard shrugged. "Alright. I'll tell her you don't want to be involved. To stop asking for your help."

"I didn't say that! I want her to know the truth, though, so she doesn't think..."

Richard raised one brow. "You want to be absolved. It doesn't work that way, my friend. Do you think it matters what your reasons are, if you don't step up?"

"Well, if I just..." Greg's hologram wrung its hands together.

"I only did it as a favor to you, as your friend, and I expect you to keep up your end." Richard's hazel-green eyes locked onto Greg's darting ones. "It stays between us."

CLOSE FRIENDS

Theresa reclined on her bed, her hand-held resting on her thighs. A glowing double helix rotated just above the surface of the console. She leaned in, wetting her lips.

"Alright. Begin simulated electrophoresis using enzyme Troy."

She narrowed her eyes, watching closely as the helix scattered and small fragments of it began reappearing in color coded groupings.

"Let's see…where is the signature fragment?"

Using the pad of her finger, she arranged the groupings of fragments by significance until the one she was looking for remained in a central location.

And there it was. Theresa's breath caught.

"Enlarge central fragment." She rubbed her cheek in frustration and then pressed her hand over her mouth.

"This isn't a signature I know. I know all of themon sight! What is this?" She let her hand slip down to her chest; Abby was asleep in her cocoon, eyelids fluttering and twitching in dream.

You know what it is, Theresa. The small hairs on her arms prickled, and a vague feeling of unease curled in her gut like a sleeping carnivore. She brushed her hands down the backs of her arms and straightened her posture.

Swiping the pads of her fingers across the edges of the holograph, she made all but the central fragment dissolve. "Compare signature fragment to AUC2's signature."

Alongside each other, the two fragments were the same aside from the tail end. AUC2 had Theresa's signature, just as all of the AUC progeny from Phase Four did, and those from Phase Three had her preceptor's. This one had a signature that she hadn't seen before.

"Incoming message." She looked up from her work, scowling in annoyance at the interruption.

"Display on the large screen."

The viewing screen on the wall came to life, colors swirling until Dr. Richard Brant appeared there. Theresa sat upright, unprepared for the image that appeared on the screen. He was as she remembered from their first meeting, white lab coat with AUC units blurred out in the background, but a dark shadow of stubble peppered his jawline and the skin under his hazel-green eyes looked bruised from lack of sleep. The recorded image rubbed a hand across his face.

"Theresa." Her name came out as more than a name. It was a plea, and she was unable to look away.

"I have no choice but to assume you are ignoring my messages. The alternatives are scenarios I don't want to imagine." Dr. Brant brushed back the hair that had fallen onto his brow. *It's longer, I think.*

"God, I've run through this message in my mind several times and now I'm rambling. I know that you reached Mars and we've had no reports back of catastrophic events since the elevator crash. No more deaths. But who's to know what information makes it through and what ends up classified." He paused again to take a deep breath and exhaled, his eyes seeming to lock with hers. "Theresa, I don't care about your secret. I can't play dumb. I have my ideas but if it's going to keep you from contacting me, the hell with my ideas and the possible benefit to be had from sharing information! Just, for the love of…Earth, Mars, whatever you value, answer me! You haven't answered my messages in weeks. I'm worried about you."

Theresa stared at the viewing screen long after it went dark, her cheeks burning, pulse thumping in her ears. *I'm worried about you?* The message replayed itself, echoing in her memory.

God, how did I misjudge this man so badly? And what did he do? Go examine the corpse and run tests? Why would he do that?

She unclipped her hair, allowing the braid to fall down from its coil. Her hands were shaking. She held one out and winced at the broken nails, the trembling paleness that highlighted how foreign her own hands had become. *Why are you so afraid of telling him? He's on Earth! He's helping us. Stop cowering.*

She stood, striding over to her computer console and planted herself in front of it.

"Prepare to record on three."

The computer counted down for her. "Three…two...one...record." The record light flashed on and she stared directly into the camera, jaw set.

"We arrived safely on Mars and are acclimating well. I took longer to adjust for a number of reasons." Her speech was stilted and formal, tone unyielding. "I was injured during the flight, a concussion and a broken clavicle. I also suffered from a severe case of space sickness." Theresa took a breath and plunged ahead. "She's safe here with me. Thank you for asking after her." She paused, lashes downturned as she gathered courage. "Your concern...your interest in us means more to me than I have shown you. I was ill, and frightened, or I would have kept in contact. Your messages have been a comfort to me. Please, keep me informed of news from Earth and I won't allow the distance or my fears to come between us again. End recording."

She sank down to the floor. She could hear the rushing of blood in her ears her heart beat so loudly. The trembling had spread from her hands to her shoulders, and she shook as if cold.

"I hope it's enough." Theresa placed a hand on the floor to stand and returned to the bench where she had left her work when Dr. Brant's message had interrupted her. *It will have to be enough. If he wants more confirmation of Abby's existence, he'll have to come to Mars, where the Reproductive Council can't reach her so easily. I'm sure they screen our incoming messages. I would if it were me.*

She tapped the screen and was rewarded by the display of Genesis's genetic code alongside Abby's. *Do I tell her? How much do I tell her?*

Glancing out the west-facing window, Theresa could just make out the ant-like trail of colonists as they made their way back down the mountain ridge, racing the blanket of fog that threatened to envelop them.

She scowled, eyelids fluttering in annoyance. *They're on the way back now. I wanted to go, dammit! As if having to stay home from group excursions is gonna make me look like less of an anomaly.* A sigh escaped her lips as she lowered her gaze.

"How much would I tell you, my little anomaly?" She loosened her blouse to gaze down at the growing child ensconced against her skin, the supple translucent dome covering Abby magnifying the small movements within.

"Good question, right?"

David leaned against a wall just inside Genesis's room, his arms crossed over his chest, and looked up at Genesis where she stood with her back to him. Several colonists' personal files were open at once on her viewing screen.

"What does mine say?" He nodded towards the screen when she glanced back at his remark.

She turned to face the screen. "The same information it has about everyone else. David Raiklin, forty-six years of age, widower, generation Z10, current assignment: Head of Department of Horticulture…Should I continue?"

He snorted. "No. I think I know my vital statistics."

"Okay. Then why are you here?" She continued to open and close folders, scanning the data within and adding notes.

David walked across the room and paused behind her. "Are you avoiding me?"

"You came to ask if I'm avoiding you?" She turned to face him and found him closer than expected.

He raised both brows and nodded. "You seem to be avoiding me, so I thought it better to ask than to assume. You haven't been by since the garden. That's been several days. And this morning on the hike you ran off without…a greeting? Something?"

Genesis shook her head. "I was busy." She turned back to the screen. "I'll come by when I want to hold hands." She flicked her wrist at him, before placing her hand back on the keyboard.

"Ouch. Tell me…how sharp does that tongue get when you're threatened with something worse than casual hand-holding? A massage that doesn't lead into foreplay, maybe?"

Her voice was flat, matter-of-fact. "Massage always leads into foreplay."

David laughed. "I'll give you usually, but not always."

Genesis blacked out the screen and turned to face him, closing the gap with a single step. The length of her body pressed against his and her eyes flickered with heat.

"Why don't we just play this my way? You forego handholding and I promise you won't miss it." She arched her feet, standing on tip-toe, allowing her lips to trail across his neck and faintly stubbled jawline. "And if you do miss casual, friendly touching, you are free to walk away." Genesis's voice found his ear, soft and purring with the unclaimed potential she offered. "Unless you're afraid of my tongue?"

He narrowed his eyes, trying to think clearly through the desire snaking through his thoughts and turning them to its purpose.

"I'm not afraid of you, Genesis."

One hand was all it took for David to lift her by her ass, fingers splaying across the muscle tightened by her tip-toe posture. He kissed her, lips parted, tongue seeking hers to caress, thrusting deeper into her welcoming mouth, a pantomime of the claiming he longed for.

Pulling away, David held back, waiting for her to initiate the next kiss. When she did, hands sliding into his hair, arms twined around his neck, she pressed her mouth to his, soft, wet, inner lips tasting him; he returned the kiss, but held back. He teased, lips gliding, tasting, all breath and promise as he met her lips with his, over and over again, pulling away before satisfying their thirst.

"I agree to your terms." His voice wavered, thrumming in his chest with his quickened breath. "If you'll agree to the same. Let me show you what warmth is, the slow burn of tenderness. Let me redefine it for you. If you don't like it you can pull away, or walk."

Genesis groaned, bending back at the waist with her hips still against his, held there by his hand, hot through her clothing.

"Alright, alright!" She slid both hands under his collar, clasping them behind him. "It sounds awfully close to playing games, you know."

David leaned down to kiss her arched neck. "No, more like setting ground-rules…mmm…every relationship needs them…" His lips trailed, leaving a damp, tingling path in their wake.

The door chime sounded. "Theresa Marin requests entry."

David paused mid-kiss and raised his eyes to hers. "You could ignore it…I'm sure she'll leave in a moment…"

"No. We have business to attend to." She slid out of his arms and straightened the front of her blouse. "The council meeting is in three weeks. In fact, that reminds me. You need to prepare a list of the produce we can expect to have access to as well as a time-frame for when it can be expected and in what amounts, to present at the meeting. And if you intend to make a play for

Head of the Mars Council you'll want to come up with a game plan."

He licked his lips. "All business now, aren't we? You switch gears so quickly my head spins."

"You'll get used to it." She raised up on tiptoe once more and placed a quick kiss on his lips before walking to the entryway to greet her guest. "Admit her, please."

David narrowed his eyes, following her with his gaze. "Head of the Mars Council? Is that where you see me?"

Genesis shrugged. "I said if…it *would* suit you though, and you're well-liked."

He snorted. "The Captain does just fine. Think I'll stick to my plants, thank you very much."

The door slid open to reveal Theresa where she stood neatening her braid and murmuring under her breath.

"I'm glad you came. We have matters to attend to, don't we?" Genesis smiled in welcome and placed a hand on Theresa's shoulder as she led her into the room.

"Oh, David." Theresa stopped short when she noticed him standing next to Genesis's viewing screen. "I didn't know you were busy, Genesis. Should I come back later?" Theresa blushed, eyebrows pulling together as she looked from one to the other.

"Mmm…not at all, Theresa. David and I had already agreed to finish what we started at a later time."

Genesis turned to David. "In fact, why don't we go over your agricultural report tomorrow morning?"

David headed for the door. a slight smirk on his lips. "Sure, Genesis. You can check me for typos. Good to see you, Theresa." The door opened to admit him into the hallway.

Theresa's gaze followed David out, one hand in her pocket pulling strings as she surveyed the room for things other than the business at hand to hold her interest.

Genesis walked over to the wall and pushed a button. "Are you hungry? Of course you are. Let's see…steak and greens for two with red potatoes."

"Preparation of this meal will require ten minutes and will use up your quota of meat for the week. Would you like to confirm your order?"

"Yes, confirmed." Genesis walked over to where Theresa sat and handed her a thin cushion, placing another on the bench before sitting herself. "At least they've been distributing these."

"Wow. You're cheerful. I don't think I can eat while we talk. I might waste your steak by choking on it or spitting it back up." Theresa grimaced at the nervous rambling she let slip out. "Um, that was not what I planned to say."

Genesis wet her lips with the tip of her tongue and nodded. "Okay. Eat after we talk. Or at least after you get past whatever part is making you nervous."

Theresa sighed, adjusting the cushion under her and rubbed the seal of the RPU just under the edge of her neckline, where it itched. "You don't have…no that's not really…" She paused to collect her jumbled thoughts before trying again.

"I examined your genetic code and, as I expected, instead of a generational serial number like the rest of the population has, I found a signature." Theresa bit the tip of her pinky nail and flinched when the edge pulled off too deep.

"A signature?"

"Yes. A signature is used when a progeny's genetics are entirely engineered using several parent sources. Each genetic engineer has their own personal signature that can be recognized by other engineers."

"Like yourself." Genesis's face was placid as she waited for confirmation of her assumption.

"Ah, yes. Or I wouldn't have been able to recognize the signature." Theresa frowned.

"These progeny…are they grown like yours there?" Genesis gestured to the bulge of Theresa's shirt where Abby was concealed."

Theresa answered without thinking. "Oh, that would be entirely inefficient. It's too great a strain on the carrier's body. This was…impromptu." She stopped, biting her lip, aware that she had shared more than intended.

Genesis sat facing her, hands resting in her lap, and caught Theresa's flitting gaze with her own. "Theresa. You wouldn't be here if you didn't have something more to tell me."

Theresa opened her mouth to speak, paused, then pushed ahead.

"I didn't recognize the signature. I thought I knew all of them. Have them memorized. But the one in your coding is unique." She hesitated again. "I believe it indicates that you were the first."

"The first what?" Genesis blinked, intrigued.

"The first phase. There are four phases of progeny within the program that you come from. All of them younger than you and with different signatures. So it stands to reason that you are the product of an experimental Phase." Theresa's words increased in speed as she gained confidence in her theory; hearing it aloud lent even more credence.

"The first portion of the signature, AUC, designates the project. The second the Phase. The third is unique to the engineer, usually part of a name or some reference to an inside joke, a pet...like a password. AUCPH6CB. But yours... AUCPHA9BR; it has a letter included in the phase number, and I don't recognize the signature."

Theresa reached for the water glass on the table between them, her fingertips bumping the side instead of grasping. The glass tipped, then toppled as she overcompensated, attempting to avert the crisis. "Shit!" She grabbed the glass by the rim before it could roll off the edge. "Sorry." Theresa bit her lip, handing the empty glass to the other woman before continuing. "Genesis, this is private, classified information I'm sharing with you."

"Just like little Abby, right?"

Theresa froze. Something in Genesis's voice caused her to look up and search her face for the hint of threat, menace, that seemed to seep through the woman's words.

"I would like to run more tests...would you agree to that?" She met Genesis's gaze, eyes wide, a slight tremble to her lips.

Genesis looked down, a wry smile appearing as she nodded, realization dawning.

"Now I see. You want to continue your research on me...The research you started on Earth? That would make me your only candidate, wouldn't it? Or her." She gestured with an inclination of her head.

"She isn't involved in this." Theresa's eyes flashed, brows dipping, lips tightening.

"She had better be involved if you expect me to be. Do you realize how unreasonable it is for you to ask this of me and offer nothing in return?" Genesis stretched her arms and slid her fingers through the back of her hair, locking them behind her head.

Theresa's brows tipped upward as she let her words rush out. "It would give you insight into your own character. Allow you to know yourself far better than most people do and…and improve upon…any issues you may have."

"Really?" Genesis's words dipped and rose with laughter. "I have been myself for twenty-eight years. I'm very confident in my knowledge of self. I also prize my privacy."

Genesis removed one hand from her hair and held it out in front of her, palm upward, in one fluid gesture. "If I were to agree to this…" She paused and leaned close. "If. You would have to realize how much power that would give you over me. I don't give up my power lightly…"

Theresa's words tumbled out one on top of the other in her hurry to give assurances. "Genesis, I would never share information that wasn't mine to share. I have had the top clearance within the Reproductive Council since I was fourteen."

Genesis held up a hand. "You just, moments before now, shared classified information with me." She pushed the sharply nailed hand forward again when Theresa opened her mouth to defend. "It doesn't matter that we are on Mars or the circumstances are dire in your mind. My personal information is more vital than any level of security clearance you have ever qualified for and I require assurances."

Theresa took a breath, brow furrowed, and met Genesis's eyes. "I mentioned you have a signature like Abby…"

Genesis nodded for her to continue.

"If you *are* like Abby, and I think you are, then you likely share certain deficits." She picked up speed, rushing to finish before Genesis could refuse her again. "If my preliminary research proves out then it isn't genetic but environmental, an adaptation of sorts."

Genesis frowned, her eyes taking on a look of true concern. "Where did she come from? What is this secret?"

Theresa curled her shoulder's inward, lifting her hand to rest over Abby, eyes dipping down. "I can't allow her secret to ever reach the Reproductive Council… or anyone, for that matter."

Genesis shrugged, a look of sympathy crossing her features as she stood. "I can't allow anyone to have my secrets either. I hope you understand."

Theresa spoke without looking up, hand still resting on the capsule that held Abby, gathering strength from the warmth that emanated from within. *God, this better not be a mistake! But we need to know more, Abby. I don't want to screw you up worse.*

"Abby is from Phase Four of the AUC program where progeny are grown in a lab from conception to birth. All progeny in the program show signs of abnormal development…manifesting as sociopathy in brain scans…" Theresa looked up to gauge Genesis's reaction and found her eyes unreadable.

"Phase Four was slotted for termination, all one hundred of them under my care. I fought the council. They reassigned me to Mars." Theresa sighed, trying to release the tension that shook her voice. "Abby was the smallest and least likely to survive. I transferred her to the RPU and installed it on myself before turning the project over."

Genesis's eyes glowed and a slight smile widened her lips. "You're stronger than I thought. And more capable of forethought."

Theresa grimaced. "It was more desperation than forethought, but thank you." Her eyes were wet with emotion and she rubbed her arm with one hand, leaving a red pressure mark. "If my actions got back to the Council...I wouldn't …"

"I'll submit to any research you want to conduct...within reason. If Abby and I are one and the same as you say, then it would be equally detrimental to the both of us for me to reveal her secret. You needn't worry."

"Except that the Reproductive Council already knows what you are."

"Yes. True. But the other colonists do not. You have that to hold over me if you are concerned about me sharing this information."

Theresa bit her lip. "I guess that helps...but for Abby and I the repercussions would likely be worse. Keep that in mind."

"Abby and I will be good friends." Genesis walked over to where the food waited, still hot. "We should eat to seal the deal."

Theresa tried to smile and accepted the plate.

Carla leaned in for an eye-scan, tapping her foot. "I don't have time for this...you just tell him it's Carla and her seeds."

"Scan complete. Your identification is confirmed as Carla Schoen, mental health specialist."

"Like I said. Carla and her seeds." She rolled her eyes and scratched the tip of her nose.

Another moment later the door slid open and a fine warm mist dampened her cheeks. Taking a step into the room to allow the door to slide shut, she breathed in the heavy scent of wet soil and crisp green foliage. The domed room was large and opened up into a larger central dome with several smaller domes attached like a flower.

"What can I do for you?" David's voice echoed across the central dome to where Carla stood mesmerized, lips parted and eyes wide as she looked up at the transparent ceiling of the dome complex and the lichen covered walls leading up to it.

"Hello? I'm in the central dome if you're there." His voice was light and playful.

"Oh! Here I come." She weaved her way through the circular rows of half-grown plants rooted at waist level in hydroponics channels, allowing her fingers to trail over the leaves as one would the toes of a sleeping newborn.

David crouched in the central dome, a large tray of Martian soil in front of him with several transplants firmly packed within. He glanced up at Carla. His eyes were bright, twinkling, and his breaths deep and peaceful as he savored his task. Large competent hands moved in swift, sure motions that could only be achieved with muscle memory. He hollowed a small crater in the soil, cupped water into it, and lifted a seedling from the hydroponics tray into the waiting space.

He used both hands to fill the hole and pull a mountain of soil up around the fragile plant, covering all but the leaves and a small portion of the top stalk. Standing, he brushed the wet loam, the color of clotted blood, off onto a work apron.

"How are you, Carla?" His smile was large and genuine, without the shadows that usually haunted his face.

"Better now." She wiped the corners of her eyes, her smile just as true, breaking through maudlin thoughts of home. "I have troubles, though…" She held up two withered seedlings, no larger than three centimeters each.

David leaned in, squinting at the tiny shriveled scraps of plant matter that she placed in his palm. "Where did these come from?" His eyes widened, perplexed.

"They're mine…from my own seeds." Carla looked down and then set her jaw, tipping her face back up to speak. "I know you're altering the plants to grow on Mars, but I wanted to see what I could do with my own stock. I got impatient. I know. I know. You never rush a seedling, but I was homesick, and stubborn, and you were busy."

David snorted, but his eyes were still warm when he shook his head. "I am busy…but not too busy for this. What sort of seeds do you have? These look like tomato?"

"Yes. I have fifty different plants, all fruit and vegetable, herbs as well actually, been growing them for over sixty years on Earth. Wasn't sure if it was pointless but I wanted to…to try." Her lips quivered and then stilled as she tightened them, meeting David's gaze square on. "I wanna grow them if we can. Obviously the garden soil isn't gonna cut it, and maybe they won't grow at all here."

David turned towards a side dome with a gesture for her to follow as he untied his work apron and folded it up. "Oh, they'll grow. But they'll do better if we tweak the genetics a bit." He approached the sealed door to one of the side domes. "Open." He strode through the door, pace quickened with excitement. "Let's get these into my lab for analysis…may I?" He turned back, holding out a hand for confirmation.

Carla nodded, producing a fabric bag with an old fashioned zipper. The zipper stuck several times before she managed to produce several small paper packets, carefully folded and sealed, with handwritten labels.

"Oh, packets? I guess you wouldn't have had access to the stay-dry seed preservation kits I use, would you? Have they been kept dry?"

She pursed her lips. "Well, it's a dead hobby, isn't it? Not enough clean soil on Earth to go around outside of the agricultural sector. But, they're dry, yes, and freshly dried too. I saved them for this. Had my own garden at home, and bees." She crossed her arms over her chest.

David turned away from where he was loading the seeds for analysis, eyes wide.

"How did you manage that? The permits alone for soil are impossible to get outside of the department I worked in…and bees?"

"I've been around a long time…and I know how to hold on to what matters."

David nodded. "Alright. I can get on board with that explanation." He smiled, shaking his head as he turned back to investigate the first display of data on his viewing screen.

"Oh. Wow." Another backward glance. "The genetic diversity is staggering! What were you doing?"

"Just…keeping hold of Earth's legacy."

David exhaled, wonder crossing his face as he placed his hands behind his head and turned to Carla with growing respect in his eyes.

"So, do you want an assignment in the horticultural department? Because…you can have it."

Carla laughed. "No, no. I'm a dabbler. I have other fish on my plate. But I do want my garden back. I'd like to come in here and smell the plants and help you along." She placed a hand on his shoulder. "And I have a request. These seeds, the herbs, I need for personal use. I want them to grow, but I can't have their properties altered too much."

David rubbed his lips together, squinting as he thought. "I can do the bare minimum, make them grow in the thinner Mars atmosphere, light level, soil mineral concentration, like the others I've prepped for Mars. But, honestly, I wouldn't know which properties you are trying to preserve. And which you want to eliminate."

"If I give you that info, can we do it?" Her eyes were sharp, determined.

"Carla, I'd consider it an honor to work on this with you. If you'll allow me to work with these seeds, it will open up the diversity in our Mars species exponentially. You let me work on your seeds and I'll get you a small hydroponics set-up in your room, office, whatever. And the communal garden…honestly, the soil there needs a lot of work, but you can have it. Start fertilizing it; you have my authorization to take the materials from your personal waste composting systems and till it into the garden. The rest needs to go into the colony's fields, but yours won't make a difference. It'd be negligible anyway."

Her eyes were sad, contrasting with a wistful smile. "Where were men like you when Earth was dying?"

David shrugged. "Busy trying to keep their families fed and their debt from drowning them, if my history is accurate. I'm no unicorn, just born at the right time, I think."

She shook her head. "Alright, unicorn." She laughed. "Can I trust you with my babies while I go prepare for the women's meeting?"

"You can." David paused a moment, deciding whether or not to speak his thought. "Why a women's meeting? Isn't that a bit old-fashioned?"

"It is. But sometimes you need to take a few steps backwards to find the right path forward. Don't wanna run forward blindly tripping on the bodies of those at the front of the pack just in the name of forward motion."

His brow creased and he tilted his head, eyes taking on a sharp glint. "Okay. So what if I wanted to attend your meetings?"

"I'd invite you to the next one."

"What if I showed up tonight…would you turn me away?"

"Yes…No. None of the other men have expressed an interest. Why would you want to do that?" Carla twisted her hands, a frown accentuating the faint lines on her face. "Some of the women might not be comfortable enough to speak in front of a man." Her eyes were apologetic.

David's face twisted in doubt, confusion. "That doesn't make any sense to me. We've been working and living together as equals for generations. Misogyny died a hundred years before I was born! With all due respect, what you're suggesting is a little insulting." He blinked rapidly, agitation making his words and gestures more abrupt.

"Please. Let me try to explain this another way." Carla held up a hand. David took a breath, sliding one hand into his hair, damp from the humidity that seeped into the room from the greenhouse.

"I'm listening."

"Fruit trees…no, let's go with honey bees. Say we take their hive away and give it to…I don't know…nano-bees. If we bring them back generations later and ask them to make honey, will they? And how can we expect them to even consider making honey if the nano-bees are buzzing around the hive, whispering about them?"

David exhaled through his lips, shaking his head. "Whispering about them? Not quite getting that one either. Bee behavior is instinct, not a learned skill. They'll hive and make honey wherever you…"

"Shit! It's a damn metaphor! Just come to the meeting tonight. Come to the meeting and just…" She held her hands out, gesticulating, and then pressed her palms together, tucking them under her chin. "Just listen…okay? Listen, and afterwards we can talk about it, alright?"

Jonathan sat in front of his stone desk, gaze drifting up from the 3-D printer in front of him every few minutes to observe Emily where she sat, scrolling through clips on her hand-held viewer. He watched her, lowering a tool and opening his mouth, once, twice, completing the motion when the words welled up and stood their ground instead of falling back again in indecision.

"Is this you, Em? Or is it Carla…grandmother? I've never seen you on a crusade before, not like this…"

Emily looked up at her husband as if his voice were a gunshot. Eyes wide at first, then narrowing as she looked inward.

"Is it me?" A smile pulled at her lips. "It's more me than anything I did on Earth."

"But I don't see how her crusade fits in with what brought us here. When you want something for as long we have, does it matter in what form it comes? Don't we just want our own progeny?"

She looked down at her hands, folded in her lap, gone white at the knuckles, then tucked her hair behind her ears on both sides. Looking up then, her gaze was steady, impassioned with a slow-burning fervor that he had never seen in his wife before.

"It matters more." She spoke the words in a soft voice that drew his attention, causing him to listen more closely. "I've spent a good portion of our lives together struggling against the futility of what we wanted. Now I feel…for once…like I have some choices, or the opportunity to have some choices, if that makes any sense."

Jonathan stood and crossed the room, crouching down and taking Emily's hands in his.

"I'm tired of seeing you hurt, Em." He leaned his cheek against her palm, and looked up into her face. "You've been happier here so far. Can't we just take that? Take that and run with it. I mean, let's try for our progeny here. We can now, but do we have to make things…complicated?"

Emily looked down again, blinking. "This is the reason I've been happier. Carla, our crusade, Mars! I'm tired of being like a bird trying to fly with its foot in someone's hand!"

He rubbed his forehead, a sigh escaping his lips. "Now you're using her metaphors. That *is* one of hers, you know."

"Yes, I know! It's a good one. It's appropriate in this case because that *is* what I felt like on Earth, Jonathan!" Her voice had risen several decibels. "Like a bird with my foot caught, only they wrapped the other hand around my chest and squeezed as well!" She held up a clenched fist, her breathing ragged as if a phantom hand had indeed clamped down on her chest."

"Shh. Shh…It's okay." He wrapped his arms around his wife, cursing himself for the trembling of her shoulders against his chest. "Hey, I'm sorry. No one's gonna get hold of your feet on Mars, I'll beat the blood out of them if they try. I'll pull their wings off. You just…crusade on. Point the way…"

She winced at his words, turning her face into his chest. "Jonathan!"

"No I mean it, Em. Beat 'em bloody." He stroked her hair, leaning his face atop her head, forehead creased, smile wavering.

"I need to bring these clips to grandmother before the meeting starts."

Theresa's right hip bone pressed against the stone of the bench through the thin cushion as she slid the scanning probe in an arc upwards from her pubic bone towards her left hip. She stared, unblinking, at the viewing screen on the wall displaying the pink landscape of her abdominal cavity. A sigh escaped her lips as she shifted her hips, readjusting her right arm and flexing the wrist that held up her head and trying to find a less awkward position.

"Should have just done it on Genesis!" *She's the one who suggested we need birth control.* Theresa cursed under her breath, lifting the probe from her reddened skin and lowering it back to the starting position just below her pubic bone. *Not until I've tested it, dammit. Hmmm…I'll just follow the uterus up to the Fallopian tube from the opposite direction.*

Sliding the probe again, she narrowed her eyes, watching closely for the entryway to the left Fallopian tube.

"Internal OS, lower uterine segment, fundus approaching…there it is! Alright, so about two centimeters up we should see the implant…" Theresa slowed the movement of the probe. No need to rush and pass over the landmark she was seeking. One centimeter. One and a half. Two. She moved the probe forward an imperceptible amount. "Huh." Increasing in speed, she slid the probe downward, following the path of the Fallopian tube until the fimbria at the end came into view.

"Okay! I missed the damn thing anyway!" Jerking the probe back to the start point, Theresa traveled the path again with even greater attention to detail, she leaned in towards the screen, pausing when her vision blurred from staring and then resumed.

She stopped, two and a half centimeters from the base of her left Fallopian tube, unable to process what she saw before her. Instead of the solid wall of tissue of an implant, there was a thin, almost imperceptible ring of scar tissue.

Theresa sat upright, holding the probe in place. "Freeze frame." Tilting her head, she blinked, a weight settling in the pit of her stomach like a stone displacing the murky sediments at the bottom of a moat.

"Magnify." Standing, she took two steps towards the screen as the image enlarged. Several moments passed, with Theresa gazing at the still image, one knuckle between her clenched teeth. Abby twisted in her cocoon, her fist flailing at Theresa's ribs.

"It's not there…" She shook her head. "You son of a bitch! I don't know how you did it, but you did."

The knuckles of Theresa's fists blanched white and she channeled all of her willpower into holding back the intense urge to hurl them against the door. Breathing in through her nose and out through her lips, she attempted to simulate calm while the security system scanned her retinas for identification. *Stay calm. Breathe, or it won't let you in.*

The door opened. Jacob pressed his palms across his shirt, neatening the pleats and cuffs. "Theresa, what brings you...Is everything... ?"

She strode forward, the momentum of her suppressed anger propelling her and sending her words out like projectiles.

"All right? What do you think? Why don't *you* tell *me* if I should be all right?"

Jacob recoiled from her diatribe, his eyes going cold, smile faltering where it was forming on his lips. "I don't really know. Why don't you sit down so we can talk?" He gestured towards an examination table. "You don't look well. Is the RPU malfunctioning? The...progeny?"

Theresa's eyes flashed, not just lightning within but a full-fledged storm system coming in off the sea.

"What kind of fool do you take me for...wait, don't answer that. I can do it myself." Her lips twisted as if tasting bitter, unripe fruit. "The kind I am...was. Trusting you to honor my requests for my medical decisions." She shook her head, shoulders rising and falling with the gesture. "I am the head of Reproductive Technologies, for fuck's sake! What made you think I wouldn't check? Or barring that, 'Whoops! Looks like I'm pregnant despite fail-proof contraceptive implants! I wonder how that happened!' What were you going to tell me when that happened? Huh?"

Jacob's expression was closed off, a wall of ice behind his eyes, his arms crossed. "I'm sorry. You were overruled."

She looked askance at him. "Overruled? By who? You?"

"No. The Reproductive Council. They aren't just cutting us loose, Theresa. This is a colonization effort. Not a free-for-all. Our success depends on careful management."

Her eyes widened and she retreated, the back of her knees coming into contact with a bench and buckling. "You're in direct contact with them." She nodded, interlacing her fingers and taking a slow breath in while her mind raced, galloped. *Tread lightly. What was it Genesis said? Forethought, cunning...*

Theresa tried on a look of pity, pressing her lips together and curving them sideways, raising one brow with a shrug. *God, don't overdo it, Theresa.*

"I didn't realize you didn't have the authority to make independent decisions. But no matter, I'll just take future concerns up with the Council directly. Morton and I need to catch up anyway. Progress updates for reproductive technologies on Mars are about ready, as well as my write-up for gestation in zero-g. I'll just add in my recommendations for strategic contraception." She pulled out her hand-held device to make a note, a slight tremble in her wrist, and stood to leave.

Theresa paused at the door and turned back. "Are there any issues you would like me to bring to the CEO for you? I regret storming in here like that…"

Jacob looked away, fidgeting with one pocket of his jacket and then lifted his chin.

"Quite alright." His features relaxed, brow smoothing out as he tried on a half smile. "I'm certain we'll enjoy working together once these little kinks are smoothed out."

Theresa smiled, channeling thoughts of steak, pie, Abby safe and sleeping, anything but Jacob Emory and the missing implants. "Oh, I'm sure we will. Just the stress of moving. Chain of command confusion and all that. Really my fault for not going straight to the source."

She caught his flinch from the corner of her eye as she turned and walked out of the office.

Once in the hallway, Theresa walked as fast as her legs could manage, stride increasing in length until she broke into an all-out run. She turned corners blindly until she was out of breath, lightheaded and breathing more heavily than the running itself could have caused. Her lungs retracted at the end of each out-breath, forcing her to gasp and preventing the slow inhales that she knew could calm her. She leaned back against the nearest solid surface. *Why am I crying? I can just put them back...I can just.* Her face crumpled as she doubled over in silent sobs, shaking against the door.

A voice spoke over Theresa's low moaning sobs, repeating itself several times before she registered the sound or its source.

"To request entry, position your face in front of the retinal scanner." She opened her eyes, red and aching from squeezing shut against the storm that now shook her shoulders. Twisting at the waist, she turned to confirm that she was leaning against the surface of a door and not just a wall. It wasn't her door. Pulling herself up, she blinked to clear her blurred vision and examined the name plate on the door. *Mental Health Department. Carla Schoen.* Staring before her, Theresa waited, eyes still distant.

"Scan complete. You have been announced."

She smoothed her blouse, more habit than conscious action. The security door slid open, seal breaking with a faint hiss. A cacophony of voices enveloped her as she stepped into the room, the air warm from the gathering of many bodies. She stood just inside the full room, arms wrapped around her chest, and allowed the door to seal behind her.

Carla looked over at the sound of the door and disentangled herself from a conversation. There were too many women gathered to afford her a view of the latest addition. In the interests of greeting each new arrival personally, she headed towards the door. The crowd parted around her, clearing a path.

Standing there, eyes swollen and pink, was Theresa. She lifted a hand to push the strands from her face, scrunching her forehead as her hand touched the long braid now hanging down her back, clips missing.

She's actually here and Lord, she looks about to bolt! Carla placed one arm around Theresa's back and leaned in.

"It's good to see you. Thank you...for coming, I mean."

"Shouldn't a meeting be in the community meeting hall?" Theresa stared across the overcrowded room.

"Mmm...the community meeting hall is for public meetings. This meeting is private."

Carla led Theresa to a less crowded area to sit, a section of the floor strewn with thin, red cushions, then crouched down next to her. "Are you alright?" Her eyes dipped down to the bulge still present beneath Theresa's clothing and then back to her face. "Is it Abby? If you want to talk in private, there's another room..."

"No, Abby is fine. It's...I just want to be here for now. Is that alright?"

"Of course it's alright. You would have been welcome at any of the other meetings. I've been holding your spot for you. And Abby too." Carla smiled. *What is this? She looks like a peeled onion. All raw, but with bite.*

Pushing off from the floor with her fingertips, Carla stood. "You just get comfortable. Let me know if you need anything. Even after I've gotten started, okay?"

Carla sat on a bench at the front of the room, the other forty-six women taking up positions in a bloated semi-circle around her.

Take it down to soul-speed now. Can't water the garden well with you tripping over yourself. It'll play out how it does and no different.

She massaged one hand with the other and slowed her breathing. *Now, I'll just set everything outside this room on a shelf. I can pick my troubles back up later. Just like waiting on a baby.* Carla allowed her gaze to drift across the half-moon of women. For each pair of eyes she met, she returned a smile, or a nod, and brought to mind her clearest memory of the woman and her stories.

"Alright…"

A soft chime sounded, preceding the announcement of another arrival.

"David Raiklin and Genesis Shaw request entry." A sharp prick of anxiety pierced the calm that Carla had cultivated and then was gone. *Might as well have them all here at once, I suppose.* "Well, the more the merrier, right? Let them in please!"

The door opened and then closed behind the pair. David looked around the room, taking a hand from his pocket to raise up in a half-wave. Genesis headed straight to where Carla sat to embrace her and give her most exuberant greeting.

"Sorry, we're late! You know I wouldn't have missed the first meeting planet-side, but we got caught up in last minute planning for the Council meeting. You know how that is, don't you, with all this." She gestured towards the viewing screen behind them, and the gathering of women.

"Well you're here now, aren't you? We were just getting started so you haven't missed a thing." Carla patted Genesis's hand. "Why don't you and David sit with Theresa there? It's about the only emptyish spot."

Once everyone was seated Carla took another breath, a full smile dominating her face.

"Looks like we have new additions this evening, so we won't skip anything." Carla pulled her legs up onto the bench to sit cross-legged.

"It's important that we start with an affirmation that this is a safe place. We are all here to share, to learn, to grow, and to move forward. Our stories are a part of who we are, and while they only have as much power over us as we allow them, they are sacred. It's like handing a piece of ourselves out to our sisters."

Carla met eyes with David where he sat, hands and chin resting on his knees, and acknowledged him with a nod. "Our families. And knowing that that piece is just as safe in their hearts as it is in ours. Here in this room, in this group, we all have a safe place to receive empathy, and validation, without fear of judgment." Several of the women were nodding, others smiling with their whole faces, and still others lost in calm contemplation of the picture Carla painted with her words. More than one pair of eyes were damp.

"Now…before we move on. I feel I need to acknowledge that between meetings we have lost one of our number." Her eyes were solemn. "Nicole was a friend of mine. I was her assigned therapist in the surrogacy program back on Earth. I know many of us were close to her." The midwife's eyes shone, moisture gathering in the corners as she found Alissa in the crowd. Silent tears were making tracks down Alissa's flushed cheeks, until she buried her face against her folded knees. "I know when the service is held we'll all get our chance to say our goodbyes, so for tonight I say we hold a space open among us for Nicole, knowing she would be here with us if she could." Carla bowed her head and went silent.

Several moments later, Carla lifted her face to those assembled around her, gauging their readiness to move on by their expressions. Alissa had pulled the broken pieces of herself back into place, as had Kendra, and while the mood was a shade darker than in previous meetings, all eyes were attentive and focused on her.

"Anyone who has a story to share tonight is welcome to do so. Sit where you are or stand. Whatever makes you feel most comfortable." She looked down at her crossed legs, allowing the silence to draw out and form a blanket around them. When none spoke from the silence, she looked back up and pulled in a breath to prepare herself.

"I've shared once before. But I have another story for tonight that's been weighing on me again, pushing into my dreams, clamoring for a telling." Carla rubbed her nose, pulling it between her thumb and forefinger, and cleared her throat.

"I'm old. In case it isn't obvious." Smiles met her attempt to start light. "The Reproductive Council was just hitting its stride when I started catching babies. I'd learned it from my mother, who'd learned it from hers. Anyway. They offered us a partnership, and we took it." Her eyes were hooded, clouds forming in their depths.

"They offered us access to technology in exchange for full control of our records and oversight on our protocols. Flash forward twenty years and they were phasing us out. Said we weren't needed now that the birthrates were so low and the limit on family size had given way to the license to procreate program."

Carla stood up to stretch her legs and fell to pacing. "I called bullshit. Why wouldn't we be needed? Even the few babies being born and their mothers could still benefit from what we had to offer, would need options." She shook her right hand, pointer finger stabbing the air. "Problem was, our women wanted more children, they wanted more say-so, they represented a subculture that wasn't dying out as fast as the council wanted, and we were their support."

Carla sat down on the edge of the bench. "Pull down the trellis and the vines have nothing left to grow on." She shook her head.

"So that's a bit of history for my story. I'm going on too long, I think, so I'll just put this last part out there." She busied her hands unbraiding the thick, silver that hung down past her shoulders as she spoke.

"I was pregnant at the time. My first and only child. I think they thought issuing me a license for her would help push me out of midwifery. When they called for our mass resignation and reassignment, I flat out refused. Made a big fuss about it, talked to women, talked to their husbands, tried to get it in the news. They begged me to stop, the other midwives, my husband; they said it was a lost cause and that I had lost my mind." Carla laughed, a bitter, humorless sound, traveling to their ears from the place long past that she spoke from. "But I had nightmares about them, nightmares of their babies pulled from their arms and taken to God knows where. I saw their faces waking and dreaming, the faces of the women who had entrusted me with their care, faces I was expected to just walk away from." She lifted her chin, eyes hard and glimmering.

"I didn't walk away. I kept attending women in their homes, in my home, in private resorts arranged in advance." A smile touched her lips. "I got away with it for six more months before they took me in my sleep." Carla paused then, swallowing against the dryness that cracked her voice and dropped a hand to her flat belly. "She was gone when I woke up three days later. The only evidence of her a scar here." She slid the edge of one hand from one hip to the other. "And the pain in my breasts, raw and stuck to my gown with leaking milk."

Carla caught sight of Emily, blinking as the tears stung her eyes, and gave her a smile.

"But...Gran...Why...You didn't tell me? I don't..." Emily shook her head, shoulders following with the force of the motion.

"Em, your mother doesn't forgive me for it. She didn't want you told. The council informed me that I was unstable and therefore unfit to parent. They gave your mother to a couple who had applied to the foster program and refused to tell me who."

Emily's voice was low, but had no competition with the depth of the silence in the room. "How did you find her then?"

"I apologized to the council, apologized publicly. I requested training for a new position in mental health, and in my spare time I looked for her. It took three years." Carla blinked, the smile that touched her eyes infecting them with bitterness. I befriended her mother and played the role of 'Aunt.' When your mother was old enough to keep a secret I told her. It didn't go so well."

She laughed, wiping the moisture from her eyes and looking around the room as if she had forgotten the size of her audience until just then.

Kendra stood and took the room in several steps, wrapping her long arms around Carla. Her lips were pressed together in a thin line, her eyes red. "I didn't expect that." Her head shook back and forth rapid fire. "I didn't think they'd do that. Mine were surrogate babies…I signed on for it before I knew better." She pulled herself upright and squeezed Carla's hand. "I think I thought you hadn't been through what we had. I'm sorry you know that pain."

There were three more stories before the room stayed silent. Theresa sat, arms wrapped around her knees, and as each story unfolded, it seeped into her like lake water through the clothes of a drowning victim, filling her up with a muddled murkiness. *Is there any of me left in here? I should share something, shouldn't I? What would I share? Not Abby. Not the AUC program. Am I getting up?* As the silence pooled around them and none stood, or spoke, the sense of urgency that had taken root grew sharper. Paralysis held her to the floor.

"We've been digging out stones all night. I'd say it's time we fill in the holes. Em, can you start the clips?" Emily nodded, pulling out her hand-held device.

"Sync to resident viewing screen, passcode, IVY2034." Emily gave another nod. "It's ready. Three minutes?"

"Sure. These clips were filmed in secret with the women I served during the six months after we were ordered to resign. They might be disturbing to some of you. These things have been removed from the media. Thing about birth videos, good ones anyway…makes us want babies. Hormones make a nice antidote for cultural conditioning."

The lights dimmed and the screen lit up with images. *Two women, swaying hips, one round with child, the other so full-bellied that pink stretch marks spread like tree roots across her exposed abdomen.*

The smaller of the two, with a long golden braid, whispered something as the other's rhythmic moaning subsided, bringing laughter that was just as shared as the swaying.

One wave came after another, waves of moaning. Swaying transitioned to rocking on hands and knees, and the camera was passed as the young flaxen haired Carla traded places with a tall man, rough-featured in the dim light, but tender as he held his wife.

Sweat dripped from the laboring woman's flushed face and the moans changed in quality, becoming guttural, animal. She rose to her knees.

"Stand up!" The woman's tone was urgent, two words uttered with just enough clarity to provoke action. The man stood and his wife grabbed hold of his hand, lacing her fingers with his and arched her back.

Theresa gripped her own throat, eyebrows collided above her eyes, wide and panicked. *Why would she show us this?*

The woman roared then, one hand white-knuckled with effort, the other reaching down between her thighs to catch the child as he rushed out in a sea of amniotic fluid, mottled in color, wriggling, and coated with waxy vernix.

The woman sat back on her heels and pulled the child to her chest, her laughter welling up from somewhere deep inside and bringing tears.

The screen went black and dim lights illuminated the faces in the room.

Theresa stared at the black screen, trying to name the hollow feeling that gripped her heart as the progeny emerged from its mother's womb.

Limbs heavy, she stood and walked to the front of the room, stopping next to Carla.

She kept her voice low to cover the nervous vibrato.

"...Does anyone want to see her? It isn't the same as a pregnant belly, but she's our first progeny on Mars." Theresa looked down at her hands and then surveyed the room to see how many would meet her gaze. "I still can't answer many questions. It isn't safe." She caught Carla's gaze. Carla was trying to smooth out her features, cover the grimace caused by her words. Theresa's mouth fell open, confusion in her eyes.

Biting her lip, Carla leaned in to whisper. "Let's make it something that won't sound so secretive and robotic, why don't we? May I?"

Theresa shrugged.

Carla turned back to explain. "The Reproductive Council's policy is to terminate progeny that are not strong and healthy enough to complete gestation. Babies born early receive no extra support and are generally put out of their misery. There aren't many, mind you. The Council makes sure of that. But when it does happen, well ...Theresa was assigned within the Reproductive Council and had the opportunity to use old technology." She rested a hand on the back of Abby's cocoon. "She took pity on little Abby, born two months early, and transferred her to the RPU to give her a chance at life." Carla smiled down at Abby, her look a mix of fondness and pity and gave her a gentle pat.

"Why don't I show some of you how to feel for baby parts? It'll be good practice for when it's your turn." Carla looked at Theresa for permission raising an eyebrow. Theresa nodded and, as a third of the women gathered closer, she unclasped her blouse and pulled back the sides enough to reveal the RPU that held Abby. Their expressions had changed, shifted from suspicion to something closer to compassion, awe, and cautious pity.

The upper edge of the seal was still reddened and angry looking despite the Rapid Heal ointment Carla had applied and the criss-cross of white fabric straps that held the capsule in place to prevent further tearing. Theresa's breasts were displaced to the sides of the RPU capsule, blooms of color from fading yellow and purple bruises and red and blue from newer ones evincing the strength of Abby's kicks.

Kendra stepped closer, bringing two other surrogates with her.

"That was a good thing you did." She leaned her face closer to the translucent surface of the RPU, her eyes widening as they took in the contraption, along with the delicate creature inside of it.

Abby was in light sleep, eyelids fluttering. Kendra's hand came up to touch the thin covering that held Abby and the fluid surrounding her, shaking a little at first and then just resting over the small back. Carla placed her aged hand over Kendra's pressing down and guiding the younger woman's hand.

"Feel the flatness here? The back is the only part that feels this way. The head and butt are similar but the head will wiggle separate from the body. The butt is more pointed. Oh! There she is, we've woken her." Abby's butt pushed up, stretching the confines of the RPU as she twisted to her side and tipped her head back. Theresa flinched as Abby kicked out at the side of the RPU.

"Shh, shh. Go easy on your mama. Those are some strong kicks."

Theresa's brows tipped up. *Mama. What does she...* "This *is* her going easy. You should see while I'm sleeping!"

The corners of Carla's lips twitched upwards. "That's baby witching hour."

Kendra laughed, feeling the squirming beneath her hand and smiled up at Theresa, all traces of animosity replaced with wonder. "Thank you, Theresa."

David hung back at the end of the cluster of women and Theresa beckoned him forward. "Are you sure?"

Theresa gave him a shy smile. "Well... you've been more supportive than pretty much anyone except maybe Carla. I want you to see her."

He came forward, keeping his gaze trained on the capsule and Theresa's face, and lifted a finger to press over Abby's cheek through the layer of silicone. He leaned in. "Hello, Abby."

As if in response, Abby kicked off, straining the side of her face against the capsule. The owner of the breasts she kicked clenched her teeth, struggling to maintain her composure. "She likes...your voice."

David withdrew his hand, startled, and then grinned at Theresa, tempering the smile with sympathy when he saw her pain. "Sorry."

The meeting wound down once the organized discussion transitioned organically to small side conversations and socializing. Attendees excused themselves and retired to their rooms in twos and threes, forming small clusters around Carla before taking their leave.

"Are you staying longer?" David broke his prolonged silence, looking from Theresa to Genesis. The two had fallen into their own pools of solitude despite close proximity to one another. There was a palpable tension surrounding them; the almost expressed sentiments and nearly spoken questions left faded smoke trails like rockets that had fallen back to Earth.

Theresa flinched at the sound of David's voice, eyes that had been focused on some distant train of thought clearing.

"Yes. I have questions for Carla. I'm waiting for the swarms to subside so we can speak in private."

Genesis stared, face still and expressionless. "I'm going to sleep. I have preparations to make in the morning."

David nodded. "I'll head out with you, then, if you don't mind."

David and Genesis made their way to the door, bypassing Carla and the last cluster of women exchanging farewells, waving from the doorway instead.

Theresa leaned back on the floor pillows into a semi-reclining position and closed her eyes to wait. There was just too much she wasn't ready to think about. Thoughts and questions, newly implanted, collided in her mind with what was already firmly rooted there. She squeezed her eyes shut and listened past the sounds of conversation to the Martian wind singing through the garden gates.

"Theresa." Someone shook her shoulder. "Theresa, you're asleep."

Another small shake and she was able to step out of the self-constructed whirlwind. She opened her eyes and stared as if uncertain where she was or what she was seeing.

"You fell asleep on the floor. You'll be more comfortable in your bed, I imagine."

Theresa rubbed her eyes and struggled to sit up. "I was going to ask you some questions."

"Oh?"

"I can't remember them."

Carla chuckled, sitting down next to her. "Well, you could ask later when you do remember…"

Theresa sat up farther, a frustrated scowl on her face as she struggled to recall the plethora of questions that were plaguing her before she fell asleep.

"Mmmmm...no, I just need a minute…" She stared up at the blank viewing screen, reconstructing the images recently played there, in her own mind for analysis. The fog cleared from her eyes and she nodded.

With a slant to her head and narrowed eyes, she was ready to dig in and clear out the widow-web tangles that had been growing in her thoughts.

"The woman in the clip…the women you tended to, were they all clean?"

Carla pressed her lips together, nodding. "They were, by at least three generations. That was the first thing the council took care of…Well, second thing, I guess. The first was mass sterilization. The second thing was to entirely clean the human genome within two generations."

Theresa blinked, taking in a deep breath along with the extra information that, instead of clarifying, added several more strands to the tangled web, behind which pointed black legs tapped and scrambled. Theresa shuddered at the mental image and tried to pull her focus back to the conversation at hand. *Why spiders? Ugh. Where was I?*

She looked back to Carla, the next question forming on her lips. What emerged instead was not that question. "He took out my implants." Jacob's face loomed large in her memory. <*"I was overruled."*>

"I told him to leave them in because I didn't want to worry about another pregnancy while caring for Abby."

Traitorous eyes. Never in my life have I leaked so damn much. I should have my tear-ducts removed!

She scrubbed away the moisture with the backs of her hands, brutal strokes leaving them reddened and still leaking.

"Oh." Carla's eyes clouded over, grief and anger warring within a deluge, lit by lightning strike. The older woman placed a hand on Theresa's shoulder.

"Then, that's why you came tonight. I would have preferred a less…invasive catalyst."

That made Theresa laugh, but with little humor.

"You know, when they put the implants in I was a child. Old enough to know what was being done but not old enough to question it. Or…if I did. I think I did. I asked a lot of questions generally. But it made sense, their answers, I mean.

Overpopulation dumbed down just enough for a precocious child. I never thought about what it would have been like if I had disagreed." She scowled and shook her head. "Never conceived of anyone disagreeing. They cleaned the human genome, stopped overpopulation in its tracks. They're cleaning the oceans and repopulating the animal species. What was there to argue with?"

Theresa sighed and rubbed her forehead, leaving the stress creases bunching up between her brows. "Shit! I don't even know what my problem is. I feel like…" *Spiders*. "Like a jumble of puzzle pieces with squares expected to fit with circles! I'm used to neat grids and data-blocks, dammit!" She shook her head, eyes panicked and almost pleading. "What exactly do you want from me?"

Carla squeezed Theresa's shoulder and nodded. "What do *you* want from you? That's the question. You attended the meeting for a reason. You have questions you need answered."

Theresa licked her lips, taking a breath to slow the skittering behind the webs.

"Can you give me your rates? Complications, deaths, hemorrhages, pre-terms, and that of your colleagues?"

Carla grinned. "Yes. Yes I can. I can give you several files of data, clips, and saved live-footage from way back when we were phased out." Carla rose to her feet in one fluid movement, striding over to her desk and producing a data key from within the top drawer.

"This has everything you need. It also contains the conclusions drawn at our last meeting that we would like presented to the Mars Council."

"Oh. You had this ready for tonight?" Theresa's eyes narrowed, lips twisting in confusion.

Carla gave a snort. "No, Theresa. I've had this ready for the past fifty years. Like a spider, biding my time." She laughed at herself, the sound coming out a mix between a snort and a cackle.

Theresa gaped. *Like a spider?*

"Just...Please, come to me with questions. With your decision..." The old woman frowned, and soul-deep weariness gave away the lack of youth so carefully hidden by longevity treatments.

The urgency Theresa saw in Carla's eyes made her shift her shoulders. *God, fifty years?! I can't promise her anything.*

"I'll come back with my questions before the council meeting. Okay?"

"Okay. Alright. I'll be here or the garden. Or maybe David's greenhouse." Carla patted Theresa's shoulder once more as she walked her to the door.

Theresa stepped out into the empty hallway, silence falling around her along with the warm air that prevailed in the narrow space. *It's like a cave, a spider's cave. There aren't any spiders on Mars, Theresa...only in your head.*

"You were thinking about her, weren't you, during the meeting?" They came to a stop at the end of the hall.

"Hmmm...?" David looked over at Genesis where she stood in front of her door, luminescent eyes the defining feature in the dimly-lit hall. "Her?" He squinted his eyes, leaning against the wall opposite Genesis.

"Your wife, David." Genesis's features held a look of cultivated interest that was as sharp as her tone. "Why are you so damn evasive every time she's mentioned?"

He looked down at his feet and then back up at her, still hesitating.

Genesis turned to her door with an abrupt twist of her hips and leaned in for an eye-scan. The blue light of the scanner lit her face, making her golden eyes flash white as she turned back to him.

"It's late. I'm going to bed." She stepped into the doorway as the door slid open to admit her and was stopped by David's hand on her upper arm.

"Wait. It's just not easy to talk about."

"Why don't you let me know when you're ready to talk about it. Or anything that's 'personal' or 'difficult' for that matter. Just make it after the council meeting. I'll be busy until then." Genesis peeled his hand away as he simultaneously released his grip.

"Please, stand in front of the scanner to confirm identification before entering." The voice of Genesis's security system interrupted David's train of thought.

"Okay. Okay." He took a step back, placing himself out of range of the scanner. "After the council meeting, then."

Genesis turned her back to the doorway and began undressing, starting with the outer layer of weighted clothing and then the thin shirt and leggings worn underneath. Her movements were casual, fluid, as she undressed and then turned back to face him, the last of her garments falling to the floor.

"And why don't you think about whether you are in this for sex or something else. I already gave you the green light on sex, so figure it out and stop wasting my time." She pressed the door release, allowing it to close.

David did not look away as the door slid shut, blocking the view that held his full attention, nor did he argue any further, lips gone dry, and eyes narrowed.

"Shit."

Emily walked down the domed hallway, lit from above and both sides of the floor by simple embedded track lights that extended through the thick walls to be charged by the Martian sun. *Everything is so…red.* The thought brought a smile to her lips. She trailed the fingertips of her right hand across the underside of her left arm, upwards towards her shoulder and back down to her wrist, stroking. The sensation was enlivening, as if awakening each individual cell in her body. *Delicious. How does one feel delicious?*

She blushed at her own thought. What was this? Each movement, her clothes against her skin, hair tickling the nape of her neck, even standing entirely still she had never felt so *in* herself. Each sensation radiated through her, warming her to her core. *Delicious.* The thought occurred again, bringing Emily to an abrupt stop several paces from her own door, where Jonathan would be waiting… already in bed, no doubt.

And that thought was enough. She stood trembling, fighting the urge to rush into the room and awaken him.

"What is this?" The whisper fluttered out into the empty hallway burrowing into the foot thick clay walls. This wasn't just arousal. She had felt that, yes. When the worries and stresses of a long day had fallen away after hours at home with Jonathan, a run, a shower, the lights out. She could shed inhibition along with her gown, but not like this. Not thoughts entirely unbidden emanating from her body like directives from a higher authority. No, that was too clinical. Like imperatives, for food, for sleep, but instead of some small compartmentalized basic urge, an all-encompassing desire. Delicious.

Emily touched her own lips, fingertips pressing there, as she alternated between being sensation and contemplation of it. *How long has it been like this? Six days, I think. Six very good days, or nights, rather.*

She crossed the distance to her door and, gaining entry, found that her husband was in bed as expected. She smiled noting that he had left one light on for her to find her way.

Climbing into the bed, she leaned over her husband, allowing her hair to fall into his face, tickling as she placed moist kisses on his jawline, throat.

Jonathan stirred, reaching a hand to her cheek. "Mmmm…Em?" He opened his eyes.

Emily lifted her face to his, kissing him awake, and slid one thigh over him to rest her weight there, straddling his prone form. He returned the smile, still groggy, but awake.

"You were right about Mars." He slid his fingers into Emily's hair to the back of her head.

She grinned, leaning down to kiss his chest, and breathe in his scent held in the curls of dark hair. "Was I?"

"Mmm…Very good for us."

"David Raiklin requests entry." The familiar voice of Genesis's security system woke her just as she had started the downward slide into her subconscious, like a slow sinking into the water of a still lake to the sediment-covered mossy bottom. Her eyes opened before awareness returned and the message was repeated.

"David Raiklin requests entry." Her eyes flicked to the window to confirm that the sun was indeed still sleeping, as she should be. *Interesting development.* Her thought was that of a taunted hangman adjusting the noose with sadistic pleasure. *It had better be interesting.*

"Let him in then."

Genesis leaned up in bed, propping herself on one elbow and allowing the sheets to slide down to her waist.

The door hissed open and David entered, his steps quick and energetic, eyes wide with relief.

"Genesis."

"Is it after the council meeting?" Her lips twisted in sarcasm.

He crossed the distance in two strides, answering with his lips. His mouth pressed hard against hers, tongue pushing through her slightly-parted lips before she could pull back or lean in, teeth mock biting the soft flesh of her bottom lip.

He grabbed one naked breast, covering it with his palm and squeezing. Against Genesis's lips, "Are you ready to listen, or are you going to kick me out?"

Her voice was breathy. "This doesn't seem like a conversation."

He kissed her again, longer this time, and then lifted one of her hands. She tried to withdraw it but found David's grip held.

Sliding his fingers between hers, David pinned Genesis's hand behind her head and looked down at her. Her eyes were wide, lips parted; she was off balance.

"Do you want me to talk first or…"

"If you talk right now, I'll kick you out."

"Will you kick me out afterwards, anyway?"

"I might."

He raised both brows. "I guess I don't have many options then."

"You could come back after the council meeting." Her voice mocked him, and David shook his head.

"If I come back after the council meeting you'll send me packing...this is it, if we stand a chance."

"If…" She echoed the sentiment as his mouth trailed down her neck, leaving a moist hot trail.

His lips quested downward across the soft skin of her abdomen, encouraged by her hand twisting into his hair, rough and urgent; the other, released from his grip, left pink crescent marks in his shoulder. The sharp press of Genesis's nails encouraged him, maddened him, until he was leaving light red teeth prints in her skin with each kiss.

"Yes. Mmmmm…Yes." She moaned and growled under her breath, creating something akin to a purr in response to the increasing roughness of his kisses, the tightness of his grip as his hands slid down to her ass, and his mouth reaching the triangle of fur that pointed down to the cleft between her muscular thighs.

David paused, allowing his hot breath to tease her, until she arched her back, thrashing her head and breathing in through her teeth.

He chuckled and penetrated her with his tongue, sliding it with one quick motion into the wetness that had already gathered between the petals of her vulva.

"Is that what you want?"

She growled, tightening her grip on David's hair. He laughed again.

"Mmm…say it, Genesis. Gotta be sure this isn't purposeless touching, don't I?"

She growled again. "I agreed. Remember?" Her words came out in short guttural bursts.

"Is that a yes?" David's smile was a mockery of innocence.

"Yes! Dammit!"

David covered her wet crevice with his mouth, suckling, caressing her with his tongue and lips, dipping into her as she arched against him.

She pulled him up by his hair and slid down to the front of his shirt, fingers seeking the clasps of his weighted over clothing and sliding beneath.

"Why are you dressed, dammit!" Her voice came out in one breath as if she had surfaced just long enough for that single sentence. Another breath. "Get up here!"

David stood, licking his lips, and with one hand unclasped the upper garment, allowing it to slide to the stone floor with a thud. Genesis scowled at his languorous movements and stood to close the gap between them. Sliding her fingers down the neckline of his shirt, she turned her wrists in a circular motion and pulled downward with just enough force to rip the thin fabric away from the clasps that held it together.

"You're wasting time." She hissed in his ear, nipping the lobe, and sliding her hand down into his pants.

David's hands fumbled as he undid the pants, uncaring as to whether or not she ripped them, but caring very much that this woman might decide he wasn't as interested as he was in obliging her.

Genesis grinned at the speed with which he undressed, at the skin revealed for her consumption. She placed one hand on either side of his chest.

"I want you in my mouth." She allowed her nails to slide down David's sides, leaving trails, then bent down to take him in. Suckling, she drew her tongue along the sides of his shaft. One hand gripped the muscles of his ass, the other cupping the soft tissue beneath his manhood as she took all of him.

David's head tipped back and he ran his fingers through his hair. Through sheer force of will, he lifted Genesis up, hands under her arms and pushed her back onto the bed. Her eyes glowed with excitement, with lust.

"Well played...usually once I take charge, it's entirely my game."

David shook his head as he lowered himself down between her thighs.

"Well, that sounds dull." He took a nipple into his mouth, teasing it with his teeth as he entered her, effectively ending the conversation aside from exclamations in guttural tones, and high pitched screams. If she was of a mind to care, Genesis would have been grateful for the thickness of the walls as she climaxed, hard and fast, trembling as her muscles clenched around him.

David slid one arm underneath Genesis's back and rolled over, pulling her on top of him to rest as their breathing slowed from deep and fast to a slower, more even tempo. Genesis burrowed her face into his neck, still holding him inside her and relishing the sensation.

"You can talk now." Her voice seemed to come from somewhere else and brought him back from the edges of sleep. He sighed and pulled himself more upright, shoving a pillow behind his back, without moving her off of him.

"Okay." The pause was long enough to be misconstrued as the end of conversation instead of the beginning. "We were very young when we met. I loved her and she died. I miss her every day."

Genesis leaned up to look him in the eye. "Is that what you came back to tell me? Because if that's it…I had gathered that much already."

David rubbed his forehead with one hand. "No. No, just give me a sec, okay? How much do you want to hear?"

She narrowed her eyes. "How much do you *want* me to hear?"

"All of it, I guess. Just…be patient with me. I'm not sure where to start."

"What was she like?"

David closed his eyes, trying to distance himself from the words as they came.

"Sincere. Couldn't lie worth a damn. Didn't want to. But smart. Scary smart. She gave me a run for my money even in my field, and she was assigned to Environmental Rehabilitation, totally different focus. We were both just getting started when we met, both out in the field collecting samples for entirely different reasons." He smiled, shaking his head. "There was no going back after the first date. We were married two months later. I was nineteen and she was twenty-two."

He paused, letting his breath out with a sigh and searching for the right words to continue. Genesis had lowered her head to David's chest, listening, and shivered at the sound of his heart thrumming against her ear in the absence of his voice. She grimaced, pushing away and sliding over to stretch out on the empty side of the bed; the cool sheets, crisp against her skin, elicited a smile.

He stayed on his back, resisting the urge to pull her to him.

"I guess we've entered the realm of unnecessary touching?"

"Yes." The answer was simple, tone matter-of-fact. "How did she die?"

His breath cut off in his chest at the question.

"She got pregnant. It was a fluke. She was the point one percent implant failure mentioned. It took awhile for us to realize it, because it's supposed to be virtually impossible, right? And we were busy…ignorant." David took in another breath, this one shaking on the way out.

"So when she started feeling movement and we put it all together we were just scared shitless. I mean, there were the news stories of underground implant removal. People hauled off for unauthorized breeding…Shit, we didn't want that to be us. How do you explain an impossible pregnancy, halfway through, to the Reproductive Council?"

He sat up and slid his hands into his hair, brows pulled together. "So when she started bleeding a few months later we didn't know what to do at first. It wasn't a lot, but we just didn't know what it meant."

He sucked in another breath to continue, words coming faster now. "We went to the nearest hospital and it was just like the nightmares. Joanna had been having them for months.

"They strapped her down on a gurney and rushed her into the building while I was detained outside. She was calm until they separated us, really until she saw them bind my arms." David's jaw tightened. "Then she just started begging them, over and over as they strapped her down. Didn't fight them, just over and over. 'Let him come with me. It was an accident. I'm so sorry, David. Please, just let him come with me.' Until they knocked her out with something."

Genesis stood and walked to the window, turning to listen from a distance, arms folded across her chest where she leaned. David looked across the room at her, meeting her eyes for the first time, and she flinched at the raw anguish she saw there, the unmasked version of the shadows that hovered in his eyes so often.

"I lost it. Shouldn't have done that." He laughed, the sound rough and humorless. "Kicked the nearest guy right in the crotch, then in the face when he doubled over. I think I broke something, the way the blood gushed on his white shirt." His smile was cold and hard. "I'm glad Joanna didn't see it. It would have scared her, hurt her I guess. Could have been a damn bird and she would have cried for it. I didn't see her again."

He crossed the room to the fountain for water and filled a whole glass, emptying it in three long gulps without coming up for air until it was empty. Refilling the glass, he strode over and handed it to Genesis.

"They said she bled to death when I woke up…they had knocked me out, I think. She and the baby…before they could get them into the operating room, even." He clapped his hands together, the sound making her jump with the force of it.

"Just like that." David shook his head and looked askance at Genesis, distaste curling his lips.

He doesn't believe it. It is a bit farfetched.

He paced towards the bed pausing there a moment to stare down at it and then turned back to Genesis, clenching one hand into a fist. "They can regrow limbs. Synthesize human blood or milk in a sheep's body, heal broken bones in a week's time. But they couldn't stop a slow bleed? Couldn't stop her bleeding? She wasn't bleeding that fucking much!"

Genesis stared at him as tears wet his cheeks and he sank to the bed. It was several moments before he raised his eyes back to hers, and she was still formulating the appropriate response. She phrased and rephrased, opening her mouth once and then stopping short.

"Thank you for telling me." The sound of her own heartbeat was loud in her ears, foreign and disturbing. "I'm sorry that happened." Her voice sounded stiff and unnatural to her ears. *Was that appropriate?*

David closed his eyes and nodded, inhaling through his nostrils. Not the response she expected; she searched for some other social convention to fit this situation, trying this and that one out in her head, each one feeling hollow and inadequate. *Well, it's not like he expects empathy, or even sympathy. Fuck it!*

She abandoned the search for a correct response.

"I think you're right. They probably lied. I could confirm it for you, find records if they exist." Her voice rose, filling with excitement at the prospect of vengeance on his behalf.

His brows arched together, and he laughed, rising and crossing to where she stood, her eyes alight with cunning.

Wrapping his arms around her back, David pulled her against him and stared into her golden eyes, so different from Joanna's soft green ones. He leaned down to kiss her, but stopped short.

"That sounds very sincere…and almost sweet coming from you." His lips touched hers, gentler than before. "You can if you want…but I don't want to know anymore. If she's alive, she's on Earth and has lived without me for the past twenty years. If she's not…if they killed her, I can't take it back. As for retribution, I don't see what you could do from here."

Genesis shrugged and pulled up on tip-toe to reach his lips again.

"You'd be surprised."

ALLIES

Theresa walked through the greenhouse, tucking stray hairs back up into her bun as she went, following the sounds of rustling plant leaves.

"We're in the central dome!" David's voice was louder than necessary. She approached from the left, emerging from between two rows of bean plants.

Carla turned at the sound of Theresa's footfalls, a smile spreading to her cheeks, only her eyes giving any hint of worry.

"Give it to me straight, Theresa, before my old heart gives out."

Theresa snorted. "Your heart's probably in better shape than mine at this juncture. But since I haven't been able to sleep and I've used up my coffee rations for the week, I'll try not to be circuitous."

Carla's mouth fell open and she blinked several times. "Oh, well then, why don't we sit down and talk? I didn't expect you to go over all of that in one night, you know. Two, maybe, but not one."

Theresa waved away the concern. "Cognitive dissonance is a bitch, right? And I'd rather not sleep wrapped in widow-web as I toss and turn. So I swept them out instead, squashed them, most of them anyway." Her voice came rapid fire, one thought colliding with the next like train cars overtaking one another on the tracks.

"We should speak in private, shouldn't we?" Theresa gestured towards David where he stood trimming dead leaves from an otherwise healthy plant.

Carla turned and stared at David, hands on her hips, lips pressed tight. "No. I think David needs to hear it. He's gonna hear it at the council meeting and needs to decide where he stands. Better beforehand so I can count my votes, so to speak."

"You might not like everything I have to say."

The old woman nodded her head, withholding reaction. "Just lay it on me then."

"Okay, so. The way I see it, the Reproductive Council's policies were a necessary reaction to rampant disease and extreme overpopulation; the human race was breeding itself out of space and resources, but was, by and large, sickly and dying young. Also, a logical progression of technological advancement in the field of obstetrics. Take the RPU...capable of saving progeny born anytime in the second or third trimesters, or the advancements in Caesarean technique with the Caesarean Access Panel, in and out in a matter of minutes without the risk of hemorrhage or adhesions." Carla was silent, listening with chin resting in her hand.

"So my reaction is two-fold, really. We took it too far, threw out the baby with the bathtub so to speak...is that how you say that?...and probably lost something. In my research...I've encountered the concern that without the maternal host, progeny cannot develop as intended."

Carla opened her mouth as if to speak and then, clamping her lips shut, rested a hand there instead, arms folded.

Theresa paused to catch a breath and gauge Carla's reaction. "I'm on board for stepping back a couple hundred years in terms of reproductive rights, placing it in the hands of the hosts." She noticed Carla's grimace at her choice of terms. "Women. But not without getting the obstetrics team on board with my reproductive technologies available for emergency support."

David cleared his throat and Theresa looked over to where he stood, working just a moment before, closer now, with arms crossed and dark eyes on her. "A couple hundred years? Doesn't that put us right back into the midst of chaos? A free fall into overpopulation, and that in a small colony with limited resources?"

Theresa grinned, her excitement overtaking the dark circles under her eyes. "See, that's the beauty of it! I watched Carla's live history clips. The quality's bad but they go way back...and cover things the Reproductive Council leaves out." Theresa pulled down on the edges of her top. "Yes, reproduction was unregulated and rampant...but not because people intended it or even couldn't help it. The culture of the times encouraged over-breeding, used progeny as status symbols; factions forced their numbers higher through procreation to outnumber dissenting opinions, poverty, lack of reliable birth control, abortion illegal. I mean, I could go on all day on the myriad of causes, but the short of it was that humanity was just stuck, overpopulating as if hell-bent on its own extinction. We don't have that now. Poverty, misogyny, war are non-issues for us, so if we start out right this time…I think that's what Carla was trying to get me to see, anyway."

Theresa paused, appearing to have reached the end of her report. "Wow, that was pretty circuitous. Was I clear with any of that?"

Carla dipped her head, the right corner of her mouth upturned. "Sure, I got it. But with that kind of language…not the history lesson, but your thoughts on getting the obstetrics team on board. Unless you can give them all a full-on paradigm shift, they'll only hinder us. With compromise, we start out already on the slippery slope to recreating hell-from-Earth-here-on-Mars. By all that's holy, I just can't watch that again."

Carla shook her head slowly. "Anytime there is a council over women, it will start trumping their choices, their rights. Did you look over the list of demands? Can you bring that to the Mars council, present it to them? Can you endorse it?"

Theresa spread her hands, looking from Carla to David. She wet her lips.

"Yes. I can. But it's going to turn into a negotiation quickly. I can't picture Jacob Emory or the others in the medical department agreeing to all of it. Like the Caesarean access panels, for one. No medical professional in their right mind would consent to removal when the patient intends to conceive again." Theresa's eyes held a preemptive apology.

"But the access panel is *your* technology. Can't you come up with a feasible plan for removal and recovery and what not, and pitch it to them?"

Theresa bit her lip, moving her head in a figure eight as she tried to pin herself down to an answer without the usual research and advance planning it would require. "Um, it's…possible, sure. I can look into that."

"It won't work." Genesis's voice carried across the central dome from the arched entryway where she stood, listening.

The three looked over, startled by the sudden appearance. "Did we miss the announcement?" David directed his question at his two companions.

Genesis sauntered over, joining the group. "No, I made friends with your security system. But, as I said, it won't work the way you're planning it." She smiled. "What you are playing at is a grab for power, but you're handing them the reins right off the bat."

All three pairs of eyes were now on Genesis, and her smile grew in brightness under the attention. Theresa opened her mouth twice and the third time found her missing voice. "We can't circumvent the Mars Council before it's even established. The colony would fall into chaos!"

Genesis laughed, the sound full of excitement. "I'm not suggesting we circumvent. But I know a thing or two about power plays." She gave David a meaningful glance. "If we start from a place of assumed power they will have little choice, and even if we choose to negotiate we will keep the upper hand."

Carla's full focus was now on Genesis. "I'm listening. What do you have in mind?"

"What does the Mars colony need to sustain itself? Something that we have control over?" Genesis looked from one to the other, continuing before her three listeners could make any suggestions. "Theresa is developing a user-controlled form of female birth control. The women of the community can refuse to conceive progeny so long as it is not on their terms, assuming they are as united as you suggest."

A sharp whistle came from where David stood watching the exchange. He folded both hands into fists and knocked them together in front of his chest. "That's likely to make the more obstinate on the council lock up and refuse to cave."

Theresa's eyes were wide. "I'm still testing it though, and what if Jacob informs the Earth Council and gets them involved?"

Genesis shrugged. "By the time Earth could *actually* get involved we would have the problem resolved on our own. David makes a good point though. A slower build would get better results, smoother. Each council member could be paired up with someone from our cause, to determine their position on the matter and groom them to accept our terms once we present them."

"This is sounding complicated." Theresa frowned. "I don't do subterfuge well."

All three sets of eyes turned to the RPU concealed under Theresa's shirt, staring and incredulous.

Theresa sighed. "I mean with people. I don't do well with one-on-one deception."

Genesis rolled her eyes, lips sneering. "Grow a spine, Theresa! Do you want the council deciding what direction your research into reproductive technology should take? Do you want them deciding at what age and with whom Abby performs every Martian woman's duty to produce progeny? The head of our Department of Medicine removed your implants without consent! Do you want him to continue to feel justified in his actions?"

Theresa's eyes sparked with anger, her nails making half-moons in her palms. "No. I just don't want this getting back to the Earth Council."

"Well. Then you had better work on your diplomacy and take a vested interest in how this plays out. Because it is happening, isn't it, Carla? I've chosen my side."

Theresa inhaled, looking from Genesis to Carla and then to David. "Why don't we go install your implants, Genesis?"

Genesis smiled, and with a nod, strode towards the exit. "I'll be in touch with you, Carla." Theresa took up a slow, awkward jog to catch up with her at the door, leaving David and Carla staring after them.

"She's…somethin' that one." Carla shook her head, trying to maintain some doubt to ground her against the wild hope flapping drunkenly within the walls of her chest.

David snorted. "Yeah, something. She is that, isn't she?"

She turned her stare to David, who was still gazing off at the empty space left by Genesis and Theresa. "You and Genesis, huh?"

David blinked, turning to face her. "Something like that." His smile was small and uncertain. "Maybe."

Carla nodded, biting her lip. "Can I ask you something?"

"We have several more transplants to do here, so ask away."

She bit back the urge to ask a leading question. "Where will you stand at the council meeting?"

"You need to open up your meetings to the whole colony. Get everyone involved." He scratched his neck. "Yeah, I know that's not what you asked. I'll stand with you on this if it comes down to a fight, but let's see what we can do to avoid that, huh?"

Carla smiled, reaching out a hand to pat his shoulder and turned her attention to the seedling in front of her.

Genesis reached for Jacob's personal handheld to sync it to her own. "Did you cover any and all developments within the colony, health status, pregnancies, et cetera? The Reproductive Council doesn't appreciate having to ask for more data once they've made it clear what they want reported."

"Yes, yes. I think so." A look of concern, indecision crossed Jacob's pointed features. "There was one matter that concerned me, as it were." He fumbled with the headset he had used to record his report. "The Head of Reproductive Technology."

"Theresa?" She gave him her full attention.

"Yes, Theresa. She objected quite strenuously to having her implants removed and implied that she would be speaking with Morton in the Reproductive Council from now on. Something about a proposal for birth control on Mars? Is that accurate? Doesn't she report to you as well?"

Genesis blinked, inhaling through her teeth and shaking her head. "Unfortunately not, Jacob. She reports directly to Morton Steiner. If I were in your position, I would be careful of Theresa. The birth control program she is proposing is already in the works; she has been cleared to make a proposal on it at the upcoming council meeting."

"Shit. What is that woman thinking?"

Genesis smiled, leaning in close enough for him to smell orange and cinnamon. "The same thing you're thinking. It's entirely a political move on her part."

Jacob's eyes widened and were locked to hers as Genesis spoke. "Whoever founds a Reproductive Council branch on Mars and acquires endorsement from the council on Earth, as well as the Mars colony, will hold the reins. Why would you be the only one to have thought of that?"

She stood and gathered her jacket, sliding on the sleeves and pressing a hand at the juncture to activate the magnetic closure.

Jacob pushed a hand through his hair, squeezing his lips with the other. His gaze slid from her face to the ceiling, eyes hard.

"It's unfortunate, really…that you didn't think of it first. You are going to have a hell of a fight if you go against Theresa, but if you don't, you're forfeiting your chance at heading the Reproductive Council on Mars."

She paused at the door and turned back. "Let me know if you need any help." Smiling, she exited through the side door into the garden, the wind pulling her hair up into twisting snakes.

"MmmMmm…Mmmm…Mmmmmm…Mmm. Baby I'ma' comin' through." Kendra's voice resonated, filling the stone room with her sweet contralto vibrato. Stepping across her own path as she crossed the small space, she exaggerated the sway of her hips, sliding her leggings down rounded thighs and flipping them behind her with a flick of her toes.

"I do know other songs, you know…" She rested her arms on Neil's shoulders, crossing her wrists behind his head and sitting, one leg on either side of his.

"I like that one. It brought us down safely, after-all."

Sadness filled her eyes, and she looked away. "Mostly."

Neil winced, placing a hand on her soft cheek and turning her face. "Hey. I'm sorry. I know we didn't all make it through... I just..."

She shook her head. "It's alright. I know you didn't mean it like that. I just miss her, is all." The smile that she gave him was a mixture of grief and bravery. "I'm used to it being the three of us...I wish it wasn't her, but I'm glad it wasn't me, I guess...that sounds awful."

The captain smiled, placing a kiss on her mauve-colored lips. "No, it doesn't. It sounds normal...I'm glad it wasn't you too."

Kendra allowed a soft laugh to escape her lips. "Well I am straddling you, so that's good to hear..." She mimicked his crooked grin, pushing her grief aside. "Where were we headed, now?"

"You were about to sing to me...and I might like that even better if you sing it again right here on my lap."

"Oh, is that how it is?" She laughed. "I might be able to do that. If you lose a few layers, that is." She toyed with the magnetic clasps on the captains weighted shirt.

He slid a hand between the edges of the fabric, breaking the contact between the two sides and shrugged his shoulders out of the sleeves.

"How's this?"

"Hmph. I said a few layers didn't I?" Kendra crossed her arms on her chest and leaned back, to look askance at him.

"If you insist." With one hand Neil pulled his undershirt over his head and with his other he shifted Kendra closer, pressing her against his chest, now bare.

She placed one hand on his exposed skin. "That's better, then, isn' it? Now I can sing again."

"Isn't this a little imbalanced though?"

Captain Neil gave a half smile, slipping one hand under the bottom edge of the light yellow undershirt she wore. Kendra's hand shot down to push his away and pull the shirt back in place over her lower abdomen.

"Uh-uh. This stays on."

Neil pulled his hand away and looked at her, worry etching his face.

"What is it? What did I do?"

"Nothing. It's not you. Just...the shirt stays on." Her eyes flicked away and then back to his, an apologetic frown crossing her face.

"Okay. I can respect that, but, why?" His look was perplexed.

"I was a surrogate, you know that. It's...not all me under there, and I don't want that between us, don't wanna' think about it."

He squinted, not quite understanding. "What do you mean, the scars or...?"

She sighed. "If it was just scars it'd be no worries. But I've still got the council's hardware in me..." Kendra stood up and took a seat and few feet away from him. She shuddered, trying to decide on a better explanation. "An access panel, Neil. You don't want to see it and I don't wanna talk about it. It gives me nightmares and it'll give you the creeps."

"It wouldn't bother me, really...I know about the access panels... after what...I mean, I don't care if you..." Neil paused to search for words.

"Yes. It would bother you. I liked you feeling all sexy a minute ago. Knowing and seeing are two different things altogether." She looked him in the eye, the steel of her gaze giving no room for argument. "We can either keep the shirt on or wait for another time. Get together once they've taken this thing out of me."

"Is that what they're going to do?" He looked genuinely curious, though doubtful.

"They are if they have any sense." She set her jaw. "I won't be a part of any colonization effort if it's not on my terms. Either I'll bring a baby through on my own steam or not at all."

"Okay. Alright. Why don't we speak with the head of the Medical Department tomorrow? See what he says about it. There must be a reason for leaving it in..." Neil fell short of hiding the distaste in his tone.

"I told you it would creep you out." Kendra lowered her eyelids half-mast and looked away. "How would you feel if it were you? An easy access port to your insides permanently embedded in those nice tight abs so they could pull out a bit a' Neil every so often.

His lips curled in disgust at the mental imagery. "Well, if I needed a prosthetic I'd take it. I mean, medicine is there for a reason."

"Well, I wouldn't. Not for this. I'm not very good at explaining the kind of knowing that comes from your gut, but I just know there's another way for me, and if there isn't then I'd prefer *no* progeny to this way." She pulled the bottom edge of her shirt down even lower lest it rise up without her knowledge.

"Look, if there's a better way, then I'm all for it. Let's just talk to the Medical Department tomorrow. It's what they do right?"

Kendra shook her head and licked her lips. "Sure. Why don't we just do that? We'll do it after the Council meeting."

Theresa allowed herself to slump back against the wall, rubbing a hand across her eyes to ease the gritty stinging sensation, and let out a sigh. *I'll be damned if I'm the cause of our failure. At least now it's in their hands.* She turned to where Genesis sat staring at her.

"Forty-four contraceptive implants installed in seven hours…and three early pregnancies detected." Theresa gave a weak smile. "Are you ready for the first phase of tests? Just to get base-line data for further research."

Genesis stared at her, a half smile on her lips. "This can wait until tomorrow, you know, so that you can sleep, rest…avoid falling into an exhaustion-induced coma." She made a palm up gesture, splaying her fingers as if showcasing Theresa's options.

Theresa sat up and pushed off to stand, placing one hand on the wall to steady herself when the curtain of darkness threatened to descend over her eyes. *It's getting harder again. Maybe I need to change something. See Carla about it. What do I have? Five more weeks maybe.*

Once the vertigo receded, Theresa moved with a bit more caution and went up on tip-toe in front of her storage shelf to collect a translucent helmet.

"No. I'll rest once this is done. I have you here now and it won't take long. We'll get some brain scans at resting and in response to stimuli, as well as auxiliary information: pulse, BP, perspiration."

Genesis shrugged and sat down in front of Theresa to make putting the helmet on easier. "Whatever you think you need." Tucking her hair behind her ears, she frowned. "I have a concern, though; how will we keep things on track once this is all sorted out?"

Theresa squinted her eyes, glancing away from the helmet she was adjusting and over to where Genesis sat. "Once what is sorted out?"

Genesis tilted her head one way and then the other. "Reproductive rights on Mars. How can we ensure that the protocols, or rights, as Carla would put it, we set up aren't gradually eroded and that your technologies are used as intended?"

Theresa scratched her cheek. "I don't know. I haven't really thought about it…I mean, I'm sure Carla has some plans for that?"

"Maybe, but I don't think she is thinking that far, and without someone standing guard over the rights we want to secure, how can we be sure they won't eventually be undermined. You worked in the Reproductive Council on Earth. How did they make sure that what they put in motion stuck?"

Theresa tucked the helmet, now glowing with a criss-cross grid of red light under one arm, and looked down to think. "They made sure of it. They made committees for committees and protocols to cover protocols. They made sure their technology was tamper-proof, prosecuted anyone who managed to tamper with it…" She took in a breath and shook her head. "And they had strong leadership."

Genesis's brows tipped together as she mirrored Theresa's head-shake, and threw up one hand in frustration. "We couldn't really do that here on Mars, though…"

"Huh. Well, why not? So long as we set up preservation of reproductive autonomy as the core principle, a Reproductive Council on Mars could help us avoid the kinds of problems that the council was created to solve on Earth, as well as the problems you brought up."

Genesis's eyes widened as she looked up at Theresa settling the helmet over her skull.

"You surprise me every time we come to a challenge. Honestly. I just wouldn't have expected you to volunteer to take something like that on."

Theresa pulled back as if bitten.

"I don't know that I would be the right one to hold a position like that…" Her face scrunched up at the thought of leading a council.

"Well, there's Jacob Emory, I guess. He is head of the Medical Department, so he would be an equally fitting choice. I'm not sure that would be in our best interests, though."

Theresa blinked, a grimace of distaste flashing across her lips as she keyed in the programming sequence to begin scanning Genesis's brain. "Well, *that's* not happening. I'd rather sell myself to the Council for live research than see him head up anything."

"I'm tired all the time. Getting dizzy, fuzzy gray spots when I stand up too fast, I'm itching all over…my upper back is killing me. I get numb, tingling spots between my shoulder blades when I sit upright, and headaches. I've got one now, in fact." Theresa slumped against Carla's wall, where she sat on a floor cushion, and closed her eyes, her face gaunt and bloodless. "She's still growing now, though. Oh, and everyone's new implants are in place, by the way, user-controlled. The implant attracts and holds the egg until it's no longer viable, preventing fertilization and implantation…so as long as…"

"Are you still eating, Theresa?" Carla sat down next to her, pressing a tall glass of red-colored smoothie into the other woman's hand.

"I am. Just as we discussed before, religiously even." She lifted the glass to her lips without opening her eyes. "Mmmmm." She sighed, raising it again for a gulp this time instead of a sip.

Carla smiled, still holding onto the lines of worry around her eyes. "But have you increased? You've upped your work load, based on what you've told me, and this is the last trimester. As of right now the RPU data shows a calorie deficit. You aren't as bad off as before, but we don't want you on your ass by the end of this. Abby is only going to be demanding more from you from this point on, and you've clearly lost weight. Unless we take her out early."

Theresa shook her head, opening her eyes to meet Carla's concerned gaze. "Uh-uh. She's staying in here until the end as long as she's still growing and I'm still breathing."

Carla licked her lips. "Okay then. What are you planning to do to make sure all those things keep happening for four more weeks?"

"Eat more. Definitely more of these drinks. We can request another increase to my rations. I'd promise to sleep more, but that hasn't been working so well."

"Well, the food and the overwork should be an easy fix for you then. What is it with your sleep? Insomnia, worry, nightmares, getting kicked in the ribs all night?"

"All of the above."

Carla snorted. "Well, let's start with the worries then. Number one?"

"I think you know the top worries and stressors. So how about after she's out. I've never seen this work...I mean..." Theresa shook her head, floundering for the words.

"Mothering?"

"Sort of? And what if I have no milk...what if my body doesn't respond to the RPU's preparations? I haven't had the influence of the hormones for a full pregnancy and there's nothing else here for her."

"You told me your breasts are sore, that they've changed. That means they're prepping to make milk. And with the RPU, your milk is set to start coming in just as she's ready to come out instead of just after."

Theresa scowled as she took the last gulp of Carla's concoction. "Maybe I'm just sore from being kicked incessantly."

The midwife smiled, shaking her head as she took Theresa's glass for a refill. "Most likely six of one, half a dozen of the other, but you'll know when it happens."

"So you say." Theresa rolled onto her side, trying to find a more comfortable position. *Zero-G sounds good about now.*

Returning, Carla sat down next to the younger woman's resting form, and pressed the glass into her shaking hand. "Is this your fear talking or your inner knowing?"

Theresa laughed mid-gulp, choking on the viscous fluid and turning incredulous eyes to the older woman. "Inner knowing? What does that even mean?"

Carla sighed. "Alright, if we need to keep this scientific then, is your worry stemming from amorphous and baseless fears or a collection of unbiased observations pertinent to the situation, with proper control variables, compiled to form a well-founded and complete picture of the issue?"

Theresa blinked, staring at the other woman for long moments. "You know, it's a lot harder to think...critically...when *my* physical body is involved, as opposed to being an outside observer."

Carla snorted. "Yeah...that's where inner knowing comes in, but you could use a bit of your science brain to sort out fear from fact. Why don't you try hand-expressing some colostrum from your breasts to see what's there? Might ease the worry some, and you can save it for her in cold storage."

Theresa looked deep in thought, fatigue deepening the lines in her forehead as she struggled into a sitting position, taking care not to bump Abby's capsule with her arms or knees.

Carla stood, looking around the room for several more pillows and depositing them in Theresa's reach with a smile. "It can wait, though."

Grabbing three more of the pillows, Theresa tucked them strategically to support her in a position that wouldn't crush Abby, then closed her eyes with a deep sigh. "Okay, later then."

The council room was the largest dome in the complex, central to the circle of interconnected geo-domes like the hub of a wheel. A stage was surrounded by raised tiers of immobile stone benches, a smaller version of the Roman Parthenon on Earth, and held a semi-circle of seats with a control console in the center.

A thick blanket of early morning sea-fog hovered just above the small arched windows, shifting with shadows in the wind, but the colonists within were warmed by the heat from the previous days sun still seeping out of the walls. A low din ebbed and flowed through the crowd of eighty-nine Martians awaiting the ten who would represent them at this first council meeting since their arrival on Mars.

Theresa sat, one hand in her lap, the other on her hand-held as she reviewed her notes for the portion of the meeting she would present. Her hands felt restless in her lap and, in an old unconscious gesture, she smoothed invisible stray hairs that could have fallen from her tight bun. Self-conscious of the gesture, she turned to the front row of the outer circle of colonists where Carla sat and found the sharp blue eyes of the midwife light with humor. Carla gave a small nod to her worried smile.

A voice from Theresa's left spoke low enough that it would carry no further than her ears. "The pieces are set. All you need to do is knock them down." She glanced over at Genesis.

She wasn't there for my last presentation. I think the only one I knocked down was myself. She stifled a laugh that wouldn't have conveyed humor so much as desperation. *Hold it together, Theresa.*

The semi-circle was filling up; the Departments of Engineering and Justice were the last two unrepresented within the circle.

Genesis looked out at the assembled colonists to gauge the atmosphere and, after a moment's contemplation, pulled out her hand-held device and synced it to the audio system. Stepping up to the edge of the central stage, she sat down with her legs hanging over and nodded to her audience.

"I don't remember most of my dreams. Some people, every night they have these elaborate stories in their heads." Genesis paused, waiting as she collected smiles, nods, murmurs of recognition.

"So when I do remember a dream, it's a big one, something I know is gonna come up in real time…or, if I think about it long enough, reveal something important I've been trying to figure out. And then there's the recurring dream. I've had it every few years since the first time…I was five, I think."

She spoke in slow measured tones, every word pregnant with meaning, and every set of eyes on her. "I'm walking down a tunnel, an abandoned subway tunnel, and I can hear water dripping, the scratching of rats in the side tunnels." Her eyes stared out, shimmering as if seeing the scene she described before her. "I know exactly where I'm going and I hurry, faster and faster. No matter how many times I have the dream I feel fear rising, growing into panic, as I get closer."

Genesis swung her feet, heels colliding with the edge of the platform, with the nervous energy of early childhood. "There's a door at the end of the tunnel blocked by rocks. I cut my hands on them, but still lift them and throw them behind me, one after another, until the path is clear."

The tension gathered between her brows…and then cleared, giving way to a smile that could only be seen as radiant.

"It's a forest, greener than I've ever seen outside of textbooks, and teeming with wildlife. The smell of the rain is fresh and clean. It's my safe place. I never want to wake up when I'm there."

She paused again, allowing time for each listener to picture, savor what she described. "I dreamt I was there again last night. I broke into a run. I threw the rocks, red this time before my blood smeared there, but when I opened the door the scene was different. The green crashed against great red and black rocks, foaming and spraying against my cheeks. The sand was red between my toes, and the smell was salt, algae, the rusty tang of iron, and the bitter spice of wet lichen." Genesis breathed in, as if filling her lungs with the scents she described.

"I've had this dream my whole life. Always the same. And even last night the dream was unchanged." She slid her eyes across the crowd, making eye contact with as many as she could.

"It was my safe place, still. On Mars."

There were several laughs of surprise from the audience, smiling colonists turned to one another to recount snippets of their dreams since they had arrived on Mars. In the center circle Theresa and David exchanged looks, wry smiles.

David raised both brows, leaned in to Theresa, and shook his head. "The way they lap up her every word…

She nodded and pulled her lip between her teeth. Genesis's control of the crowd was far from a comfort; instead, it burrowed in to commune with the unease growing in her mind. *'Abby and I will be great friends.' Isn't that what Genesis had said?*

Genesis stood, smoothing her clothing back in place and smiled out at the colonists, *her* colonists, before taking the seat between Theresa and David, turning a satisfied smile to each of them in turn.

David spoke under his breath. "I thought you didn't dream."

She patted David's hand once and gave him a smile. "I don't."

Eli and Melissa, the heads of Bioengineering and Justice, arrived together, flustered; they hurried to their places within the inner circle, ducking their heads in simultaneous greeting and apology.

Captain Neil clapped his hands together. "Well, it looks like we're all here now." He gave a pointed look at the latecomers. "So I'll call the first Council meeting of the Mars colony to order." Whoops of approval and excitement came from the outer circle of colonists attending.

"Now, this isn't a ball game, so let's try to keep that to a minimum once we get started...But, you know what, let's give ourselves a big long cheer for our strong start on Mars." The room was instantly filled with cheers and applause, shouts and laughter. Jubilation swept through the crowd with such force that it would have been pointless to do anything but wait it out before continuing.

"Alright, Now I think we're ready to get down to the bare-bones here, the politics, if-you-will, of forming a colony. First order of business is to set in motion the search for candidates to officially head up the Mars Leadership Council. As you know, I'm the current leader by virtue of my position as Captain of the ship that brought us here. At the next council meeting, my position will be open to other colonists with strong leadership skills and a vision for our future."

There were murmurs of disapproval from the colonists, the shaking of heads, and a few spoke out of turn.

"Well, thank you for your loyalty." Captain Neil inclined his head to the outer circle. "I'll still be a candidate, so the decision will be in your hands." He nodded and looked around the inner semi-circle.

"Second order of business. Each of you will present your current progress and concerns within your departments so that we can open up for council discussion and decision-making. We'll start with the latecomers, Bioengineering and then Justice.

Eli took the floor, a full foot shorter than Captain Neil, having yet to reach his full growth. With the press of a button, he synced his handheld device to the audio system and the large screens circling the room filled up with footage from the bioengineering lab. Large petri dishes held pulsing red tissues, growing before their eyes through time-lapse. The images were quickly transposed with ones of cold tanks filling slowly with the self-same tissues, frozen solid for long-term storage. Eli set the footage to loop.

"We are on target to ease up on rationing of lab-grown meat products within three months. A rationing system will still be necessary to ensure we don't eat through the stores too quickly. Buuuut... assuming our calculations hold, we will have enough in storage so that every colonist can expect a daily ration of meat, and we'll be able to keep enough in storage to sustain us for six months should a shut-down in production occur. Copacetic, right?"

He paused to catch his breath for the first time, smiling at the other council members for approval. There was a preponderance of approving grins.

Captain Neil nodded. "Well done, Eli; well done."

Theresa touched the screen of her hand-held, making it emit a light *tinging* sound, and all eyes turned in her direction.

"Eli, have you accounted for the increase in necessary protein intake for pregnant colonists? It is possible that half of the colony will have increased needs within our first year."

Eli blushed. "Well, um, I...er. No, I didn't think of that. I did calculate for an increase in population, though, so we're half-way there. Maybe you could send me the numbers. It'll push back the timeline for easing-up the rationing, though." He glanced over at the Captain. "Thought I'd covered all the bases...body-size, activity level, illness...sorry about that."

The Captain gave him a half-smile. "Don't feel bad about being corrected by other experts. We aren't, any of us really, used to reproductive things...except for Theresa."

Jacob Emory's hand-held indicated he wanted the floor. "It really is more within the domain of the Medical Department, I would think." Jacob raised a quizzical brow at Theresa where she sat on the edge of her seat.

"Don't you specialize in Reproductive *Technologies*? Not the *physiology* of reproduction?"

Theresa looked down, and then, tightening her lips, met his gaze. "Actually, my specialty requires that I know everything pertaining to reproduction and then some." She held Jacob's stare, unblinking, until he broke eye contact and then turned back to face center.

Captain Neil looked from one council member to the other, unsure of the cause of tension he felt or the meaning of their exchange. "Right then. If you're finished, we'll move on to the Justice Department with Melissa Espinosa."

Eli took his seat, and Melissa took control of the viewing screens with a much less visceral display. A large chart filled the screen, rows of offenses categorized and matched up with the proposed corrections. Therapeutic reeducation and mandated training sessions in morality and interpersonal interaction skills, problem solving, and emotional intelligence were the primary corrective measures she described. Her report took into consideration the success of therapeutic reeducation on Earth and the resulting low crime rates in the past century.

"The only new concept that the Mars Justice Department would like to consider may be a bit hard to swallow for some."

Her hands trembled before she clasped them together, but the steel in her eyes held firm. "Should reeducation and therapy fail repeatedly in cases of murder, torture, or treason, we propose that the only recourse we have is re-sterilization and exile. We have a fresh start on Mars. We don't want to allow diseases from Earth to follow us here and undermine that."

Melissa closed out the charts on the viewing screen and sat back in her seat, surrounded by the silence her proposal triggered.

Captain Neil took in the stunned silence, the gaping mouths, and cleared his throat. "I'm going to suggest that we put the Justice Department's proposal on hold until the next council meeting, where the council can vote at that time." He rapped on his podium with both fists while thinking. "Alright, the Medical Department followed by the Department of Horticulture, and then we'll break for lunch."

Murmurs and sighs of relief broke through the heavy atmosphere in the chamber. Brian's voice rose up from the back row, a low mumble just loud enough to get attention from the otherwise quiet gathering. "Here's hoping horticulture can bring back my appetite if Doc Emory kills it." His assertion was greeted by scattered laughter and shaking heads. The Captain cracked a smile but raised a hand to gesture for silence. "Alright now, let's give our next speaker full attention. Jacob?" He glanced over to the physician's seat on the bench, and raised his brows. Jacob was already standing with his hand-held device, ready to take the floor. "They're all yours now."

The head of the Medical Department nodded and turned to the viewing screen, lifting his hand-held closer to his face. "Display Visual A3, Colony Health Analysis." He faced the assembled colonists, smiling out at them as the screen behind him filled with a large graph. "As you can see…" He gestured with one hand. "Our two weeks in space affected all body systems." A collection of 3-D images of translucent men and women replaced the graph and filled the wall-sized screen, rotating to display all sides. Circulatory, muscular, skeletal, respiratory, all systems were represented and each one presented the effects of zero-G on the colonists' bodies. Blood pooled and collected, moving in the sluggish fashion of clogged freeways, muscle tissues thinned and shrunk before their eyes, bones took on a porous quality as if a single fall could crumble them.

"Despite the ravages of zero-G, we are recovering nicely. Lung capacity, muscle strength, and bone density are all improving steadily. Immune system functions that were also impaired during our transit are now approaching normal levels." The translucent colonists' body functions mirrored Jacob's words, blood and lymph flow taking up normal transfer rates, bones thickening, muscles swelling back to respectable size.

Jacob held his position on the floor, nodding, the smile expanding across his face as he waited for the collective exclamations of relief and excitement to dissipate. "Our retraining regimen is paying off nicely thanks to the Captain's, er—persistent—hiking schedule, the use of weighted garments, adequate nutrition and the salutary effects of Mars gravity. We are adapting well. In fact…" Jacob gave a flourish of one skilled hand for emphasis. "As of this morning, the whole colony has a clean bill of health and full medical team authorization to procreate at will. Of course, appointments have been made for all females of breeding age to be examined for early pregnancy…" A small laugh escaped his lips. "Can't really expect a whole colony cooped up in space and then released onto the surface with reproductive freedom to wait for authorization." Laughter erupted throughout the room.

"Now, that said, any and all pregnancies will be closely monitored to ensure success in our new environment. We expect a higher rate of breech births on Mars due to the lower level of gravity and, whether or not that holds true, we are fully equipped to install access panels after each delivery to ease subsequent births."

Theresa stared down at her hands on the council bench, lips pressed together. A quick glance out at the assembled colonists revealed similar closed off expressions on many of the women's faces as they tried to look anywhere except at Jacob. Carla stared straight at the man with a slight shake of her head, lips turned down in a frown.

"To wrap up the Medical Department's presentation, I'd like to touch on weighted garment compliance. We're at around 75% and that's not bad, but we can do better. While it may seem inconvenient or nonessential now that we're on Mars, the weighted clothing is intended to prevent loss of bone density." He scratched the end of his nose, glancing around to collect the eyes of the room full of wayward patients. "If we need to return to Earth in the event of a failed effort here, you'll need the strength to stand up under Earth gravity." He held his gaze on the colonists as if waiting for a hundred 'yes doctors,' and then nodded as if satisfied. "Alright. I'll turn the floor over to Horticulture, now. Thank you."

David transferred the survey to the colony's shared database, displaying the location on the viewing screens for the colonists to witness.

"So, if you feel there are any gaps in the foods we are cultivating, note that in the survey. Include things that would improve your quality of life. We've covered all the bases from a nutritional standpoint, but only you can let me know what your comfort foods are. If I can deliver, I will. A few plants are just too fickle for Mars to be worth the effort, but really, I can adapt almost anything." He rubbed his hands together, eyes shining at the prospect of developing more hybrids for the colony.

"Now, our last point." The display changed in anticipation of his change of topic. "Timelines for fresh produce availability. We'd all like some fresh fruit and veggies added to our rations, right? It's going to be at least three months until we have fruits, longer for some produce…but within the week we'll have lettuces and other greens. I could go into soil quality and readiness for larger scale farming, but I'll leave that to our planetologist since we have some overlap."

Captain Neil stood, stretching as he did so. "Alright, we'll reconvene in an hour with Reproductive Technology. Right, Theresa?"

She startled, lifting her gaze to Neil's friendly one. "Yes, Captain. I'll be ready."

He laughed at her formality. Council members and colonists alike rose from their seats, rubbing bottoms numbed by the prolonged contact with hard stone benches and migrating towards the built-in food processors at the northwest curve of the room.

The colonists broke into smaller groups, discussions varying from which foods should be cultivated in the colony's greenhouse, to the likelihood that crimes warranting exile or re-sterilization would ever be committed on Mars; after all, how many years had it been since there was a murder on Earth?

Theresa ate her rations in silence, with Genesis, David, Carla, and several others gathered nearby. The conversation flowed around her but did not pierce her thoughts. *Twenty-five minutes until I represent the whole female population of Mars. No pressure. Of course, punching so many holes in Dr. Emory's presentation that it falls around his bony ankles in shreds will be fun. And then there'll be the news broadcast from Earth.*

She pushed the mashed potatoes on her plate into a small, lumpy tower, pointed at the top like a space elevator. *I wish I knew why Richard thinks we should watch it. One sided- time delay conversations with Earth are such a pain in the ass. It makes it too easy for him to not answer my damn questions!*

"But what are they planning to classify as treason. I mean, that's totally specious, to even classify treason at this time. This is the only Martian colony." The voice of a colonist Theresa had not met in person carried from a nearby group.

"Not really. Treason could mean trying to knock off Captain Neil or whoever else we vote in, or stirring up trouble with Earth over Martian decisions that don't mesh with Earth policies. If you ask me, exile is too kind. I say we ask Earth to come pick them up. Total deportation on a planetary level, right?"

There was laughter from the small group involved in the discussion.

"That would give pause to pretty much everyone, don't you think? We left for a reason." The laughter that followed had an edge to it, raw nerves and unpleasant imaginings lurking beneath.

Theresa stared down at her hands, not really seeing them. *Guess I'd better give up my plans for treason, huh, Abby? Wonder if blackmailing the whole colony would qualify?*

"Theresa!" She looked up at the source of the voice, eyes wide.

"You just dropped half your food without noticing. Are you still with us?" Genesis frowned at her companion.

Theresa looked down at the stone floor where her steamed edamame was scattered, then gathered it up in one hand. "Sorry, I was thinking, I guess. Just running over things in my head."

"Better to speak on the fly. It comes out more sincere."

"Ha! Maybe for you. For me it comes out more jumbled and neurotic." Theresa laughed, the sound shaky with tension. She squeezed a green pod, popping the beans into her mouth and scraping the soft outer skin between her teeth.

"We aren't all naturals at public-speaking, recounting our dreams like legends and weaving a spell on listeners." David grinned at Genesis and she gave a half-smile back, shrugging.

"No, I guess not. All the same, the important thing is the information you convey and the confidence you display. If you believe what you say, your audience will believe it. Trust me."

The group turned in unison at the sound of approaching steps, their light shuffle deceiving as to the size of the feet due to Mars's low gravity. Captain Neil stood over them, accompanied by Kendra, her hand on the Captain's arm.

"Theresa, how long do you expect your briefing to take? I'd like to get an idea of how much longer we can expect the council meeting to last." Neil smiled, his crooked grin lightening the weight of authority his voice naturally carried. "In other words, will we be able to squeeze in an afternoon nap when we're through?"

"Oh, um, unlikely. The nap, I mean. There are four more departments presenting after Reproductive Technologies, and that doesn't include the news broadcast from Earth."

"Right, right. Well, the other four have said they can keep it under ten minutes each...What about you?"

She blinked several times. "It will likely be more than ten minutes, but I'll do what I can."

"Sure. Of course. Whatever it takes to cover everything important. I guess it's time to dig in."

"The Reproductive Technologies Department has three orders of business to share with the council." Theresa paused, hearing the tell-tale tremor in her own voice and pulled down on the hems of her clothing, still in place. She pressed a hand over Abby's hidden cocoon as if to assure herself of its presence as well as the position of the scarf covering it. *This is Mars, not the Reproductive Council...*you *are the authority here.*

She pulled in a breath, releasing it at half the rate and felt a measure of calm descend. *If you believe it...so will they.*

"In order to meet the needs of the women of the colony, and at their behest, I have developed and installed user-controlled contraception in all but four female colonists. I have also developed user-controlled male contraception. This technology will allow..."

Jacob Emory broke in, interrupting her mid-sentence. "You did what? That is in direct violation of the Earth Council's directives!"

Theresa turned to face Jacob, waiting for him to finish his statement and then, raising an eyebrow, glanced over to Captain Neil.

The Captain held up a hand and gestured towards her. "The Head of Reproductive Technology has the floor, Jacob. Let's not forget the rules. Theresa, if you will...make certain to go into the reasoning behind your decision, even if it takes more time." He inclined his head in her direction, working to keep his tone in check, though the strain showed in the tightness of his jaw and the glint in his eyes.

She smiled and inclined her head in assent. "While we are no longer tripping over ourselves, physiologically, we are still recovering from the effects of zero-G and acclimating to life on Mars. As Jacob demonstrated, we may be through the hardest parts of recovery, but two weeks planet-side is not enough for the intricate workings of reproductive systems to normalize. It would be detrimental to our colony's health and the well-being of the next generation to allow pregnancies to occur before the women who will sustain those pregnancies are in peak condition and before they feel ready." The more Theresa spoke, the better the words flowed. "It is also my expert opinion that we must grant the approval of the surrogates request to remove their Caesarean Access Panels."

She caught Jacob Emory's eye. He was flipping his hand-held in his right palm and shaking his head, cheeks and forehead suffused with redness. She continued. "Caesarean Access Panels are designed to last through three pregnancies and then are removed in order to retire the surrogate host. Their safety has not been proven through a fourth pregnancy, and I don't recommend using half of our population as test subjects. Furthermore, our first-time mothers should be given the agency to determine how they will birth: surgically, and with the subsequent insertion of an access panel, or in the physiological manner—vaginally." Theresa drew in a breath and released it slowly in an attempt to steady herself before continuing. "As we have recently seen, access panels were never tested in scenarios that involve a more active lifestyle, like that required for a colonization effort...nor were they tested in high impact scenarios." There were faint murmurs of conversation in the crowd. "In support of this, our mental health expert Carla Schoen has submitted reports indicating Caesarean Access Panels are a detriment to mental and emotional stability and overall psychological well-being."

Theresa didn't bother to look back at Jacob again to gauge his reaction; she could picture the deepening purple-red of his cheeks well enough on her own. Taking a breath before continuing, she felt a twinge of doubt, a twist of electric fear in her gut. *Here's the kicker, ladies and gents.*

"The Reproductive Council on Earth has a vested interest in our success on Mars, but I think none has a greater interest in our well-being then we ourselves. The idea of a Reproductive Council on Mars may be distasteful to some of you." A strangled sound escaped from where Jacob sat, but Theresa kept her attention on the colonists sitting upright on their benches, listening, as well as the other council members. "But that is precisely why we need one. If we don't set up a council of our own to protect the reproductive rights we were promised as Martian colonists, we will be at the mercy of the Earth Council and what they think is best for us." She raised a hand and placed it over the scarf that covered Abby, lifting her chin as her words grew more impassioned. "Abby was slated for death until I stepped in and proposed further research. Our implants were removed with the timing designated by the Earth Council, with or without our consent." Theresa met Jacob's eyes then, her stare cold and purposeful.

"I believe we can do better for ourselves. A lot better." She sat back on the bench and used her hand-held to signal that she was giving up the floor. "Thank you."

Conversations broke out all over the room, some heated. The instant Theresa sat, Jacob claimed the floor, standing before his hand-held could even signal his intent, and pacing as he spoke. "It seems to me that the Reproductive Technologies Department is trying to make medical decisions, which is outside of their purview. We *have* a Medical Department for that! Or were you planning to perform the removal of Caesarean Access Panels in your bedroom on the sly, like your birth control?" Jacob blinked at Theresa, unveiled hostility in his eyes and she stared back, face immobile.

He turned to address the head of the council. "I will not participate in something I consider foolhardy and downright dangerous. All of the women who consented to birth control implants are in direct violation of their agreements with the Earth Council and are committing an act of treason against the colony!"

Captain Neil held up a hand. "Woah, Jacob. Those are strong words there. Let's just back up."

Theresa signaled for the floor. "I have a statement signed by forty-six female members of the colony stating the only conditions under which they are willing to take on the responsibility of procreation. The document is publicly available in the colony's open database."

Jacob Emory broke in. "You're holding the colony hostage?"

Mario Palmares leaned in, interlacing his tanned fingers. "That is like threatening the colony with extinction before it even gets started."

Eli signaled for the floor. "Let's say the council doesn't agree to the terms…or maybe agrees to some but not all of them. I'm not saying my opinion, just hypothetically speaking…or wants to add in some more…what then?" Eli's face was animated, as he dove in to the debate.

"All of the terms are non-negotiable. Look, these are very basic, core rights that we want to set forth, and they have been considered carefully." She spread her hands in appeal.

The air in the room seemed several degrees warmer and electric with tension. The floor passed from one to the other of the council members with no semblance of order; interjections from the colonists in the outer circle further obliterated that order. Theresa sat still in the midst of this whirlwind, in awe of what she had started. Maybe David was right, and more of the male colonists should have been included from the beginning and not just in the last few stages. But Carla had been insistent that it would erode the movement before it even started.

Captain Neil stood and gave his signal to clear the floor, much louder than the other council member's, once, twice, a third time, until the room returned to relative silence, if not peace. "This issue may be larger than we can resolve within the course of one council meeting. A second meeting will therefore be set for two weeks from now, at which time…we will bring the issue to a vote." Captain Neil's lips were tight, his brows knit as he fell back on formal phrasings, unearthed from the recesses of memory.

"Earth news broadcast downloaded and beginning playback." The voice of the AI system cut in to the conversation.

The viewing screens glowed to life, filling with a jumble of images: throngs of Earth citizens amassed outside the Reproductive Council, expressions screaming outrage, personal-hand-held devices projecting statements onto the outside of the tinted reflective windows of the Council Headquarters; *Let Them Live! Overpopulation Is A Dead Issue!*

The caption at the bottom of the screen gave only enough information to further confuse. *The Source Live Broadcast: Mass protests outside Reproductive Council Headquarters met by silence.*

A brunette, tan-skinned, with hair swept up into a cascade of waves, filled half of the screen, her expression a controlled mix of mild displeasure and sympathy.

"It seems late last night, classified information and live footage was broadcast into homes and offices across the globe via hand-held devices and the world-wide web. According to our sources, that broadcast was made by a Dr. Richard Brant, Head of the Reproductive Technologies Department within the Reproductive Council."

The anchorwoman's nose wrinkled in a look of distaste as the second half of the screen split to display a photograph of Dr.

Brant on the top half and a clip of live footage on the bottom half.

Theresa's shoulders tightened, her hand rising to cover her mouth.

The bottom half of the screen showed the glowing curve of an AUC unit, the unfinished progeny stretching within, dark eyes open and blinking as it lifted a small round fist to its lips to practice suckling. Theresa did not look to see how many pairs of eyes glanced her way. There were several.

"While I don't doubt that most of you have a copy of Dr. Brant's message to the public saved on your hand-helds, what follows is a replay of that message."

The viewing screen filled with Dr. Brant at an angle that made the self-recorded nature of the video obvious. He wore a lab coat and stood in front of the many rows of translucent AUC's. He looked as if he had not slept in at least a week, with purple brown bruises framing his hazel- green eyes.

"This is the AUC project. Artificial Uterine Chambers, where progeny are being grown through ectogenesis, outside of the human body. I'm going to make my point quickly. They could shut me down at any moment." He rubbed a hand across his eyes.

"The project, and all of the Progeny in it, are slotted for termination tomorrow morning. The council claims they are defective, despite my effccts to show them that any deficits these progeny might have because of the way they were created can be made up through nurture. These Progeny, children, are not parentless experiments crafted out of nothing and easy to throw away. They are the children of Dr. Theresa Marin and Dr. Gregory Matthews, former scientists who started this project, and they are five short weeks from their delivery date." Dr.

Brant turned the camera to focus directly on the nearest AUC unit and the sleeping progeny within. "The Reproductive Council has refused all of my requests to continue the project. So this is my last ditch effort. These are *our* progeny, after all, and I think we should have a say in whether they deserve a chance or should be thrown away. Contact the Council. Take to the streets. Do what you can."

The clip ended freezing on the final image and was replaced by the impassive face of the Anchorwoman. "Dr. Brant's current whereabouts are unknown, as are the whereabouts of the two scientists who presumably started the AUC project, and the Reproductive Council has, as yet, made no statement in response to the information leak or the unprecedented response of the public. The WGC has responded, saying they are watching the situation closely."

The broadcast ended. The edge of Theresa's right hand had migrated to a position between her teeth, blanching whiter with the pressure, whiter than her face by only a small measure. She squeezed her eyes shut. *If I could just disappear. Or strangle him and his good intentions.* Unable to disappear or avoid it any longer, she looked to see how many eyes were on her.

All of them. A sea of windows that she wished she could slam shut. Anger, disgust, pity. None of it what she would have wanted directed at her, or at Abby. *Maybe Carla should have chosen someone else for her spokesperson.*

Theresa choked back a bitter laugh, and sat up straighter by will alone; placing her hands on either side of the stone bench to stop their trembling, she turned her head to face the head of the Council.

Her voice was low; she couldn't trust it with the force of volume behind it. "May I be excused from the council meeting, Captain?"

Captain Neil opened his mouth to answer and then closed it again, shaking his head. "No. You don't want that, do you? Speculation behind your back. Let's finish this here and now."

She blinked back the moisture gathering in her lashes and inclined her head.

"In light of the news from Earth and how it effects certain members of our colony, the reports from our remaining four departments will be postponed until our follow-up meeting in two weeks. Theresa, would you like to explain your role in the…"

"The AUC project."

"Alright, the AUC project, to explain it for us, or to field questions?"

She took in a breath. "Questions may be quicker." *Possibly not painless, though.*

The first question confirmed her fears.

"Why did you leave them on Earth?" Kendra's voice was angry, incredulous.

"There are a hundred of them." Theresa unwound the scarf covering Abby, ignoring the way some of the colonists averted their eyes, and others that made small sounds of disgust.

"The project was being terminated. I was reassigned. The council refused my appeals to continue the project, so when I found out I was being reassigned to Mars, I took Abby, thinking I could keep her safe."

Her lips curled in a half smile as she shook her head, belying the pain in her eyes. "I couldn't walk out of the Reproductive Council with one hundred progeny. They weren't mine."

Jacob Emory spoke next, a satisfied smile on his lips. "Is *this* what you have in mind for a Reproductive Council on Mars, Theresa? Because if it is, I don't think…"

Her face twisted into a grimace as she stood and took a step towards the Head of the Medical Department. "Seriously? Does that even make sense? If we lost every woman able to bear children on Mars, I could recreate the AUC project within a month. But we're trying not to repeat Earth's mistakes here, right?" She turned to face the rest of the colonists.

"The AUC project was the logical next step for the Reproductive Council. The culmination of the steps they began a century before, when they took reproduction into their own hands. That is why we need to remove the Caesarean Access Panels, and grant ourselves reproductive freedom. If my involvement with the council on Earth creeps you out…makes you unable to trust me? Fine. Choose someone else. Carla, or Kendra or someone else, but for God's sake make it someone with a uterus that will be affected by the decisions made!"

David's voice came out of the silence that followed Theresa's impassioned speech, calm and measured by comparison. "So the council believes there is something wrong with the progeny. Is that possible?"

She turned to meet his question head on. "Yes. Absolutely. They show signs of deficits in their ability to feel empathy. Adjustments have been made at every phase to correct that, to lessen the effects. But it's a pretty huge concern. Yes …and valid."

David looked down, blinking a few times before looking back up at her from under his brows. "And if it can't be corrected, what will you do about Abby?"

Theresa stared, feeling two heart rates beating against her chest and in her ears, unable to respond at first. "I don't know. I guess I'll do what feels right in the moment, like I did when I took her." With one hand, she pulled the scarf back over Abby's RPU, covering her, and found herself unable to lower the hand that rested there when she finished.

Captain Neil, with a crease still etched between his brows where it set up camp during Theresa's presentation, signaled for the floor and stood. "Theresa, you look more than ready to be done here for the day, as am I."

Her brows pulled up in agreement and she let out a staccato sigh, half held in. "Yes."

"Then I would like a detailed report of your intentions for a Reproductive Council and the rationale and research behind it on my hand-held in three days, and, please, include further back-up for your request on behalf of the Mars colony women." He turned to face Jacob and the rest of the council. "Anyone with a contrasting view needs to provide the same. I now call the first Mars council closed until two weeks from today."

Theresa moved for the nearest exit, the Southeast hallway that would lead back to the housing complex, trying to acknowledge the many faces turned towards her as she went without encouraging conversation. Her heart galloped ahead of her, filling her ears with a thrumming din as she entered the hall, dulling the rising voices of argument that boiled in the meeting room.

It's so damn close in here, and red.

She veered to the right, requesting exit at a sealed door leading out to the central garden, and plunged into the heavy wind that greeted her there. *It's blowing in rain again.* She passed the darkened, fertilized, and tilled patch of soil in the center of the garden, Carla's patch, and, despite feeling out of breath, broke into a clumsy headlong run towards the entrance to the hallway that would lead home.

Her VR glasses were on and connecting before the door to her room sealed behind her.

"Why did you tell them that?! All of Earth and Mars did not need to know the genetic contributors to the AUC project!" Theresa's voice rose in volume and intensity as the pent up frustration and anger, some of it twisted inward as a sharp stinging shard of shame, boiled up and vented into the virtual message she recorded.

"It wasn't your information to give. If that was the only way you could save them…then yes, leak all the damn classified information you want, but I don't see how information about their parentage needed to be shared. And what about the additions and alterations to their DNA? They aren't my children, Richard."

She pulled the glasses from her face and authorized its delivery. Her heart-rate thundered on and her mouth tasted sour, the heaviness that generally preceded a bout of vertigo descending onto her limbs. *Maybe if we could have a two-fucking-way conversation it would be more satisfying.* She pulled in a breath, and another, then lay down on her bed, inviting quick oblivion with the darkness of covers over her head. Sleep came, but not peace.

Every single one of them had been delivered, a mass of one-hundred squirming and wriggling around her legs, her waist. The pile reached that high. Their stubby arms and legs were still wet and coated with waxy lanugo. One hundred sets of eyes, not the unfocused eyes of newborns, stared at her, and small hands grasped the cords still attached at their navels. Grasped and pulled.

She cried out as sharp pains, one after another, like shards of glass shot, through her abdomen. She pressed her hand against her belly where the pain seared her, and warm wetness trickled, and felt a gap, rigid on the sides, not flesh but something man-made. The light was dim, the light of the AUC lab, but she could see the Caesarian access panel installed just above her pubic bone, and the gaping space where it had been opened, the hundred cords emerging from within the bleeding space, each attached to a child.

"Where is Abby?" The thought was her own. She grasped the bundle of cords and sifted through, searching. She would know it if she found it, wouldn't she?

And there it was. The thinnest cord, drained of blood and no longer pulsing. Theresa held the cord in one hand and followed it with her eyes. *She's on the bottom.* The thought was louder than the insistent cries from the ninety-nine other progeny in the room. *My child.*

Leaning down, Theresa ducked her head and arms down into the pile, submerging her upper half as if in water, holding the single cord, Abby's cord, as she swam towards her. With each stroke more pairs of arms grabbed hold of her ankles, cords tangled and wrapped around her throat. That single thought propelled her. *She's on the bottom.*

She pulled the cord, a final effort to bring Abby closer to her through the mass of progeny that clung to her arms, legs, waist, throat.

The cord snapped.

Theresa opened her eyes; a sound had woken her. The chime of her message inbox alert.

COUNCIL VOTE

The grainy grinding of lichen and stone underfoot made Kendra's approach less stealthy than intended.

"Watch the bench. About two meters ahead." Neil's voice gave little of his mood away in the darkness.

"Someone needs to wrap those moons in foil or something. I can't see shit. Okay, I can see my feet, but that's it."

He let out a chuckle. "Phobos and Deimos, black as the space around them. I'll just go wrap those up for you." He laughed again, the sound complex with undertones.

"No, thank you. Someone else can do it. I like you here just fine." Kendra felt the edge of the bench with her hand and then sat, allowing the faint glow from her shoes to go out.

Neil sat, hands behind his head, elbows out, with his gaze turned to the stars.

"Where would be the fun in sending someone else?" He didn't bother to look over at her in the pitch black.

"You get sick every time you leave zero-G. You didn't seem to have much fun with that."

"Hm." It was a grunt more than anything.

"Am I going to have to wonder if you're taking the next ship out every time you get angry?" Kendra's tone was low, but less than gentle.

"Angry? No. I'm disappointed, surprised, sure. Wondering if this is the right assignment for me."

"You did fine."

"That's not it. You knew all this was coming. You lied to me, humored me…said sure, we'd go to the medical department together. And you let me walk into that council meeting unprepared."

"Well, you sound pretty pissed-off. Pissed for you, anyway. I'd be pissed if it were me. But this started before we did."

Neil groaned from the darkness. "I think this is just more of your stubbornness. A way to take control after surrogacy and I can sympathize but—Tell me I'm wrong. I know when I look that your name will be on that manifesto—declaration—whatever you want to call it."

"You're wrong. I want this damn thing out of me. I do. I've hated it since I woke up with it there after they took my first child out of me. But I want it out of all those other women too, don't want to see one put into my children and grandchildren if I have them."

He sighed. "I just want to do what's best for the colony, and for you, and it looks like the whole Medical Department is against this."

"Well, then you should get why I'm doing this. Because we want the same thing."

"I wanted to wait longer, to be sure, but with everything going on now...I just." Emily's smile permeated not only her eyes but the very breath that passed her lips, warm, and trembling like a child's witness of a miracle.

"Em, say it." Jonathan found his smile echoing hers, unable to hold back despite his lack of insight into her delight.

"It's a baby. I'm one of the three. Theresa confirmed it when we talked about the implants. It's me. We're going to have one, our own." Emily blinked, her smile parting into a full-on grin.

Jonathan wrapped his arms around his wife, laughter coming from deep inside his chest He wiped his eyes with one hand over her shoulder. "Emily...Really?"

"I wondered when I was so..."

Jonathan pulled back, holding her at arms-length to look at her. "So sexy?"

A laugh. "Yeah. For so long." Her skin pinked, remembering.

"How far along?"

"Only a few weeks."

"Wonderful." He shook his head. "You'll do wonderfully."

Theresa sipped the hot broth and stared across the room at her door, the red stone arch above it blurring out, her mind millions of miles away on Earth. Time delay was a bitch for conversations. A lot of time to think and formulate, and rethink, but no satisfying back and forth. She replayed the conversation, taking another sip of broth, imagining hot chocolate as it had been the last time she was in the same room with Dr. Brant.

"Are you ashamed?" His eyes were soft, sympathetic, or so she imagined them.

"What? Of the progeny? Of myself? No, if that's what you're asking. But, I'm not their mother." Her eyes flicked up to his, flinching away from his sharp gaze. "They don't have one. They should, but they don't. How does anyone mother one hundred? Quick answer: they don't." The look in her eyes was bitter.

Richard Brant leaned in, in her mind's eye, making a steeple with his sinewy fingers.

"You did your assignment, Theresa, like a good girl. So did I. But at this point we get to decide who and what we are, what we are willing to do." He pushed a hand through the forelock of his hair. "I am not willing to back out of what I've started. If that makes me father to a hundred, then so be it."

His lips were set in a firm line, his gaze direct and unwavering. Theresa looked up from her hands where she pulled flaky pieces from her croissant, allowing them to fall back onto the top of the mutilated pastry and met his gaze.

"What about Greg? Isn't he a part of this?"

Dr. Brant blinked, withholding further reaction. "Greg? He's holed up in the Reproductive Council Headquarters and has made no statement. It would help if he stepped up and spoke to the World Governing Council on the matter."

"The World Governing Council? Have they gotten involved?" Her heart tripped over itself. That could be the key.

He nodded and spread his hands. "They have. They've taken temporary custody of the AUC lab and the Phase Four progeny until such a time as they can determine the correct action to take.

Earth is fairly divided on the matter, if you'll watch more recent broadcasts. The one I sent was from three days ago and things are heating up quickly."

"Send them, please. I want to stay involved." A small voice in the corner of her mind, feeling the concern blooming there, called her hypocrite. *You can't deny them and then say you want to be involved. Make a choice.*

"Alright, I'll send them. There are calls to clean-out the Reproductive Council leadership, to abolish the reproductive program and their research now that overpopulation is a non-issue and the human genome is clean. That comes from a small but vocal sect. And there is a large faction that are in support of the Council's decision to terminate. Abominations, they called them."

Theresa's lips took on a sneer. "They wouldn't say that if they had a walkthrough of the surrogate program."

"No. They probably wouldn't."

"What can I do, Richard? I'm so far away. How can I help them from here?" Theresa stood up from the table, following Dr. Brant's lead, and placed her hand in the one he offered. The ground would be slippery with rain and slush from the late-spring hail storm that was just abating, the air heavy with the smells of carbon and sulfur.

"Anything you can do could be what saves them. You'll think of something."

She hadn't answered yet. Theresa looked down at the mug of broth, no longer steaming or warming her hands. Richard's hands were gone. *They were never there.*

The door chime she was expecting sounded, louder than she was ready for in the relative silence.

"A party of three requests entry, Carla Schoen, Genesis..."

Theresa didn't wait for the announcement to finish. "Let them in, please."

"My pleasure."

The party's voices preceded them as soon as the door slid open, raised and impassioned.

"This is exactly why I recommended you involve the whole colony instead of splitting off the women and excluding the men. How can joint decisions be made, at least for those paired up already, if they feel pitted against each other?" David gesticulated with one hand, a frown on his lips.

"You're still not getting it, David!" Carla shook her head.

"I get your campaign, your demands. I signed it, didn't I? But you're right, I don't get your tactics."

Genesis turned to walk backwards, facing him. "You aren't a tactician. Carla isn't either, intellectually, but her instincts were spot on, whether this pans out or not. If the women weren't firm in their own views on the matter, then they would have been forced to choose between budding relationships and ideas that were hard to swallow. Most would have been turned away from Carla's words by their own fears compounded by their partners' fears. Add to that the very real risk that complaints would have been made to the Captain and the meetings would have been forbidden."

David pressed his lips together and stopped next to Theresa's desk. "I don't think you are giving the men enough credit. How do you know they wouldn't have come around if they had attended your meetings?"

Carla took a breath before answering. "Maybe they would have, and they still can. That's not really the point here. What we are asking is that they acknowledge that these are not their decisions to make."

The three who had entered Theresa's room fell silent. Theresa sipped her broth.

"So are we good? Was that what you came to discuss with me?"

Genesis smiled. "No. We came to discuss strategy. Plans of action for the time between now and the next council meeting."

"I wrote up the extra information the Captain requested. Last night. When Jacob and any others submit theirs, I'll update it to counter their objections. What else can I do?"

Carla fingered her braid, looking at Theresa with an advance apology clear in her eyes. "There's still a lot of talk about Earth, confusion, assumptions, judgment. The best you can do is get out there and talk to people. Answer their questions."

Theresa blinked and looked from Carla to the other two assembled. David and Genesis's looks mirrored Carla's.

"Like I said, I'm not social. Maybe it was a mistake to set me up as your leader...figurehead?"

Genesis rolled her eyes. "Then I guess you don't mind taking on the role of unscrupulous mad-scientist, entirely lacking in ethics or humanity, that half the colony is cooking up for you? Because if you're aloof and inaccessible, they'll reach their own conclusions about you."

Theresa opened her mouth to speak, and then closed it again.

"Fine. What about Jacob and the Captain? Will Captain Neil side with us over the whole Medical Department?"

"Don't worry about the medical department, I'll be sending them to you prepped and ready to listen."

Theresa blinked a few times, startled. "Okay then."

Carla spoke up from her silence, moving her knuckle from between her lips and gestured towards David. "You need to gather with all the men in the colony and have a heart to heart. You have faith they'll come around, and I think you're right…so that makes you our man."

Before David could speak, Genesis smiled, her teeth showing with the fullness of her grin. "Brilliant! Yes, he could certainly do that. Couldn't you?" She turned to David, the shark-like grin having vanished, her eyes softer, like a damsel requesting a boon.

David inhaled and fell to nodding. "Yes. I could do that. My audiences generally have yellow and green ears and don't talk back, but for the colony, yes I could. I will."

Genesis squeezed her hands together, the pointed nails clicking. "Perfect. Then we know what our roles are. Oh, except for Carla…"

Carla raised her eyebrows. "I'll be running damage control for all of the colonists burnt out and angry from standing their ground."

Green foam sprayed into Theresa's face, the waves crashing into the red and black rocks that she placed her feet upon, taking care not to slip on the damp lichen. Streams of plant matter, like clumps of black rat-tails, trailed from the lower edges of the rocks and into the green water, swaying in the receding waves.

Theresa pushed back the hair that whipped from her braids and put out a hand for balance. "Donovan! Do you have a minute?"

Several steps ahead and to her right, Donovan crouched, leaning over the edge of the rocks and reaching into the water.

He started at the sound of her voice, placing a hand onto the rock to rebalance. "Theresa? Um…sure, I guess…let me just…" Donovan lifted a sealed tube out of the water, and stood upright. He held it up to the sunlight, shaking it as he squinted into the green liquid, before turning to face her. "Alright. What did you need?"

Theresa hesitated.

"What are you testing the water for?"

Donovan blinked. "Everything. Algae types and properties, mineral concentrations, bacteria and any other life forms."

She smiled. "That *is* a lot then, isn't it?"

Donovan shrugged, dipping his finger into the water and tasting it with the tip of his tongue.

"Aren't you afraid of…"

He licked his lips. "Not really. This is the third round of tests. Nothing dangerous here for now."

Theresa stifled a look of distaste. "Okay, then."

Donovan laughed and rubbed his hand on his clothes, heading back towards the colony complex. "You didn't come out here to look over my shoulder while I take samples, did you?"

Theresa blushed, turning to follow after him. "Well, no. Though I'm interested. I actually wanted to talk about the council meeting with you." Theresa struggled to match his pace.

"You don't need to worry about what you did…on Earth, I mean. Not my thoughts on it anyway. I understand doing your assignment. They all should. This is a fresh start, right?"

She couldn't help but smile. "Thank you. I don't know how many agree with you."

He nodded, slowing down for her to keep pace.

"I was hoping to talk to you about something else, though."

"Your cause, right? What is it? Reproductive freedom?" Donovan stopped and turned to face her, speaking before she could.

"Sorry to say…I'm against it. Entirely."

Theresa's mouth fell open. "Oh. Um…why?"

His mouth was a slash across his face. "You don't really know me yet. Planetology specialist." He tapped his own chest. "I like animals more than I like people. Algae, lichen even, are more worthwhile as a species. I mean, as individuals, people are okay, some of them anyway, but as a species? Not so much." He grew more animated as he spoke.

"So reproductive freedom from my perspective equals unrestricted breeding of an invasive species. How many planets do we need to ruin before we realize breeding like…well not rabbits, they make more sense, reabsorbing their young and all that, that breeding indiscriminately doesn't make sense." Donovan stopped for a breath.

Theresa jumped at the opportunity, wetting her lips. "So, birth control, then. You'd be in favor of that. I'm developing one for men as well as women, fail-safe but not permanent."

"The implants were better, in my opinion."

Theresa stared at him, struggling not to be flustered. "I don't think you realize that, on Earth, reproductive freedom meant overpopulation, whereas here it means we can control our population from the beginning. The Reproductive Council on Earth just took out our implants, so if we don't set up our own council and set up guidelines, then we're in the same boat as the one that wrecked Earth."

Donovan had his fist to his lips and was looking down, nodding as he listened.

"So reproductive freedom here will let the surrogates decide to remove their access panels, will let us set guidelines or regulations for spacing births. It would just put the decisions here with us on Mars instead of the Earth Council. Am I making sense?"

He scratched his nose. "A little bit. What makes you think Earth won't just veto all of this?"

"I don't know. But we don't have any chance if we assume they will."

Donovan turned back to the nearest security entrance and leaned in for a scan.

"Identity verified and access approved. One moment, please."

The security door light turned from red to green and back to red.

"Shit."

Theresa looked at the door over his shoulder. "Should I try it?"

"No. The damn thing keeps doing this. It'll let us in in a minute, though."

"Are you sure?"

"Well, it has every time before. And Mario is supposed to be fixing it. See, there it goes."

The light changed back from red to green and the door slid open with a carbonated beverage hiss.

Theresa followed him through the door and into the domed room. "What about what we were talking about? Did you have any questions, maybe…?"

He shook his head. "I'm going to think about it. Read your reports and all. That's the most I can say for it."

"What can I do to help?" Genesis pivoted at her desk to face Jacob Emory as he entered, a smile of welcome resting between her lips.

Jacob looked around the room, his glances furtive, his very person emanating tension and unease.

"How did you know she would make a play for starting a Reproductive Council? Did she tell you?"

Genesis's brows pulled up as she laughed. "No, she didn't tell me. I've worked with her before. She hides her ambition well. From herself even. But a woman doesn't spend her entire apprenticeship fifteen years working in the Reproductive Council with the highest level of security clearance, without ambition." She spread her hands before him.

"I need to know what her next move is. There's nothing in her supplemental reports that could push this over the edge in their favor." He shoved a hand through his hair. "Absolutely nothing! I've looked over them. Read them fifteen-fucking times at least."

Genesis stood to walk over to where he was, just across her threshold, and, taking one of his sweat-damp hands in hers, placed the other hand on his shoulder. Her short stature was convenient. No matter the height of the man, she could look up at him, and what the angle did for her tawny eyes bordered on magic. She leaned just close enough so that he could feel the heat of her, or imagined he could through his thin shirt, without making contact, and looked up at him from under her lashes.

"I've been trying to help you, Jacob. I have. But you keep fucking it up. I warned you about Theresa and you did nothing. I'm afraid I've wasted my effort. Given my support to the wrong side…"

"No. I still have some options…plans…I'm grateful for your help. But if you could just inform the colony of where you stand, then…"

Genesis leaned back and gave him a look that would have made Nikola Tesla feel a dunce. "You can't be serious."

"Well…" He hesitated, but then pushed forward. "Yes. The colonists respect you. They trust your judgement."

She shook her head back and forth. "My vote is the tipping vote. The small amount of respect I've earned will carry perhaps ten percent of the colony, no more. It would be foolhardy to try and use it as more. If I stand against popular opinion, I will lose that hard-won esteem. You need to make it worth my while and bring the other eighty to ninety percent with you."

Jacob breathed in through his nose, pursing his lips and nodding at her assessment.

"Well, I have the whole Medical Department with me. That's a start."

"If you can keep them."

He snorted. "Of course I can keep them."

Genesis raised a brow and placed a hand on Jacob's cheek. "Because you're still confident, and you want my continued support, I'm going to help you. I called you here because I became aware that Theresa has requested audience with your department to discuss her plans. I don't know what time the meeting begins, but it would be in your best interest to find out and be there."

Jacob's face turned red and his eyes widened. "I wasn't informed...invited?"

Her eyes were sympathetic.

"Well, she wouldn't invite you, would she?"

The confusion, hurt, in his eyes crystalized, hardened. "Well, I'll just have to crash the meeting, then.

Genesis smiled. "Good. And don't let her walk all over you with all of your colleagues in the room, for God's sake."

Jacob nodded and moved towards the door. "I'll keep you informed."

She waited until the door whooshed closed behind him to wipe her hands against her pants-suit and release the shudder she held back from the contact with his skin. *How does David think hand-holding is at all appealing?*

Turning on her heels, Genesis strode to the dark screen on her wall.

"Display room 59."

The viewing screen glowed to life and she leaned back to watch, sliding her hands through her hair, making a black waterfall of it against the wall, resting them on the back of her head.

"For your viewing pleasure." Her laugh echoed in the empty chamber.

There were eight of them. Five men and three women, sitting around Theresa on cushions engaged in lively discussion. Drinks were in several hands around the circle, and outer garments were draped in a pile on the nearest stone bench.

"Look at this one." She held up her hand-held, enlarging the display and projecting it above the screen as a three-dimensional image. A woman on all fours rocked back and forth, whispering, the sound all but lost, and moments later reached between two round thighs to produce a small wet progeny, cone-headed and mottled.

Theresa grinned. "I almost peed myself laughing the first time I saw this one."

The laugh was infectious, spreading between the physicians.

"Like a rabbit out of a hat. Surprise!" Her smirk held and then gave way as she tried to hold back from another bout of runaway humor.

The woman on her right took up Theresa's laughter. "I wanna see her pop it back in and repeat the trick!"

"I know! Right?!"

Another joined in, struggling to get out his full sentence through his chortling. "Shows scheduled every nine months, no encores!"

Desmond, the only man who had not entirely succumbed to his laughter, leaned further into the circle, holding a hand up.

"See, that's my big concern. My last hold-out. Who was this woman? What's her background? I mean were these isolated incidences, freak-shows? We can't have a whole colony of women emulating a 'don't try this at home' extreme sports scenario, and falling on their asses." He took a large gulp of water, wiping his mouth with a cloth napkin from his pocket. "I mean, maybe under other circumstances, but in a colony situation, their failure is our failure."

"He just wants to watch more." Theresa raised a brow at the physician. "I have more."

"How many?"

"Two-hundred-thirty-five. Two hundred with their colorful medical records attached. These women were old-school. Some with their genetics as flawed as a white sheet dragged through the mud, and with what they called 'unproven pelvises.' At first I was just laughing my ass off watching these things. I mean, I was told progeny didn't fit out that way, and the positions these women are in. You gotta be kidding me!"

Small answering snickers came from several of the physicians. She had their full attention now.

"But then I started noticing things, the way they arch their backs in the final moments, the ones that seemed to have an easier time of it and what they had in common. That's when I got excited." Her eyes sparkled. "Do you realize the opportunity this gives us? I already have ideas for complementary technologies and a system that would let them pull the rabbit out of the hat, and allow us to swoop in if it gets stuck."

"I would love to get in on that. I considered transferring into Reproductive Technologies on Earth, actually, fascinating stuff."

Theresa's grin was a combination of surprise and pleasure. "Really, Erik? I would be happy to apprentice you. They sent me by myself in the expectation that I would build the department through apprenticeship. Wonderful. Now I'm even more giddy."

"Now here's a thought…" One of the three female physicians leaned in, placing a hand on Theresa's knee. "If we can get Jacob on board, we could set up an apprenticeship exchange program. You could apprentice in obstetrics and the other areas of medicine that interest you, and we could take turns apprenticing in your department. After all, crossover ability is going to be important, considering we have a smaller pool to draw from than on Earth."

"Now, if we did that…"

"Jacob Emory requests entry." The announcement interrupted Erik's train of thought and elicited several abashed looks between the assembled physicians.

"Oh. Let him in then, I guess." Theresa raised her eyebrows and looked at her colleagues. "I thought he had decided not to come."

The door slid open to reveal the man in question, hair mussed from a shortcut through the garden, and eyes alight with the fire of a cuckold having caught the adulterers in the act.

"So this is how you work. Inviting my colleagues to meet behind my back?"

"Uhhh…" Theresa rubbed her forehead. "Well, more in front of you, really."

Jacob snorted, folding his arms and standing over the circle of physicians who were still sitting, some craning their necks to look up at him and others avoiding eye-contact.

"Now that you're here…we've come up with some, well I think, really brilliant ideas for cross-department collaboration." Erik stood and invited him into the casual circle with a gesture of his arm.

Jacob took a half step toward the open space and then a sneer crept across his cheeks, wrenching his lips into a smirk and obliterating whatever thought had motivated the step forward. "You're letting yourselves be wooed by a woman who is posing as a medical professional. What is it? The progeny grafted between her breasts? I promise you'll have other opportunities to interact with progeny on Mars. At least if we don't let her hold us hostage."

Theresa sat, unmoving, a look of incredulity frozen on her face as she watched the head physician become more and more agitated.

"I don't think that's really called for, Jacob. Can't we be civil here? Medical professional or not, she is an expert in an area that intersects with ours."

"Well, I guess I know where you stand, Erik. And the rest of you? We have limited time to write up our department's objections. I'll need you in my office in twenty minutes."

Theresa watched Jacob leave, the crease between her brows still in evidence. *When exactly did 'let's work together, babe' turn into, 'I hate your soul' with the requisite Nosferatu hiss added in for good measure?*

"Well. That was colorful." She pressed her lips and took a breath before standing to refill her water. "I guess you have work to attend to…If any of you have more questions about my proposal, you know, when you get in there and sit down with the details, feel free to ask me. I want to make sure everyone's input is considered so we're all on board, or at least so we know for sure why some are overboard." Theresa laughed. "Well, it made sense in my head anyway."

Erik took one of her hands in his. "You handled that quite well."

"Yeah, not bad for being reduced to a walking science experiment, I guess."

Erik gave a half smile. "Yeah. The man has quite a temper. I've been on both sides of it, but he usually sees reason eventually."

She bit her lip and shrugged one shoulder. "Well, I'll keep trying, then. Maybe he'll meet with me in private."

The other physicians had risen from their comfortable floor nests and were straightening their clothing while listening in.

"I haven't seen him change his mind."

"Or admit he was wrong."

Erik glanced over but continued to refasten his weighted outer garment. "You have to earn his respect first, Johnson, and that takes time."

Johnson gave a skeptical glare to Erik's back. "Uh-huh. I won't hold my breath." The other physicians laughed, trying to keep the exchange light.

Theresa shook Erik's hand, followed by Johnson and the others. "Thank you all for coming to talk. I look forward to working together."

Dr. Alexander hung back, raising a hand to his colleagues as they went on without him. When the door sealed shut behind them, Theresa turned to face him. "You were awfully quiet... care to let me in on your thoughts?"

The older man nodded, his look serious. "Thank you for this...forum, as it were. I admit that I had started to wonder if my initial esteem for you was brought about by our shared experience..."

A small smile held place on her lips. "And now?"

He paced closer, taking a seat on the nearest cushion. "Now, I at least understand your perspective, and your goals for the colony." He shook his head. "I do wish we could see eye to eye, though."

She pulled at the edges of her collar, displaced by the enlarged RPU capsule. "Perhaps with further discussion…"

He held up a hand and shook his head with a sad smile. "If I could bridge the gap between our perspectives, then it would be me bringing you over to my way of thinking." His eyes held just enough humor to temper any insult. "I believe that you have only the best intentions, but years of research and personal experience backs my perspective. Your work in reproductive technology is unparalleled, and I respect that…but consider this: your skills would never have been needed if human reproduction was not innately perilous-flawed, if you will."

Theresa frowned, fidgeting with a drinking glass left empty. "The process is no more flawed than any part of human biology, and if we circumvent it, then we take on the flaws and risks of the technologies we use…so it's a trade-off. Like with the access panels-if not for that, then Nicole may have survived."

He grimaced. "Theresa, that argument isn't logical…"

"You can't deny that the access panel caused the rupture and her death!"

"That's neither here nor there. If not for the access panel she may have died in childbirth in any of her previous pregnancies. We could pick apart and argue probabilities all day, and any one of our colonists could have died in that crash."

A sigh escaped Theresa's lips, sped by frustration and uncertainty. "What of the woman's experience? What about what they want for themselves and the benefits of birth for host and progeny?"

Dr. Alexander stood to pace. "You seem to think Jacob and I intend something inhumane for the colony. With the help of your technology, we can provide safety and an uplifting, positive experience." A deep frown pulled his lips and eyebrows down. "By setting these women up for something unrealistic and unachievable, you're making it impossible for us to do that. Expectations are the main factor in a woman's level of satisfaction in birth."

"I've read that study. But how is it ethical to tailor a woman's expectations to meet what we are willing to provide?"

"Not willing but able…with a modicum of safety. You could show me two hundred birth videos, and it isn't going to convince me that a 'natural experience' for thousands of women is worth risking even one catastrophic rupture or hemorrhage." His eyes were apologetic but unwavering, and he leaned over to shake her hand. "I'll need to report to Jacob shortly…help him with his presentation."

"Just a second…if you have it…"

He nodded.

"This isn't mine or even Carla's brain-child. This was set in motion because the women themselves wanted options, control, and-"

The physician stood and headed to the door indicating that she should follow. "We can give them options. Safe ones. And control over the things that don't impact safety." He spread his hands before him. "But a layperson…male or female, is not the best suited to make decisions about life and death…the future of our species. If there is to be a council, then it must be a council of experts, as opposed to people who are too close to the issue, thereby…emotionally compromised."

Theresa bit back a hasty reply, trying to remain impassive, and instead nodded agreeably. "Let's talk again… If I can't win you over now, then maybe once you see what I described in action."

"We will, yes, and I'm certain I'll find your innovations…intriguing."

She gave a wry smile with equal parts exhaustion and humor as the door closed behind him.

She turned to face the empty room, eyes wide and glassy, shellshocked. Thoughts in a tangle, she sank down on the nearest cushion, leaning back and exhaling slowly. Her cheekbones stood out in sharp relief to her face and dark circles rimmed her eyes, the color incongruous with the sallow tint of her skin.

With one hand she unwound the light scarf that concealed the RPU unit and rested a hand over the flat of Abby's back before allowing sleep to take her.

"I don't really want to spend my night here, wasting time on the same damn arguments; argued with Grantley for a full forty-five minutes after the last council meeting. So you tell me right up front. Which side are you for?" Brian, a heavyset colonist with hazel eyes, leaned in, pinning David with his glare.

"I wouldn't talk to me either if I'd spent forty-five minutes arguing with Grantley. Man can't convey a full thought without switching metaphors five times. But, honestly I just think we need to swap stories, bounce ideas off each other…you know?" David handed a warm drink to Brian and another to Eli on his right, and sat down between them. Five others sat across from the trio.

Brian laughed, the sound pinched by his reticence. "I guess if they're holding 'exclusive' women's meetings, we can have men's meetings, huh?"

David snorted. "Sure we can. Of course they weren't exclusive, just not well advertised. I was at one, actually. " He took a sip of his drink, breathing in the steam and the strong spicy smell of it.

Brian chewed his lip, taking in this new bit of information.

David smiled. "So, for my part I had a couple problems with the whole thing when I first heard about it." Another sip. "One, if we could just go back to some other way of delivering progeny, then why did the Reproductive Council on Earth start doing things this way? Two, I don't want to be the cause of a woman in our colony dying or even suffering just because I got them pregnant. And three, shouldn't we have some say over the thing? It takes two to tango right?"

Brian was nodding so hard some of his drink dribbled down the front of his shirt, eliciting a hiss and a hurried attempt to wipe the hot tea from his skin. "I couldn't've put it better. I tried to tell Grantley that, and he acted like he wasn't getting it. Course, if he had a girlfriend then he'd relate better."

David looked from one man to the next. Some of them were nodding, others deep in thought. Eli had one hand pinching his lips as he contemplated the situation. "Eli?"

The young man raised his eyes, startled. "Well…I'm still back-and-forth with the whole thing. I mean, part of me thinks…just leave it to the professionals and then the other half'll chime in with questions. Melissa and I talked about it and she's not so sure either…"

David sat forward, his full attention on Eli. "Did she sign the paper they all signed?"

"Well, yeah…"

Brian interrupted. "Why would she sign it if she's not on board with it?"

Eli cocked his head. "If I understood her, it's because she's not sure for *her*, what she wants. But she said some of her friends are so adamant about what they want that she would feel wrong doing anything else."

"Sounds like she's just jumping on the bandwagon." Mario stood up to stretch and shrugged before pulling one arm and then the other across his chest. "How much integrity does she have if she won't stand up for her ideas against her friends?"

Eli frowned and jumped in, his tone sharper than the other men had yet to witness. "No, no. It's not like that. I think you're forgetting her assignment. She heads up the Justice Department. She's clear on her beliefs about justice…just not what she'll do if she has progeny." Eli glanced over at David before continuing and found support in the other man's near imperceptible nod to continue. "In fact, she said as far as she is concerned, it would be very easy to start the colony off down the wrong path if we limit personal freedom too much."

Mario crouched down at the edge of the circle. "Personal freedom…medical freedom…too much of either of them leads to bad things for us as a species. We are innately lazy, gluttonous, and self-serving. I think Donovan would agree if he wasn't out keeping company with the lichen…"

There were murmurs of agreement and some of dissent. Mario opened his mouth to continue, but stopped when David raised a hand.

"We could go round and round with this, for hours. I'm just gonna tell you what made me change my mind. Okay?"

Brian frowned. "See, I told you I needed to know right off the bat what side you were takin' cuz forty-five minutes was enough." He started to stand.

"Sit down Brian. This'll only take ten." David passed the man a bowl of dried fruits and nuts, eliciting a begrudging nod.

"So, one, the council wasn't looking out for Earth women or the progeny when they set things up. What's their bottom line, guys? Come on, we've all had it drilled into us."

Eli recited in a dead-pan tone. "To definitively halt overpopulation and the mechanisms that caused it, and to produce clean, genetically diverse, and specialized progeny in carefully controlled numbers." He trailed off, looking from one man to the next for any dispute.

Mario added in just loud enough to be heard. "That's not such a bad mission."

David ignored the comment. "Thanks, Eli. Two, the second argument I mentioned is all ignorance and ego. Ignorance because we don't know a damn thing about how birth worked before the council stepped in, and ego because, well, it's any morenot my place...our place, to decide what the women are going to do with their bodies, be it eat, sleep, piss, or climb mountains, than it is their place to decide for us. Which brings us to three. Shouldn't we have a say?"

David glanced around to gauge the group's reaction thus far. They seemed to be listening, if not agreeing. "Well, we have a say in who we hook up with, and with the men's birth control being set up for us, we'll have a say in whether we want to procreate at all. That should be enough. Anything more is just greedy."

"Man, I don't have to listen to this." Brian crossed his arms on his chest.

"No. You don't. But I don't recommend trying to talk to Marina again until you've thought real hard about what you're telling her by voting against her getting to make decisions about…"

"I haven't voted shit yet!"

Eli shook his head. "Yeah, but we can all guess what you want to vote, Brian. David makes some good points here. I'm not fully convinced on the safety…I mean, I have questions still."

"Yeah, but, If this was so damn reasonable, why didn't they just tell us what they wanted? No threats."

"Because it goes against the grain. How many of us jumped up and told the Captain, 'Hey, with all due respect, we don't need time to think, or to take a vote?'"

A tall thin man with an aquiline nose and frowning lips tapped the edge of his tea cup. "You said there were clips to watch? Old films? I'd like to see them before we argue any further. What sort are they?"

David wet his lips and grinned. "Good plan, Alan. I don't think anyone'll be disappointed. You game, Eli? Brian? Mario."

Eli shrugged. Brian scratched his head and stretched one shoulder. "Fine."

Mario inclined his head, acquiescing.

Carla stared out the small, arched window across from her bed at the heavy darkness, roiling over itself in the Martian sky. Deep blues, purples, and charcoal-gray filled the dim morning sky, blocking out the sunrise that the songbirds had been heralding for the past hour.

She sat up, forcing herself out from under the last few veils of sleep all at once. She rubbed a hand across the space between her eyes and her silver brows. The storm clouds were still there, but the songbirds were gone. When had she last seen songbirds? Years, it seemed. *There were crusty old ravens in the cities on Earth, but the songbirds were relegated to poetry and history books long before. Unless they could be brought back like they hoped.*

Carla stood up and stretched out her back, sending out a chorus of crackling pops as she twisted in either direction. *Where is your mind, Carla? This is the day and you're thinking about songbirds?*

She dropped down to the floor, chest parallel to the surface as she fell into the comfortable rhythms of her morning exercises. Her arms shook after the first fifty. "Fifty to go, old woman…keep it coming." The words were ragged, forced out between breaths. *What if they say no, and the women cave in? Get all wobbly-legged and back down?*

She pushed harder, channeling her nervous energy, and, reaching one hundred, transitioned to a squat, her thighs like strong pistons as she stood and then crouched repeatedly.

The first rumbles of thunder resonated through the stone walls while Carla drank her breakfast, but were still quite distant by the time her door sealed shut behind her.

"Perfect weather for a shortcut through the garden!" Another deep rumble echoed her sentiment, grumbling from the western mountain ridge. "Appropriate, I guess."

The door slid open and she stepped out, letting the damp wind enfold her. The moist air was heavy with the smells of

Mars as it whipped the midwife's braid back behind her while she crossed the garden, and unlike the soft warm air that blew in from the north, this was ice cold.

David rubbed his eyes, squeezing them shut and blinking in an attempt to banish the aching sandpaper feel in the corners before leaning in for a scan.

He jerked back from the light before it completed its arc across his face, startled by a hand on his shoulder, and turned.

"I've heard good things about your meetings." Genesis smiled at David's bleary raise of brow.

"It was just last night. How have you heard anything yet?"

She shrugged, twisting a lock of hair around her index finger. "The colonists respect you very much, it seems; your concern for others, active involvement in the community…there's a lot you could do with that."

Catching her meaning, he shook his head. "As I said before, I have zero interest in politics." He turned back to the scanner. "Shouldn't we go in?"

"Wait. I wanted to talk to you about something."

"Does it have to be before the meeting? I don't want to be late." He turned back to face her, stifling a yawn.

"This will only take a moment." She closed the gap between them, looking up at him, eyes wide and full of emotion.

David raised a hand, aiming to caress her cheek, but held back at the last moment, closing it and bringing it back to his side. "What's this, then?"

She looked down before meeting his gaze again. "We've been so busy preparing for the council meeting the past couple weeks that it took me longer than I expected."

She searched his face for a reaction, and found him half-smiling, attentive. "I've been looking into your wife's medical records as I promised I would."

David's jaw tightened. "Okay."

Genesis's brows pulled together and she opened her mouth to speak, false starting once before finding the words. "If you don't want me to tell you, I don't have to." She bit her lip and waited.

David pushed a hand through his hair and shrugged. "If there's something I don't know, then just say it."

He looked away, pulling in a shaky breath. When she didn't respond, David looked down and found Genesis's yellow-gold eyes on his, sharp and unblinking.

"It wasn't a hemorrhage. She and the child were both labeled 'do not resuscitate' or provide care."

David turned back to the scanner, his movements stilted.

"There's more." She placed a hand on his back, the warmth sinking through the layers. "The attending physician's name was included in the records." She let the silence grow between them. "I guess it doesn't matter now. If you'd rather not know..."

His voice was sharp, each syllable clear. "Who was it?"

"It was Jacob Emory."

He stiffened, straightening out of range of the door's sensors a second time, and she could feel the muscles in his back tighten, along with the sharp intake of breath.

The moments stretched out. David stood facing the door, his breathing uneven, lacking the ease and rhythm that comes with peace of mind. His voice was barely audible when it came, as if he didn't trust it to hold steady with any force of volume behind it.

"Thank you."

He dipped his head low enough for the scan, walked into the Council chamber, and was swallowed up by the noise of conversation and the warmth of many bodies gathered indoors.

Half asleep, Theresa brushed the tips of her nails across her skin where the RPU made a seal with her tender flesh, irritated from weeks of contact, and pulling, despite the support straps. She opened her eyes without thought or hesitation and sat up. Gray-spots swirled and speckled the edges of her vision. *Slow down…*

There were damp tracks on her skin and the RPU unit, moist in the center with dried edges that scraped away like crystals of caramelized sugar. She opened her eyes again and held her fingers an inch from her nose, inhaling. *What is this? Shit! Are we leaking amniotic fluid?*

With panicked, clumsy movements, Theresa followed the trails on her skin, searching the edges of the seal and then moving out to the central portions of the RPU where Abby's growing form stretched the material to its thinnest. Her right forearm brushed her breast. *What is that?* She pulled aside the fabric of her nightshirt on the right side, expecting bruising.

Well, she was kicking all night…Oh.

"Oh." She grinned, stretching the corners of her lips past what her heart could contain. Her breast was full and heavy, with an ache that pushed the dull pain of the past few weeks, which she had become accustomed to, to the back of her memory, reclassifying it entirely. Her mauve-brown nipple stood out from the areola, held erect by the pressure from within. That was where the trails emanated from.

She grasped the nipple between two fingers and squeezed, causing a few small drops of liquid to bead, collecting into a thin stream.

Theresa pulled the shirt back over her exposed skin, both hands spreading across Abby's back with light pressure. Her hands shook with withheld excitement.

"Shit! I've gotta tell Carla before the council meeting." She glanced at the time on the viewing screen and blinked. *And I better pump some of this…*

Outside of the central meeting chamber, Theresa twisted her hair for the third time, pulling it into place, tightening, clip and release. Despite years of practice, her fingers again, and several strands of hair slid down into her face. Moisture sprang to her eyes.

"Shit! Shit! Shit! And that's going to be your first word right, Abby? If I keep this SHIT up anyway! Oh. I didn't braid it first. No damn wonder. Ten minutes. Just get it done."

The room was alive with colonists when the door between Theresa and the meeting chamber slid open. She made mental comparisons between the silent, patient scene from two weeks before and that of today. The colonists were animated by the booming of the storm overhead as well as the debate that dominated their minds.

Theresa made her way to her seat in the council circle, struggling to block out the murmurs of gossip that assaulted her ears.

"Mother of a hundred."

"Yeah, but she bailed out right?"

"Can you picture all of them strapped to her chest?"

She grimaced at the mental image and took a short detour around the cluster of colonists that glanced her way.

"Carla." She beckoned the older woman from the edge of the dais a few feet away and awaited her approach. Carla held up a finger, while nodding to the woman in front of her who was gesticulating, a look of distress pinching her features.

"But if they don't agree to the terms we'll have a cat's game. And they can hold it over our heads that we want progeny too."

Carla nodded again. "That could happen. We have a chance if we stand together now. You do what's in your heart, Ellen."

"Couldn't we negotiate the terms, keep the parts we can all agree on and just let the others slide?"

Carla inhaled through her nose. She had heard this before on Earth. "Who decides which points to fight for? Do we keep the points that matter most to me? To you? Kendra and her surrogate sisters? The surrogates will be holding their ground, and I won't be throwing them under the bus."

Ellen's nose crinkled and she tilted her head at the unfamiliar euphemism.

"Pulling them with the weeds? Culling with the sheep? Never mind. I'll be standing with them." She placed a hand on Ellen's shoulder and gave it a squeeze. "I'll be back in a moment. Save me a seat?"

Theresa steepled her hands in front of her lips, looking over the top at Carla as she approached.

"I have milk." Theresa's eyes glowed and she pulled her bottom lip between her teeth to hold back a grin.

Carla widened her eyes and inclined her head. "When? Just now?"

"I love that I don't have to explain any further. No, last night. It was all …" Theresa noticed some of the colonists straining in their direction to catch the conversation and lowered her voice. "It was all over me this morning! So tonight. We'll be delivering her tonight after the council meeting, okay? Its three weeks early but the RPU's data indicates readiness, lung-maturity, reflexes. Apparently the RPU reached its threshold at two in the morning and…" She struggled to maintain a whisper throughout the effusive explanation.

"We?"

"Well, yeah. I want you there. I mean I can deliver progeny from AUC's. I've done it more times than I can count and an RPU delivery is supposed to be the same, so I don't really *need* you." Theresa noticed Carla's smirk. "Well, I don't really mean I don't need you exactly…"

"Sure you do, Theresa." She snorted. "I don't need to be needed, honey. I'm glad to be wanted. Honored to be there for you."

"It's just I don't want to do it like we do in the lab. Cut them out and pass them off. So maybe you can help me make it more…" Theresa floundered for the right words. "Like in your old clips."

"Like a birth. Yes, I can help you do that. However this turns out." She placed a hand over Theresa's and smiled, then gestured over her shoulder with her eyes.

Theresa turned her head and answered the question in Captain Neil's eyes with a thumbs up. She took the steps one at a time despite the strong urge to leap and take them by threes. *Probably trip if I tried, tasty hormones or not…mmm, oxytocin, prolactin, endorphins… Nothing better than a natural high to make a girl feel invincible. I think I'll need it.* A brilliant grin glowed on her wan face as she took her seat, contrasting with hollow cheeks and fatigue-bruised eyelids.

The thunder in the mountains drew closer, a panther with deep throaty growls of warning rumbling in the back of its throat. Captain Neil took the floor.

"Good morning, everyone." The thunder boomed overhead and Neil increased the volume for the speakers and glanced up at the sky-light with mock concern. "Looks like I have some competition for the floor." He cleared his throat, eliciting a ripple of nervous laughter. "Good morning. This second meeting of the Mars Council has been called to determine the extent of reproductive rights within the Mars colony, as well as to establish a separate council to govern matters of reproduction within the colony." He paused to clear his throat, which had gone dry despite the humidity in the room, before continuing.

"The supporting documents of those against, as well as those for reproductive autonomy, as presented by the Head of Reproductive Technologies, were submitted and reviewed. Are there any points that either side would like to add before we move ahead? As long as we can be civil we can share the floor in the interests of time. Jacob?"

Jacob rubbed the point of his index finger across his lips. "I've included my concerns that removal of the Caesarean Access Panels will result in catastrophic ruptures during a subsequent pregnancy and that the lack of an access panel will make it harder to check for and repair damage to the uterus, causing death of both the surrogate and the progeny, so…"

"Yes. You did, and it's noted along with the chances of that occurring. Is there something new you'd like to add?"

"Yes. It's likely that in one-third Earth's gravity the progeny won't settle into cephalic, or head down rather, presentation, and will therefore be born breech with all of the incumbent risks. None of the physicians in my department are trained to deliver breech without an access panel or a primary caesarean section."

Captain Neil gave a slight nod, turning to the head of reproductive technologies. "Theresa? Do you have any rebuttal?"

"No, not really, but Carla can speak to that, I'm sure."

Captain Neil turned to face the sea of colonists, scanning the rows until his eyes fell on Carla.

"Carla, are you trained to deliver breech progeny?"

"Sure I am, Captain. Funny thing, you catch a breech the same way you catch a cephalic baby." She smiled. "With your hands." There were several laughs from around the room. "I can teach every single colonist. And assuming we do get a rash of breech babies, it'll go even faster."

"With all due respect, Captain Neil, Carla Schoen is a psychologist, not an obstetrician."

The Captain pursed his lips, running his tongue across his teeth under them. "Noted. But I'm going to have to submit about a hundred video clips worth of evidence on her behalf that prove she knows what she's talking about, considering I was up all damn night watching them." He raised both brows for emphasis.

A light chime sounded from Jacob's hand-held and he glanced down to see the message heading.

"Alright, any other points to raise?" Captain Neil looked at each of the council members and then opened his mouth to speak.

Jacob spoke first. "If you'll forgive me... I have one more thing I would like to share with the council."

"Look, I think we've covered this from every angle and should move on." The Captain's brows pulled together and he scratched his head.

"With all due respect. We've all taken the time to watch Carla's 'clips,' and I've just obtained supporting evidence to further elucidate my concerns for the safety of this colony." He stood and held up his hand-held as if presenting it to the assembly. "It's only fair to allow me the same chance to present my case."

The Captain took a breath, smoothing his expression through force of will.

"You've just acquired this 'evidence'?"

"Yes. Only moments ago, or I would have included it in my report. It takes time to dig up information that's all the way back on Earth."

The Captain nodded. "Fine." He gestured towards the viewing screens. "You've got the floor."

Jacob returned the nod. "Thank you." The corners of his mouth twitched upwards as if trying to draw his lips into the same smirk that lit his eyes.

Wetting his lips, he lifted his hand-held closer to his face, and gave the command. "Sync and begin playback." He turned a solemn gaze to his audience. "There can be no doubt that the proponents for medical autonomy have good intentions. After all, we were promised reproductive freedom on Mars, were we not?"

Murmurs of assent rose from the crowd, heads nodding along with the physician's words. "The freedom to answer our biological urgings with a renewed ability to procreate, to bring forth and raise young." He paced along the dais, painting the scene for his audience with gestures of hand and tone of voice.

"But herein lies the rub, if you will. If we are to obtain reproductive freedom, we must not be tied down by our flawed biology. Even in best case scenarios, human reproduction is fraught with peril. We are but few here on Mars." Jacob's voice took on the raw quality of withheld emotion, a slight tremor slipping through his control. "How many of our own can we afford to lose, and if we could choose instead of playing victim to the caprices of childbirth, who would we sacrifice in the name of control, in the name of nature? Emily? Bethany? Kendra? Perhaps Alissa?" His eyes were pleading as he scanned the crowd, each name spoken as one would the name of a cherished lover.

He cleared his throat and gestured to the screen behind him. "I refuse to reduce the dangers of what you ask for to numbers, lest we reduce the lives of our own to just numbers. Any number of the complications shown in these clips could happen each time you flout medical progress and put the complicated and perilous process of childbirth into the hands of the untrained and ill-equipped."

The screen lit up with a stark scene, naked flesh, splashed with blood, masked attendants rushing with equipment in hand, raising needles and masks, the stamp of fear apparent on their brows.

"Postpartum hemorrhage, placenta accreta, abruption, stillbirth."

The scene changed. Rows of silent progeny awaiting their turn, T-shaped incisions on chests, the only color on their skin the glow from the incinerator.

"Shoulder dystocia, internal decapitation, asphyxiation, meconium aspiration, cord entanglement. How many deceased progeny do we want to burn and spread in our gardens?" The physician's voice was low, gentle, audible only by way of the amplification provided by his hand-held. The eyes of the crowd that met his ran with tears.

The sound from the next clip filled the chamber, the screams echoing from the walls and forcing many to cover their ears. Lying on a wheeled gurney the woman struggled against the straps, head whipping back and forth as she screamed, breaking down into incoherent sobs. "Make it stop! God, make it stop!"

The screen froze with a collage of graphic still-shots, and Jacob bowed his head a moment, and then nodded once to the audience, rubbing a hand across his eyes as he took his seat among the council members.

Theresa stood, heart pounding in her ears and looked from Captain Neil to Carla. The Captain gave a small shrug, his eyes wide and glassy with residual shock.

"Carla?" She took a step towards the older woman. "It would... give unfair advantage if we were not allowed a rebuttal." She turned to Captain Neil once more for approval, and was satisfied by a nod. "Maybe you should come up here to speak?"

"Nope. I can speak just fine from right here. As impressively gory and one-sided as that presentation was, it isn't going to take much to address it." Her voice was calm, though Theresa could see the bunches around her narrowed eyes and the twitch of her tensed jaw. "How much context did we have for those images? When were they taken? Who were they? And what circumstances led up to the so called 'complications'? Were they complications of labor and birth, or complications of archaic and unnecessary interventions, or perhaps side-effects of the epidemic of poor health in the twenty-first century?"

She stood and looked around the room, brows raised in challenge. "How many of you would have felt confident going up on the space elevator if they'd shown us footage of all the early test runs where the shuttles crashed and burned or got lost in space? Hm?" She shook her head. "Not much more to say, except I'm tired of this overblown misogyny!"

Jacob laughed and turned in his seat, his look incredulous. "Misogyny? We've not seen true misogyny for centuries. Do you even know what the word means?"

Carla snorted, her sharp blue eyes boring into the physician. "Hatred of women, sir. Just because you and your ilk separated us from our biology and called one half useful and the other deficient does not make you a champion of women!"

Her words came in a torrent, pouring forth with years of pent up frustration. "So, yes, I call it misogyny when you deem women 'ill-equipped' to carry out their own bodily functions. You may have succeeded in terrifying the whole colony, but that's about it. You can't erase knowledge with fear."

The physicians gaze was cold as he turned back to face the Captain without response to Carla's accusations. He took a slow breath in, allowing silence to reclaim the chamber before he spoke.

"Should my recommendations be ignored, I must make you aware of the Medical Department's request. Considering that the female colonists have put forth demands that require our expertise, we would like to put forth a counter-measure that states we will not be required to perform procedures that go against our recommendations. Our rights as physicians should be held as equally important." Jacob spoke each word with a level of calm confidence, his tone quite reasonable.

"Captain. May I share the floor as well?" David leaned in to get the Captain's attention without speaking over anyone.

"Of course. Go ahead." He spoke through a faint grimace.

David's eyes were trained on Jacob Emory, narrowed as he wet his lips and pulled in a breath. "So, say one of the colonists had a prosthetic heart left-over from the old days. And say the capacity of the prosthesis prevents him from running, heavy lifting, and good sex." Scattered, nervous laughter ensued. "Now bear with me. It could happen, right? So we now have the capacity to grow him a replacement heart that would allow him to do strenuous work again. He wants that heart now, risks be damned. But you are not in favor of it. Who chooses?"

Jacob pushed his lips out and brushed the air aside with a flip of his hand. "That is not an appropriate comparison."

"Sure it is. Just answer the question. Who chooses?"

"If the man's quality of life and bodily function is at stake, then it is generally considered patient choice." The words were spoken one at a time as if Jacob knew once released they could not be called back.

"Ah, I see. Then quality of life and bodily function should be respected above the physicians' recommendations. I call bullshit on your counter measure." David threw his hands in the air and looked around at the council chamber for support. It came in overwhelming measure, as the room filled with applause.

"No. No. The example you gave does not involve progeny. The women are asking for agency over not only themselves but the future of our colony by claiming full responsibility for the progeny they carry."

The light that filtered in the small arched windows and through the octagonal skylight at the top of the domed chamber dimmed.

"Let's make this clear real quick." David walked over to where Jacob sat in the circle and with a slashing gesture he drew a gash on Jacob's lower abdomen with the side of his hand.

"We'll get you an access panel and implant your very own progeny. Hell, we could even get you a uterus. So then you can make all of the choices you like on its behalf…oh, wait…That's what you're arguing against. Scratch that. We'll put it in on our schedule and take it out when we feel the urge and we'll just strap you down and knock you out if you argue with our timetable. Wouldn't want you screaming while we cut it out of you, would we, you son-of-a-bitch." David was leaning down, his face bare inches away from Jacob's blanched one.

The cinder colored clouds overhead sparked to life, crackling with purple fire, the sound of the lightning strike mere seconds after, and loud enough to make everyone in the room flinch. Captain Neil signaled for the floor.

"Alright then. If we could all just take our seats. I think we've had about enough of this. I have anyway." The agitation that had been building was clear on the Captain's face as he watched David back away from the physician and take his seat.

"Here's what we're going to do now. I'm going to propose a solution and we will bring it to a vote within the Mars governing council. Any objections?"

"I would like the measure ratified by a full-colony vote."

Captain Neil stared at Jacob. "Fine. Agreed."

"A Reproductive Council will be formed to safeguard the reproductive freedoms set forth during this council. The council will be headed by Theresa Marin. She will be assisted by Jacob Emory, Erik Garner, Carla Schoen, and Kendra Soulie." The Captain's voice increased in volume as he spoke.

. "Now here's the crux of it. All medical and reproductive decisions are to be made by the most invested individual, the man or woman whose personal safety and well-being is at stake, with the exception of safety measures affecting the colony at large."

Jacob signaled his desire to take the floor. The Captain held up his hand.

"Unless you are objecting to your appointment to the Mars Reproductive Council, I'd like you to hold your comments until after the vote is taken. Thank you."

Theresa sat up straighter on the bench, staring around the circle to glean information. How many would stand with them? *Well, they say if they won't look you in the eye they're gonna vote against you, I think.*

Donovan was staring down at his nails, bitten too low for further nibbling. Melissa looked from Donovan's face to Theresa and gave her a friendly smile before looking back to the Captain. *Is that one? How the hell does this work if they don't look at you or look away?*

Genesis sat straight-backed in her seat, hands behind her head as she scanned the inner circle just as Theresa did. When she met Theresa's gaze, her expression gave Theresa no confidence. Theresa watched Genesis's eyes move on from her face to Jacob Emory's. There was still no smile or other encouragement, but Genesis and Jacob locked eyes for quite some time. *Did Jacob smile?* It was just a moment, before he turned his eyes on Theresa, and the hatred that bubbled and seethed in his face was quite clear. She turned away and then back to Captain Neil, awaiting the vote. *What was that? Half and half? And Genesis looked at both of us, Jacob had no problem looking at me. Pretty sure that look said something like 'Burn in hell,' though, not 'you have my vote!' What a bullshit theory.*

The Captain stood. "Initiate council vote. Fifty percent plus one."

The viewing screens glowed to life. "Private or public tally mode?"

The Captain hesitated a moment and then sighed. "Private tally."

"Council vote commencing. Each council member has ten minutes to send in their final vote." The automated voting system's volume increased to compete with the rumbling overhead. Every few seconds, another flash lit the chamber with white-blue light.

Within a moment each council member's hand-held lit up with the same contents as the large viewing screen, containing the voting options, for or against.

"One vote against." The computer's voice echoed in the chamber

"One for."

"Two for."

"Two against."

Theresa scanned the outer circle for Carla's face and found her to the right, three rows back, holding Kendra's hand. *Who's supporting who? Maybe it's mutual. Like if one of them moves the other will just fall over. Dominoes in the colosseum.* Theresa breathed in through her nose, noticing the edge of hysteria in her thoughts.

Carla's lips were tight, her jaw locked, and the hand that held Kendra's was blanched white at the knuckles. *She looks...old. Tired. Fifty years in the making riding on a ten person vote.*

"Three against." The computer voice broke in on Theresa's thoughts and a sharp knife of alarm lanced through her. Another breath. She looked around the inner circle again for a sign, some clue as to who had voted already and how they had voted.

"Three for."

It was impossible to watch the voters' hovering fingers for a single click, but she tried. *Was that the Captain's?* Captain Neil glanced down at his handheld and then at the outer circle of colonists. He nodded to someone there, an almost imperceptible gesture, coupled with a transient smile.

"Five for."

Theresa exhaled. *This is torture. Why didn't he make it silent too?*

"Six for, four against. The majority is for the initiative."

"Thank you." The Captain glanced over at Jacob and was met by a look of smug expectation. "Commence colony vote for same initiative. Make it silent this time as well as private tally. Ten minute time frame."

Theresa's head throbbed and the burning in her chest alerted her that she had better take a breath if she didn't want to end up on the floor.

Doubt descended like a cloud of locusts, picking apart her actions, motivations and the wisdom of what she was supporting, each leggy winged insect taking a bite of her confidence as it flew by. Could she even run a council? Assuming they got what they asked for, how many of the surrogates would survive removal of the access panels and any subsequent births? *God, is this all a pride thing? He went against your wishes, so you need to prove something? Prove what?*

For seven minutes Theresa floundered, the sharp, sour tang of anxiety permeating her thought processes. Seven minutes into the vote Genesis stood, and, walking over to Theresa, her steps echoing in the silent chamber, pulled her to standing. With both hands on Theresa's shoulders, Genesis nodded and smiled before speaking in a low voice.

"It's going to work out. The vote is yours. I guarantee it."

Theresa's eyes narrowed and she shook her head in confusion. "How would you..."

"Just trust me."

Theresa looked away, just long enough to miss the direction of Genesis's gaze over her shoulder as well as the slight shake of her head.

The Head of the Medical Department stood, his eyes wide with shock. He took a step forward and then glared up at the viewing screen as the computer voice spoke.

"All votes have been cast. Seventy-two in favor, twenty-two against, five abstentions. The Colony majority vote confirms the council vote. Initiative passed."

The tension holding the silence in the chamber broke as did the storm clouds, pouring out a torrent of liquid from the heaving clouds as relief, jubilation, and triumph poured from the colonists' eyes and lips. Laughter rang out, lifting above the crowd and joined by echoes of the same. Kendra's eyes were wet, as were Carla's…and they were not alone.

Jacob Emory's red-rimmed eyes were wild, contrasting with the brown of his irises as he strode towards Theresa, arm outstretched.

"You. You think you know what you're doing. You don't, you sick, angry fool. Who will you turn to when my patients are bleeding out into your hands? Who will bury the progeny you needlessly send to their deaths for the sake of your pride?"

He choked on his next words, before regaining some composure. "I pictured a golden age for us on Mars. Reproductive freedom *and* safety such as we've never experienced, and you want to drag us back into the dark ages." The physician's eyes narrowed. "Well, I won't be a part of it!"

Jacob turned and pushed away the hand on his shoulder. Erik and Dr. Alexander, his colleagues, stood at his side, concern clear in their eyes.

"Jacob, please. Let's go talk…Please." Erik placed his hand back on Jacob's shoulder and pulled. "Please."

Theresa watched as the two men made their way to the nearest door. Her eyes were wide, lips resting in neutral, unable to craft a smile to meet the occasion with so many locusts of doubt whispering in her ears, their wings creating a crackling, clicking hum as they knocked together like cards in the spokes of a bicycle.

Jacob's accusations echoed in her mind. *Who will you turn to when my patients are bleeding out into your hands? Who will bury the progeny you needlessly send to their deaths for the sake of your pride?*

Was it pride?

Theresa silenced her inner voice, turning her attention outward to the multitude around her. The volume of their voices, rising, falling, and melding together into one voice. The voice of the colony. The vote was not unanimous, and yet that voice was filled with excitement and hope.

Theresa found Carla in the crowd with her eyes, surrounded by the beaming faces of Kendra, Emily, and so many others. Her cheeks were damp and the light had returned to her face, almost erasing the signs of age Theresa had noticed creeping in over the past few days.

She found her smile then, and, climbing down from the central stage, started navigating the crowd to reach her friend and mentor.

The first volleys of hail went unnoticed, the sound lost in the din of exultation. The shattering of the outer layer of the skylight above the colonists, however, drew their full attention. All eyes turned upward to see the cracked and pitted glass and the melon sized balls of hail falling from the black, swirling clouds. The sound of hail ricocheting off of the stone dome was deafening, only muted a degree by the thickness of the walls.

The council members remaining in the center of the dome made their way into the outer circle of colonists, trying not to rush or look overly concerned as they put some distance between themselves and the fractured glass above them.

"Looks like the meeting is officially over then. Though I recommend taking the halls." Captain Neil gestured towards the cracked skylight with a crooked half-grin.

Pairs and trios meandered toward the exits, leaning in to the sensors to be scanned.

"Identity confirmed. Just a moment please." The security light blinked from red to yellow and then back to red.

Donovan scratched the tip of his nose with his index finger and turned to Mario, who waited just to his left.

"Mario, hey. Didn't you get to that yet? I told you these doors had a problem with me!"

"Yeah, about that...so just wait, what, two minutes you said?

Two minutes later the security light was still red. The security lights on all of the doors were red, in fact, and long lines had formed behind each one.

"Try it again, man." Mario pulled his handheld out of his pocket and pulled up the code for the colony security systems. Donovan leaned forward again, closer this time.

"Identity confirmed. One moment, please."

"Yeah. I'm not gonna hold my breath here. Anyone else want to give it a try?" Donovan stepped back from the scanner and gestured to the next in line just as Captain Neil joined them.

Mario shook his head. "I wouldn't bother for now. It's not you. See?" He gestured with a sweep of his hand towards the other doors placed at each point of the compass around the chamber. "Wait ten minutes and then we'll try it again."

He turned to the Captain and inclined his head. "Captain."

"Ten minutes then? Is that a guess, an estimate, or a prayer?"

Mario tightened his lips against a smile. "Wishful thinking, and a first step to solving the problem."

"Alright, what's the second step?"

"Turn off the system and restart it."

"How long?"

Mario ran his tongue across his large white teeth and clicked his tongue. "At least an hour. Maybe two, depending on how bad it is."

The Captain raised his brows and pulled out his handheld to sync up with the audio system as he turned to face the room.

"Looks like we're having lunch here today, folks. The doors are malfunctioning and need to be reset. Right now, it looks like a two hour wait, so instead of sittin' and bitchin' I say we eat and then check back in with Mario." The Captain clapped him on the shoulder and tapped his hand-held. "Keep me posted."

Mario gave an exaggerated salute to the Captain and then set up at the main console to get started.

Kendra took the Captain's hand in hers, reaching out and claiming it as soon as he approached.

"Sittin' and bitchin' huh? I think that's one of mine." She gave Captain Neil a wide grin as she went up on tip-toe to kiss his cheek.

"Well, they all know where I'm spending my time these days...and it fit, right?"

Kendra laughed out loud, a deep rumbling laugh lacking the dark notes that were often there. The smile stayed long after she stopped. "You are just on a roll, aren't you, Captain?"

Neil slid an arm around her waist, noticing the smile that spread all the way to her eyes and showed no signs of receding. When he turned to include the women she had been speaking with, he found similar smiles. Carla, Theresa, and Emily, along with Alissa, were gathered close. Carla and Theresa had fallen to discussion at his arrival.

"So we need to ensure that it'll hold up to the pressure during labor." Theresa's look was one of deep contemplation. After a few moments she looked over at Kendra and held up a finger, biting her top lip.

"Kendra, I need at least a month to run simulations so I can come up with the safest and most effective way to remove the panel and repair damage. After that, Carla says you'll need at least six months before trying to conceive."

Kendra looked askance at Carla. "Psh! I didn't even get that between my pregnancies. What are you thinking?"

Carla laughed. "We'll talk about it. It's not my uterus, so how about I give you my reasoning and you make that call."

"Alright, alright. Let's get some lunch. All this talk of surgery has me hungry."

Carla snorted. "I can eat covered in blood if I have to, so you're not scaring me off."

"Hm. I'm going to go check with Mario about those doors and leave you ladies to the blood, viscera, and brunch."

The group fell to laughing, spirits so high that the laughter bordered on cackling.

"You do that, amou. I'd like to sleep in my bed tonight." Kendra gave Captain Neil a wink before heading over to the lunch lines that had formed.

Deep purples and reds glowed through the arched windows and the fractured skylight as the sun hovered on the horizon, a luminous red ball sinking as if being submerged into the murky green ocean.

The hail had given way to flurries of snow some hours earlier, frosting the glass and accumulating on the edges of the skylight. The colonists were scattered about the room in various stages of relaxation. Most had given up on standing in clusters and had instead formed small circles, others reclined on the benches napping or entertaining themselves with their hand-helds.

"Carla. I want to do it here." Theresa opened her eyes and looked over at Carla from where she was resting on her side.

Carla tried to hold her eyes open and moistened her lips, dry with sleep. Her eyes had just started to close before Theresa spoke, and her hand-held was resting in her lap where it had fallen a moment before.

"Mmmm. Do it here? What were we talking about now?"

Theresa smiled. "We weren't. We were sleeping. Supposed to be anyway. I can't sleep. I don't want to wait anymore. I want to deliver her here."

Carla sat up straight and leaned forward. "Say again."

Theresa swung her legs over the edge of the bench and sat up. "I want to deliver Abby here. Tonight. Like now, actually."

"Oh. OH! Here? With all these people? Are you sure about that? Because this isn't a show or a spectator sport. You might feel watched, nervous."

"No, I've considered all that. It's time. And more than that, don't you think it would be good for them? For the colony, I mean. To see the first progeny delivered on Mars."

"Birthed, not delivered. It's not about them, though. It's about you and Abby." Carla held her tone to a quiet and gentle one.

Theresa's smile was small, barely reshaping her lips and leaving her eyes hooded and dark.

"It hasn't been about just me and Abby since I consented to cultivate her in an AUC unit."

"Then isn't it about time it *was* about you? You'll be the one mothering her."

Theresa shook her head. "I can't do it by myself."

Carla started to protest but Theresa held a hand up. "I don't mean the delivery…or birth. I mean…maybe seeing her from the beginning, being here for it, will make them…I don't know. Take some ownership?"

Carla twisted her braid around one finger, listening.

"How much chance does she have if she just has me? In a small colony like this, with everyone looking askance at her as she grows, when she apprentices. Whispering as she skips by. Waiting for her to be different." Theresa's lips were tight, curling with emotion as she spoke.

"Okay. Let's do it then." Carla nodded, pressing her lips together and pushing silver strands of stray hair back from her face.

Theresa took a breath, the exhale shaking on the way out.

"I'll go tell the Captain. Do you have what you need?" Carla was standing now, her energy sharp and focused on the task at hand.

"No. But one of the physicians will have their bag for emergencies."

"Get Kendra if you want her there. She's my apprentice now, so she can help you get comfortable."

"Uh…okay."

Carla gave Theresa's shoulder a light squeeze and turned to scan the room for the Captain. As expected, he was leaning next to the main computer console speaking with Mario while the other man worked.

The Captain smiled as Carla approached, his expression quizzical.

"Mario's working as fast as he can. Or so he assures me."

"Well, it's either I comb through the code piece by piece at this point or I rewrite it." Mario smiled at Captain Neil.

"I vote rewrite it. And give it a friendly voice and a sense of humor this time." Carla punctuated her assertion with a nod. "I'm not here to complain about the doors, though, Captain. It's time for little Abby to be born. It's going to be a community effort. Well, so much as watching quietly and keeping their distance takes effort."

"Oh. I guess it can't wait then?"

She pursed her lips and shook her head at Captain Neil's nervous expression. "It can't wait—oh, and Captain, consider this my formal request to take on another assignment and begin my practice of midwifery. I hope you don't need the approval of the medical department…"

The Captain barked a laugh and shook his head. "I think the ship sailed on that one already. Just tell me what you need, Carla."

Theresa knelt in a sea of cushions and blankets with Kendra on one side and Emily on the other. She pulled a thin sheet up over her shoulders. Fingers trembled as she detached the magnetic clasps on the top half of her weighted over shirt and then the thin blouse underneath.

She slid them both off to expose the RPU sealed to her skin and the tubes that strapped to her chest and shoulder, inserting into her brachial plexus artery and vein. The translucent capsule was stretched and thin, bulging out on both sides and pressing against her breasts, which were themselves swollen and mapped with blue veins. Sunset bruises made sharp contrast to the overall thin, and sallow look of her skin, and an inch-wide patch surrounding the seal on all sides was reddened and peeling in some places; and in others it wept from minute fissures. Where the straps made contact with her shoulders and undersides of her breasts there were angry red abrasions that had bled at some point and left a faint stain on the white fabric.

Theresa breathed in, filling her lungs as best she could with the extra weight on her chest, and placed a hand on Abby's back, a tender smile on her chapped lips. She heard Carla's footsteps approach but did not look up. Abby was awake, her eyes wide open and locked on Theresa's.

"I want it recorded." Theresa twisted the ends of the sheet around her arms to free them from their draping coverage, leaving only her breasts covered. "There's someone on Earth who needs to see this."

Carla put her hands on her hips, nodding understanding as she surveyed the set-up. "Sure. We can make that happen."

"Where do we start? I've delivered from an AUC using the automated program, and also manually." Theresa made a slicing gesture with one hand. "But not an RPU, and not slowly. I want it to be as…normal? As possible for her."

Carla nodded and knelt down next to Theresa, placing a medical bag to her right.

"Contractions then. Is the RPU set to full output of oxytocin and endorphins yet?"

"No, it's up to the first setting for early labor. I was waiting for you."

"Set it to gradually increase over the course of an hour then."

Theresa took the control in her hand and adjusted the setting, looking back to Carla when she finished.

"Okay, let's do it this way. I'll tell you your options now so you can move ahead as you like without interruption. Physiologically this is different than a uterine labor and birth, but for you it's gonna feel like one, and you'll have cramping and bleeding as well. On a hormonal level, the RPU will mimic that for you and Abby. So contractions…Wait, we need to talk position first."

"Position?" Theresa's eyes were wide and receptive when she looked up at Carla.

"You've got her head up, butt down. Breech. We can do it that way or you can squeeze her through the top. That or invert yourself."

"Upside down?"

Carla's eyes sparkled with humor at the mental image of Theresa upside down.

"Well, no, but butt in the air and leaning forward."

Theresa wet her lips. "We expect more breeches here on Mars, so why not get some practice?"

"Okay. Breech then. You'll start with some warm-up contractions. Squeeze firmly with both hands at the bottom of the RPU and slide your hands gradually up to the fundus, increasing pressure as you go. Make it last about a minute and then rest about half that. No need to count though."

"Before or after we make an incision?"

"Before. We want to do the warm up with the fluid for cushioning. So after you've done that for awhile and you are getting close to peak oxytocin levels, or your arms feel like they're gonna fall off, you'll make the incision. Smaller than you normally would. It'll stretch over her with the next few contractions and then she'll come out along with the waters. You'll get pretty wet."

"Okay." Theresa took another breath, nodding as she made mental notes. "What about after that?"

"After that you'll have a baby."

"What about the RPU?" Theresa blinked back thoughts of what that meant, preferring to focus on her immediate task.

"It'll start to separate once it hits peak levels of oxytocin, but I'll rub something on topically to get it off faster if you want."

"Please. Yes. It itches and it aches. God, I just want it off me."

Carla patted Theresa's hand, eyes filling with sympathy as the universal distress of late pregnancy, magnified by the unusual circumstances of this one, seeped from Theresa's quavery voice into her consciousness.

"When you're ready." Carla sat back on her heels, hands in her lap.

Genesis stood against the western wall, leaning back with her arms crossed against her chest. Her eyes stared forward from the shadow, sparking like fool's gold in the side of a dark mine where water trickled down over the cold stone walls.

David leaned next to her, one arm crossed over his chest, the other in front where he could examine his nails in between glances at Genesis's face. Looking up again, he followed her gaze to the central stage where Carla and her assistants formed a circle around Theresa.

He lifted a hand to the back of Genesis's neck, brushing his fingertips against the line where fine hairs started. She flinched, recoiling from the touch.

"You're watching as if you can't not. But you don't seem to want to." He pulled his hand away and placed it behind his head, lips tightening. "Why? Why don't you go ask to join the circle? Be closer?"

"I don't want to be closer."

David waited to see if she had anything to add before continuing.

"The Captain said the doors are working again. We could leave then. Go to our room?" The suggestion was subtle but there.

"No."

She didn't look away from the scene. Up above the circle of women, the viewing screen displayed a closer view. Genesis alternated between watching the smaller real life version and the closer, more intimate one on the screen.

"One word answers don't really further conversation." David waited for an answer and then started to speak. "We could just…"

She cut him off with her sudden movement, pulling herself into his arms for a kiss. It was wet, desperate, and full of lust.

"Go back to our room for this? Just this? Without anything else?"

He pulled back enough to look into her eyes. "Genesis."

"Don't tell me you don't want more! I know you well enough. You want things I don't have." She inclined her head towards the viewing screen, her face tight, eyes dark with something resembling grief.

David followed her gaze again to the larger than life picture of Abby, still held in the RPU, tiny feet kicking against the cocoon as Theresa's hands slid up over her chest and head, squeezing upwards.

"What, progeny?"

Genesis just stared at him.

"We could. If you wanted. Is that what you want?"

Her lips twisted into a scowl, pulling back from her teeth as she spoke.

"No. No we couldn't. You could, David." A sardonic smile spread across her lips. "Can't stand to be touched unless it's erotic. Is that a mother you'd want?"

She threw a hand out towards the viewing screen. "The thought of something like that depending on me, touching me. Makes me nauseous. Makes my skin crawl."

David blinked several times. "Okay. That's okay."

Genesis backed away from him. "Are you kidding me? You are delusional. A total fucking lunatic."

"Genesis. You don't need to do this."

"Yes, I do. I put my fucking cards on the table, but you forgot what game we're playing. This isn't a friendly game of go fish, where we sit by the fire and cuddle afterwards."

David pushed a hand through his hair.

"What game is it, then?"

"War. We take each other's cards and burn them. And if there's any left at the end we might form some alliances and enjoy a good fuck, but that's where it ends."

She turned to walk away, but was stopped by his hand.

"I wasn't playing any games. And I don't have any deal-breakers…God, these fucking metaphors keep coming out of my mouth, but I'm all in. You don't want progeny, fine. You don't want to be touched unless we're fucking, fine. I'm a big boy. You don't have to call me names to scare me off."

"Let go of my arm. Or I'll scream and ruin their little sacred ritual." Genesis widened her eyes, threatening.

David released her arm and watched her walk to the nearest security door, watched the blue glow of the retinal scan wash across her face, the light turn from red to green and the door slide shut behind her. He put both hands behind his head in unconscious mimicry of Genesis's resting stance as he looked up at the viewing screen.

"See you tomorrow, then."

Theresa's arms were heavy. The muscles had settled into a cycle of dull ache during each rest and a throbbing burn while she wrapped her hands around the RPU, squeezing and massaging. Her hands reached the top of the cocoon, maintaining the squeeze for several seconds. Beads of sweat gathered on her skin, making the loose hairs on her forehead curl and stick. Dropping her arms to her sides and closing her eyes, she took a slow shaky breath.

"I want her out now." She didn't open her eyes, but smiled when she felt the cool cylindrical metal of a cauterizing scalpel pressed against her palm.

"Thank you." She opened her eyes and activated the tool. With one smooth motion she sliced a two-inch opening into the bottom of the RPU. The fluid gushed out, pouring down her abdomen in warm rivulets, soaking into the blanket on her lap.

The next simulated contraction squeezed Abby's bottom through the opening. Theresa reached down and felt the soft wrinkled skin. Her own laugh surprised her and she broke into a smile. "Come on, Abby. We're so close!"

She squeezed the top of the RPU. Taking the empty space that Abby left and balling it between her hands she pulled upward over Abby's head and pushed down. Abby's abdomen and legs slid out, releasing another gush of warm liquid, and dangled from the RPU.

"Is she okay like this?" Theresa glanced at Carla, uncertain.

Carla nodded, her eyes warm and reassuring.

"I want to catch her. Can you do this?" She removed her hands from the RPU so that Carla could take over.

"Just don't pull."

It was Theresa's turn to nod as she slid one arm under Abby's back and hovered the other hand over her chest. "Okay."

Carla gathered the loose silicone into her fists as Theresa had and squeezed it together, pushing Abby down. The opening stretched, catching on Abby's arms.

"She's stuck." Theresa looked over at Carla in alarm.

"She'll come. See that." The baby wiggled, pulling her arms down and, with another squeeze from above, her body was entirely out.

"She's blue. I want her now." Theresa reached up with one hand and squeezed Abby's head out in one motion,

"Oh, thank God!" She leaned back against the bench behind her, staring at the minute form in the crook of her arm.

Carla folded her hands between her knees and watched, suppressing the urge to help and catching Kendra's concerned gaze before her apprentice succumbed to the same impulse. She shook her head, and, turning to Emily, gave her a squeeze on the shoulder. A finger to her lips reminded all present not to disturb the pair.

Theresa closed her eyes, feeling a wave of exhaustion and overwhelming numbness. "At this point, I would have already passed the progeny to an aide for assessment and removal to the nursery. Just pinking up and crying... She isn't crying."

Theresa looked down into her arms and found Abby staring back. Her eyes were a dim grey and her eyelids were swollen and mottled. Swirls of vernix clung to her bluish skin in patches, and her breathing sounded wet. Abby kicked her legs and pulled her arms in, her face crinkling into a grimace as she let out a weak sound that was half cough and half cry.

Theresa pushed herself into a sitting position with her free hand and lifted Abby up to her chest. "Here I am, Abby. Here I am." She glanced up at Carla. "She's gurgling."

"Postural drainage. And if that doesn't fix it, a few breaths will. See how she's pinking up? And no chest retractions. Just lay her over your arm with a downward tilt to her head."

Theresa lifted Abby with both hands under her arms, struggling with her floppiness as well as the folds of silicone and cords draping on her own chest.

After a few attempts, she succeeded in turning Abby onto her stomach with her small round cheek resting in her palm. Abby wailed in protest, the sound echoing around the chamber much like the cry of a newborn goat.

Theresa's brows pulled together as she curled herself instinctively around her progeny, crossing her legs on the floor and using her free hand to stroke and pat Abby's damp, sticky back.

Her shoulders relaxed and her own breathing slowed as Abby's breathing took on a dryer, less irregular quality. Her fingertips traced the dark, wet curls on the back of the tiny head that rested in her palm.

"Carla. Can you please get this contraption off of me now? It's in the way, and it's wet, and I'm itching."

Carla smiled and reached into the medical bag for a vial of oxytocin and a thin flexible tool to help separate the RPU. "Yes, I can. I was just waiting for you to be ready."

"Why is everyone so quiet? Is the display screen working so they can see her?"

Carla chuckled. "It's working. Captain let 'em know they'd better not let out a peep to disturb you during the birth. But would you like to see their faces?"

Theresa nodded, trepidation crinkling her brow. Carla grabbed her hand-held, already synched up to the main system.

"Why don't you reverse the display for us?"

"Awaiting your command."

Carla scowled. "I said...whatever. Reverse the damn display!"

"Command confirmed."

The large display screen, as well as the several positioned around the meeting hall shifted, the live footage of Theresa and Abby replaced by the faces of the crowd. Their eyes glowed with emotion, many smiling, others covering their mouths with brows upturned. Not one among them was unaffected, and only a few stopped the tears from running down their cheeks.

Genesis slid her gaze across the message blinking on her handheld.

"Jacob Emory is the best candidate to lead the Mars branch of the Reproductive Council. Were you able to place him?"

Genesis rolled her eyes and shook her head despite the absence of an audience, and voiced her reply to the device.

"Jacob Emory was unstable. He was found in his chambers with his own knife in his throat this morning. So, clearly not a good candidate. You gave me this position because you trust my judgment."

She walked over to the window and looked out. A small crowd had formed in the garden. The ground was damp and the light crust of snow from the night before had already melted under the rays of the sun.

Carla handed a thin-trunked sapling to Donovan, laughing as she spoke. David passed the next to the colonist on his right, gesticulating and pantomiming, his hands digging, burying, and patting down in mid-air.

The walls were too thick to hear the words that passed between them. Carla bent over laughing and patted David's shoulder. David's eyes crinkled around the corners as he spoke through his grin.

Genesis stared out at the jovial interaction, her features smooth. *They'll be spreading ashes by nightfall, assuming he tells them.* She glanced down at the screen of her hand-held to see the reply that had arrived.

"Who do you intend to place in the position?"

"I've already placed the best candidate. She has more strings to pull than a marionette."

Theresa forced herself up out of the heavy folds of sleep that had enveloped her.

"Abby. Oh God, she's underneath them all. Abby!"

Her hand came up in a panic, feeling between her breasts. She was there. Not the RPU, but Abby, warm and soft with sleep, face resting over the ring of raised scars left behind by the seal. Theresa listened to the soft sound of her breathing, smiling at light hitches of newborn respiration. She sighed, feeling the drowsiness of chronic sleep deprivation returning in place of the panic she had felt moments before.

That damn dream again. The sea of progeny. She turned to find the source of the blue glow that illuminated her room. The viewing screen showed a pool of blue water, rippling in concentric rings as droplets of water fell into them.

"What was I watching?" Her voice was low so as not to wake Abby but loud enough to wake the viewing screen. The blue puddles dissolved to reveal her screen paused on an image from her AUC lab on Earth. Dr. Brant was frozen in a smile with a single progeny held against his lab coat. It was AUC6, the one Dr. Brant called Gavin. He was wet and milk- skinned, as Abby had been short weeks ago, almost twice her size, with a barrel chest and a large head. *But his eyes are the same…*

Abby stretched in her sleep and nuzzled into the side of her mother's breast, rooting. Theresa slid one hand under her head to direct the search, and smiled at the tiny squeaking sounds made with each suck once she got ahold of the nipple.

Theresa's gaze returned to the frame of the clip she had been watching when she fell asleep.

"No wonder I keep dreaming about them. I'm the one that asked for the footage, though."

She unfroze the screen and watched as one progeny after another was delivered from the AUC units and passed to an assistant or to Dr. Brant. *He really thinks he can raise them all? If the Council lets him. Still no decision there.*

Theresa froze as an electric pulse of anxiety flooded her.

"I could give them their decision. I could just…"

She tried to close her eyes and found them open again and staring at the screen. Sliding one arm over Abby's back to hold her in place Theresa put her feet on the ground her heart rate increasing to rabbit's pace with the commitment getting up implied. *Am I really doing this? Can I?*

She moved on autopilot with a speed borne of fear. Fear that she would follow through…and also that she wouldn't. Pulling on a white robe one arm at a time, half-covering Abby with the silken material as she pulled it together in the middle, Theresa sat down in front of her computer console and took her headset out of her desk. She flicked it open with her free hand and placed it over her eyes.

"Address the message to the World Governing Council of Earth."

"Addressed and ready to broadcast. Proceed when ready."

She smoothed back the hair that flowed around her shoulders and placed her free hand on the edge of the desk to still its shaking. Taking a breath and wetting her lips, she began.

"As head of the Mars Reproductive Council, I am authorized to inform the Earth Reproductive Council that the AUC program progeny must be considered the offspring of Dr. Theresa Marin, and therefore citizens of the Mars colony by blood. As such, I request that their caretaker, Dr. Brant, be allowed to care for them on Earth until such a time that they can be transported to Mars."

Theresa removed the headset and released her breath. She was unable to pin down one thought with the multitude of conflicting ones swirling in her head, unable to stop looking at the headset in anticipation of a reply. After several minutes she stood and took up pacing in a convoluted star-shaped pattern around the chamber, from desk to viewing screen, viewing screen to window, window to kitchen bot, and back to the desk again.

The reply came two hours later, once Theresa was beginning to doze at her desk, having placed the sleeping Abby on her bed.

She lifted the headset and placed it over her eyes, heart rate rising to meet the occasion. The reply was not from the World Governing Council. It was from Dr. Brant, his eyes bright with excitement.

"Didn't I say you would come up with something? Clever girl. The WGC is keeping us in protective custody and the Reproductive Council can't touch us. They're sending us to Mars."

The end

CL FORS

An artist of multiple mediums with a myriad of interests, CL Fors is a multipotentialite, mother, author, and adventurer. Refusing to take the conventional route after high school, she moved to Hollywood to act in films and later joined the army as a military intelligence linguist. She now spends her days writing, illustrating, and publishing with her husband and partner is wizardry Jason P. Crawford, while raising their four children. When she isn't writing or painting, you may find her bellydancing, running, hiking, metal-smithing, sculpting, or volunteering at the local gallery.

Cradle of Mars is the first installment of the Primogenitor series and is followed by three more parts. Follow CL Fors on Social Media Sites and subscribe to her newsletter for updates and exclusive gifts!

Instagram: @C.L.Forsauthor
Facebook: CL Fors
Facebook Page: https://www.facebook.com/cl.fors
Facebook Page: Progeny@CLForsauthor
Twitter: @CLFors
Subscribe to her newsletter here: http://eepurl.com/cidcjX
Website: https://www.clforsauthor.com/